heard the one about...?

heard the one about...?

Over 3,500 of the funniest jokes...ever

Collins

First published in 2006 by Collins
an imprint of
HarperCollins Publishers
77-85 Fulham Palace Road
London
W6 8JB

The Collins website address is:
www.collins.co.uk

A CIP catalogue record for this book is
available from the British Library

ISBN-13 978-0-00-724255-9
ISBN-10 0-00-724255-7

Collins uses papers that are natural,
renewable and recyclable products made
from wood grown in sustainable forests.
The manufacturing processes conform to
the environmental regulations of the country
of origin.

Printed and bound in Great Britain by
Clays Ltd, St Ives plc

Contents

family

Birth Pangs

Labour pains had started. The anxious father-to-be called the doctor and told him. The doctor said, 'How far apart are the pains?' The father-to-be replied, 'I'm not absolutely sure, but I think they're in the same place.'

We've been married 30 years now. Our idea of birth control is to turn the lights on.

Doctor: A glass of water is a cheap and effective contraceptive.
Patient: Do I take it before or after intercourse?
Doctor: Instead of.

My dad was so delighted when I was born that he rushed out to tell all his friends. We're expecting him back any day now.

They've just invented the most effective birth-control pill ever. It weighs two and a half tonnes and when you jam it up against your bedroom door, there's no way your husband can get in.

When he was born he was so ugly that the doctor slapped his mother.

Midwife: It's a girl!
Father: Oh.
Midwife: Are you disappointed?
Father: Not really. A girl was my second choice.

I was an unwanted child. After I was born, my father spent a month trying to find a loophole in my birth certificate.

I know a woman who just had triplets. Heavens. Do you know that triplets happen only once in every 15,000 births? I wonder when she ever had time to do the housework.

Should women have children over 40? No. Forty are quite enough!

I want to have children, but my friends scare me. One of them told me she was in labour for 36 hours. I don't even want to do anything that feels good for 36 hours.
Rita Rudner

Don't ask me why I was in hospital when I was born. Up till then I'd never had a day's illness in my life.

They call us 'coaches'. The job is to remind your wife to breathe. Think about that for a second. You realise exactly how worthless you are in this thing. When was the last time you had to be reminded to breathe? It's like saying, 'Digest!' ***Robert Klein***

I was born on 24 December. I wanted to be home for Christmas!

After going through many antenatal classes with his expectant wife, the proud new father remained by his wife's bedside throughout labour and the delivery. Wanting to be as sympathetic as possible, he took her hand afterwards and said emotionally, 'Tell me how it was, darling. How it actually felt to give birth.' 'Okay, sweetheart,' his wife replied. 'Smile as hard as you can.' Beaming down beautifully at his wife and newborn child, the man followed her instructions. 'That's not so hard.' She continued, 'Now stick a finger in each corner of your mouth.' He obeyed, smiling broadly. 'Now stretch your lips as far as they'll go,' she went on. 'Still not too tough,' he remarked. 'Right,' she snapped. 'Now pull them over your head.'

How come you were born in Scarborough? I wanted to be near my mother.

A woman entered the hospital to deliver her tenth child. 'Congratulations,' said the nurse, 'but don't you think this is enough?' The woman replied, 'Are you kidding? This is the only holiday I get each year.'

I weighed only 6 oz when I was born. Good Heavens! Did you live? I certainly did! You should see me now!

This guy came into work the other day with a fistful of cigars and started passing them out left and right to celebrate the birth of his son. 'Congratulations, Eric,' said his boss. 'How much did the baby weigh?' 'Four and a half pounds,' reported the father proudly. 'Wow, that's quite small.' 'What did you expect?' retorted Eric indignantly. 'We've only been married three months.'

I was so surprised when I was born that I couldn't talk for a year and a half.

Tell me, doctor, is it a boy? Well, the middle one is!

In this day and age, women can have kids for other women, through surrogate motherhood. Is that the ultimate favour or what? I think I'm a good friend. I'll help you move. Okay. But whatever comes out of me after nine months, I'm keeping. I don't care if it's a shoe. ***Sue Kolinsky***

Birth control is a way of avoiding the issue.

You have this myth you're sharing the birth experience. Unless you're passing a bowling ball, I don't think so. Unless you're circumcising yourself with a chainsaw, I don't think so. Unless you're opening up an umbrella up your ass, I don't think so!
Robin Williams

Gracie: My sister had a baby.
George: Boy or girl?
Gracie: I don't know, and I can't wait to find out if I'm an uncle or an aunt.
George Burns and Gracie Allen

But Doctor, I thought if you did it standing up, you couldn't get pregnant. Ah, yes, a popular misconception.

Doctor to parents of ugly baby: I charge £5 if it's a boy and £5 if it's a girl. Let's just say this one's on the house.
Bob Hope

What do you call people who use the rhythm method of birth control? Parents.

A young woman was sitting on the bus cooing to her baby when a drunk staggered aboard and down the aisle. Stopping in front of her, he looked down and pronounced, 'Lady, that is the ugliest baby I have ever seen.' The woman burst into tears and there was such an outcry of sympathy among the other passengers that they kicked off the drunk. But the woman kept on sobbing and wailing so loudly that finally the driver pulled the bus over to the side of the road. 'Look, I don't know what that guy said to you,' the driver told his inconsolable passenger, 'but to help you calm down I'm going to get you a cup of tea.' And off he went, coming back shortly with a cup of tea from the corner deli. 'Now please calm down,' soothed the driver, 'everything's going to be okay. See, I brought you a cup of nice hot tea, and I even got a banana for your pet monkey.'

A baby is a perfect example of minority rule.

We delivered our child by natural childbirth, the procedure invented by a man named Lamaze. The Marquis de Lamaze, a disciple of Dr Josef Mengele, who concluded that women could counteract the incredible pain of childbirth by breathing. I think we can all agree that breathing is not a reasonable substitute for anaesthesia. That's like asking a man to tolerate a vasectomy by hyper-ventilating. ***Dennis Wolfberg***

A baby is something that gets you down in the daytime and up at night.

We call our baby 'Teeny'. We'd call him 'Martini' but he isn't dry enough.

A boy went to visit his mother in hospital and to see his new baby brother. While there, he slipped into an adjoining ward and started talking to a woman with her leg in traction. 'How long have you been here?' he asked. 'Six weeks,' she replied. 'Can I see your baby?' 'I haven't got a baby.' 'Wow, you're slow. My mum's only been here two days but she's got one!'

They said the baby looked just like me. Then they turned him the right way up!

The baby is great. My wife and I have just started potty training. Which I think is important because when we want to potty train the baby, we should set an example.
Howie Mandel

I have a friend called Tuesday. I know it's unusual but when he was born his parents thought they'd call it a day.

As babies, we used to share the same nappy. It was the only way to make ends meet.

Parenthood Changes
Yes, parenthood changes everything, but it also changes with each baby. Here are some of the ways having a second and third child differs from having your first.

Your clothes:
First baby: You begin wearing maternity clothes as soon as your pregnancy is confirmed.
Second baby: You wear your regular clothes for as long as possible.
Third baby: Your maternity clothes are your regular clothes.

The baby's name:
First baby: You pore over baby-name books and practise pronouncing and writing combinations of all your favourites.
Second baby: Someone has to name their kid after your great-aunt Mavis, right? It might as well be you.
Third baby: You open a name book, close your eyes, and see where your finger falls. Bimaldo? Perfect!

Preparing for the birth:
First baby: You practise your breathing religiously.
Second baby: You don't bother practising because you remember that last time, breathing didn't do a thing.
Third baby: You ask for an epidural in your eighth month.

The layette:
First baby: You pre-wash your newborn's clothes, colour-coordinate them, and fold them neatly in the baby's little bureau.
Second baby: You check to make sure that the clothes are clean and discard only the ones with the darkest stains.
Third baby: Boys can wear pink, can't they?

Worries:
First baby: At the first sign of distress – a whimper, a frown – you pick up the baby.
Second baby: You pick up the baby when its wails threaten to wake your firstborn.
Third baby: You teach your three-year-old how to rewind the mechanical swing.

Activities:
First baby: You take your infant to Baby Gymnastics, Baby Swing and Baby Story Hour.
Second baby: You take your infant to Baby Gymnastics.
Third baby: You take your infant to the supermarket and the dry cleaners.

Going out:
First baby: The first time you leave your baby with a sitter, you call home five times.
Second baby: Just before you go out, you remember to leave a number where you can be reached.
Third baby: You leave instructions for the sitter to call only if she sees blood.

At home:
First baby: You spend a good bit of every day just gazing at the baby.
Second baby: You spend a bit of every day watching to be sure your older child isn't squeezing, poking or hitting the baby.
Third baby: You spend a little bit of every day hiding from the children.

I was a premature baby – my father wasn't expecting me.

A man took his pregnant wife to the hospital to give birth. Once there, the doctor revealed that he had developed an experimental machine, which could take some of the pain of childbirth away from the mother and give it to the father instead. He asked the couple whether they were interested in giving it a try, and they agreed. Since the machine was largely untested, the doctor thought it wise to start at the lowest setting. He strapped the man down, switched on the machine and asked him whether he could feel any pain. 'No, I feel fine,' said the man. So the doctor turned the machine to a slightly higher setting. Again the man reported feeling no discomfort. All the while the wife was going through pain-free childbirth. Greatly encouraged, the doctor turned the machine to its highest setting. Still the man felt no pain. 'This is truly amazing,' said the doctor excitedly. 'A veritable breakthrough in childbirth.' After his wife had given birth, the husband climbed off the machine and calmly drove home. There he found the postman dead on the doorstep.

Darling, can you get up and go see why the baby isn't crying?

People who say they sleep like a baby usually don't have one.

It's easy to look after a baby. All you've got to do is keep one end full and the other end empty.

If I were a new baby I don't think I could stand knowing what I was going to have to go through. That's why they don't show them any newspapers for the first two years. ***Charles M Schulz***

One of the first things you learn from a baby is that you should never change nappies midstream.

In the woods, in a shack with no electricity, a man's wife went into labour in the middle of the night. The local doctor was fetched to help with the delivery. The doctor gave the nervous father-to-be a lantern to hold, partly to keep him occupied and partly so that he could see what he was doing. After a few minutes, a baby boy was born and the husband put down the lantern to hold him. 'Don't put that lantern down just yet,' said the doctor. 'I think there's another one on the way.' Shortly afterwards, a baby daughter was born and the husband put down the lantern to hold her. 'Don't put that lantern down yet,' said the doctor. 'I think there may be another one still to come.' Sure enough, a few minutes later, another baby girl was born. The father scratched his head and said to the doctor, 'Do you think it's the light that's attracting them?'

The baby was christened 'Glug-Glug'. The vicar fell into the font!

A group of pregnant women and their partners were attending the antenatal class. The instructor was emphasising the importance of keeping healthy during pregnancy. 'Ladies, exercise is good for you. Walking is particularly beneficial. And, gentlemen, it wouldn't hurt you to take the time to go walking with your partner.' Hearing this, a male voice asked, 'Is it all right is she carries a golf bag while we walk?'

The baby's father and mother were first cousins. That's why he looks so much alike.

The only thing that prevented a father's love from faltering was the fact that there was in his possession a photograph of himself at the same early age, in which he, too, looked like a homicidal fried egg.
PG Wodehouse

When the baby cries at night, who gets up? The whole street!

There's nothing like having a baby to make you realize it's a changing world.

Thanks to the miracle of fertility treatment, a woman was able to have a baby at 65. When she was discharged from hospital, her relatives came to visit. 'Can we see the baby?' they asked. 'Not yet,' said the 65-year-old mother. Twenty minutes later, they asked again. 'Can we see the baby?' 'Not yet,' said the mother. Another 20 minutes later, they asked again. 'Can we see the baby?' 'Not yet,' said the mother. The relatives were growing impatient. 'Well, when can we see the baby?' 'When it cries.' 'Why do we have to wait until the baby cries?' they asked. 'Because I forgot where I put it,' replied the mother.

You know what they say: out of the mouths of babes comes... cereal.

On the way to pre-school, the doctor had left her stethoscope on the car seat, and her little girl picked it up and began playing with it. 'Be still, my heart,' thought the doctor. 'My daughter wants to follow in my footsteps!' Then the child spoke into the instrument: 'Welcome to McDonald's. May I take your order?'

Now you've had the baby, you must be worried about getting the father back!

But, darling, this isn't our baby! I know, but it's a much nicer pram!

Mr and Mrs Harris were desperate to start a family, but after trying for years, they became convinced that it was not meant to happen. So, as a last resort, they decided to employ the services of a proxy father whom they had never met. On the morning the sperm donor was due to call, Mr Harris set off for work as usual and wished his wife good luck. She wasn't looking forward to it. As chance would have it, that same morning a travelling baby photographer was also in the area and called at the Harris' house. Mrs Harris answered the door. She was expecting the sperm donor. 'Good morning, madam,' said the photographer. 'You don't know me, but I've come to...' 'Yes, I know,' she interrupted. 'There's no need to explain. Come in. I've been expecting you.' 'Really?' said the photographer, thinking that his advertising must have paid off. 'I must say I have made a speciality of babies.' 'That's what my husband and I were hoping,' she said. 'So where do we start?' 'Well, I usually try two in the bathtub, one on the couch and perhaps a couple on the bed. That seems to work for me.' 'No wonder George and I haven't had much luck...' 'If we try several different positions and I shoot from six or seven angles, I'm sure you'll be pleased with the results.' 'I do hope so,' she said nervously. 'Can we get this over with quickly?' 'In my line of work, I have to take my time,' he replied. 'It's no good rushing these things. I'd love to be in and out in five minutes, but I think you'd be disappointed with that.' 'That's true,' she sighed knowingly. The photographer opened his briefcase and pulled out a portfolio of baby pictures. 'This one was done on top of a bus,' he explained. 'Oh my!' exclaimed Mrs Harris. 'And these twins turned out really well considering the fact that their mother was difficult to work with.' 'In what way was she difficult?' asked Mrs Harris anxiously. 'She insisted we go out outdoors, so I had to take her over to Hyde Park to get the job done properly. People were crowding four deep to watch. It took over three hours in all. It was really exhausting.' By now Mrs Harris was looking decidedly worried. 'Right,' he said. 'I'll just get my tripod.' 'Tripod?' 'Yes, I need a tripod on which to rest my Canon.' At that point Mrs Harris fainted.

After all, I'm your father. It's true if it hadn't been me it would have been someone else. But that's no excuse.

Samuel Beckett

My father was very disappointed when I was born. Why? Did he want a girl? No, he wanted a divorce.

I've got a baby brother. He's called Onyx. Why Onyx? Because he was 'onyxpected'.

How come the Greens have started taking French lessons? Didn't you know their adoption plans finally came through? They've gotten an adorable French baby, and they want to understand what she says when she begins to talk.

For weeks, a six-year-old lad kept telling his teacher about the baby brother or sister that was expected at his house. One day the mother allowed the boy to feel the movements of the unborn child. The boy was obviously impressed, but he made no comment. Furthermore, he stopped telling his teacher about the impending event. The teacher finally said, 'Tommy, whatever became of that baby brother or sister you were expecting at home?' Tommy burst into tears and confessed, 'I think Mummy ate it!'

It must be time to get up, darling. How do you know? The baby's fallen asleep.

There is no finer investment for any community than putting milk into babies.

Winston Churchill

Is your baby a boy or a girl? Of course. What else could it be?

Pregnancy Q & A

Q. I'm two months' pregnant now. When will my baby move?
A. With any luck, right after he finishes college.

Q. How will I know if my vomiting is morning sickness or the flu?
A. If it's the flu, you'll get better.

Q. What is the most common pregnancy craving?
A. For men to be the ones who get pregnant.

Q. What is the most reliable method to determine a baby's sex?
A. Childbirth.

Q. The more pregnant I get, the more often strangers smile at me. Why?
A. 'Cause you're fatter than they are.

Q. My wife is five months pregnant and so moody that sometimes she's borderline irrational.
A. So what's your question?

Q. What's the difference between a nine-month pregnant woman and a model?
A. Nothing (if the pregnant woman's husband knows what's good for him).

Q. How long is the average woman in labour?
A. Whatever she says divided by two.

Q. My childbirth instructor says it's not pain I'll feel during labour, but pressure. Is she right?
A. Yes, in the same way that a tornado might be called an air current.

Q. When is the best time to get an epidural?
A. Right after you find out you're pregnant.

Q. Is there any reason I have to be in the delivery room while my wife is in labour?
A. Not unless the word 'alimony' means anything to you.

Q. Is there anything I should avoid while recovering from childbirth?
A. Yes, pregnancy.

Q. Does pregnancy cause haemorrhoids?
A. Pregnancy causes anything you want to blame it for.

Q. Our baby was born last week. When will my wife begin to feel and act normal again?
A. When the kids are away at college.

The phrase itself – birth control – doesn't make sense. It's nine months earlier that you need the control.

Looking at their new baby the mother said, 'Those tiny arms, he'll never be a boxer. Those tiny legs, he'll never be a runner.' The father said, 'He'll never be a porn star either.' ***Bob Hope***

My sister is expecting a little stranger. Oh, I'm sure they'll soon get to know each other.

A man was pushing a pram containing a screaming baby along the street. All the while the man kept repeating quietly, 'Keep calm, George.' 'Don't scream, George.' 'It'll be okay, George.' A woman heard this and said to the man, 'You really are doing your best to soothe your son George.' The man looked at her and replied stonily, 'I'm George.'

Proud father: My new baby looks just like me!
Nurse: Well, never mind, as long as it's healthy.

What's the new baby's name? I don't know. We can't understand a word he says!

He's just like his father. I know – bald, sleepy and uneducated.

The first-time father, beside himself with excitement over the birth of his first son, was determined to follow all the rules to a T. 'So tell me, Nurse,' he asked as his new family headed out the hospital door, 'what time should we wake the little guy in the morning?'

If men got pregnant ... women would rule the world.

I was born because it was a habit in those days; people didn't know anything else. ***Will Rogers***

When they brought their first baby home from hospital, the wife suggested to her husband that he should have a go at changing the baby's nappy. 'I'm busy,' he said. 'I'll change the next one.' So three hours later, she tried again. 'Darling, will you change the baby's nappy?' 'No,' he said. 'I meant the next baby.'

What is the difference between a man and childbirth? One is a constant pain and almost unbearable, the other is simply having a baby.

What do you get when you cross LSD with a birth control pill? A trip without the kids.

A father asked his young daughter what she would like for Christmas. She said that what she wanted more than anything else was a baby brother. And it so happened that on Christmas Eve her mother came home from hospital clutching a baby boy. The following year, the father again asked his daughter what she would like for Christmas. 'Well,' she replied, 'if it's not too uncomfortable for Mummy, I'd like a pony.'

Definition of 'baby': A loud noise at one end and no sense of responsibility at the other.

If the baby does not thrive on fresh milk it should be boiled. ***Women's magazine***

'Do you mind if I sit down, 'cause I'm pregnant?' a woman said. I said in reply, 'You don't look it. How long have you been pregnant?' She said, 'Only ten minutes – but doesn't it make you feel tired?' ***Max Miller***

A pregnant woman is involved in a car accident and falls into a deep coma. Asleep for nearly six months, she wakes up and sees that she is no longer pregnant. Frantically, she asks the doctor about her baby. The doctor replies, 'Ma'am, you had twins! A boy and a girl. The babies are fine. Your brother came in and named them.' The woman thinks to herself, 'Oh no, not my brother – he's an idiot!' Expecting the worst, she asks the doctor, 'Well, what's the girl's name?' 'Denise,' the doctor says. The new mother thinks, 'Wow, that's not such a bad name! Guess I was wrong about my brother. I like Denise!' Then she asks the doctor, 'What's the boy's name?' The doctor replies, 'DeNephew.'

Grandchildren are God's rewards to grandparents for not shooting their children.

A little girl came home from school and said to her mother, 'Mum, guess what! We learned how to make babies today.' The mother, more than a little surprised, asked fearfully, 'That's interesting. How do you make babies?' 'It's simple,' replied the little girl. 'You just change 'y' to 'i' and add 'es'.'

Children are a great comfort in your old age – and they help you to reach it faster, too. ***Lionel Kauffman***

Why is a baby like an old car? It never goes anywhere without a rattle.

The first-time dad was taking a turn at feeding the baby some strained peas. Naturally, there were traces of the food all over the baby. His wife comes in, looks at the infant, then at her husband, who is just staring off into space and says, 'What in the world are you doing?' He replied, 'I'm just waiting for the first coat to dry, so I can put on another.'

I'm on a plane and it hits me: when did it become federal regulation that you have to have at least seven crying babies on every flight? I just want to know – where are they going? Why are they on planes? They have no appointments, they were born just days ago. Our times are so hectic that babies are born and go, "I just popped out of the womb. I gotta dry up, learn to breathe – I'll be on the two o' clock, it's the best I can do." ***Paul Reiser***

A couple are attending Lamaze class. The instructor tells the husband, 'Try to imagine that you are the one carrying the baby. How would you pick up that pen that's on the floor?' The husband thinks for a moment, tugs at his wife's sleeve, and says, 'Honey, pick up that pen for me, will you?'

Little girl to her friend: 'I'm never having kids. I hear they take nine months to download.'

A man and his wife were making their first doctor visit, the wife being pregnant with their first child. After everything checked out, the doctor took a small stamp and stamped the wife's stomach with indelible ink. The couple was curious about what the stamp was for, so when they got home the husband got out his magnifying glass to try to see what it was. In very tiny letters, the stamp said, 'When you can read this, come back and see me.'

I hear that God has sent you two more brothers. That's right. And He knows where the money's going to come from too, I heard Dad say last night.

The Perils of Parenting

The First Parent
Whenever your kids are out of control, you can take comfort from the thought that even God's omnipotence did not extend to his kids. After creating Heaven and Earth, God created Adam and Eve. And the first thing He said to them was: 'Don't.' 'Don't what?' Adam replied. 'Don't eat the forbidden fruit.' 'Forbidden fruit? Really? Where is it?' 'It's over there,' said God, wondering why He hadn't stopped after making the elephants. A few minutes later, God saw the kids having an apple break and He was angry. 'Didn't I tell you not to eat that fruit?' the First Parent asked. 'Uh huh,' Adam replied. 'Then why did you?' 'I dunno,' Adam answered. God's punishment was that Adam and Eve should have children of their own. Thus the pattern was set and it has never changed. But there is reassurance in this story. If you have persistently and lovingly tried to give them wisdom and they haven't taken it, don't be hard on yourself. If God had trouble handling children, what makes you think it would be a piece of cake?

Be nice to your kids – they'll choose your nursing home.

A father spotted his four-year-old daughter out in the backyard brushing the family dog's teeth. 'What are you doing?' he asked. 'I'm brushing Bruno's teeth,' she replied. 'But don't worry, I'll put your toothbrush back, like I always have.'

I remember the time I was kidnapped and they sent a piece of my finger to my father. He said he wanted more proof. ***Rodney Dangerfield***

Why is Christmas just like a day at the office? Because you do all the work and the fat guy in the suit gets all the credit.

A man passed out in a dead faint as he came out of his front door onto the porch. Someone dialled 999. When the paramedics arrived, they helped him regain consciousness and asked if he knew what caused him to faint. 'It was enough to make anybody faint,' he said. 'My son asked me for the keys to the garage, and instead of driving the car out, he came out with the lawn mower.'

A teenager is...

- → A person who can't remember to walk the dog but never forgets a phone number.
- → A weight watcher who goes on a diet by giving up chocolate bars before breakfast.
- → A youngster who receives his/her allowance on Monday, spends it on Tuesday, and borrows from his/her best friend on Wednesday.
- → Someone who can hear a rock song played three blocks away but not his mother calling from the next room.
- → A whiz who can operate the latest computer without a lesson but can't make a bed.
- → A student who will spend 12 minutes studying for her history exam and 12 hours for her driver's licence.
- → A youngster who is well informed about anything he doesn't have to study.
- → An enthusiast who has the energy to ride a bike for miles, but is usually too tired to dry the dishes.
- → A connoisseur of two kinds of fine music: Loud and Very Loud.
- → A young woman who loves the cat and tolerates her brother.
- → A person who is always late for dinner but always on time for a rock concert.
- → A romantic who never falls in love more than once a week.
- → A budding beauty who doesn't smile until her braces come off.
- → A boy who can sleep until noon on any Saturday when he suspects the lawn needs mowing.
- → An original thinker who is positive that her mother was never a teenager.

When our second child was on the way, my wife and I attended a pre-birth class aimed at couples who had already had at least one child. The instructor raised the issue of breaking the news to the older child. It went like this: 'Some parents,' she said, 'tell the older child, "We love you so much we decided to bring another child into this family." But think about that. Ladies, what if your husband came home one day and said, "Honey, I love you so much I decided to bring home another wife." One of the women spoke up immediately. 'Does she cook?'

My salary goes into five figures – my wife and four kids.

Once I was lost. I saw a policeman and asked him to help me find my parents. I said to him, 'Do you think we'll ever find them?' He said, 'I don't know, kid – there are so many places they can hide.'
Rodney Dangerfield

'I'm glad you named me John,' said the small boy. 'Why?' asked his mother. 'Because that's what all the kids at school call me.'

There was this little kid who had a bad habit of sucking his thumb. His mother finally told him that if he didn't stop sucking his thumb, he'd get fat. Two weeks later, his mother had her friends over for a game of bridge. The boy points to an obviously pregnant woman and says, 'Ah! I know what you've been doing!'

She has her own apartment, in mine. ***Jean Carroll, about her teenage daughter's lifestyle***

Martin has just received his brand new driver's licence. The family troops out to the driveway and climbs into the car, as he is going to take them for a ride for the first time. Dad immediately heads for the back seat, directly behind the newly minted driver. 'I bet you're back there to get a change of scenery after all those months of sitting in the front passenger seat teaching me how to drive,' says the beaming boy to his father. 'Nope,' comes dad's reply, 'I'm going to sit here and kick the back of your seat as you drive, just like you've been doing to me all these years.'

My husband and I are either going to buy a dog or have a child. We can't decide whether to ruin our carpet or ruin our lives. ***Rita Rudner***

A very successful businessman had a meeting with his new son-in-law. 'I love my daughter, and now I welcome you into the family,' said the man. 'To show you how much we care for you, I'm making you a 50-50 partner in my business. All you have to do is go to the factory every day and learn the operations.' The son-in-law interrupted, 'I hate factories. I can't stand the noise.' 'I see,' replied the father-in-law. 'Well, then you'll work in the office and take charge of some of the operations.' 'I hate office work,' said the son-on-law. 'I can't stand being stuck behind a desk all day.' 'Wait a minute,' said the father-in-law. 'I just made you half-owner of a moneymaking organisation, but you don't like factories and won't work in an office. What am I going to do with you?' 'Easy,' said the young man. 'Buy me out.'

Remember that as a teenager you are at the last stage in your life when you will be happy to hear that the phone is for you. ***Fran Lebowitz***

One day, Joe's mother turned to Joe's father and said, 'It's such a nice day, I think I'll take Joe to the zoo.' 'I wouldn't bother,' said father. 'If they want him, let them come and get him!'

I've got nothing against kids. I just follow the advice on every bottle in my medicine cabinet – 'keep away from children'.

As a kid I used to have a lemonade stand. The sign said, 'All you can drink for a penny.' So some kid would come up, plunk down the penny, drink a glass, and then say, 'Refill it.' I'd say, 'That'll be another penny.' 'How come? Your sign says...' 'Well, you had a glass, didn't you?' 'Yeah.' 'Well, that's all you can drink for a dime.'

Flip Wilson

Four guys were sitting in a bar when one got up to go to the toilet. In his absence, the other three started to talk about their sons. The first said, 'Mine was a big worry to me. I really didn't think he was ever going to make anything of himself. But I'm happy to say he's doing okay now. He owns a car dealership and just bought his best mate a new car.' The second said, 'Mine was hopeless at school. He had failure written all over him. But he's pulled through. I'm really proud of him. He owns a bank and just gave his best friend a £1-million savings bond.' The third said, 'My son was bad at school too, but I'm glad to say he's doing fine now. He owns a pet shop and just gave his best pal a puppy.' Just then the fourth guy returned from the toilet. 'We were talking about our sons,' said the others. 'Mine was a real headache,' said the fourth guy. 'He's gay, but he's turned out okay. And he sure is popular. Just recently one of his boyfriends gave him a new car, another gave him a £1-million savings bond and another gave him a puppy.'

Children are stupid. That's why they're in school. I'd lecture for an hour about percentages and interest rates and at the end I'd ask one simple question: you put £10,000 in the bank for one year at five and a half per cent and what do you get? Some kid would always yell out, 'A toaster!'

Many a man wishes he were strong enough to tear a telephone book in half – especially if he has a teenage daughter. ***Guy Lombardo***

Adolescence is a period of rapid and remarkable change. Between the ages of 12 and 17, for instance, a parent can age as much as 20 years.

Great Truths About Life That Adults Have Learned

→ Raising teenagers is like nailing jelly to a tree.
→ There is always a lot to be thankful for if you take the time to look. For example, sitting and thinking how nice it is that wrinkles don't hurt.
→ One reason to smile is that every seven minutes of every day someone in an aerobics class pulls a hamstring.
→ Car sickness is the feeling you get when the monthly payment is due.
→ The best way to keep kids at home is to make a pleasant atmosphere and let the air out of their tyres.
→ Families are like fudge – mostly sweet, with a few nuts.
→ Today's mighty oak is just yesterday's nut that held its ground.
→ Laughing helps. It's like jogging on the inside.
→ Middle age is when you choose your cereal for the fibre, not the toy.
→ My mind not only wanders; sometimes it leaves completely.
→ If you can remain calm, you just don't have all the facts.

A teenage girl was forced to stay at a friend's house overnight and called her mother first thing in the morning to let her know she was safe. The words came out in a breathless torrent. 'Mum, it's Caroline. I'm fine. I knew you'd be worried, but I didn't get a chance to call you last night. My car broke down and I had to stay at Monica's house, and by the time I got there it was gone midnight so I knew you'd be asleep. Please don't be angry with me.' By now, the woman on the other end of the phone realised that the caller had got the wrong number. 'I'm sorry,' she said, 'I don't have a daughter named Caroline.' 'Wow, Mum, I didn't think you'd be this mean!'

My mother never saw the irony of calling me a son-of-a-bitch. ***Rich Jeni***

The small girl was allowed to stay up for the start of her parents' dinner party and as a treat was given the chance to say grace. 'But I don't know what to say,' she whispered nervously in front of the guests. Her mother helped her out. 'Just say what Daddy said before breakfast this morning. You know, "Oh God..."' 'Oh yes, I remember,' said the little girl. 'Oh God, why have we got to have these boring people to dinner tonight?'

Teenage is the period between hopscotch and real scotch.

Are You Ready for Children?

Mess Test
Smear peanut butter on the sofa and curtains. Now rub your hands in the wet flowerbed and rub on the walls. Cover the stains with crayons. Place a fish stick behind the couch and leave it there all summer.

Toy Test
Obtain a 55-gallon box of Lego (if Lego is not available, you may substitute with roofing tacks or broken bottles). Have a friend spread them all over the house. Put on a blindfold. Try to walk to the bathroom or kitchen. Do not scream (this could wake a child at night).

Grocery Store Test
Borrow one or two small animals (goats are best) and take them with you as you shop at the grocery store. Always keep them in sight and pay for anything they eat or damage.

Dressing Test:
Obtain one large, unhappy, live octopus. Stuff into a small net bag making sure that all arms stay inside.

Feeding Test:
Obtain a large plastic milk jug. Fill halfway with water. Suspend from the ceiling with a stout cord. Start the jug swinging. Try to insert spoonfuls of soggy cereal (such as Fruit Loops or Cheerios) into the mouth of the jug, while pretending to be an airplane. Now dump the contents of the jug on the floor.

Night Test:
Prepare by obtaining a small cloth bag and fill it with 8-12 pounds of sand. Soak it thoroughly in water. At 8pm begin to waltz and hum with the bag until 9pm. Lay down the bag and set your alarm for 10pm. Get up, pick up the bag, and sing every song you have ever heard. Make up about a dozen more and sing these too until 4am. Set alarm for 5am. Get up and make breakfast. Keep this up for five years. Look cheerful.

Physical Test (Women):
Obtain a large beanbag chair and attach it to the front of your clothes. Leave it there for nine months. Now remove ten of the beans.

Physical Test (Men):
Go to the nearest pharmacy. Set your wallet on the counter. Ask the assistant to help himself. Now proceed to the nearest supermarket. Go to the head office and arrange for your paycheque to be directly deposited to the supermarket. Purchase a newspaper. Go home and read it quietly for the last time.

Final Assignment:
Find a couple who already has a small child. Lecture them on how they can improve their discipline, patience, tolerance, toilet training and child's table manners. Suggest many ways they can improve. Emphasise to them that they should never allow their children to run riot. Enjoy this experience. It will be the last time you will have all the answers.

My daughter is a very popular young woman. The only time the phone doesn't ring is when it's for me.

A girl invited her boyfriend to come to her parents' house for dinner. She realised it was a daunting prospect but as an incentive, she said that after the dinner she wanted to go out with him and lose her virginity. To prepare for this, the boy, who was also a virgin, went to a pharmacist to buy a packet of condoms. The pharmacist was extremely helpful and told him everything he wanted to know about sex. Finally, he asked the boy whether he wanted a three-pack, a six-pack or a family pack. 'I think I'd better take a family pack,' said the boy, 'because I think I'm going to be busy over the next few nights.' The boy showed up on time for dinner and was greeted at the front door by his girlfriend. She then showed him to the dining room where her parents were already seated at the table. Sitting down, the boy quickly offered to say grace and bowed his head. After ten minutes his head was still down. When after 20 minutes the boy's head was still bowed, his girlfriend leaned over and whispered, 'I had no idea you were so religious.' The boy whispered back, 'And I had no idea your father was a pharmacist.'

Never forget: a mother's place is in the wrong.

My teenage son said to me last night, 'Dad, how do you expect me to be independent, self-reliant and stand on my own two feet on the tiny allowance you give me?'

I could tell that my parents hated me. My bath toys were a toaster and a radio.
Rodney Dangerfield

George knocked on the door of his friend's house. When his friend's mother answered, he asked, 'Can Albert come out to play?' 'No,' said the mother. 'It's too cold.' 'Well, then,' said George, 'can his football come out to play?'

A little girl was attending a church service with her mother when she started to complain that she was feeling unwell. 'I think I need to throw up,' said the girl. 'Well, go outside,' said the mother, 'and use the bushes by the front door of the church.' The little girl went off but was back less than a minute later. 'That was quick,' said the mother. 'Did you throw up?' 'Yes, but I didn't need to go outside,' replied the little girl. 'I used a box near the door that says "For the sick".'

Never raise your hands to your kids. It leaves your groin unprotected. ***Red Buttons***

A man answered the phone. 'Yes, Mother,' he sighed. 'I've had a hard day. Mildred has been in one of her difficult moods ... I know I ought to be firmer with her, but it's not easy. You know what she's like ... Yes, I remember you warned me ... Yes, I remember you told me she was a vile creature who would make my life a misery ... Yes, I remember you begged me not to marry her. You were right ... You want to speak to her? Okay.' He put down the phone and called to his wife in the next room, 'Mildred, your mother wants to talk to you!'

I did something really special for my mum on Mother's Day. I opened the door for her when she put my laundry in the washing machine!

A Parent's Dictionary of Meanings

DUMBWAITER: one who asks if the kids would care to order dessert.
FEEDBACK: the inevitable result when the baby doesn't appreciate the strained carrots.
FULL NAME: what you call your child when you're mad at him.
GRANDPARENTS: the people who think your children are wonderful even though they're sure you're not raising them right.

Once upon a time, a four-year-old boy was visiting his aunt and uncle. He was a very outspoken little boy and often had to be censured to say the right thing at the right time. One day at lunch, when the aunt had company, the little boy said, "Auntie, I want to tinkle." Auntie took the little boy aside and said, "Never say that, Sonny. If you want to tinkle, say, 'I want to whisper'." And the incident was forgotten. That night when Uncle and Auntie were soundly sleeping, the little boy climbed into bed with them. He tugged at his uncle's shoulder and said, 'Uncle, I want to whisper.' Uncle said, 'All right, Sonny, don't wake Auntie up. Whisper in my ear.' The little boy was sent back to his parents the next day.

George Jessel

Top Ten Things You'll Never Hear a Dad Say

10 Well, how 'bout that? I'm lost! Looks like we'll have to stop and ask for directions.
9 You know, Pumpkin, now that you're 13, you'll be ready for un-chaperoned car dates. Won't that be fun?
8 I noticed that all your friends have a certain 'up yours' attitude – I like that.
7 Here's a credit card and the keys to my new car – go crazy.
6 What do you mean you want to play football? Figure skating not good enough for you, son?
5 Your Mother and I are going away for the weekend – you might want to consider throwing a party.
4 Well, I don't know what's wrong with your car. Probably one of those thingummybobs – you know – that makes it run or something. Just have it towed to a mechanic and pay whatever he asks.
3 No son of mine is going to live under this roof without an earring – now stop your moaning and let's go shopping.
2 What do you want to get a job for? I make plenty of money for you to spend.
1 Father's Day? Aahh – don't worry about that – it's no big deal.

Somewhat sceptical of his son's newfound determination to become Charles Atlas, the father nevertheless followed the teenager over to the weight-lifting department. 'Please, Dad,' whined the boy, 'I promise I'll use them every day...' 'I don't know, Michael. It's really a commitment on your part,' the father pointed out. 'Please, Dad?' 'They're not cheap either.' 'I'll use them Dad, I promise. You'll see.' Finally won over, the father paid for the equipment and headed for the door. From the corner of the store he heard his son yelp, 'What? You mean I have to carry them to the car?'

My mother had morning sickness after I was born.
Rodney Dangerfield

The rotten kid next door isn't completely clueless – at least ten parents use him as a bad example.

If your parents never had children, chances are you won't either. ***Dick Cavett***

The boss of a big multinational company urgently needed to speak to one of his management team at the weekend, so he phoned him at home. A small boy's voice answered the phone in hushed tones. 'Hello,' said the boss. 'Is your daddy home?' 'Yes,' whispered the child. 'May I talk with him?' 'No.' The boss was not used to hearing the word 'no'. 'Well, is your mummy there?' 'Yes,' whispered the child. 'May I talk with her?' 'No.' Knowing that it was unlikely that a small boy would have been left home alone, the boss tried again. 'Is anyone else there?' 'Yes,' said the boy. 'A policeman.' The boss was startled to hear that the police were there. 'Well, may I speak with him?' 'No, he's busy,' whispered the boy. 'Busy doing what?' asked the boss, beginning to wonder what was going on at the house. 'Talking to Daddy, Mummy and the firemen.' Just then, the boss heard the sound of a helicopter down the phone. 'What's that noise?' he asked. 'A helicopter,' whispered the boy. 'Exactly what's going on there?' 'The search team just landed the helicopter,' confided the boy. 'What are they doing there?' 'They're looking for me.'

Adults are always asking little kids what they want to be when they grow up because they're looking for ideas.

Paula Poundstone

Children – creatures who disgrace you by exhibiting in public the example you set for them at home.

Things Mum Would Never Say

'How on earth can you see the TV sitting so far back?'

'Yeah, I used to skip school a lot, too.'

'Just leave all the lights on – it makes the house look more cheery.'

'Let me smell that shirt – yeah, it's good for another week.'

'Go ahead and keep that stray dog, darling. I'll be glad to feed and walk him every day.'

'Well, if Timmy's mum says it's okay, that's good enough for me.'

'The curfew is just a general time to aim for. It's not like I'm running a prison around here.'

'I don't have a tissue with me – just use your sleeve.'

'Don't bother wearing a jacket – the wind-chill is bound to improve.'

Raj had been talking on the phone for about half an hour before he hung up. His father said, 'Wow! That was short. You usually talk for an hour. What happened?' Raj replied, 'It was a wrong number.'

Adolescence is the time when your daughter starts to put on lipstick and your son starts to wipe it off.

In a certain suburban neighbourhood, there were two brothers, eight and ten years old, who were exceedingly mischievous. Whatever went wrong in the neighbourhood, it nearly always turned out they had a hand in it. Their parents were at their wits' end trying to control them and after hearing about a priest nearby who worked with delinquent boys, the mother suggested to the father that they ask the priest to talk to them. The mother went to the priest and made her request. He agreed, but said he wanted to see the younger boy first and alone. So the mother sent him to the priest. The priest sat the boy down across from the huge, impressive desk he sat behind. For about five minutes they just sat and stared at each other. Finally, the priest pointed his forefinger at the boy and asked, 'Where is God?' The boy looked under the desk, in the corners of the room, all around, but said nothing. Again, louder, the priest pointed at the boy and asked, 'Where is God?' Again the boy looked all around but said nothing. A third time, in a louder, firmer voice, the priest leaned far across the desk and put his forefinger almost to the boy's nose, and asked, 'Where is God?' The boy panicked and ran all the way home. Finding his older brother, he dragged him upstairs to their room and into the closet, where they usually plotted their mischief, and quickly said, 'We're in big trouble!' The older boy asked, 'What do you mean, big trouble?' His brother replied, 'God is missing and they think we did it!'

I worry about my kid dating these days. Kids go out and they have to worry about things like herpes and AIDS. I want my son to meet an old-fashioned girl – one with gonorrhoea. ***Norm Crosby***

Did you read about the woman who hadn't used a telephone in more than 30 years? That's what happens when you have teenagers in the house!

I figure if the children are alive when he gets home, I've done my job. ***Roseanne***

A mother had twin children, Will and Jenny. The two had entirely different outlooks on life – Will was a born pessimist while Jenny was an eternal optimist. These attitudes caused the mother a great deal of concern, particularly when it came to buying presents for them. So she decided to consult a child psychiatrist with regard to what she should buy them for Christmas. The psychiatrist told her to spend as much as she could afford on Will the pessimist but said that Jenny would probably be happy with anything. 'Why not get a pile of manure and wrap that up for Jenny?' he suggested. 'I'm sure she'd be fine with that.' The mother took his advice and spent £300 on presents for Will and wrapped up a heap of manure for Jenny. Christmas morning arrived and the kids were opening their presents. 'What has Santa Claus brought you?' she asked Will. He answered gloomily, 'A bike, but I'll probably get run over while riding it; football boots, but I'll probably break my leg while playing; and an electric train set, but I'll probably electrocute myself.' Realising this wasn't going as planned, she turned swiftly to Jenny. 'And what has Santa Claus brought you?' 'I think I got a pony,' said Jenny, up to her elbows in manure, 'but I haven't been able to find him yet!'

Last year on Father's Day, my son gave me something I've always wanted: the keys to my car.

A fraught housewife answered the phone and was relieved to hear a friendly voice on the other end. 'Oh Mother,' she sobbed. 'I've had a terrible day. I sprained my ankle this morning so I haven't been able to go shopping. The washing machine's broken, the baby won't eat, the house is a mess and I'm supposed to be hosting a dinner party tonight.' 'Now, don't you worry about a thing,' came the reply. 'I'll be over in half an hour. I'll do the shopping, clean up the house and cook your dinner. I'll feed the baby and I'll call a repairman to fix the washing machine. I'll do everything. And I'll call George at the office and tell him he ought to come home and help.' 'George? Who's George?' said the woman. 'George – your husband! This is 314 4628?' 'No, this is 314 4629.' 'Oh,' said the voice. 'Does this mean you're not coming over?'

I love children, especially when they cry, for then someone takes them away.
Nancy Mitford

A young man agreed to babysit one night so a single mother could have an evening out. At bedtime he sent the youngsters upstairs to bed and settled down to watch football. One child kept creeping down the stairs, but the young man kept sending him back to bed. At 9pm the doorbell rang. It was the next-door neighbour, Mrs Brown, asking whether her son was there. The young man brusquely replied, 'No.' Just then a little head appeared over the banister and shouted, 'I'm here, Mum, but he won't let me go home!'

She's at that awkward age when she's stopped asking us where she comes from and started refusing to tell us where she's going.

A man went to the supermarket with his three-year-old daughter in tow. Since he was just there to grab some essentials like milk and bread, he opted to save some time by not pushing a trolley around the shop. 'That's not the way Mummy does it,' his daughter informed him. 'I know, dear, but Daddy's way is okay, too,' he replied. Leaving the supermarket in the rain and without a trolley, he carried the bag of groceries, his daughter and the milk quickly to the car. Not wanting to set anything down on the wet ground, he put the milk on top of the car, efficiently whisked open the car door with his now free hand, scooted the groceries in and lifted his daughter into the car seat in one swift motion. Then he hopped in himself. 'That's not the way Mummy does it,' his daughter informed him again. 'Sweetheart, there's more than one way to do things,' he replied patiently. 'Daddy's way is okay, too.' As they pulled out and headed down the street, he became aware of the scraping sound on the roof as the milk slid down the length of the rooftop, bounced off the bonnet of the car and splattered to the ground, sending a froth of white milk in every direction. In the millisecond he took to process his mistake, his young daughter looked at him, and in a most serious voice said, 'That's NOT the way Mummy does it.'

It's not easy arguing with my kids. My trouble is, I'm not young enough to know everything.

Two kids are talking to each other. One says, 'I'm really worried. My dad works twelve hours a day to give me a nice home and good food. My mum spends the whole day cleaning and cooking for me. I'm worried sick!' The other kid says, 'What have you got to worry about? Sounds to me like you've got it made!' The first kid says, 'What if they try to escape?'

Father: When I was your age I worked 16 hours a day in this business, seven days a week!
Son: I really appreciate it, Dad. If it wasn't for all your ambition, determination and hard work, I might have had to do that myself.

A father was trying to teach his young son the evils of alcohol. He put one worm in a glass of water and another worm in a glass of whisky. The worm in the water lived, while the one in the whisky curled up and died. 'All right, son,' asked the father, 'what does that show you?' 'Well, Dad, it shows that if you drink alcohol, you will not have worms.'

If a mother's place is in the home, how come I spend so much time in the car?

Bumper sticker

A four-year-old boy and his father went to the beach. There was a dead seagull lying on the sand. The boy asked his father, 'Dad, what happened to the birdie?' His dad told him, 'Son, the bird died and went to Heaven.' Then the boy asked, "And God threw him back down?'

I come from a big family. There were 19 of us. I didn't know what it was like to sleep on my own until I got married.

Teddy came thundering down the stairs, much to his father's annoyance. 'Teddy,' he called, 'how many more times have I got to tell you to come down the stairs quietly? Now, go back up and come down like a civilised human being.' There was a silence, and Teddy reappeared in the front room. 'That's better,' said his father. 'Now will you always come down stairs like that?' 'Suits me,' said Teddy. 'I slid down the banister.'

One day a little girl was sitting watching her mother do the dishes at the kitchen sink. She suddenly noticed that her mother had several strands of white hair sticking out in contrast on her brunette head. She looked at her mother and asked inquisitively, 'Why are some of your hairs white, Mum?' Her mother replied, 'Well, every time that you do something wrong and make me cry or unhappy, one of my hairs turns white.' The little girl thought about this revelation for a while and then said, 'Mummy, how come all of grandma's hairs are white?'

I don't know what to do. My boss won't let me make personal calls at the office and my wife and daughter won't let me make them at home.

A six-year-old boy called his mother from his friend Charlie's house and confessed he had broken a lamp when he threw a football in their living room. 'But, Mum,' he said, brightening. 'You don't have to worry about buying another one. Charlie's mother said it was irreplaceable.'

I think I'd be a good mother. Maybe a little overprotective. Like I would never let the kid out – of my body.

Wendy Liebman

50 Things That Change After University

1 6am is when you get up, not when you go to sleep.
2 Having sex in a single bed is absurd.
3 You keep more food than beer in the fridge.
4 Your fantasies of having sex with three women with lesbian tendencies are replaced by fantasies of having sex with anyone at all.
5 You don't volunteer for clinical trials at the local hospital.
6 You know all of the people sleeping in your house.
7 You hear your favourite song in the lift at work.
8 Informative TV does not include Richard and Judy.
9 The bank manager doesn't write threatening letters any more.
10 You carry an umbrella.
11 Seven-day benders are no longer realistic.
12 You don't go to Tesco with all your friends.
13 You have standing orders and direct debits.
14 The heating works in your house.
15 Your friends marry and divorce instead of get together and break up.
16 You pay the government thousands of pounds every year.
17 You go from 130 days of holidays to 20.
18 Jeans and a jumper no longer qualify as 'dressed up'.
19 You're the one calling the police because those damn kids next door won't turn down the stereo.
20 You get out of bed in the morning even if it's raining.
21 Washing up is not an annual ritual.
22 Older relatives feel comfortable telling sex jokes around you.
23 You don't know what time the kebab shop closes anymore.
24 Your car insurance goes down and your car payments go up.
25 You feed your dog Pal instead of McDonalds.
26 You don't get ideas for drinks from local tramps.
27 You don't put half-finished curries in the fridge to eat later.
28 You don't spend half your day strategically planning pub crawls.
29 You 'hate scrounging students'.
30 You no longer have a strange attraction to road signs when drunk.
31 Sleeping in the lounge is a no-no.
32 You can't persuade your flatmates to 'drink till dawn'.
33 You don't spend Wednesday afternoons in the pub.

34 You always know where you are when you wake up.
35 You no longer take naps from noon to 6pm.
36 A fire in the kitchen is not a laugh.
37 You go to the chemist for Panadol and antacids, not condoms and pregnancy test kits.
38 A £3 bottle of wine is no longer 'pretty good stuff'.
39 You can remember the name of the person you wake up next to.
40 You actually eat breakfast foods at breakfast time.
41 You don't have mice living in your kitchen.
42 Grocery lists are longer than pot noodles and cans of lager.
43 You don't go to Liquor Save to buy vodka.
44 You have hoovered.
45 Breaking the law means doing 40 in a 30 zone.
46 'I just can't drink the way I used to' replaces 'I'm never going to drink that much again'.
47 Over 90 per cent of the time you spend in front of a computer is for real work.
48 You don't experiment with banned substances.
49 You don't get drunk at home, to save money, before going to a pub.
50 You don't find a 'dump' left in the toilet hysterically funny any more.

A young man moved away from his parents to become a student. Proudly showing off his new apartment to a couple of his friends late one night, he led the way to his bedroom where there was a big brass gong. 'What's that big brass gong?' one of the guests asked. 'It's not a gong. It's a talking clock,' the man replied. 'A talking clock? Seriously?' asked his astonished friend. 'Yup,' replied the student. 'How's it work?' the second guest asked, squinting at it. 'Watch,' the student replied. He picked up a hammer, gave it an ear-shattering pound and stepped back. The three stood looking at one another for a moment. Suddenly, someone on the other side of the wall screamed, 'You idiot, it's ten past three in the morning!'

My dad used to play games with me as a kid. He used to throw me in the air – and walk away.

An irate woman burst into the baker's shop and said, 'I sent my son in for 2lb of cookies this morning, but when I weighed them there was only 1lb. I suggest that you check your scales.' The baker looked at her calmly for a moment or two and then replied, 'Ma'am, I suggest you weigh your son.'

We've given my son a hint. On his bedroom door we've pinned a sign: check-out time is 18.

Today's teenagers are alike in many disrespects.

'Mum, can I please change my name right now?' asked Ben. 'But why would you want to do that, dear?' said his mum. 'Because Dad said he's going to spank me as sure as my name's Benjamin!'

One night, a teenage girl brought her new boyfriend home to meet her parents, and they were appalled by his appearance: leather jacket, motorcycle boots, tattoos and pierced nose. Later, the parents pulled their daughter aside and confessed their concern. 'Dear,' said the mother diplomatically, 'he doesn't seem very nice.' 'Oh please, Mum,' replied the daughter, 'if he wasn't nice, why would he be doing 500 hours of community service?'

The teenager approached the sales clerk in the dress shop with a large bag. 'My mother likes this outfit – may I exchange it?'

The policeman got out of his car and the kid, who was stopped for speeding, rolled down his window. 'I've been waiting for you all day,' the policeman said. The kid replied, 'Yeah, well I got here as fast as I could.'

You're twelve years old? Heavens, when I was your age I was 16!

I'll never forget Father's Day last year. I called my dad on the phone, wished him happy Father's Day and had a really good conversation that went on for ages, all about Mum and when I was a kid and playing in the park and going for rides in the car. It was great. As we were saying goodbye, there was a catch in his voice and he said three words which, as long as I live, I'll never forget. He said, 'Who are you?'

You can see why grandparents and grandchildren get on well with each other. They have a common enemy.

We've been married for six years, so people are trying to force us to have kids; it's like we're cheating or something. They all say the same thing, "Kids, they're a lot of work, but they're worth it." But have you noticed something? They never look you in the eye when they say that.

Wanda Sykes-Hall

Adolescence is the age when a child feels that its parents should be taught the facts of life.

A family is just like a bath. At first it's okay but later on it's not so hot.

For their anniversary, a couple went out for a romantic dinner. Their teenage daughters said they would fix a dessert and leave it waiting. When they got home, they saw that the dining room table was beautifully set with china, crystal and candles, and there was a note that read: 'Your dessert is in the refrigerator. We are staying with friends, so go ahead and do something we wouldn't do!' 'I suppose,' the husband responded dryly, 'we could clean the house.'

They treated the au pair like one of the family – so she left.

Son: Dad, I'm afraid the car's got water in the carburettor.
Dad: Where is the car?
Son: In the lake.

What did your daughter do last weekend? Her hair and her nails.

Donald MacDonald from the Isle of Skye left home for the first time and went to study at an English university, living in the halls of residence with all the other students there. After he had been there a month, his mother came to visit him. 'And how do you find the English students, Donald?' she asked. 'Mother,' he replied, 'they're such terrible, noisy people. The one on that side keeps banging his head on the wall and won't stop. The one on the other side screams and screams all night.' 'Oh Donald! How do you manage to put up with these awful noisy English neighbours?' 'Mother, I do nothing. I just ignore them. I just stay here quietly, playing my bagpipes.'

A boy was teaching a girl arithmetic, he said it was his mission.
He kissed her once; he kissed her twice and said, 'Now that's addition.'
In silent satisfaction, she sweetly gave the kisses back and said, 'Now that's subtraction.'
Then he kissed her, she kissed him, without an explanation.
And both together smiled and said, 'That's multiplication.'
Then her Dad appeared upon the scene and made a quick decision.
He kicked that boy three blocks away and said, 'That's long division!'

Little Johnny

One day the teacher wanted the class to use the word 'definitely' in a sentence. Suzy raised her hand so she called on her. She said, 'The sky is definitely blue!' 'I'm sorry Suzy,' said the teacher, 'but that's wrong. The sky sometimes turns different colours, like red or grey etc. Anybody else?' Timmy raised his hand and said, 'The grass is definitely green.' 'I'm sorry Timmy, that's not true either. Sometimes the grass dies and it may turn brown. Anybody else?' Little Johnny raises his hand and says, 'Teacher, do farts have lumps?' The teacher says, 'No, why?' Johnny says, 'Then I definitely shit my pants!'

Little Johnny was sitting in class one day. All of the sudden, he needed to go to the bathroom. He yelled out, 'Miss Jones, I need to take a pee!' The teacher replied, 'Now, Johnny, that is NOT the proper word to use in this situation. The correct word you want to use is 'urinate'. Please use the word 'urinate' in a sentence correctly, and I will allow you to go.' Little Johnny thinks for a bit, then says, 'You're an eight, but if you would let me go pee, you'd be a ten!'

A teacher cautiously approaches the subject of sex education with her class because she realises Little Johnny's propensity for sexual innuendo. But Johnny remains attentive throughout the entire lecture. Finally, towards the end of the lesson, the teacher asks for examples of sex education from the class. One little boy raises his hand, 'I saw a bird in her nest with some eggs.' 'Very good, William,' said the teacher. 'My mummy had a baby,' said little Esther. 'Oh, that's nice,' replied the teacher. Finally, little Johnny raises his hand. With much fear and trepidation, the teacher calls on him. 'I was watching TV yesterday, and I saw the Lone Ranger. He was surrounded by hundreds and hundreds of Indians. And they all attacked at one time. And he killed every one of them with his two guns.' The teacher was relieved but puzzled. 'And what does that have to do with sex education, Johnny?' 'It'll teach those Indians not to f*** with the Lone Ranger.'

A Sunday School teacher of pre-schoolers was concerned that his students might be a little confused about Jesus Christ because of the Christmas season emphasis on His birth. He wanted to make sure they understood that the birth of Jesus occurred a long time ago, that He grew up, etc. So he asked his class, 'Where is Jesus today?' Steven raised his hand and said, 'He's in Heaven.' Mary was called on and answered, 'He's in my heart.' Little Johnny, waving his hand furiously, blurted out, 'I know! I know! He's in our bathroom!' The whole class got very quiet, looked at the teacher, and waited for a response. The teacher was completely at a loss for a few very long seconds. He finally gathered his wits and asked Little Johnny how he knew this. Little Johnny said, 'Well, every morning, my father gets up, bangs on the bathroom door, and yells "Jesus Christ, are you still in there?'"

'Johnny,' scolded the small boy's mother. 'Your face is clean but how did you manage to get your hands so dirty?' 'Washing my face,' replied Johnny.

At school Little Johnny was told by a classmate that most adults are hiding at least one dark secret, and that this makes it very easy to blackmail them by saying, 'I know the whole truth.' Little Johnny decides to go home and try it out. He goes home, and as he is greeted by his mother he says, 'I know the whole truth.' His mother quickly hands him £20 and says, 'Just don't tell your father.' Quite pleased, the boy waits for his father to get home from work, and greets him with, 'I know the whole truth.' The father promptly hands him £40 and says, 'Please don't say a word to your mother.' Very pleased, the boy is on his way to school the next day when he sees the postman at his front door. The boy greets him by saying, 'I know the whole truth.' The postman immediately drops the mail, opens his arms and says, 'Then come give your real father a big hug.'

As a special treat, little Johnny was allowed to stay up for a dinner party which his parents were giving for friends. As his mother collected the plates after the main course, Johnny piped up 'Is the dessert not good for me or is there enough to go round?'

Little Johnny's neighbour has just had a little boy. The only problem is that the baby doesn't have any ears. Everyone who comes to see the baby compliments the woman on its looks, but no one mentions the fact that it doesn't have any ears. Suddenly, the mother sees Little Johnny coming over from next door. She becomes very worried because she thinks that he is going to make fun of the baby. When he enters the house, he compliments the baby on everything without mentioning its ears. Without warning, he says, 'He has beautiful eyes, does he have 20/20 vision?' She thanks him, says yes and asks why. Finally he says, 'Well, it's a good job, because if he didn't he wouldn't have a damn thing to hang his glasses on now, would he?'

The summer holidays were over and Little Johnny returned to school. Only two days later his teacher phoned his mother to tell her that he was misbehaving. 'Wait a minute,' she said. 'I had Johnny with me for three months and I never called you once when he misbehaved!'

Little Johnny was attending his first day of school. The teacher advised the class to start the day with the pledge of allegiance, and instructed them to put their right hands over their hearts and repeat after him. He looked around the room as he started the recitation, 'I pledge allegiance to the flag.' When his eyes fell upon Little Johnny, he noticed his hand over the right cheek of his buttocks. 'Little Johnny, I will not continue until you put your hand over your heart.' Little Johnny replied, 'It is over my heart.' After several attempts to get Little Johnny to put his hand over his heart, the teacher asked, 'Why do you think that is your heart?' 'Because every time my Grandma comes to visit, she picks me up, pats me here, and says, "Bless your little heart", and my Grandma wouldn't lie!'

Little Johnny wasn't getting good marks in school. One day he surprised the teacher with an announcement. He tapped her on the shoulder and said, 'I don't want to scare you, but my daddy says if I don't start getting better grades, somebody is going to get a spanking!'

Little Johnny's kindergarten class was on a field trip to their local police station where they saw pictures, tacked to a bulletin board, of the ten most wanted men. One of the youngsters pointed to a picture and asked if it really was the photo of a wanted person. 'Yes,' said the policeman. 'The detectives want him very badly.' So Little Johnny asked, 'Why didn't you keep him when you took his picture?'

Little five-year-old Johnny was in the bath, and his mum was washing his hair. She said to him, 'Wow, your hair is growing so fast! You need a haircut again.' Little Johnny replied, 'Maybe you should stop watering it so much.'

Little Johnny was going to his father's house so he packed everything in his room and put it in his little red wagon. He was walking to his father's house with his wagon behind him, when he came to this hill. He started up the hill but was constantly swearing, 'This God damn thing is so heavy.' A priest heard him and came out. 'You shouldn't be swearing,' said the priest. 'God hears you. He is everywhere. He's in the church. He's on the pavement. He's everywhere.' Then Little Johnny says,

'Oh, is he in my wagon?' The priest replies, 'Yes, Johnny, God is in your wagon.' Little Johnny says, 'Well tell him to get the hell out and start pulling!'

Little Johnny's new baby brother was screaming up a storm. He asked his mum, 'Where'd we get him?' His mother replied, 'He came from Heaven, Johnny.' Johnny said, 'Wow! I can see why they threw him out!'

In Sunday School, they were teaching how God created everything, including human beings. Little Johnny seemed especially interested when they told him how Eve was created out of one of Adam's ribs. Later in the week, his mother noticed him lying down as though he were ill, and said, 'Johnny, what's the matter?' Little Johnny responded, 'I have a pain in my side. I think I'm going to have a wife.'

Little Johnny's pre-school class went on a field trip to the fire station. The fireman giving the presentation held up a smoke detector and asked the class, 'Does anyone know what this is?' Little Johnny's hand shot up and the fireman called on him. Little Johnny replied, 'That's how Mummy knows supper is ready!'

Little Johnny says to Grandpa, 'Grandpa, please can you make a noise like a frog?' 'Now why should you want me to do that?' says Grandpa. 'Well,' replies Little Johnny, 'Mum said that when you croak we can all go to Disneyworld.'

The vicar was talking to a group of young children about being good and going to Heaven. At the end of his talk, he asked, 'Where do you want to go?' 'Heaven!' Suzy cried out. 'And what do you have to be to get there?' asked the vicar. 'Six feet under!' yelled Little Johnny.

Little Johnny's father said, 'Let me see your report card.' Johnny replied, 'I don't have it.' 'Why not?' His father asked. 'My friend just borrowed it. He wants to scare his parents.'

Little Johnny sees his father's car passing the playground and going into the woods. Curious, he follows the car and sees Daddy and Aunt Jane kissing. Johnny finds this so exciting and can barely contain himself as he runs home and starts to tell his mother excitedly. 'Mummy, mummy! I was at the playground and Daddy and...' His mother tells him to slow down, but that she wants to hear the story. So Johnny tells her. 'I was at the playground and I saw Daddy's car go into the woods with Aunt Jane. I went to look and Daddy was giving Aunt Jane a big kiss, then he helped her take off her shirt, then Aunt Jane helped Daddy take his pants off, then Aunt Jane laid down on the seat, then Daddy...' At this point, his mother cut him off and said, 'Johnny, this is such an interesting story, suppose you save the rest of it for supper time. I want to see the look on Daddy's face when you tell it tonight.' At the dinner table, Johnny's mother asks him to tell his story. He describes the car going into the woods, the undressing, the laying down on the seat, and, 'then Daddy and Aunt Jane did that same thing Mummy and Uncle Jeff used to do when Daddy was in the Army.'

Little Johnny came running into the house and asked, 'Mummy, can little girls have babies?' 'No,' said his mum, 'of course not.' Little Johnny then ran back outside and his mum heard him yell to his friends, 'It's okay, we can play that game again!'

Little Johnny was sitting on a park bench munching on one chocolate bar after another. After the sixth one a man on the bench across from him said, 'Son, you know eating all that chocolate isn't good for you. It will give you acne, rot your teeth and make you fat.' Little Johnny replied, 'My grandfather lived to be 107 years old.' The man asked, 'Did your grandfather eat six chocolate bars at a time?' Little Johnny answered, 'No, he minded his own business!'

Teachers never give up, and neither does Little Johnny. She asks him, 'Can you name the Great Lakes?' You know Johnny, he is always fast with an answer, and he pipes up with, 'I don't need to. They've already been named.'

Little Johnny was in the garden filling in a hole when his neighbour peered over the fence. Interested in what the cheeky-faced youngster was doing, he politely asked, 'What are you up to there, Johnny?' 'My goldfish died,' replied Johnny tearfully, without looking up, 'and I've just buried him.' The neighbour was concerned. 'That's an awfully big hole for a goldfish, isn't it?' Johnny patted down the last heap of earth and then replied, 'That's because he's inside your cat.'

The arithmetic teacher had written 10.9 on the blackboard and had then rubbed out the decimal point to show the effect of multiplying this number by ten. 'Johnny,' the teacher asked, 'where is the decimal point now?' 'On the eraser!' came back the quick reply.

Little Johnny was heard by his mother reciting his homework: 'Two plus two, the son of a bitch is four; four plus four, the son of a bitch is eight; eight plus eight, the son of a bitch...' 'Johnny!' shouted his mother. 'Watch your language! You're not allowed to use the swear words.' 'But Mum,' replied the boy, 'that's what the teacher taught us, and she said to recite it out loud till we learned it.' The next day, Johnny's mother went right into the classroom to complain. 'Oh, Heavens!' said the teacher. 'That's not what I taught them. They're supposed to say, "Two plus two, the sum of which is four".'

Coming through the door after school one day, Little Johnny hollers out, 'Okay, everyone in the house, please stand advised that I, Little Johnny, have on this date made a complete fool of myself in sex education class by repeating stories concerning storks as told to me by certain parties residing in this house!'

'Hey, Mum,' asked Little Johnny, 'can you give me £20?' 'Certainly not!' answered his mother. 'If you do,' Little Johnny went on, 'I'll tell you what Dad said to the maid when you were at the beauty shop.' His mother's ears perked up and, grabbing her purse, she handed over the money. 'Well? What did he say?' 'He said, "Hey, Juanita, make sure you wash my socks tomorrow."'

It was the first day of class in a new town for Little Johnny. As a test, his teacher went around the room and asked each of the students to count to 50. Some did very well, counting as high as 30 or 40 with just a few mistakes. Others couldn't get past 20. Little Johnny, however, did extremely well; he counted past 50, right up to 100 without any mistakes. He was so excited that he ran home and told his dad how well he had done. His dad nodded and told him, 'That's because you are from Alabama, son.' The next day, in language class, the teacher asked the students to recite the alphabet. It's third grade, so most could make it half way through without much trouble. Some made it to S or T, but Little Johnny rattled off the alphabet perfectly right to the end. That evening, Johnny once again bragged to his dad about his prowess in his new school. His dad, knowingly, explained to him, 'That's because you are from Alabama, son.' The next day, after physical education, the boys were taking showers. Johnny noted that, compared to the other boys in his grade, he seemed overly 'well endowed'. This confused him. That night he asked his dad, 'Dad, they all have little tiny ones, but mine is ten times bigger than theirs. Is that because I'm from Alabama?' he asked. 'No, son,' explained his dad, 'That's because you're 18.'

A teacher decides to teach sex education to her class. She starts out by drawing a penis on the blackboard and asks the class, 'Does anyone know what this is?' Little Johnny jumps up and says, 'Yes, my dad has two of them!' 'Are you sure about that Johnny?' asks the teacher, somewhat stunned. And little Johnny says, 'Yep, he uses a small skinny one to go to the bathroom, and a big long one to brush the babysitter's teeth.'

Little Johnny came into the kitchen where his mother was making dinner. His birthday was coming up and he thought this was a good time to tell his mother what he wanted. 'Mum, I want a bike for my birthday,' he said. Little Johnny was a bit of a troublemaker. He had been in trouble at school and at home. Johnny's mother asked him if he thought he deserved to get a bike for his birthday. Little Johnny, of course, thought he did. Johnny's mother, being a Christian woman, wanted him to reflect on his behaviour over the last year and write a letter to God to tell him why he deserved a bike for his birthday. Little Johnny stomped up the steps to his room and sat down to write God a letter.

The first letter:

Dear God,
I have been a very good boy this year and I would like a bike for my birthday. I want a red one.
Your friend,
Johnny

Johnny knew this wasn't true. He had not been a very good boy that year, so he tore up the letter and started over.

The second letter:

Dear God,
This is your friend Johnny. I have been a pretty good boy this year and I would like a red bike for my birthday.
Thank you,
Johnny

Johnny knew this wasn't true either. He tore up the letter and started again.

The third letter:

Dear God,
I have been an okay boy this year and I would really like a red bike for my birthday.
Johnny

Johnny knew he could not send this letter to God either. He was very upset. He went downstairs and told his mother he wanted to go church. 'Just be home in time for dinner,' his mother said. Johnny walked down the street to the church and up to the altar. He looked around to see if anyone was there. He picked up a statue of the Virgin Mary and slipped it under his shirt and ran out of the church, down the street, into his house and up to his room. He shut the door to his room and sat down with a piece of paper and a pen. Johnny began to write his letter to God.

The fourth letter:

I'VE GOT YOUR MUM. IF YOU WANT TO SEE HER AGAIN, SEND THE BIKE.
Signed
YOU KNOW WHO

Little Johnny returns from school and says he got an F in maths. 'Why?' asks his father. 'The teacher asked "How much is 2 x 3?" I said 6. 'But that's right!' 'Then she asked me "How much is 3 x 2?"' 'What's the f**king difference?' asks his father. 'That's what I said!'

The summer holiday was over and the teacher asked Little Johnny about his family trip. 'We visited my grandmother in Minneapolis, Minnesota.' The teacher asked, 'Good, can you tell the class how you spell that?' Little Johnny said, 'Actually, we went to Ohio.'

Little Johnny watched, fascinated, as his mother gently rubbed cream on her face. 'Why are you rubbing cold cream on your face, Mummy?' he asked. 'To make myself beautiful,' said his mother. A few minutes later, she began removing the cream with a tissue. 'What's the matter?' asked Little Johnny. 'Giving up?'

On the last day of kindergarten, all the children brought presents for their teacher. The florist's son handed the teacher a gift. She shook it, held it up and said, 'I bet I know what it is - it's some flowers!' 'That's right!' shouted the little boy. Then the sweet shop owner's daughter handed the teacher a gift. She held it up, shook it and said, 'I bet I know what it is - it's a box of sweets!' 'That's right!' shouted the little girl. The next gift was from the off licence owner's son, Little Johnny. The teacher held it up and saw that it was leaking. She touched a drop with her finger and tasted it. 'Is it wine?' she asked. 'No,' Little Johnny answered. The teacher touched another drop to her tongue. 'Is it champagne?' she asked. 'No,' he answered. Finally, the teacher said, 'I give up. What is it?' Little Johnny replied, 'A puppy!'

Little Johnny is sitting in a biology class, and the teacher says that an interesting phenomenon of nature is that only humans stutter, no other animal in the world does this. Johnny's hand shoots up. 'Not correct, Miss!' he says. 'Please explain, Johnny,' replies the teacher. 'Well, Miss, the other day I was playing with my cat on the veranda. The neighbours' Great Dane came around the corner, and my cat went "ffffffffff! ffffffffffff! ffffffffff!", and before he could say "F*** OFF!", the dog ate him!'

Little Johnny was starting his first day at a new school and his father called the teacher to tell her that Little Johnny was a big gambler. She said that it was no problem and she had seen worse than that. After Little Johnny's first day at his new school, his father called the teacher to see how it went. She said, 'I think I broke his gambling.' His father asked how and she said, 'He bet me £5 that I had a mole on my bum, so I pulled down my pants and won his money.' 'Damn!' said Little Johnny's father. 'What's wrong?' the teacher asked, to which Little Johnny's father replied, 'This morning he bet me £100 he would see his teacher's bum before the day was over!'

A schoolteacher asked her students to use the word 'fascinate' in a sentence. Molly put up her hand and said, 'My family went to my grandad's farm, and we all saw his sheep. It was fascinating.' The teacher said, 'That was good, but I wanted you to use the word fascinate, not fascinating.' Sally raised her hand. She said, 'My family went to Graceland and I was fascinated.' The teacher said, 'Well, that was good Sally, but I wanted you to use the word fascinate, not fascinated.' Little Johnny raised his hand. The teacher hesitated because she had been burned by Little Johnny before. She finally decided there was no way he could damage the word 'fascinate', so she called on him. Little Johnny said, 'My Aunt Gina has a shirt with ten buttons, but her boobs are so big she can only fasten eight.' The teacher cried.

Little Johnny had been misbehaving and was sent to his room. After a while, he emerged and said to his mother that he had thought it over and said a prayer. 'Fine,' said his mother, pleased. 'If you asked God to help you not misbehave, He will help you.' 'Oh, I didn't ask him to help me not misbehave,' said Johnny. 'I asked him to help you put up with me.'

Finding one of her students making faces at others on the playground, Ms Smith stopped to gently reprimand the child. Smiling sweetly, the Sunday School teacher said, 'Johnny, when I was a child, I was told that if I made ugly faces, it would freeze and I would stay like that.' Little Johnny looked up and replied, 'Well, Miss Smith, you can't say you weren't warned.'

The department store Santa has Little Johnny on his lap and says to him, 'I bet I know what you want for Christmas, Little Johnny. You want some t-o-y-s,' he says, touching Johnny's nose with his finger as he spells out the word toys.

'No, I've got plenty of toys,' replies Little Johnny. 'Then I bet you want some g-a-m-e-s,' replied Santa, touching Johnny's nose with his finger as he spells out the word games. 'No, I've got all the games I want,' came Little Johnny's reply. 'Well, Little Johnny, you don't want any toys or games for Christmas, what do you want?' asked Santa. 'I want some p-u-s-s-y,' Johnny replied, touching Santa's nose with each letter, 'And don't tell me you don't have any because I can smell it on your finger.'

One day, Little Johnny came home from school, and said to his mother, 'Mummy, today in school I was punished for something that I didn't do.' The mother exclaimed, 'But that's terrible Johnny dear! I'm going to have a talk with your teacher about this. By the way, what was it that you didn't do?' Little Johnny replied, 'My homework.'

Little Johnny comes home from school with a note from his teacher, indicating that 'Johnny seems to be having some difficulty with the differences between boys and girls,' and would his mother '...please sit down and have a talk with Johnny about this.' So, Little Johnny's mother takes him quietly by the hand upstairs to her bedroom, and closes the door. 'First Johnny, I want you to take off my blouse...' So he unbuttons her blouse and takes it off. 'Okay, now take off my skirt...' And he takes off her skirt. 'Now, take off my bra...' He does. 'And now, Johnny, please take off my panties...' And when Johnny finishes removing these, she says, 'Johnny, *please* don't wear any of my clothes to school any more! What were you thinking?'

A young female teacher is giving an assignment to her class one day. It is a large assignment so she starts writing high up on the blackboard. Suddenly there is a giggle from one of the boys in the class. She quickly turns and asks, 'What's so funny, Pat?' 'I just saw one of your suspenders!' 'Get out of my classroom,' she yells, 'I don't want to see you for three days!' Then she turns back to the blackboard. Realising she has forgotten to title the assignment, she reaches to the very top. Suddenly there is an even louder giggle from another male student. She quickly turns and asks, 'What's so funny, Billy?' 'I just saw both of your suspenders!' Again, she yells, "Get out of my classroom! This time the punishment is more severe, I don't want to see you for three weeks!' Embarrassed and frustrated, she drops the eraser when she turns around again. So she bends over to pick it up. This time there is a burst of laughter from another male student. She quickly turns to see Little Johnny leaving the classroom. 'Where do you think you're going?' she asks. 'From what I just saw,' replies Little Johnny, 'my school days are over!'

Losing It

A reporter was interviewing a 104-year-old woman: 'And what do you think is the best thing about being 104?' the reporter asked. She replied, 'No peer pressure.'

At my age I do what Mark Twain did. I get my daily paper, look at the obituaries page and if I'm not there I carry on as usual. ***Patrick Moore***

An elderly gentleman had had serious hearing problems for a number of years. He went to the doctor and the doctor was able to have him fitted for a hearing aid that allowed the gentleman to hear 100%. The elderly gentleman went back in a month to the doctor and the doctor said, 'Your hearing is perfect. Your family must be really pleased that you can hear again.' To which the gentleman said, 'Oh, I haven't told my family yet. I just sit around and listen to the conversations. I've changed my will three times!'

Middle age is when it takes longer to rest than to get tired.

For the first time in many years, an old man travelled from his rural town to the city to go to the cinema. After buying his ticket, he stopped at the concession stand to purchase some popcorn. Handing the attendant £3.50, he couldn't help but comment, 'The last time I came to the cinema, popcorn was only sixpence.' 'Well, sir,' the attendant replied with a grin, 'You're really going to enjoy yourself. We have sound now.'

Three retirees, each with hearing loss, were taking a walk one fine March day. One remarked to the other, 'Windy, isn't it?' 'No,' the second man replied, 'It's Thursday.' And the third man chirped up, 'So am I. Let's have a Coke.'

God, grant me the senility
To forget the people
I never liked anyway,
The good fortune
To run into the ones I do,
And the eyesight
To tell the difference.

A wise old gentleman retired and purchased a modest home near a junior high school. He spent the first few weeks of his retirement in peace and contentment. Then a new school year began. The very next afternoon three young boys, full of youthful, after-school enthusiasm, came down his street, beating merrily on every rubbish bin they encountered. The crashing percussion continued day after day, until finally the wise old man decided it was time to take some action. The next afternoon, he walked out to meet the young percussionists as they banged their way down the street. Stopping them, he said, 'You kids are a lot of fun. I like to see you express your exuberance like that. In fact, I used to do the same thing when I was your age. Will you do me a favour? I'll give you each a pound if you'll promise to come around every day and do your thing.' The kids were elated and continued to do a bang-up job on the rubbish bins. After a few days, the old-timer greeted the kids again, but this time he had a sad smile on his face. 'This recession's really putting a big dent in my income,' he told them. 'From now on, I'll only be able to pay you 50 pence to beat on the bins.' The noisemakers were obviously displeased, but they accepted his offer and continued their afternoon ruckus. A few days later, the wily retiree approached them again as they drummed their way down the street. 'Look,' he said, 'I haven't received my Social Security cheque yet, so I'm not going to be able to give you more than 25 pence. Will that be okay?' 'A lousy 25 pence?' the drum leader exclaimed. 'If you think we're going to waste our time, beating these bins around for that, you're nuts! No way, mister. We quit!' And the old man enjoyed peace.

Middle age is having a choice of two temptations and choosing the one that will get you home earlier.

First you forget names, then you forget faces. Next you forget to pull your zipper up and finally, you forget to pull it down. ***George Burns***

Three ladies were discussing the travails of getting older. One said, 'Sometimes I catch myself with a jar of mayonnaise in my hand, while standing in front of the refrigerator, and I can't remember whether I need to put it away, or start making a sandwich.' The second lady joined in with, 'Yes, sometimes I find myself on the landing of the stairs and can't remember whether I was on my way up or on my way down.' The third one responded, 'Well, ladies, I'm glad I don't have that problem. Knock on wood,' as she rapped her knuckles on the table, and then said, 'That must be the door, I'll get it!'

You know you're getting older when...

Everything that works hurts, and what doesn't hurt doesn't work.

You feel like the morning after, and you haven't been anywhere.

Your little black book only contains names ending in MD.

Your children are beginning to look middle-aged.

Your mind makes contracts your body can't keep.

You look forward to a dull evening.

Your knees buckle and your belt won't.

Your back goes out more than you do.

You sink your teeth into a steak, and they stay there.

You know all the answers, but nobody asks you the questions.

An 80-year-old couple was having problems remembering things, so they decided to go to their doctor to get checked out to make sure nothing was wrong with them. When they arrived at the doctor's, they explained to him about the problems they were having with their memory. After checking the couple out, the doctor told them they were physically okay, but might want to start writing things down and make notes to help them remember things. The couple thanked the doctor and left. Later that night while watching TV, the old man got up from his chair and his wife asked, 'Where are you going?' He replied, 'To the kitchen.' She asked, 'Will you get me a bowl of ice cream?' He replied, 'Sure.' She then asked him, 'Don't you think you should write it down so you can remember it?' He said, 'No, I can remember that.' She then said, 'Well, I also would like some strawberries on top. You had better write that down because I know you'll forget that.' But he said, 'I can remember that. You want a bowl of ice cream with strawberries.' She replied, 'Well, I would also like whipped cream on top. I know you will forget that so you'd better write it down.' With irritation in his voice, he said, 'I don't need to write that down, I can remember that.' He then fumed into the kitchen. After about 20 minutes, he returned from the kitchen and handed her a plate of bacon and eggs. She stared at the plate for a moment and then said, 'You forgot my toast.'

As a senior citizen was driving along the M25, his car phone rang. Answering, he heard his wife's voice urgently warning him, 'Herman, I just heard on the news that there's a car going the wrong way on the M25. Please be careful!' 'Heck,' said Herman. 'It's not just one car. It's hundreds of them!'

A woman walked up to a little old man rocking in a chair on his porch. 'I couldn't help noticing how happy you look,' she said. 'What's your secret for a long, happy life?' 'I smoke three packs of cigarettes a day,' he said. 'I also drink a case of whisky a week, eat fatty foods, and never exercise.' 'That's amazing,' the woman said. 'How old are you?' 'Twenty-six,' he said.

I don't feel old. I don't feel anything till noon. That's when it's time for my nap.
Bob Hope

Two policemen saw an old woman staggering down the street. Stopping her, they could tell she had had far too much to drink, but instead of taking her to jail they decide to simply drive her home. They loaded her into the police car and one of the officers got in the back with the drunk woman. As they drove through the streets they kept asking the woman where she lived. All she would say as she stroked the officer's arm was 'You're passionate'. They drove a while longer and asked again. Again the same response as she stroked his arm, 'You're passionate'. The officers were getting a little upset so they stopped the car and said to the woman, 'Look, we've driven around this city for two hours and you still haven't told us where you live.' To which the old woman replied, 'I keep trying to tell you - you're passing it!'

Don't worry about avoiding temptation. As you grow older, it will avoid you.

A kind-hearted fellow was walking through Hyde Park and was astonished to see an old man, fishing rod in hand, fishing over a beautiful bed of red roses. 'Tsk, tsk!' said the passer-by to himself. 'What a sad sight. That poor old man is fishing over a bed of flowers. I'll see if I can help.' So the kind fellow walked up to the old man and asked, 'What are you doing, my friend?' 'Fishing, sir.' 'Fishing, eh? Well how would you like to come have a drink with me?' The old man stood, put his rod away and followed the kind stranger to the corner bar. He ordered a large glass of vodka and a fine cigar. His host, the kind fellow, felt good about helping the old man, and he asked, 'Tell me, old friend, how many did you catch today?' The old fellow took a long drag on the cigar, blew a careful smoke ring and replied, 'You are the sixth today, sir!'

I chanced to pass a window
While walking through a mall
With nothing much upon my mind,
Quite blank as I recall.
I noticed in that window
A cranky-faced old man,
And why he looked so cranky
I didn't understand.
Just why he looked at me that way
Was more than I could see
Until I came to realise
That cranky man was ME!

There was an old man whose family could no longer afford to take care of him. So the family decided that a nursing home for the aged would be appropriate. On his first day at the home, he spent most of his time lying in bed reflecting on life, feeling lonely. A while later, a care worker stopped by to see how the old man's first day was going. 'How are you doing today?' she said to the old man. 'First day I see.' The old man replied with a nod. In no time the two began talking up a storm. As the conversation began to drag on, the care worker was eyeing the room filled with fresh flowers, cards and balloons from friends and relatives. She noticed a bowl full of peanuts sitting on top of the table next to the bed, and helped herself to a handful. As the two continued to converse with each other, the care worker kept eating more helpings of the peanuts. She looked at her watch and noticed that nearly two hours had passed and said, 'My goodness, the time has gone by quickly. I have to tend to other people here too.' 'That's okay,' said the old man, 'I feel so much better being able to talk to someone.' Looking into the bowl, the care worker said, 'I feel awful! I ate almost all of your peanuts!' The old man responded, 'That's okay. Ever since I got these false teeth, all I could do was suck the chocolate off them anyway.'

Retirement at 65 is ridiculous. When I was 65 I still had pimples. ***George Burns***

A couple goes out to dinner to celebrate their 50th wedding anniversary. On the way home, she notices a tear in his eye and asks if he's getting sentimental because they're celebrating 50 wonderful years together. He replies, 'No, I was thinking about the time before we got married. Your father threatened me with a shotgun and said he'd have me thrown in jail for 50 years if I didn't marry you. Tomorrow I would have been a free man!'

You're getting old when you're sitting in a rocking chair and can't get it started.

The Burglar

A story I'll tell of a burglar bold
Who started to rob a house.
He opened the window, and then
crept in
As quiet as a mouse.
He looked around for a place to
hide,
'Till the folks were all asleep,
Then said he, 'With their money
I'll take a quiet sneak.'
So under the bed the burglar crept,
He crept up close to the wall
He didn't know it was an old maid's
room,
Or he wouldn't have had the gall.

He thought of the money that he
would steal,
As under the bed he lay,
But at nine o'clock he saw a sight
That made his hair turn grey.
At nine o'clock the old maid
came in
'I am so tired,' she said.
She thought that all was well that
night
So she didn't look under the bed.
She took out her teeth and her big
glass eye,
And the hair from off her head.

The burglar, he had forty fits
As he watched from under the bed.
From under the bed the burglar
crept,
He was a total wreck!
But the old maid wasn't asleep
at all
And she grabbed him by the neck.
She didn't holler, or shout or call,
She was as cool as a clam
She only said, 'The Saints be
praised,
At last I've got a man!'

From under the pillow a gun she
drew,
And to the burglar she said,
'Young man, if you don't marry me,
I'll blow off the top of your head!'
She held him firmly by the neck,
He hadn't a chance to scoot
He looked at the teeth and the big
glass eye,
And said, 'Madam, for Pete's sake,
shoot!'

I am a senior citizen...

- I'm the life of the party – even when it lasts 'till 8pm.
- I'm very good at opening childproof caps with a hammer.
- I'm usually interested in going home before I get to where I'm going.
- I'm good on a trip for at least an hour without my aspirin, antacid...
- I'm the first one to find the bathroom wherever I go.
- I'm awake many hours before my body allows me to get up.
- I'm smiling all the time because I can't hear a word you're saying.
- I'm very good at telling stories – over and over and over and over.
- I'm aware that other people's grandchildren are not as bright as mine.
- I'm so cared for: long-term care, eye care, private care, dental care.
- I'm not grouchy, I just don't like traffic, waiting, children, politicians...
- I'm positive I did housework correctly before the internet.
- I'm sure everything I can't find is in a secure place.
- I'm wrinkled, saggy and lumpy, and that's just my left leg.
- I'm having trouble remembering simple words like ... uh ...
- I'm realising that ageing is not for sissies.
- I'm walking more (to the bathroom) and enjoying it less.
- I'm sure they are making adults much younger these days.
- I'm wondering, if you're only as old as you feel, how could I be alive at 150?
- I'm anti-everything now: Anti-fat, anti-smoke, anti-noise, anti-inflammatory.
- I'm a walking storeroom of facts ... I've just lost the key to the storeroom.
- I'm a senior citizen and I think I am having the time of my life ... Aren't I?

An elderly woman from Brooklyn decided to prepare her will and make her final requests. She told her rabbi she had two final requests. First, she wanted to be cremated, and second, she wanted her ashes scattered over Bloomingdales. 'Bloomingdales?'' the rabbi exclaimed. 'Why Bloomingdales?' 'Then I'll be sure my daughters visit me twice a week.'

I do wish I could tell you my age but it's impossible. It keeps changing all the time.
Greer Garson

A shop owner hires a young female shop assistant who likes to wear very short skirts and G-string panties. One day a young man enters the store, glances at the assistant and then looks at the loaves of bread behind the counter. Noticing the length of her skirt (or general lack thereof) and the location of the raisin bread, he has a brilliant idea. 'I'd like some raisin bread, please,' the man says politely. The assistant nods and climbs up a ladder to reach the raisin bread, which is located on the very top shelf. The young man standing almost directly beneath her is provided with an excellent view, just as he surmised he would be. Once she descends the ladder he muses that he really should get two loaves as he's having company for dinner. As the assistant retrieves the second loaf of bread, one of the other male customers notices what's going on. Thinking quickly, he requests his own loaf of raisin bread so he can continue to enjoy the view. With each trip up the ladder the young lady seems to catch the eye of another male customer. Pretty soon each male patron is asking for raisin bread, just to see the assistant climb up and down. After many trips she's tired, irritated and thinking that she is really going to have to try this bread for herself! Finally once again atop the ladder, she stops and fumes, glaring at the men standing below. She notices an elderly man standing amongst the crowd staring up at her. Thinking to save herself a trip, she yells at the elderly man, 'Is yours raisin, too?' 'No,' croaks the old man. 'But it's starting to quiver.'

You're getting old when getting lucky means you find your car in the parking lot.

Two elderly women were out driving in a large car. Both could barely see over the dashboard. As they were cruising along they came to a crossroads. The traffic light was red but they just went on through. The woman in the passenger seat thought to herself, 'I must be losing it, I could have sworn we just went through a red light.' After a few more minutes they came to another crossroads and the light was red again and again they went right though. This time the woman in the passenger seat was almost sure that the light had been red but was really concerned that she was losing it. She was getting nervous and decided to pay very close attention to the road and the next crossroads to see what was going on. At the next intersection, sure enough, the light was definitely red and they went right through and she turned to the other woman and said, 'Mildred! Did you know we just ran through three red lights in a row? You could have killed us!' Mildred turned to her and said, 'Oh, am I driving?'

In the dim and distant past
When life's tempo wasn't so fast,
Grandma used to rock and knit,
Crochet, tat and babysit.

When the kids were in a jam,
They could always call on Gram.
But today she's in the gym
Exercising to keep slim.

She's checking the web or surfing the net,
Sending some e-mail or placing a bet.
Nothing seems to stop or block her,
Now that Grandma's off her rocker.

Worried because they hadn't heard anything for days from the widow in the neighbouring apartment, Mrs Silver said to her son, 'Timmy, would you go next door and see how old Mrs Kirkland is?' A few minutes later, Timmy returned. 'Well?' asked Mrs Silver, 'Is she all right?' 'She's fine, except that she's angry at you.' 'At me?' the woman exclaimed. 'Whatever for?' 'She said "It's none of your business how old I am,"' snickered Timmy.

When I was a boy the Dead Sea was only sick. ***George Burns***

A young man asked an old rich man how he made his money. The old guy fingered his worsted wool vest and said, 'Well, son, it was 1932. The depth of the Great Depression. I was down to my last penny.' 'I invested that penny in an apple. I spent the entire day polishing the apple and, at the end of the day, I sold the apple for ten pennies.' 'The next morning, I invested those ten pennies in two apples. I spent the entire day polishing them and sold them at 5pm for 20 pence. I continued this system for a month, by the end of which I'd accumulated a fortune of £1.37. Then my wife's father died and left us £2 million.'

A young man saw an elderly couple sitting down to lunch at McDonald's. He noticed that they had ordered one meal, and an extra drink cup. As he watched, the gentleman carefully divided the hamburger in half, then counted out the fries, one for him, one for her, until each had half of them. Then he poured half of the soft drink into the extra cup and set that in front of his wife. The old man then began to eat, and his wife sat watching, with her hands folded in her lap. The young man decided to ask if they would allow him to purchase another meal for them so that they didn't have to split theirs. The old gentleman said, 'Oh no. We've been married 50 years, and everything has always been and will always be shared, 50/50.' The young man then asked the wife if she was going to eat, and she replied, 'It's his turn with the teeth.'

You know you're getting old when you stoop to tie your shoelaces and wonder what else you could do while you're down there. ***George Burns***

Just before the funeral service, the undertaker came up to the very elderly widow and asked, 'How old was your husband?' 'Ninety-eight,' she replied. 'Two years older than me.' 'So you're 96,' the undertaker commented. 'Hardly worth going home, is it?'

Now that I'm older, here's what I've discovered:

I started out with nothing, I still have most of it.
My wild oats have turned to prunes and All Bran.
I finally got my head together, now my body is falling apart.
Funny, I don't remember being absent-minded.
If all is not lost, where is it?
It is easier to get older than it is to get wiser.
Some days you're the dog, some days you're the lamppost.
I wish the buck stopped here, I could use a few.
Kids in the back seat cause accidents; accidents in the back seat cause kids.
It's hard to make a comeback when you haven't been anywhere.
Only time the world beats a path to your door is if you're in the bathroom.
If God wanted me to touch my toes, he would have put them on my knees.
When I'm finally holding all the cards, why does everyone decide to play chess?
It's not hard to meet expenses, they're everywhere!
The only difference between a rut and a grave is the depth.

A small-town prosecuting attorney called his first witness to the stand in a trial – a grandmotherly, elderly woman. He approached her and asked, 'Mrs Jones, do you know me?' She responded, 'Why, yes, I do know you Mr Williams. I've known you since you were a young boy. And frankly, you've been a big disappointment to me. You lie, you cheat on your wife, you manipulate people and talk about them behind their backs. You think you're a rising big shot when you haven't the brains to realise you never will amount to anything more than a two-bit paper pusher. Yes, I know you.' The lawyer was stunned. Not knowing what else to do he pointed across the room and asked, 'Mrs Williams, do you know the defence attorney?' She again replied, 'Why, yes I do. I've known Mr Bradley since he was a youngster, too. I used to babysit him for his parents. And he, too, has been a real disappointment to me. He's lazy, bigoted, he has a drinking problem. The man can't build a normal relationship with anyone and his law practice is one of the shoddiest in the entire state. Yes, I know him.' At this point, the judge rapped the courtroom to silence and called both counsellors to the bench. In a very quiet voice, he said with menace, 'If either of you asks her if she knows me, you'll be in jail for contempt within five minutes!'

It's hard to be nostalgic when you can't remember anything.

Two elderly couples were enjoying friendly conversation when one of the men asked the other, 'Fred, how was the memory clinic you went to last month?' 'Outstanding,' Fred replied. 'They taught us all the latest psychological techniques – visualisation, association – it made a huge difference for me.' 'That's great! What was the name of the clinic?' Fred went blank. He thought and thought, but couldn't remember. Then a smile broke across his face and he asked, 'What do you call that flower with the long stem and thorns?' 'You mean a rose?' 'Yes, that's it!' He turned to his wife. 'Rose, what was the name of that clinic?'

People ask me what I'd most appreciate getting for my 87th birthday. I tell them, a paternity suit. ***George Burns***

An old man, Mr Smith, resided in a nursing home. One day he went into the nurses' office and informed Nurse Jones that his penis had died. Nurse Jones, realising that Mr Smith was old and forgetful, decided to play along with him. 'It did? I'm sorry to hear that,' she replied. Two days later, Mr Smith was walking down the halls at the nursing home with his penis hanging outside his pants. Nurse Jones saw him and said, 'Mr Smith, I thought you told me your penis died.' 'It did,' he said. 'Today is the viewing.'

23 signs that you are getting old

1 You're asleep, but others worry that you're dead.
2 You stop trying to hold your stomach in, no matter who walks into the room.
3 You buy a compass for the dashboard of your car.
4 You are proud of your lawn mower.
5 Your best friend is dating someone half their age, and isn't breaking any laws.
6 Your arms are almost too short to read the newspaper.
7 You sing along with lift music.
8 You would rather go to work than stay home sick.
9 You enjoy hearing about other people's operations.
10 You no longer think of speed limits as a challenge.
11 People call at 9pm and ask, 'Did I wake you?'
12 You answer a question with, 'Because I said so.'
13 The end of your tie doesn't come anywhere near the top of your trousers.
14 You take a metal detector to the beach.
15 You know what the word 'equity' means.
16 You can't remember the last time you laid on the floor to watch television.
17 Your ears are hairier than your head.
18 You talk about 'good grass' and you're referring to someone's lawn.
19 You get into a heated argument about pension plans.
20 You got cable for the weather channel.
21 You can go bowling without drinking.
22 You have a party and the neighbours don't even realise.
23 People send you this list.

A little old lady went to the grocery store to buy cat food. She picked up three cans and took them to the check-out counter. The girl at the cash register said, 'I'm sorry, but we cannot sell you cat food without proof that you have a cat. A lot of old people buy cat food to eat, and the management wants proof that you are buying the cat food for your cat.' The little old lady went home, picked up her cat and brought it back to the store. They sold her the cat food. The next day, she tried to buy three cans of dog food. Again the cashier demanded proof that she had a dog, because old people sometimes eat dog food. She went home and brought in her dog. She then got the dog food. The next day she brought in a box with a hole in the lid. The little old lady asked the cashier to stick her finger in the hole. The cashier said, 'No, you might have a snake in there.' The little old lady assured her that there was nothing in the box that would harm her. So the cashier put her finger into the box and pulled it out and told the little old lady, 'That smells like shit.' The little old lady said, 'It is. Now can I buy three rolls of toilet paper?'

I don't plan to grow old gracefully. I plan to have face-lifts until my ears meet.

Rita Rudner

Here are some good things that happen as you grow older:

- Your investment in health insurance is finally beginning to pay off.
- Kidnappers are not very interested in you.
- It's harder and harder for sexual harassment charges to stick.
- If you've never smoked, you can start now and it won't have time to hurt you.
- Your secrets are safe with your friends because they can't remember them either.
- Your eyes won't get much worse.
- Things you buy now don't have time to wear out.
- In a hostage situation, you are likely to be released first.

An elderly widow and widower had been dating for about five years. The man finally decided to ask her to marry him. She immediately said 'yes'. The next morning when he awoke, he couldn't remember what her answer was. 'Was she happy? I think so. Wait, no, she looked at me funny...' After about an hour of trying to remember to no avail, he got on the telephone and gave her a call. Embarrassed, he admitted that he didn't remember her answer to the marriage proposal. 'Oh', she said, 'I'm so glad you called. I remembered saying yes to someone, but I couldn't remember who it was.'

What is the best birth control method for really old seniors? Nudity.

A retiring farmer, in preparation for selling his land, needed to rid his farm of animals. So he went to every house in his town. To the houses where the man was the boss, he gave a horse. To the houses where the woman was the boss, a chicken was given. He got toward the end of the street and saw a couple outside gardening. 'Who's the boss around here?' he asked. 'I am,' said the man. 'I have a black horse and a brown horse,' the farmer said. 'Which one would you like?' The man thought for a minute and said, 'The black one.' 'No, no, no, get the brown one,' the man's wife said. 'Here's your chicken,' said the farmer.

A young man was walking through a supermarket to pick up a few things when he noticed an old lady following him around. Thinking nothing of it, he ignored her and continued on. Finally he went to the checkout line, but she got in front of him. 'Pardon me,' she said. 'I'm sorry if my staring at you has made you feel uncomfortable. It's just that you look just like my son, who just died recently.' 'I'm very sorry,' replied the young man. 'Is there anything I can do for you?' 'Yes,' she said, 'As I'm leaving, can you say "Good bye, Mother"? It would make me feel so much better.' 'Sure,' answered the young man. As the old woman was leaving, he called out, 'Goodbye, Mother!' Then he stepped up to the checkout counter, and saw that his total was £127.50. 'How can that be?' He asked, 'I only purchased a few things!' 'Your mother said that you would pay for her,' said the checkout assistant.

Games For The Elderly

Sag, you're it.
Pin the toupee on the bald guy.
Twenty questions shouted into your good ear.
Kick the bucket.
Red Rover, Red Rover, the nurse says bend over.
Simon says something incoherent.
Hide and pee.
Spin the bottle of mylanta.
Musical recliners.

A family took their frail, elderly mother to a nursing home and left her, hoping she would be well cared for. The next morning, the nurses bathed her, fed her a tasty breakfast, and set her in a chair at a window overlooking a lovely flower garden. She seemed okay, but after a while she slowly started to tilt sideways in her chair. Two attentive nurses immediately rushed up to catch her and straighten her up. Again she seemed okay, but after a while she slowly started to tilt over to her other side. The nurses rushed back and once more brought her back upright. This went on all morning. Later, the family arrived to see how the old woman was adjusting to her new home. 'So Ma, how is it here? Are they treating you all right?' 'It's pretty nice,' she replied. 'Except they won't let me fart.'

You know you're into middle age when you realise that caution is the only thing you care to exercise.

There was this couple who had been married for 50 years. They were sitting at the breakfast table one morning and the old gentleman said to his wife, 'Just think honey, we've been married for 50 years.' 'Yeah,' she replied. 'Just think, 50 years ago we were sitting here at this breakfast table together.' 'I know,' the old man said. 'We were probably sitting here as naked as jaybirds 50 years ago.' 'Well,' the little old lady snickered, 'What do you say – should we?' Whereupon the two stripped to the buff and sat down at the table. 'You know honey,' the little old lady said, 'My nipples are as hot for you as they were 50 years ago.' 'I wouldn't be surprised,' replied the old man, 'One's in your coffee and the other one's in your porridge.'

A young and beautiful woman gets into the lift, smelling like expensive perfume. She turns to an old woman in the corner and says arrogantly, 'Giorgio Beverly Hills, £100 an oz!' Another young and beautiful woman gets into the lift and also smells of very expensive perfume. She arrogantly turns to the old woman and says, 'Chanel No. 5, £150 an oz!' About three floors later, the old woman has reached her destination and is about to get out. Before she leaves, she looks both beautiful women in the eye, turns and squeezes out a fart, declaring 'Broccoli – 49p a lb!'

A 75-year-old groom and the young wife caused a lot of attention as he checked into the resort hotel. The following morning, the old boy came strutting into the dining room, looking great with a big smile on his face. He proceeded to order an enormous breakfast. He laughed and joked and was in obvious good spirits, whereas his young wife, who came into the room half an hour later, looked worn out. She ordered coffee in a voice so weak the waiter had to ask her to repeat the order. The old man finished his breakfast, excused himself and left for their room. This gave the waitress a chance to ask the bride, 'Honey, I can't figure it out. The old geezer, your husband, looks like a million dollars and you look like two cents. What's wrong?' 'That guy double-crossed me,' the bride said. 'He told me he'd saved up for 50 years, and all the time I thought he was talking about money!'

Twin sisters were just turning 100 years old in St Luke's Nursing Home, and the editor of the Cambridge rag, *The Cambridge Distorter*, told a photographer to get over there and take the pictures of these 100-year-old twin biddies. One of the twins was hard of hearing and the other could hear quite well. The photographer asked them to sit on the sofa and the deaf one said to her twin, 'WHAT DID HE SAY?' He said, 'WE'VE GOT TO SIT OVER THERE ON THE SOFA!' said the other. 'Now get a little closer together,' said the photographer. Again, 'WHAT DID HE SAY?' 'HE SAYS SQUEEZE TOGETHER A LITTLE.' So they wiggled up close to each other. 'Just hold on for a bit longer, I've got to focus a little,' said the photographer. Yet again, 'WHAT DID HE SAY?' 'HE SAYS HE'S GOING TO FOCUS!' With a big grin the deaf twin shouted out, 'OH MY GOD – BOTH OF US?'

- → At age 4, success is not peeing in your pants.
- → At age 12, success is having friends.
- → At age 17, success is having a driver's licence.
- → At age 20, success is having sex.
- → At age 35, success is having money.
- → At age 50, success is having money.
- → At age 60, success is having sex.
- → At age 70, success is having a driver's licence.
- → At age 75, success is having friends.
- → At age 80, success is not peeing in your pants.

An elderly lady was stopped, waiting to pull into a parking space, when a young man in his new red Mercedes went around her and parked in the space she was waiting for. The sweet little old lady was so upset that she went up to the man and said, 'I was going to park there you rude man!' The man was a real Smart Alec and said, 'That's what you can do when you're young and bright.' Well, this upset the lady even more, so she got in her car and backed it up and then she stomped on the gas and smashed right into his Mercedes, trashing the front end. The young man ran back to his car and asked, 'What did you do that for you, crazy old woman?' The little old lady smiled and told him, 'That's what you can do when you're old and rich!'

An old man visits his doctor for a routine check-up and everything seems normal. Then, the doctor asks him about his sex life. 'Well...' the man said, 'not bad at all to be honest. The wife ain't all that interested anymore, so I just cruise around. In the past week I was able to pick up and bed three girls, none of whom were over 30 years old.' 'My goodness, Frank, and at your age too,' exclaimed the doctor. 'I hope you took some precautions.' 'Yep. I may be old, doc, but I ain't senile yet... I gave 'em all a false name.'

Middle age is the age half way between your present age and 100.

A retired gentleman went to apply for Social Security. After waiting in line for quite a long time, he arrived at the counter. The woman behind the counter asked him for his identification to verify his age. He looked in his pockets and realised he had left his wallet at home. He told the woman that he seemed to have left his wallet at home. 'Will I have to go home and come back now?' he asks. The woman says, 'Unbutton your shirt.' He opens his shirt revealing lots of curly silver hair. She says, 'That silver hair on your chest is proof enough for me,' as she processes his Social Security application. When he gets home, the man excitedly tells his wife about his experience at the Social Security office. She says, 'You should have dropped your trousers – you might have qualified for disability, too.'

An elderly couple came back from a wedding one afternoon and were in a pretty romantic mood. While sitting on their loveseat, the elderly woman looked at her companion and said, 'I remember when you used to kiss me every chance you had.' The old man, feeling a bit obliged, leaned over and gave her a peck on the cheek. Then she said, 'I also remember when you used to hold my hand at every opportunity.' The old man, again feeling obligated, reached over and gently placed his hand on hers. The elderly woman then stated, 'I also remember when you used to nibble on my neck and send chills down my spine.' This time the old man had a blank stare on his face and started to get up off the couch. As he began to walk out of the living room his wife asked, 'Was it something I said? Where are you going?' The old man looked at her and replied, 'I'm going in the other room to get my teeth!'

Quick Quips 1

The old system of having a baby was much better than the new system, the old system being characterised by the fact that the man didn't have to watch.
Dave Barry

I was a bottle baby. My mum said she liked me as a friend, but it had to stop there.
Ken Dodd

My parents used to beat the shit out of me. And, looking back on it, I'm glad they did. I'm looking forward to beating the shit out of my own kids, for no reason whatsoever. ***Denis Leary***

Somewhere on this earth, every ten seconds, a woman gives birth to a child. We must find that woman and stop her. ***Sam Levenson***

Babies are such a nice way to start people. ***Don Herold***

My friend has a 16-month-old. The baby's crawling round and he has an accident in his diaper. And the mother comes over and says, "Isn't that adorable? Brandon made a gift for Daddy." I'm thinking this guy must be real easy to shop for on Father's Day.
Garry Shandling

One of the best things people could do for their descendants would be to sharply limit the number of them. ***Olin Miller***

Beverly Hills is so exclusive that when a woman gives birth she breaks Perrier.
Freddy Roman

I told my mother I was going to have natural childbirth. She said to me, "Linda, you've been taking drugs all your life. Why stop now?"
Linda Maldonado

I have never understood this liking for war. It panders to instincts already well catered for in any respectable domestic establishment.
Alan Bennett

I remember a lot of things before I was even born. I remember going to a picnic with my father and coming home with my mother.
Foster Brooks

I was born by Caesarean section, but not so you'd notice. It's just that when I leave a house, I go out through the window.
Steven Wright

Contraceptives should be used on every conceivable occasion. ***Spike Milligan***

Don't tell your kids you had an easy birth or they won't respect you. For years I used to wake up my daughter and say, "Melissa you ripped me to shreds. Now go back to sleep..." ***Joan Rivers***

When I was a boy of 14, my father was so ignorant I could hardly stand to have the old man around. But when I got to be 21, I was astonished by how much he'd learned in seven years. ***Mark Twain***

I have good-looking kids. Thank goodness my wife cheats on me. ***Rodney Dangerfield***

Mother Nature is wonderful. She gives us 12 years to develop a love for our children before turning them into teenagers. ***Eugene Bertin***

The baby is fine, the only problem is that he looks like Edward G Robinson.
Woody Allen

If a man smiles in his own house someone is sure to ask him for money. ***William Feather***

Remember, blood is not only much thicker than water, it's much more difficult to get out of the carpet. ***Phyllis Diller***

Insanity is hereditary: you can get it from your children.
Sam Levinson

I once bought my kids a set of batteries for Christmas with a note on it saying 'toys not included'. ***Bernard Manning***

My mother's menu consisted of two choices: take it or leave it. ***Buddy Hackett***

Children are the most desirable opponents at Scrabble as they are both easy to beat and fun to cheat.
Fran Lebowitz

I understand the importance of bondage between parent and child. ***Dan Quayle***

Until I was 13 I thought my name was "Shutup".
Joe Namath

Watching your daughter being collected by her date feels like handing over a million dollar Stradivarius to a gorilla. ***Jim Bishop***

I have a stepladder. It's a very nice stepladder but it's sad that I never knew my real adder. ***Craig Charles***

Parents are not interested in justice, they're interested in peace and quiet. ***Bill Cosby***

Babies don't need a vacation but I still see them at the beach. I'll go over to them and say, "What are you doing here? You've never worked a day in your life!" ***Steven Wright***

There are two things that a child will share willingly – communicable diseases and its mother's age.
Benjamin Spock

My husband and I have decided to start a family while my parents are still young enough to look after them. ***Rita Rudner***

When you see a married couple walking down the street, the one that's a few steps ahead is the one that's mad. ***Helen Rowland***

Having a family is like having a bowling alley installed in your head. ***Martin Mull***

There are two things in life for which we are never truly prepared: twins. ***Josh Billings***

I've got the brain of a four-year-old. I'll bet he was glad to be rid of it. ***Groucho Marx***

Childhood is that wonderful time when all you need to do to lose weight is take a bath.
Richard Zera

Don't bother discussing sex with small children. They rarely have anything to add.
Fran Lebowitz

My 11-year-old daughter mopes around the house all day waiting for her breasts to grow. ***Bill Cosby***

The real menace in dealing with a five-year-old is that in no time at all you begin to sound like a five-year-old.
Jean Kerr

My unhealthy affection for my second daughter has waned. Now I despise all my seven children equally.
Evelyn Waugh

The worst sensation I know of is getting up at night and stepping on a toy train.
Kin Hubbard

No wonder people are so horrible when they start life as children. ***Kingsley Amis***

When you're eight years old nothing is your business.
Lenny Bruce

I have just returned from a children's party. I'm one of the survivors. ***Percy French***

To be a successful father there is one absolute rule: when you have a kid, don't look at it for the first two years. ***Ernest Hemingway***

In general my children refuse to eat anything that hasn't danced in television.
Erma Bombeck

Never underestimate a child's ability to get into more trouble. ***Martin Mull***

Children nowadays are tyrants. They contradict their parents, gobble their food and tyrannise their teachers.
Socrates

I never met a kid I liked.
W C Fields

There is nothing so aggravating as a fresh boy who is too old to ignore and too young to kick. ***Kin Hubbard***

Teenagers, are you tired of being harassed by your stupid parents? Act now. Move out, get a job and pay your own bills – while you still know everything. ***John Hinde***

My mother was like a sister to me, only we didn't have sex quite so often. ***Emo Philips***

Only the young die good. ***Oliver Herford***

Parents are the last people on earth who ought to have children. ***Samuel Butler***

I do wish that my parents could have been present today. My father would have liked what was said about me; my mother would have believed it. ***Lyndon B Johnson***

Any kid'll run an errand for you if you ask at bedtime. ***Red Skelton***

Here's a gentleman who made a fortune by putting children on his lap and talking to them. I got an uncle did the same thing; he's now serving 10 to 20. ***Joey Bishop, about Art Linkletter***

Ah, the patter of little feet around the house. There's nothing like having a midget for a butler. ***WC Fields – attributed***

A child develops individuality long before he develops taste. I have seen my kid straggle into the kitchen in the morning with outfits that need only one accessory – an empty gin bottle. ***Erma Bombeck***

Ask your child what he wants for dinner only if he's buying. ***Fran Lebowitz***

I've got two wonderful children – and two out of five isn't bad. ***Henny Youngman***

In America there are two classes of travel: first class, and with children.
Robert Benchley

Alligators have the right idea. They eat their young. ***Ever Arden***

I don't have any kids. Well, at least none that I know about. I'd like to have kids one day, though. I want to be called Mommy by someone other than Spanish guys in the street. ***Carol Leifer***

When I was a kid, I had two imaginary friends. They would only play with each other. ***Rita Rudner***

When I was a kid, we had a quicksand box in the backyard. I was an only child ... eventually. ***Steven Wright***

Before I was married I had six theories about bringing up children. Now I have six children – and no theories.
Earl of Rochester

There's not a man in America who, at one time or another, hasn't had a secret desire to boot a child in the ass.
W C Fields

We're trying to bring them up the right way. We're not spanking them. We find that we don't have to spank them. We find that waving guns around pretty much gets the job done. ***Denis Leary***

Children should neither be seen nor heard from – ever again. ***W C Fields***

There may be some doubt as to who are the best people to have charge of children, but there can be no doubt that parents are the worst.
George Bernard Shaw

Don't have any children. It makes divorce so much more complicated. ***Albert Einstein***

My father was not a failure. After all, he was the father of a President of the United States. ***Harry S Truman***

There are few things more satisfying than seeing your children have teenagers of their own. ***Doug Larson***

I love to go to the playground and watch the children jumping up and down. They don't know I'm firing blanks. ***Emo Philips***

I must have been an insufferable child; all children are. ***George Bernard Shaw***

One thing they never tell you about child raising is that for the rest of your life, at the drop of a hat, you are expected to know your child's name and how old he or she is. ***Erma Bombeck***

My parents are certainly great role models for me. Thanks to them, I certainly know how not to raise a child. ***Drew Barrymore***

I like children – fried. ***W C Fields***

Parenthood remains the greatest single preserve of the amateur. ***Alvin Toffler***

Because of their size, parents may be difficult to discipline properly. ***P J O'Rourke***

Most of us become parents long before we have stopped being children. ***Mignon McLauglin***

Human beings are the only creatures on earth that allow their children to come back home. ***Bill Cosby***

My mother had a great deal of trouble with me, but I think she enjoyed it. ***Mark Twain***

Like its politicians and its war, society has the teenagers it deserves. ***J B Priestley***

Never lend your car to anyone to whom you have given birth. ***Erma Bombeck***

The trouble with children is that they're not returnable. ***Quentin Crisp***

men and women

Boys

Men are like mascara – they usually run at the first sign of emotion.

A girl and a boy had been in a relationship for four months. One Friday night they met in a bar after work, stayed for a few drinks, then went to get some food at a local restaurant. They ate, went back to his house and she stayed over. Her story: He was in an odd mood when I got to the bar. I thought that it might have been because I was a bit late, but he didn't say much about it. The conversation was quite slow going, so I thought we should go off somewhere more intimate to talk. We went to this restaurant and he was still a bit strange. I tried to cheer him up, but it didn't seem to make any difference. I asked him if the problem was me, but he just put his arm around me. I didn't know what the hell that meant because he didn't say he loved me in return. By the time we got back to his place, I actually wondered if he was going to dump me. I tried to ask him about it, but he just switched on the TV. Reluctantly, I told him that I was going to bed. After ten minutes he joined me and we made love. But he still seemed really distracted, and afterwards I just wanted to leave. I don't really know what he thinks any more. I wonder if he's met someone else. His story: Bad day at work, but at least I got laid.

Men are like parking spots – the good ones are already taken and the ones that are left are handicapped.

A man is designed to walk three miles in the rain to phone for help when the car breaks down, and a woman is designed to say, 'You took your time' when he comes back dripping wet. ***Victoria Wood***

Men are like blenders – you need one, but you're not quite sure why.

Men are like bananas – the older they get, the less firm they are.

Men are like mini-skirts – if you're not careful, they'll creep up your legs.

Men are like cement – after getting laid, they take ages to get hard.

If men can run the world, why can't they stop wearing neckties? How intelligent is it to start the day by tying a little noose around your neck? **Linda Ellerbee**

Men are like computers – hard to figure out and they never have enough memory.

Men are like lava lamps – fun to look at, but not all that bright.

Men are like bank accounts – without a lot of money, they don't generate much interest.

Men are like coolers – load them with beer and you can take them anywhere.

Men are like fragments of soap – they get together in bars.

Men are like holidays – they never seem to last long enough.

Men are like chocolate bars – sweet, smooth and they usually go straight to your hips.

How to impress a woman:
Compliment her, cuddle her, kiss her, caress her, love her, tease her, comfort her, protect her, hug her, hold her, spend money on her, wine and dine her, listen to her, care for her, stand by her, support her, go to the ends of the earth for her.

How to impress a man:
Turn up naked with beer.

Men are like place mats – they only show up when there's food on the table.

Men are like commercials – you can't believe a word they say.

A couple was having a discussion about family finances. Finally the husband exploded, 'If it weren't for my money, the house wouldn't be here!' The wife replied, 'My dear, if it weren't for your money I wouldn't be here.'

Men are like curling irons – they're always hot and always in your hair.

Why is a launderette a really bad place to pick up a woman? Because a woman who can't even afford a washing machine will never be able to support you.

60 things you shouldn't say to a naked man:

1 I've smoked fatter joints than that.
2 Ahh, it's cute.
3 Who circumcised you?
4 Why don't we just cuddle?
5 You know they have surgery to fix that.
6 It's more fun to look at.
7 Make it dance.
8 You know, there's a tower in Italy like that.
9 Can I paint a smiley face on that?
10 It looks like a night crawler.
11 Wow, and your feet are so big.
12 My last boyfriend was four inches bigger.
13 It's OK, we'll work around it.
14 Is this a mild or a spicy Slim Jim?
15 Eww, there's an inch worm on your thigh.
16 Will it squeak if I squeeze it?
17 Oh no, a flash headache.
18 (giggle and point)
19 Can I be honest with you?
20 My eight-year-old brother has one like that.
21 Let me go get my tweezers.
22 How sweet, you brought incense.
23 This explains your car.
24 You must be a growing boy.
25 Maybe if we water it, it'll grow.
26 Thanks, I needed a toothpick.
27 Are you one of those pygmies?
28 Have you ever thought of working in a sideshow?
29 Every heard of Clearasil?
30 All right, a treasure hunt!
31 I didn't know they came that small.
32 Why is God punishing you?
33 At least this won't take long.
34 I never saw one like that before.
35 What do you call this?
36 But it still works, right?
37 Damn, I hate babysitting.
38 It looks so unused.
39 Do you take steroids?
40 I hear excessive masturbation shrinks it.
41 Maybe it looks better in natural light.
42 Why don't we skip right to the cigarettes?
43 Oh, I didn't know you were in an accident.
44 Did you date Lorena Bobbitt?
45 Aww, it's hiding.
46 Are you cold?
47 If you get me really drunk first.
48 Is that an optical illusion?
49 What is that?
50 I'll go get the ketchup for your French fry.
51 Were you neutered?
52 It's a good thing you have so many other talents.
53 Does it come with an air pump?
54 So this is why you're supposed to judge people on personality.
5 Where are the puppet strings?
56 Your big gun is more like a BB gun.
57 Look, it fits my Barbie clothes.
58 Never mind, why bother?
59 Is that a second belly button?
60 Where's the rest of it?

Men are like horoscopes – they always tell you what to do and are usually wrong.

Men are like popcorn – they satisfy you, but only for a short while.

Men do not like to admit even momentary imperfection. My husband forgot the code to turn off the house alarm. He turned himself in. ***Rita Rudner***

How Dogs and Men Are The Same:
Both mark their territory.
Neither understands what you see in cats.
The smaller ones tend to be more nervous.
Both are threatened by their own kind.
Neither of them notices when you get your hair cut.
Both take up too much space on the bed.
Both have irrational fears about vacuum cleaners.

Men are like noodles – they're always in hot water and they lack taste.

Men are like lawn mowers – if you're not pushing one around, then you're riding it.

Why do men chase women they have no intention of marrying? For the same reason dogs chase cars they have no intention of driving.

Men are like copiers – you need them for reproduction, but that's about it.

How do you scare a man? Sneak up behind him and start throwing rice over him.

What is the difference between going to a singles bar and going to a circus? At a circus the clowns don't talk.

What's the difference between a savings bond and a typical male? At some point the savings bond will mature.

What's the difference between a new husband and a new dog? After a year, the dog will still be excited to see you.

Why is it difficult to find men who are sensitive, caring and good looking? Because they already have boyfriends.

15 reasons why it's great to be a man:

1 Your toilet queues are 75 per cent shorter.
2 Same work, more pay.
3 You can write your name in the snow.
4 People never glance at your chest when you're talking to them.
5 Hot wax never comes near your pubic area.
6 If another guy turns up at a party wearing the same outfit, you might become lifelong friends.
7 Phone conversations are over in 30 seconds flat.
8 One mood, all the time.
9 Car mechanics tell you the truth.
10 None of your co-workers has the power to make you cry.
11 A five-day holiday requires only one suitcase.
12 You don't have to shave below your neck.
13 You don't have to clean your flat if the meter reader is coming by.
14 You can watch a game for hours in silence with your friends without thinking 'He must be mad at me'.
15 You can go to the toilet without a support group.

How does a man show that he's planning for the future? He buys two cases of beer instead of one.

What's the one thing worse than a male chauvinist pig? A woman who won't do what she's told.

How can you tell if a man is a male chauvinist pig? He thinks 'harass' is two words.

Why did God create woman? Because after creating man, he was sure he could do better.

Why do black widow spiders kill their males after mating? To stop the snoring before it starts.

There are only two four-letter words that are offensive to men: 'Don't' and 'Stop' (unless they are used together).

How do you get a man to exercise? Tie the TV remote control to his shoelaces.

How do men exercise on a beach? By sucking in their stomach every time they see a bikini.

How do you get a man to stop biting his nails? Make him wear his shoes.

When is the only time a man thinks about a candlelit dinner? When there's a power cut.

What does a man consider to be a seven-course meal? A hot dog and a six-pack.

What's the definition of a man with manners? One who gets out of the bath to pee.

What do you call a man who has lost 90 per cent of his brain? A widower.

If one man can wash one pile of dishes in on hour, how many piles of dishes can four men wash in four hours? None – they'll all sit down together and watch TV.

What should you give a man who has everything? A woman to show him how to work it.

Did you hear about the new 'morning after' pill for men? It changes their blood type.

Jesus was a typical man. They always say they'll come back but you never see them again.

What do you call a man with three eyes? Seymour.

Why dogs are better than men

Dogs do not have problems expressing affection in public.
Dogs miss you when you're gone.
Dogs feel guilt when they've done something wrong.
Dogs don't criticize your friends.
Dogs admit when they're jealous.
Dogs are very direct about wanting to go out.
Dogs do not play games with you, except Frisbee (and they never laugh at how you throw).
Dogs don't feel threatened by your intelligence.
You can train a dog.
Dogs are easy to buy for.
You are never suspicious of your dog's dreams.
The worst social disease you can get from dogs is fleas. (OK. The really worst disease you can get from them is rabies, but there's a vaccine for it, and you get to kill the one that gives it to you.)
Dogs understand what no means.
Middle-aged dogs don't feel the need to abandon you for a younger owner.
Dogs admit it when they're lost.
Dogs aren't threatened if you earn more than they do.
Dogs mean it when they kiss you.

A guy was stranded on a desert island with Cindy Crawford. At first, she tried to keep her distance but, out of sheer loneliness, the relationship became physical and for the next four months they enjoyed glorious sex. Then one day the guy said to her, 'Can I borrow your eyebrow pencil?' Cindy was surprised to say the least, all the more so when he then asked, 'Can I use it to draw a moustache on you?' 'I suppose so,' she said warily. So he drew a moustache on her. Then he said, 'Will you wear some of my clothes?' Cindy was really disappointed, but reluctantly agreed. So he got her to put on an old check shirt and trousers. Then he said, 'Would you mind if I called you Bill?' By now, Cindy was really fed up with this apparent change in their relationship, but she went along with it. 'OK, I guess you can call me Bill,' she said. Then he grabbed her by the arm and said, 'Hey, Bill, you won't believe who I've been sleeping with these last four months!'

A woman needs a man like a fish needs a bicycle.

Gloria Steinem

A woman's work that is never done is the stuff she asked her husband to do.

How can you tell if a man is sexually excited? He's breathing.

Man to God: God, why did you make woman so beautiful?
God: So that you would love her.
Man: But why did you make her so dumb?
God: So that she would love you.

What is a man's idea of foreplay? Half an hour of begging.

Husbands are like children – they're fine if they're somebody else's.

Diamonds are a girl's best friend. Dogs are man's best friend. So which is the dumber sex?

What do you call a man with a spade on his head? Doug.

Reasons Computers Must Be Male:
They have a lot of data but are still clueless.
A better model is always just around the corner.
They look nice and shiny until you bring them home.
It is always necessary to have a backup.
They'll do whatever you say if you push the right buttons.
The best part of having either one is the games you can play.
The lights are on but nobody's home.

Q. **HOW CAN YOU TELL WHEN A MAN IS WELL HUNG?**
A. **WHEN YOU CAN JUST BARELY SLIP YOUR FINGER IN BETWEEN HIS NECK AND THE NOOSE.**

Women will never be equal to men until they can walk down the street bald and with a beer gut and still think they're beautiful.

What do you call a man without a spade on his head? Douglas.

Women's faults are many. Men have only two – everything they say and everything they do.

What do you call a man with a car on his head? Jack.

How do men define a 50-50 relationship? You cook, we eat.

How many men does it take to open a beer? None – it should be opened by the time she brings it to the couch.

How many men does it take to change a roll of toilet paper? Nobody knows – it's never happened.

Why are blonde jokes so short? So men can remember them.

Advice from men to women:

→ Never buy a 'new' brand of beer because 'it was on sale'.
→ If we're in the backyard and the TV in the den is on, that doesn't mean we're not watching it.
→ Don't tell anyone we can't afford a new car. Tell them we don't want one.
→ Whenever possible, please try to say whatever you have to say during commercials.
→ Please don't drive when you're not driving.
→ Don't feel compelled to tell us how all the people in your stories are related to one another: We're just nodding, waiting for the punch line.
→ The scrum-half who just got pummelled isn't trying to be brave. He's just not crying. Big difference!
→ When the waiter asks if everything's okay, a simple 'Yes' is fine.

Why did God create men? Because a vibrator can't mow the lawn.

Why are men like paper cups? They're dispensable.

Q. **WHY DON'T WOMEN BLINK DURING FOREPLAY?**
A. **THEY DON'T HAVE TIME.**

What do you call a man with a seagull on his head? Cliff.

Guys will actually judge women based on the way they're built. A lot of guys think the larger a woman's breasts are, the less intelligent she is. I don't think it works like that. I think it's the opposite. I think the larger a woman's breasts, the less intelligent men become.
Anita Wise

Q. **HOW DO YOU KEEP YOUR HUSBAND FROM READING YOUR E-MAIL?**
A. **RENAME THE MAIL FOLDER 'INSTRUCTION MANUAL'.**

What's the difference between a man and ET? ET phoned home.

How can a real man tell when his girlfriend's having an orgasm? Real men don't care.

How is a man like the weather? Nothing can be done to change either of them.

What is the difference between men and women? A woman wants one man to satisfy her every need while a man wants every woman to satisfy his one need.

Where do you have to go to find a man who is truly into commitment? A mental hospital.

What is the difference between men and pigs? Pigs don't turn into men when they drink.

Q. **WHY DO ONLY 10 PER CENT OF MEN MAKE IT TO HEAVEN?**
A. **BECAUSE IF THEY ALL WENT, IT WOULD BE HELL.**

How many men does it take to wallpaper a feminist's house? Only four if you slice them thin enough.

Q. **HOW IS COLONEL SANDERS LIKE THE TYPICAL MALE?**
A. **ALL HE'S CONCERNED WITH IS LEGS, BREASTS AND THIGHS.**

Women dream of world peace, a safe environment and eliminating hunger. What do men dream of? Being stuck in an elevator with the Doublemint twins.

If men made the rules:

1 Anything we said six or eight months ago is inadmissible in an argument. All comments become null and void after seven days.
2 If you don't want to dress like Victoria's Secret, don't expect us to act like soap opera guys.
3 If we say something that can be interpreted in two ways, and one of the ways makes you sad or angry, we meant the other way.
4 It is in neither of our best interests to make us take those stupid Cosmo quizzes together.
5 Let us ogle. If we don't look at other women, how can we know how pretty you are?
6 Don't rub the lamp if you don't want the genie to come out.
7 You can either ask us to do something OR tell us how you want it done – not both.
8 Christopher Columbus didn't need directions and neither do we.
9 Women who wear Wonderbras and low-cut blouses lose their right to complain about having their boobs stared at.
10 When we're turning the wheel and the car is nosing onto the off- ramp, you saying 'This is our exit' is not necessary.

A smart husband is one who thinks twice before saying nothing.

What's the difference between a new husband and a new dog? A dog only takes a couple of months to train.

Q. **WHAT'S THE DIFFERENCE BETWEEN BIG FOOT AND AN INTELLIGENT MAN?**
A. **BIG FOOT'S BEEN SPOTTED SEVERAL TIMES.**

What do you call a man with 50 rabbits up his arse? Warren.

Q. **WHY CAN'T MEN GET MAD COW DISEASE?**
A. **BECAUSE THEY'RE ALL PIGS.**

Men are like toilets – either they're taken, or full of crap!

Q. **WHY DO MEN WHISTLE WHEN THEY'RE SITTING ON THE TOILET?**
A. **BECAUSE IT HELPS THEM REMEMBER WHICH END TO WIPE.**

Whenever you meet a man who would make a good husband, you usually find that he is.

Why are gingerbread men the best men of all? They are cute, they are sweet, and if they give you any lip, you can bite off their heads.

What is a man's idea of safe sex? A padded headboard.

Why don't men eat more M&M's? They're too hard to peel.

What do you call a man with an IQ of 50? Gifted.

What do men and beer bottles have in common? They are both empty from the neck up.

What's a man's idea of housework? Lifting his legs so you can vacuum.

Q: Why do men like blonde jokes? A: Because they can understand them.

Why are men and spray paint alike? One squeeze and they're all over you.

How do you save a man from drowning? Take your foot off his head.

How many men does it take to pop popcorn? Three. One to hold the pan and two others to act macho and shake the stove.

Only a man would buy a £500 car and put a £4000 stereo in it.

A woman of 35 thinks of having children. What does a man of 35 think of? Dating children.

Why do men take showers instead of baths? Peeing in the bath is disgusting.

Why do men buy electric lawn mowers? So they can find their way back to the house.

What is the thickest book in the world? What Men Think They Know About Women

Why do men find it difficult to make eye contact? Breasts don't have eyes.

If all brides are beautiful, where the hell do ugly wives come from?

Did you hear about the woman who finally figured out men? She died laughing before she could tell anybody.

Which of the following lines will do a better job of frightening away a man?
1 Get away or I'll call the police!
2 I love you and want to marry you and have your children.

... And Girls

One day three men are out having a relaxing day fishing, when suddenly they catch a mermaid. After hauling the mermaid up in a net, she promised that if the men set her free, she'd grant each of them a wish in return. The first man doesn't believe it, so he says, 'Alright, if you can really grant wishes, then double my IQ.' The mermaid says, 'Done,' and suddenly the first man starts to recite Shakespeare flawlessly and analyse it with extreme insight. The second man is so amazed, he looks at the mermaid and says, 'Triple my IQ.' The mermaid says, 'Done,' and the second man starts to recite solutions to mathematical problems that have been stumping all of the scientists in various fields from physics to chemistry, etc. The third man is so enthralled with the changes to his friends, he says to the mermaid, 'Quintuple my IQ.' The mermaid looks at him and says, 'You know, I normally don't try to change people's minds when they make a wish, but I really wish you'd reconsider.' The man responds, 'Nope, I want you to increase my IQ five times, and if you don't do it, I won't set you free.' 'Please,' said the mermaid, 'you don't know what you're asking. It'll change your entire view on the universe. Won't you ask for something else, a million pounds, anything?' But no matter what the mermaid said, the third man insisted on having his IQ increased by five times its usual power. So the mermaid finally relented and said, 'Done.' And the third man became a woman.

Why don't women have any brains? Because they don't have any testicles to put them in.

What do you call a woman with a toothpick in her head? Olive.

What is the difference between a pit bull and a woman with PMS? Lip gloss.

How can you tell which bottle contains the PMS medicine? It's the one with the bite marks on the cap.

Girls have got balls. They're just a little higher up, that's all. ***Joan Jett***

15 reasons why it's great to be a woman:

1 You can put a duvet cover on a duvet without asphyxiating yourself.
2 Your ability to concentrate is not inversely proportionate to the bust size of adjacent females.
3 You can appreciate why double E-cups might sometimes be a disadvantage.
4 You can urinate without leaving a small reservoir on the bathroom floor.
5 You can wear women's underwear without being arrested.
6 You can observe a barbecue without feeling the urge to intervene.
7 You can wear a ponytail and not look like a total jerk.
8 You can correctly estimate the dimensions of male genitalia.
9 You will never feel your sexuality threatened by large root vegetables, pepper grinders or photographs of Nelson's column.
10 When you reach your sexual peak, you are old enough to appreciate it.
11 You can recall anniversaries other than Exeter City's fifth round win over Newcastle United.
12 You can appreciate why scarlet crotchless leather panties are not, in fact, daily work wear for the female executive.
13 You can remain silent whilst in a car with a female driver.
14 You don't have to worry that you might not be the real parent of your children.
15 You can ask for directions from a stranger.

With the plane about to plunge into a mountain, a female passenger stood up and shouted, 'If I'm going to die, I want to die feeling like a woman.' Then she took off her top and cried, 'Is there someone on this plane who is man enough to make me feel like a woman?' Hearing this, a man stood up, took off his shirt and said, 'Iron this.'

Real women don't have hot flashes, they have power surges.

I hate women because they always know where things are. ***James Thurber***

Women: You can't live with them, and you can't get them to dress up in a skimpy Nazi costume and beat you with a warm squash. ***Emo Phillips***

What does PMS stand for? Probably moving to the sofa.

For Mothers-in-Law Day do something nice for the lady: take her out to dinner, send her flowers, divorce her daughter. ***Joey Adams***

Getting a Haircut...

Women's Version:
Woman 1: Oh! You got a haircut! That's so cute!
Woman 2: Do you think so? I wasn't sure when she gave me the mirror. You don't think it's too fluffy?
Woman 1: Oh God, no! No, it's perfect. I'd love to get my hair cut like that, but I think my face is too wide. I'm pretty much stuck with this stuff I think.
Woman 2: Are you serious? I think your face is adorable. And you could easily get one of those layer cuts – that would look so cute, I think. I was actually going to do that except that I was afraid it would accentuate my long neck.
Woman 1: Oh – that's funny! I would love to have your neck! Anything to take attention away from my awful shoulder line.
Woman 2: Are you kidding? I know girls that would love to have your shoulders. Everything drapes so well on you. I mean, look at my arms – see how short they are? If I had your shoulders I could get clothes to fit me so much easier.

Men's Version:
Man 1: Haircut?
Man 2: Yeah.

Reasons why bicycles are better than women:

Bicycles don't get pregnant.
You can ride your bicycle any time of the month.
Bicycles don't have parents.
Bicycles don't whine unless something is really wrong.
You can share your bicycle with your friends.
Bicycles don't care how many other bicycles you've ridden.
When riding, you and your bicycle can arrive at the same time.
Bicycles don't care if you look at other bicycles.
If your bicycle is too loose you can tighten it.
You can stop riding your bicycle as soon as you want and it won't get frustrated.
Bicycles don't care if you buy bicycle magazines.
A bicycle never wants a night out with other bicycles.
If you say horrible things to your bicycle, you don't have to apologise before you can ever ride it again.
You can ride your bicycle as long as you want to and it won't get sore.
Your parents won't keep in touch with your old bicycle after you dump it.

Why do women play with their hair at traffic lights? Because they don't have any balls to scratch.

On one issue at least, men and women agree. They both distrust women. ***H L Mencken***

What's the difference between a terrorist and a woman with PMS? You can negotiate with a terrorist.

My friend Myron tells me, 'Last year on Mother's Day the whole family got together for a big dinner and afterward, when Mum started to clean up, I said to her, "Don't bother with those dishes, Mum. Today is Mother's Day. You can always do them tomorrow."

The trouble with young wives today is that all they've learned to do is defrost frozen food. Why can't they learn to open tins like their mothers used to do?

There are two ways to handle a woman, and nobody knows either of them. ***Kin Hubbard***

Never argue with a woman when she's tired – or when she's rested.

Women who think they are the equal of men lack ambition.

More reasons why it's great to be a woman:

- → You never have to buy your own drinks.
- → You can get laid any time you want.
- → You can get out of speeding tickets by crying.
- → You're not expected to know how cars work.
- → You can sleep your way to the top.
- → You don't worry about losing your hair.
- → You always get to choose the movie.
- → You don't have to mow the lawn.
- → PMS is a legal defence for murder.
- → You don't have to understand the offside rule.
- → You don't have to adjust your genitals constantly.
- → Sweat is sexy on you.
- → You can marry rich and then not have to work.
- → You never have to use a power drill.
- → You never run out of excuses.
- → You get expensive jewellery as gifts that you never have to give back.
- → You get gifts all the time because men mess up so often.
- → You can give 'the look' that makes any man cower in the corner.
- → You can dance.
- → You look good in shorts.
- → You don't have to worry about being able to get it up.
- → You have mastered civilised eating.
- → You are better gossips.
- → You look better naked than men.
- → Women do less time for violent crime.
- → You can wear no underwear and be considered wild and sexy; a man who does the same thing is merely thought of as disgusting.
- → Short women are petite; short men are just short.
- → You don't need an excuse to be in a bad mood.
- → A pointy-shaped vegetable is all you need for a good time.
- → You piss sitting down, so it's easier to pass out on the toilet when drunk.

Women today may not know how to cook, but they sure know what's cooking.

There's not a lot of warmth between me and my mother. I asked her about it. I said, "Mrs Stoller..." ***Fred Stoller***

It was early evening in a casino and the two dealers at the craps table were waiting patiently for the first punters to arrive. Just then a woman came over and said that she wanted to bet £25,000 on a single roll of the dice. 'Certainly, madam,' they said, happy to relieve the boredom. 'There's just one thing though,' she added. 'I hope you don't mind, but going bottomless always brings me luck. So since there's hardly anyone about, is it all right with you two if I pull down my skirt and knickers?' She then stripped off, threw the dice and yelled, 'I've won! I've won!' Then she scooped up the money, picked up her clothes and left. The two dealers were dumbfounded. 'What did she roll anyway?' asked one. 'I don't know,' said the other. 'I thought you were watching the dice!'

A woman said to her friend, 'I made my husband a millionaire.' 'And what was he before you married him?' 'A billionaire.'

How do you know when a woman's about to say something smart? When she starts her sentence with 'A man once told me...'

My mom was a little weird. When I was little she would make chocolate frosting. And she'd let me lick the beaters. And then she'd turn them off. ***Marty Cohen***

At various times in her life, a woman is like the continents of the world. From 13 to 18, she's like Africa – virgin territory; from 18 to 30, she's like Asia – hot and exotic; from 30 to 45 she's like America – fully explored and free with her resources; from 45 to 55 she's like Europe – exhausted but not without places of interest; from 55 onwards, she's like Australia – everyone knows it's down there, but nobody cares.

A woman is like a teabag – you never know how strong she is until she gets in hot water. ***Nancy Reagan***

Did you hear they finally made a device that makes cars run 95% quieter? Yeah, it fits right over her mouth.

'Women Seeking Men' classifieds:

40-ISH: 48
ADVENTURER: Has had more partners than you ever will
AFFECTIONATE: Possessive
ARTIST: Unreliable
AVERAGE-LOOKING: You figure this out
BEAUTIFUL: Pathological liar
COMMITMENT-MINDED: Pick out curtains, now!
COMMUNICATION IMPORTANT: Just try to get a word in edgeways
CONTAGIOUS SMILE: Bring your penicillin
EDUCATED: College dropout
EMOTIONALLY SECURE: Medicated
EMPLOYED: Has part-time job stuffing envelopes at home
ENJOYS ART AND OPERA: Snob
ENJOYS NATURE: Bring your own muesli
EXOTIC BEAUTY: Would frighten a Martian
FINANCIALLY SECURE: One paycheque from the street
FREE SPIRIT: Substance abuser
FRIENDSHIP FIRST: Trying to live down reputation as slut
FUN: Annoying
GENTLE: Comatose
GOOD LISTENER: Hard to pull a word from her
INTUITIVE: Your opinion doesn't ever count
IN TRANSITION: Needs new sugar daddy to pay the bills
LIGHT DRINKER: Lush
LOOKS YOUNGER: If viewed from far away in bad light
LOVES TRAVEL: If you're paying
LOVES ANIMALS: Cat lady
NON-TRADITIONAL: Ex-husband lives in the basement
OPEN-MINDED: Desperate
PASSIONATE: Loud
POET: Depressive schizophrenic
REDHEAD: Shops on the Clairol aisle
RELIABLE: Frumpy
RUBENESQUE: You can figure this one out
ROMANTIC: Looks better by candlelight
SELF-EMPLOYED: Jobless
SMART: Insipid
SPECIAL: Rode the small school bus with tinted windows
SPIRITUAL: Involved with a cult
STABLE: Boring
TALL AND THIN: Anorexic
TANNED: Wrinkled
WANTS SOUL MATE: One step away from stalking
WIDOW: Nagged first husband to death
WRITER: Pompous
YOUNG AT HEART: How about the rest

Women's compact instruction book

- Never do housework. No man ever made love to a woman because the house was spotless.
- Remember you are known by the idiot you accompany.
- Don't imagine you can change a man – unless he's in nappies.
- What do you do if your boyfriend walks out? Shut the door.
- So many men – so many reasons not to sleep with any of them.
- If they can put one man on the moon, they should be able to put them all there.
- Tell him you're not his type – you have a pulse.
- Never let your man's mind wander – it's too little to be left out alone.
- Go for younger men. You might as well – they never mature anyway.
- Never marry a man for money. You'll have to earn every penny.
- Definition of a bachelor: a man who has missed the opportunity to make some woman miserable.
- The best way to get a man to do something is to suggest he is too old for it.
- If he asks what sort of books you're interested in, tell him cheque books.
- A man's idea of serious commitment is usually, 'Oh all right, I'll stay the night.'
- Women sleep with men who, if they were women, they wouldn't even have bothered to have lunch with.
- Remember a sense of humour does not mean that you tell him jokes, it means you laugh at his.
- If he asks you if you're faking it tell him no, you're just practising.
- When he asks you if he's your first tell him, 'You may be, you look familiar.'

What do cow pats and cowgirls have in common? The older they get the easier they are to pick up.

The way to fight a woman is with your hat – grab it and run. ***John Barrymore***

A husband was late home from work one evening. 'I'm sure he's having an affair,' said his wife to her mother. 'Why do you always think the worst?' said the mother. 'Maybe he's just been in an accident.'

Women would rather be right than reasonable. ***Ogden Nash***

Why do women have smaller feet than men? So they can stand closer to the sink.

Women are meant to be loved, not understood.
Oscar Wilde

A man took his dog to the vet and asked the vet to cut off its tail. The vet wanted to know why. 'Because,' said the man, 'my mother-in-law is arriving tomorrow, and I don't want anything to make her think she's welcome.'

The top six reasons computers must be female

6 As soon as you have one, a better one is just around the corner.

5 No one but the creator understands the internal logic.

4 Even your smallest mistakes are immediately committed to memory for future reference.

3 The native language used to communicate with other computers is incomprehensible to everyone else.

2 The message 'Bad Command or File Name' is about as informative as 'If you don't know why I'm mad at you, then I'm certainly not going to tell you'.

AND THE NUMBER ONE REASON COMPUTERS ARE FEMALE...

1 As soon as you make a commitment to one, you find yourself spending half of your pay cheque on accessories for it.

Continuing education courses for women

Silence, the Final Frontier: Where No Woman Has Gone Before
The Undiscovered Side of Banking: Making Deposits
Parties: Going Without New Outfits
Man Management: Discover How Minor Household Chores Can Wait Until After the Game
Bathroom Etiquette I: Men Need Space in the Bathroom Cabinet Too
Bathroom Etiquette II: His Razor Is His
Valuation: Just Because It's Not Important to You...
Communication Skills I: Tears – The Last Resort, Not the First
Communication Skills II: Thinking Before Speaking
Communication Skills III: Getting What You Want Without Nagging
Driving a Car Safely: A Skill You CAN Acquire
Party Etiquette: Drinking Your Fair Share
Telephone Skills: How to Hang Up
Introduction to Parking
Advanced Parking: Reversing Into a Space
Overcoming Anal Retentive Behaviour: Leaving the Towels on the Floor
Water Retention: Fact or Fat
Cooking I: Bringing Back Bacon, Eggs and Butter
Cooking II: Bran and Tofu are Not for Human Consumption
Cooking III: How Not to Inflict Your Diets on Other People
Compliments: Accepting Them Gracefully
Dancing: Why Men Don't Like to Dance
Classic Clothing: Wearing Outfits You Already Have
Household Dust: A Harmless Natural Occurrence Only Women Notice
Integrating Your Laundry: Washing It All Together
Ballet: For Women Only
Oil and Gas: Your Car Needs Both
Appreciating the Humour of the Three Stooges
'Do These Jeans Make Me Look Fat?' – Why Men Lie
TV Remotes: For Men Only

The front doorbell rang and a man opened the door to find his mother-in-law on the step with a suitcase. 'Can I stay here for a few days?' she asked. He said, 'Sure you can,' and shut the door in her face.

Very few things upset my wife, and it makes me feel special to be one of them.

No matter how much a woman loves a man, it would still give her a glow to see him commit suicide for her.
H L Mencken

Why did God make man first? He didn't want woman looking over his shoulder.

What would have happened if there had been three wise women? They would have asked for directions, arrived on time, helped deliver the baby, cleaned the stable, made a nice casserole and given practical gifts for the home.

Women complain about pre-menstrual syndrome, but I think of it as the only time of the month that I can be myself. ***Roseanne***

In the beginning, God created Earth and rested. Then God created man and rested. Then God created women. Since then, neither God nor man has rested.

My wife, inviting me to sample her very first soufflé, accidentally dropped a spoonful of it on my foot, fracturing several small bones. ***Woody Allen***

A woman was overweight so her doctor put her on a diet. 'I want you to eat regularly for two days, then skip a day, and repeat the procedure for two weeks. Next time I see you, you'll have lost at least 5 lbs.' But when the woman returned two weeks later, she had lost 20 lbs. The doctor was amazed. 'Did you follow my instructions?' 'Yes,' she said, 'but I thought I was going to drop dead that third day.' 'From hunger, you mean?' 'No, from skipping.'

A man's only as old as the woman he feels. ***Groucho Marx***

What does a woman make best for dinner? Reservations.

When does a woman enjoy a man's company? When he owns it.

25 things a girl would never say:

1 You know, I've been complaining a lot lately. I don't blame you for ignoring me.
2 The new girl in my office is a real beauty, and a stripper, too! I invited her over for dinner on Friday.
3 Honey, did you leave that skid in the toilet? Good one!
4 While you were in the bathroom, they went for it on fourth down and missed. If they can hold them to a field goal they'll still cover.
5 Bar food again? Wicked.
6 I liked that wedding even more than ours. Your ex-girlfriend has class.
7 That girl is wearing the same outfit as I am. Cool, I'm gonna go over and talk to her.
8 Let's just leave the toilet seat up at all times, then you don't have to mess with it anymore.
9 I've decided to buy myself a boob job. How big do you want them?
10 It's only the first half, you should order a couple more pitchers.
11 Honey, come over here! Watch me do a tequila shot off Stephanie's bare ass!
12 My mother is going to take care of the tab, so order another round for you and your friends.
13 I'm so happy with my new hairstyle, I don't think I'll ever change it again.
14 I love it when my pillow smells like your cigars and beer. You passed out before brushing your teeth again, you big silly guy!
15 You are so much smarter than my father.
16 If we're not going to have sex, then you have to let me watch football.
17 Are you sure you've had enough to drink?
18 I've decided to stop wearing clothes around the house.
19 You're so sexy when you're hung over.
20 I'd rather watch football and drink beer with you than go shopping.
21 Let's subscribe to Hustler, my treat.
22 I'll be out painting the house.
23 I love it when you ride in your hot sports car; I just wish you had more time to ride.
24 Darling, our new neighbour's 18-year-old daughter is sunbathing in the nude again, come see!
25 No, no, I'll take the car to have the oil changed.

A big game hunter went on safari with his wife and mother-in-law. One evening, the husband and wife were sitting around the camp fire having supper when she realised that her mother was missing. The hunter picked up his rifle and, with his wife close behind, set off into the jungle to look for the missing woman. After searching for over an hour, they finally spotted her backed up against a cliff with a huge lion facing her. 'What are we going to do?' shrieked the wife. 'Nothing,' said the husband. 'The lion got himself into this mess...'

What is the definition of mixed emotions? When you see your mother-in-law backing off a cliff in your new car.

Why did the woman cross the road? More to the point, what was she doing out of the kitchen?

Women have a passion for mathematics. They divide their age in half, double the price of their clothes and always add at least five years to the age of their best friend.
Marcel Achard

What do you call a woman tied up at a jetty? Maud.

What's six inches long, two inches wide and drives women wild? Money.

I said to my mother-in-law, 'My house is your house.' She said, 'Get the hell off my property.' ***Joan Rivers***

The police chief addressed a new recruit. 'As a recruit, you'll be faced with some difficult issues. For example, what would you do if you had to arrest your wife's mother?' 'Call for back-up.'

Women are like guns – keep one around long enough and you're going to want to shoot it.

A lady goes to Toys R Us to buy a Barbie doll. She tells the shop assistant that she needs to buy a Barbie but doesn't know what's available or the price. The assistant replies, 'We have Tennis Barbie and she's £28.' The lady asks, 'Well, anything else?' 'We have Equestrian Barbie, and she's £28'. The lady asks, 'Anything else?' 'Well, we have Divorced Barbie and she's £250.' The lady replies, 'I don't understand why Divorced Barbie is so expensive. The others were only £28. What's so special about Divorced Barbie?' The assistant replies, 'Simple, she comes with Ken's car, his house, and all his other stuff.'

Delia's Way
Stuff a miniature marshmallow in the bottom of a sugar cone to prevent ice-cream drips.
The Real Woman's Way
Just suck the ice cream out of the bottom of the cone, for God's sake. You're probably lying on the couch with your feet up eating it anyway.

Delia's Way
To keep potatoes from budding, place an apple in the bag with the potatoes.
The Real Woman's Way
Buy Smash and keep it in the cupboard for up to a year.

Delia's Way
When a cake recipe calls for flouring the baking tin, use a bit of the dry cake mix instead and there won't be any white mess on the outside of the cake.
The Real Woman's Way
Tesco sell cakes. They even do decorated versions.

Delia's Way
Wrap celery in aluminium foil when putting in the refrigerator and it will keep for weeks.
The Real Woman's Way
It could keep forever. Who eats celery?

Delia's Way
If you accidentally over-salt a dish while it's still cooking, drop in a potato slice.
The Real Woman's Way
If you over-salt a dish while you're cooking, tough shit. Please recite with me the Real Woman's motto: 'I made it and you will eat it and I don't care how bad it tastes.'

Delia's Way
Cure for headaches: Take a lime, cut it in half and rub it on your forehead. The throbbing will go away.
The Real Woman's Way
Cure for headaches: Take a lime, cut it in half and drop it in 8 oz of vodka. Drink the vodka. You might still have the headache, but you wont give a sh*t.

Delia's Way
If you have a problem opening jars, try using latex dishwashing gloves. They give a non-slip grip that makes opening jars easy.
The Real Woman's Way
Why do I have a man?

Delia's Way
Freeze leftover wine into ice cubes for future use in casseroles.
The Real Woman's Way
Left over wine? Hello!

Horse and Carriage?

A couple was going out for the evening. The last thing they did was put the cat out. The taxi arrived, and as the couple walked out of the house, the cat shot back in. So the husband went back inside to chase it out. The wife, not wanting it known that the house would be empty, explained to the taxi driver, 'He's just going upstairs to say goodbye to my mother.' A few minutes later, the husband got into the taxi and said, 'Sorry I took so long, the stupid thing was hiding under the bed and I had to poke her with a coat hanger to get her to come out!'

Marriage is not a word. It is a sentence – a life sentence.

A young couple got married, and celebrated their first night together, doing what newlyweds do, time and time again, all night long. Morning arrived and the groom went into the bathroom but couldn't find a towel when he emerged from the shower. He asked his bride to bring him one from the bedroom. When she got to the bathroom, he opened the door, exposing his body to his bride for the first time in the morning light. Her eyes went up and down and at about midway, they stopped and stared, and she asked shyly, 'What's that?', pointing to a small part of his anatomy. He, also being shy, thought for a minute and then said, 'Well, that's what we had so much fun with last night.' And she, in amazement, asked, 'Is that all we have left?'

Married life is full of excitement and frustration:

In the first year of marriage, the man speaks and the woman listens.
In the second year, the woman speaks and the man listens.
In the third year, they both speak and the neighbours listen.

It is true that love is blind but marriage is definitely an eye-opener.

A husband is living proof that a wife can take a joke.

Son: How much does it cost to get married then, Dad?
Father: I don't know son, I'm still paying for it.

Marriage is not just a having a wife, but also worries inherited forever.

A little boy at a wedding looks at his mum and says, 'Mummy, why does the girl wear white?' His mum replies, 'The bride is in white because she's happy and this is the happiest day of her life.' The boy thinks about this and then says, 'Well then, why is the boy wearing black?'

Getting married is very much like going to the restaurant with friends. You order what you want, and when you see what the other person has, you wish you had ordered that.

A Code of Honour: Never approach a friend's girlfriend or wife with mischief as your goal. There are just too many women in the world to justify that sort of dishonourable behaviour. Unless she's really attractive. ***Bruce Friedman***

Love is one long sweet dream, and marriage is the alarm clock.

There was this man who muttered a few words in the church and found himself married. A year later he muttered something in his sleep and found himself divorced.

Jill tells her husband, 'Jack, that young couple that just moved in next door seem such a loving twosome. Every morning, when he leaves the house, he kisses her goodbye, and every evening when he comes home, he brings her a dozen roses. Now, why can't you do that?' 'Gosh,' Jack says, 'I hardly know the girl.'

There was a man who said, 'I never knew what happiness was until I got married – and then it was too late!'

The newlywed wife said to her husband when he returned from work, 'I have great news for you. Pretty soon, we're going to be three in this house instead of two.' Her husband ran to her with a smile on his face and delight in his eyes. He was glowing with happiness and kissing his wife when she said, 'I'm glad that you feel this way since tomorrow morning my mother moves in with us.'

Husband: a man who buys his football tickets four months in advance and waits until 24 December to do his Christmas shopping.

They say when a man holds a woman's hand before marriage, it is love; after marriage, it is self-defence.

When a newly married man looks happy, we know why. But when a ten-year married man looks happy, we wonder why.

There was this lover who said that he would go through hell for his woman. They got married, and now he's going through hell.

A gentleman is one who never swears at his wife while ladies are present.

Son: Dad, I heard that in ancient China, a man doesn't know his wife until he marries her. Is this true?
Father: That happens everywhere, son, everywhere!

Correction: Instead of being arrested, as we stated, for kicking his wife down a flight of stairs and hurling a lighted kerosene lamp after her, the Rev James P Wellman died unmarried four years ago.

Marriage is like a mousetrap. Those on the outside are trying to get in and those on the inside are trying to get out.

As he lay on his deathbed, the man confided to his wife, 'I cannot die without telling you the truth. I cheated on you throughout our whole marriage. All those nights when I told you I was working late, I was with other women. And not just one woman either, I've slept with dozens of them.' His wife looked at him calmly and said, 'Why do you think I gave you the poison?'

Always talk to your wife while you're making love ... if there's a phone handy.

A young couple drove several miles down a country road, not saying a word. An earlier discussion had led to an argument, and neither wanted to concede their position. As they passed a barnyard of mules and pigs, the husband sarcastically asked, 'Are they relatives of yours?' 'Yes,' his wife replied. 'I married into the family.'

Bachelor: the only man who has never told his wife a lie.

Marriage requires a man to prepare four types of 'rings':

The Engagement Ring
The Wedding Ring
The Suffe-Ring
The Endu-Ring

Some people ask the secret of Anthony's long marriage. They take time to go to a restaurant two times a week: a little candlelit dinner, soft music and a slow walk home. The Mrs goes Tuesdays; he goes Fridays.

Bride: A woman with a fine prospect of happiness behind her.

Don't marry for money; you can borrow it cheaper.

May you be too good for the world and not good enough for your wife.

May you grow so rich your widow's second husband never has to worry about a living, God forbid.

May you live happily ever after with a poor, ugly, shrewish wife.

May you never leave your marriage alive.

May your wife be a witch who takes after her mother, and may you all live together in a one-room house.

I am in total control, but don't tell my wife.

A young couple were on their honeymoon. The husband was sitting in the bathroom on the edge of the bath saying to himself, 'Now how can I tell my wife that I've got really smelly feet and that my socks absolutely stink? I've managed to keep it from her while we were dating, but she's bound to find out sooner or later that my feet stink. How do I tell her?' Meanwhile, the wife was sitting in bed saying to herself, 'Now how do I tell my husband that I've got really bad breath? I've been very lucky to keep it from him while we were courting, but as soon as he's lived with me for a week, he's bound to find out. How do I break it to him gently?' The husband finally plucks up enough courage to tell his wife so he walks into the bedroom. He walks over to the bed, climbs over to his wife, puts his arm around her neck, moves his face very close to hers and says, 'Darling, I've a confession to make.' And she says, 'So have I, love.' To which he replies, 'Don't tell me, you've eaten my socks.'

Marriage is very much like a violin; after the sweet music is over, the strings are attached.

Marriage is love. Love is blind. Therefore, marriage is an institution for the blind.

Marriage is an institution in which a man loses his Bachelor's degree and the woman gets her Masters.

Marriage is a thing that puts a ring on a woman's finger and two under the man's eyes.

There is no realisable power that man cannot, in time, fashion the tools to attain, nor any power so secure that the naked ape will not abuse it. So it is written in the genetic cards – only physics and war hold him in check. And the wife who wants him home by five, of course.
Encyclopedia Apocryphia

I tried a mail-order bride once, but she was damaged in the mail, and I had to return the unused part for my full refund.

My darling wife was always glum.
I drowned her in a cask of rum,
And so made sure that she would stay
In better spirits night and day.

To keep your marriage brimming
With love in the marriage cup:
Whenever you're wrong, admit it,
Whenever you're right, shut up.
Nash

I think of my wife and I think of Lot, and I think of the lucky break he got.

I've been trying desperately to save my marriage for the last 35 years.

A police officer in a small town stopped a motorist who was speeding. 'But officer,' the man began, 'I can explain.' 'Just be quiet,' snapped the officer. 'I'm going to let you calm down in a cell back at the station until the chief gets back.' 'But, officer, I just wanted to say...' 'And I said to keep quiet! You're going to jail!' A few hours later the officer looked in on his prisoner and said, 'Lucky for you that the chief's at his daughter's wedding. He'll be in a good mood when he gets back.' 'Don't count on it,' answered the fellow in the cell. 'I'm the groom.'

If all men were brothers, would you let one marry your sister?

Marriage: a ceremony in which rings are put on the finger of the lady and around the hands and feet of the man.

After shopping for most of the day, a couple returns to find their car has been stolen. They go to the police station to make a full report. Later on, a detective drives them back to the car park to see if any evidence can be found at the scene of the crime. To their amazement, the car has been returned. There is an envelope on the windshield with a note of apology and two tickets to a music concert. The note reads, 'I apologise for taking your car, but my wife was having a baby and I had to hot-wire your ignition to rush her to the hospital. Please forgive the inconvenience. Here are two tickets for tonight's concert of Garth Brooks, the country and western music star.' Their faith in humanity restored, the couple attend the concert and return home late. They find their house has been robbed. Valuable goods have been taken from throughout the house, from basement to attic. And, there is a note on the door reading, 'Well, you still have your car. I have to put my new-born kid through college somehow, don't I?'

If your wife wants to learn how to drive, don't stand in her way.

In marriage, as in war, it is permitted to take every advantage of the enemy.

In marriage, the bridge gets a shower. But for the groom, it's curtains!

A woman yelled at her husband, 'You're going to be really sorry. I'm going to leave you!' He said, 'Make up your mind. Which is it going to be?'

What's the difference between a rubbish bag and a wife? The rubbish bag gets taken out once a week.

Many a wife thinks her husband is the world's greatest lover. But she can never catch him at it.

Marriage is a mutual relationship if both parties know when to be mute.

'So, as I told you, when my step-daughter married my dad, she was at once my stepmother! Now, since my new son is brother to my stepmother, he also became my uncle. As you know, my wife is my step-grandmother since she is my stepmother's mother. Don't forget that my stepmother is my stepdaughter. Remember, too, that I am my wife's grandson. But hold on just a few minutes more. You see, since I'm married to my step-grandmother, I am not only the wife's grandson and her hubby, but I am also my own grandfather. Now can you understand how I got put in this place?' After staring blankly with a dizzy look on his face, the psychiatrist replied: 'Move over!'

University courses for men and women:
Whatsamatta University's Seminars for Men – Autumn Catalogue

Once again, the female staff at Whatsamatta University will be offering courses for men of all marital status in an attempt to help males and females understand each other better. Attendance in at least ten of the following is required:

1 Combatting Stupidity
2 You Too Can Do Housework
3 Resistance to Beer
4 How To Fill An Ice Tray Properly
5 We Do Not Want Sleazy Underwear For Christmas (Give Us Credit Cards)
6 Understanding The Female Response To Coming Home Drunk At 4am
7 Wonderful Laundry Techniques (also called 'Don't Wash My Silks')
8 Get A Life – Learn To Cook
9 How Not To Act Like An Idiot When You Are Obviously Wrong
10 Spelling – Even You Can Get It Right
11 Understanding Your Financial Incompetence
12 You, The Weaker Sex
13 Reasons To Give Flowers
14 Garbage – Getting It To The Curb
15 You Cannot Always Wear Whatever You Please
16 How To Put Down A Toilet Seat
17 Give Me A Break – Why We Know Your Excuses Are Lies
18 How To Go Shopping With Your Mate Without Getting Lost
19 The Remote Control – Overcoming Your Dependency
20 Helpful Posture Hints For Couch Potatoes
21 Mother-in-Laws Are People Too
22 The Weekend And Sports Are Not Synonymous
23 How Not To Act Younger Than Your Children
24 You Too Can Be A Designated Driver
25 Male Bonding – Leave Your Friends At Home
26 Attainable Goal – Omitting Foul Expletives From Vocabulary
27 You Don't Really Need That Porsche

The theory used to be you marry an older man because they are more mature. The new theory is that men don't mature. So you might as well marry a younger one.

A dietician was once addressing a large audience. 'The material we put into our stomachs is enough to have killed most of us sitting here, years ago. Red meat is awful. Vegetables can be disastrous, and none of us realises the germs in our drinking water. But there is one thing that is the most dangerous of all and we all of us eat it. Can anyone here tell me what lethal product I'm referring to? You, sir, in the first row, please give us your idea.' The man lowered his head and said, 'Wedding cake.'

Love thy neighbour, but make sure her husband is away first.

Love: an obsessive delusion that is cured by marriage.

Losing a wife can be hard. In my case, it was almost impossible.

'I am' is said to be the shortest sentence in the English language. 'I do' is the longest.

Common wedding questions and answers:

Q: Is it all right to bring a date to the wedding?
A: Not if you are the groom.

Q: How many showers is the bride supposed to have?
A: At least one within a week of the wedding.

Q: What music is recommended for the wedding ceremony?
A: Anything except 'Tied to the Whipping Post'.

If it's true that girls are inclined to marry men like their fathers, it is understandable why so many mothers cry so much at weddings.

Marriage is a rest period between romances.

Whatsamatta University's Seminars for Women - Autumn Catalogue

Once again, the male staff at Whatsamatta University will be offering courses for women of all marital status in an attempt to help males and females understand each other better. Attendance in at least ten of the following is required:

1 Combating The Impulse To Nag
2 You Can Change The Oil Too
3 How To Properly Fill A Beer Mug
4 We Do Not Want Ties For Christmas
5 Understanding The Female Causes Of Male Drunkenness
6 How To Do All Your Laundry In One Load And Have More Time To Watch Football
7 Parenting - Your Husband Gave You Children So You Could Have Someone Other Than Him To Boss Around
8 How To Encourage Your Husband To Cook More And Be Able To Stomach His Slop
9 How Not To Sob Like A Sponge When Your Husband Is Right
10 Get A Life - Learn To Kill Spiders Yourself
11 Balancing A Chequebook - Even You Can Get It Right
12 Payday And Shopping Are Not Synonymous
13 Comprehending Credit Card Spending Limits And Financial Responsibility
14 You, The Whining Sex
15 Shopping - Doing It In Less Than 16 Hours
16 If You Want To Know How That Looks On You, Ask Your Mother
17 How To Close The Garage Door
18 If You Don't Want An Excuse, Don't Demand An Explanation
19 How To Go Fishing With Your Mate And Not Catch Pneumonia
20 Living Without Power Windows - How To Turn A Crank
21 Romanticism - The Whole Point Of Caviar, Candles, And Conversation
22 How To Retain Your Composure While Your Husband Is Relaxing By Himself
23 Why You Don't Need To Invite Your Mother Over Every Weekend
24 How To Act Younger Than Your Mother
25 You Too Can Carry A Backpack
26 Female Friendship - Why Your Best Friends Are Not The Women Who Complain About You The Most
27 Learning To Appreciate The Beer Belly And Lard Butt Male Morphologies

Marriage is the process of finding out what kind of man your wife would have preferred.

At a friend's wedding, everything went smoothly until it was time for the flower girl and her young escort to come down the aisle. The boy stopped at every pew, growling at the guests. When asked afterward why he behaved so badly, he explained, 'I was just trying to be a good ring bear.'

Did you hear about the scientist whose wife had twins? He baptised one and kept the other as a control.

Marriage is an institution – but who wants to live in an institution?

Husband: This coffee isn't fit for a pig!
Wife: No problem, I'll get you some that is.

Marriage means commitment. Of course, so does insanity.

When marriage is outlawed, only outlaws will have in-laws.

Marriage still confers one very special privilege – only a married person can get divorced.

Marriage: the only sport in which the trapped animal has to buy the licence.

Marriage is the sole cause of divorce.

My parents want me to get married. They don't care who any more, as long as he doesn't have a pierced ear, that's all they think about. I think men who have pierced ears are better prepared for marriage. They've experienced pain and bought jewellery. ***Rita Rudner***

Marry not a tennis player. For love means nothing to them.

Nuns: women who marry God. If they divorce Him, do they get half the universe?

The only one of your children who does not grow up and move away is your husband.

A man and woman were having dinner in a fine restaurant. Their waitress, taking another order at a table a few steps away, suddenly noticed that the man was slowly sliding down his chair and under the table, but his companion acted unconcerned. The waitress watched as the man slid all the way down his chair and out of sight under the table. Still, the woman dining across from him appeared calm and unruffled, apparently unaware that her dining companion had disappeared. After the waitress finished taking the order, she came over to the table and said to the woman, 'Pardon me, Ma'am, but I think your husband just slid under the table.' The woman calmly looked up at her and said, 'No he didn't. He just walked in the door.'

I had some words with my wife, and she had some paragraphs with me.

A man really loved a woman, but he was just too shy to propose to her. Now he was much older and neither of them had ever been married. Of course, they had dated about once a week for the past six years, but he was so timid he just never got around to suggesting marriage, much less living together. But one day he became determined to ask her the question. So he calls her on the phone, 'June.' 'Yes, this is June.' 'Will you marry me?' 'Of course I will! Who's this?'

Shotgun wedding: a case of wife or death.

A person receives a telegram informing him about his mother-in-law's death. It also enquires whether she should be buried or burnt. He replies, 'Don't take any chances. Burn the body and bury the ashes.'

Republican boys date Democratic girls. They plan to marry Republican girls, but feel they're entitled to a little fun first.

Spinster: a bachelor's wife.

I was cleaning out the attic the other day with the wife. Filthy, dirty and covered with cobwebs – but she's good with the kids. ***Tommy Cooper***

To hell with marrying a girl who makes biscuits like her mother – I want to marry one who makes dough like her father.

Why bother with marriage? Just find a woman you hate and buy her a house.

A young husband with an inferiority complex insisted he was just a little pebble on a vast beach. The marriage counsellor, trying to be creative, told him, 'If you wish to save your marriage, you'd better be a little boulder.'

The difference between marriage and death? Dead people are free.

What's new? Most of my wife.

Wife: the perfect acquisition for any gentleman feeling himself to have excessive control over his personal affairs.

A recent survey done by marriage experts shows that the most common form of marriage proposal these days consists of the words: 'You're what?!'

All marriages are happy – it's the living together afterward that causes all the problems.

The gods gave man fire and he invented fire engines. They gave him love and he invented marriage.

A woman accompanied her husband to the doctor's office. After his check-up, the doctor called the wife into his office alone. He said, 'Your husband is suffering from a very severe disease, combined with horrible stress. If you don't do the following, your husband will surely die. Each morning, fix him a healthy breakfast. Be pleasant, and make sure he is in a good mood. For lunch make him a nutritious meal. For dinner prepare an especially nice meal for him. Don't burden him with chores, as he probably had a hard day. Don't discuss your problems with him, it will only make his stress worse. And most importantly, make love with your husband several times a week and satisfy his every whim. If you can do this for the next ten months to a year, I think your husband will regain his health completely.' On the way home, the husband asked his wife, 'What did the doctor say?' 'You're going to die,' she replied.

Marriage is a trip between Niagara Falls and Reno.

In olden times, it is reported that sacrifices were made at the altar. Since then, weddings have been held there, and times haven't changed at all!

Jack was living in Arizona during a heat wave when the following took place. 'It's just too hot to wear clothes today,' complained Jack as he stepped out of the shower. 'Honey, what do you think the neighbours would think if I mowed the lawn like this?' 'Probably that I married you for your money.'

At a local coffee bar, a young woman was expounding on her idea of the perfect mate to some of her friends. 'The man I marry must be a shining light amongst company. He must be musical. Tell jokes. Sing. And stay home at night!' An old granny overheard and spoke up, 'Honey, if that's all you want, get a TV!'

A good marriage lasts for ever. A bad one just seems to.

Every morning I take my wife her tea in my pyjamas. She loves it but my pyjamas are getting a bit soggy.

Finally I took her for my wife. Trouble was, my wife didn't want her.

Two deaf men were in a coffee shop discussing their wives. One signs to the other, 'Boy, was my wife mad at me last night! She went on and on and wouldn't stop!' The other guy says, 'When my wife goes off on me I just don't listen.' 'How do you do that?' says the other. 'It's easy. I turn off the light!'

Five years ago I asked for her hand – and it's been in my pocket ever since.

For 25 years my husband and I were deliriously happy. Then we met.

A boy is about to go on his first date, and is nervous about what to talk about. He asks his father for advice. The father replies, 'My son, there are three subjects that always work. These are food, family and philosophy.' The boy picks up his date and they go to a soda fountain. Ice cream sodas in front of them, they stare at each other for a long time, as the boy's nervousness builds. He remembers his father's advice, and chooses the first topic. He asks the girl, 'Do you like spinach?' She says 'No,' and the silence returns. After a few more uncomfortable minutes, the boy thinks of his father's suggestion and turns to the second item on the list. He asks, 'Do you have a brother?' Again, the girl says 'No' and there is silence once again. The boy then plays his last card. He thinks of his father's advice and asks the girl the following question: 'If you had a brother, would he like spinach?'

Her husband is not exactly homeless – but he's home less than most husbands.

I can remember when I got married. And where I got married. What I just can't remember is why.

I told my wife that I don't believe in combining marriage and a career – which is why I haven't worked since our wedding day.

Every man waits for the right girl to come along, but in the meantime he gets married.

My husband added some magic to our marriage. He disappeared.

I'm so looking forward to being married - coming home from work, opening a beer, sitting on the sofa and spending the evening watching my wife's favourite television shows.

In many Eastern countries a woman never sees her husband before marriage. In many Western countries, she doesn't see him very much afterwards.

An old gentleman was reminiscing to a fellow pensioner about his late wife. 'Yes, she was a remarkable woman - extremely religious. When she woke up in the morning, she would sing a hymn, then she would ask me to join her in prayer. Then, over breakfast, she would recite a psalm, and that's how it went all day - praying, singing and reciting until she finally climbed into bed, said her prayers, sang a hymn and said her prayers again. And then one morning, she was dead.' 'What happened?' 'I strangled her.'

Marriage is just another union that defies management.

Marriage is the price men pay for sex; sex is the price women pay for marriage.

My granny told me that all girls should learn how to cook and clean the house. She said it would come in handy in case I couldn't find a husband.

One time, Billy was in Chicago to speak and there was a problem with the hotels because there was a big convention in town. And he was with his assistant, Lacy. All the rooms were booked and there was only one room left, but it had two beds in it and they decided to share the room. Lacy said, 'You know, Billy, I'm cold.' And Billy said, 'Well, Lacy, how'd you like to be Mrs Crystal for the night?' She said, 'I'd love to be Mrs Crystal for the night!' And Billy said, 'Then get up and shut the fuckin' window.'

Jim Belushi, about Billy Crystal

I think my wife's tired of me. She keeps wrapping my sandwiches in a road map.

My parents were absolutely inseparable. In fact, it used to take six people to pull them apart.

My wife should get a job in earthquake prediction. She can find a fault quicker than anyone!

Of course, I'm the master in my own house. I run everything: the parties, the holidays, the gardening, the errands.

Dan: I'm a man of few words.
Loz: Yeah, I'm married, too.

Our marriage was a love match pure and simple – she was pure and I was simple.

She wanted to marry a big movie star or nothing. She got her wish – she married a big nothing.

A wife told her husband that the vacuum cleaner was broken and asked her husband to fix it. 'Do I look like the Hoover repair man?' he asked indignantly and carried on reading the newspaper. The next day she told him that the washing machine had broken and asked him to fix it. 'Do I look like the Zanussi repair man?' he snapped and carried on reading the paper. The day after, she told him the computer was broken and asked him to fix it. 'Do I look like the IBM repair man?' he moaned and carried on reading the paper. A few weeks later the husband said, 'I see you got everything fixed. How did you get it all done so cheap?' 'Well,' said the wife, 'you know Pete next door? He agreed to do the repairs for free if I'd sleep with him or sing him a song.' 'What song did you sing?' asked the husband. The wife replied, 'Do I look like Tina Turner?'

Something terrible has happened. My best friend has run away without my wife!

The first part of our marriage was blissfully happy. Then, on the way back from the ceremony...

A best man's speech should be like a mini-skirt: short enough to be interesting, but long enough to cover the bare essentials.

We had a perfectly happy marriage until my wife found out that the Book of the Month Club doesn't hold meetings.

Marriage is a ceremony that turns your dreamboat into a barge.

A wedding is a funeral where a man smells his own flowers.

How to shower – like a woman:

1 Take off clothing and place it in sectioned laundry basket according to lights and darks.
2 Walk to bathroom wearing long dressing gown. If you see your husband along the way, cover up any exposed flesh and rush to the bathroom.
3 Look at your womanly physique in the mirror and stick out your gut so that you can complain and whine even more about how you're getting fat.
4 Get in the shower. Look for facecloth, armcloth, legcloth, long loofah, wide loofah and pumice stone.
5 Wash your hair once with Cucumber and Lamfrey shampoo with 83 added vitamins.
6 Wash your hair again with Cucumber and Lamfrey shampoo with 83 added vitamins.
7 Condition your hair with Cucumber and Lamfrey conditioner enhanced with natural crocus oil. Leave on hair for 15 minutes.
8 Wash your face with crushed apricot facial scrub for ten minutes until red raw.
9 Wash entire rest of body with Ginger Nut and Jaffa Cake bodywash.
10 Rinse conditioner off hair (this takes at least 15 minutes as you must make sure that it has all come off).
11 Shave armpits and legs. Consider shaving bikini area but decide to get it waxed instead.
12 Scream loudly when your husband flushes the toilet and you freeze/roast.
13 Turn off shower.
14 Squeegee off all wet surfaces in shower. Spray mould spots with Mould and Mildew Remover.
15 Get out of shower. Dry with towel the size of a small African country. Wrap hair in super absorbent second towel.
16 Check entire body for the remotest sign of a blemish. Attack with nails/tweezers/stanley knife/sander/power drill if found.
17 Return to bedroom wearing long dressing gown and towel on head.
18 If you see your husband along the way, cover up any exposed areas and then rush to bedroom to spend an hour and a half getting dressed.

The aged farmer and his wife were leaning against the edge of the pig-pen when the old woman wistfully recalled that the next week would mark their golden wedding anniversary. 'Let's have a party, Homer,' she suggested. 'Let's kill the pig.' The farmer scratched his grizzled head. 'Gosh, Elmira,' he finally answered. 'I don't see why the pig should take the blame for something that happened 50 years ago.'

You know the honeymoon's over when the groom stops helping his wife with the dishes – and starts doing them himself.

There's only one thing that keeps me from being happily married – my wife.

You may marry the man of your dreams, but 14 years later you're married to a couch that burps. ***Roseanne***

There is something magical about the fact that success almost always comes faster to the guy your wife almost married.

Did your wife have anything to say when you got home late last night? No, but it didn't stop her talking for hours.

They say that in some parts of the East, a man doesn't know his wife until she marries him. Isn't that true everywhere?

'Tis better to have loved and lost than to have loved and married.

If you marry two men it's bigamy. What is it if you marry just one man? Monotony.

Did you know that once you get married, you can look forward to three different kinds of sex? First there's house sex, when you make love all over the house; on the floor, on the kitchen table, in the garage, anywhere, any time. Then comes bedroom sex; after the kids are bathed and fed and asleep, the shades are pulled down and the door locked, you make love in the bedroom. Last comes hall sex. That's when you pass each other in the hall and snarl, 'F**k you.'

The truth is, I regret the day I was married. You're lucky, I was married for a whole month!

What did you do before you married? Anything I wanted to!

Husband: Put your coat on, love, I'm going to the bar.
Wife: Are you taking me out for a drink?
Husband: Don't be silly, woman, I'm turning off the heating!

What do you normally have for breakfast? Arguments about dinner.

You know that beautiful film star you were talking about? Is she married? Occasionally.

As aspiring actor called home to announce with great pride that he'd been cast in an off-Broadway play. 'It's a real opportunity, Dad,' he said, 'I play this guy who's been married for 25 years.' 'That's great, son,' enthused his father. 'And one of these days you'll work up to a speaking part.'

A man took his wife along to a marriage counsellor. The counsellor asked him to explain their problem. The man said, 'What's 'er name here claims I don't pay her enough attention.'

Bigamy is having one wife too many. Monogamy is the same thing.

The new bride gushed to her mother, 'My husband is very good to me. He gives me everything I ask for.' Her mother said, 'That only shows you're not asking for enough.' ***Joey Adams***

An extravagance is anything you buy that is of no use to your spouse.

What do you call a woman who knows where her husband is every night? A widow.

What's the best way to have your husband remember your anniversary? Get married on his birthday.

A couple in their nineties appeared before a judge to ask for a divorce. The wife moaned, 'He gambles, he stays out nights, he runs around with women. I can't take any more.' The husband countered, 'She doesn't do any housework, her cooking is atrocious, she has no time for me, she sleeps around.' 'How long has this been going on?' asked the judge. 'About 70 years,' they chorused. The judge was bemused. 'So why did you wait till now to get a divorce?' 'Well, we were waiting for the kids to die.'

The honeymoon period is over when the husband calls home to say he'll be late for dinner, and the answering machine says it's in the microwave.

When a man opens the door of his car for his wife, you can be sure of one thing: either the car or the wife is new.

How to shower – like a man:

1 Take off clothes while sitting on the edge of the bed and leave them in a pile.
2 Walk naked to the bathroom. If you see your wife along the way, shake your willy at her and make a 'wey hey' sound.
3 Look at your manly physique in the mirror, suck in your gut, look for pecs. Generally admire yourself.
4 Get in the shower.
5 Don't bother to look for a washcloth (you don't use one).
6 Wash your face.
7 Wash your armpits.
8 Crack up at how loud your farts sound in the shower.
9 Wash your privates and surrounding area.
10 Ensure you leave 'special' hair on the soap bar.
11 Shampoo your hair (do not use conditioner).
12 Make a shampoo Mohawk.
13 Pull back shower curtain and look at yourself in the mirror.
14 Pee (in the shower).
15 Rinse off and get out of the shower. Fail to notice water on the floor because you left the curtain hanging out of the bath the whole time.
16 Partially dry off.
17 Look at yourself in the mirror, flex muscles. Admire self again.
18 Leave shower curtain open and wet bath mat on the floor.
19 Leave bathroom light on.
20 Return to the bedroom with towel around waist. If you pass your wife, pull off towel, grab willy, repeat 'wey hey sound.
21 Throw wet towel on the bed. Take two minutes to get dressed.

A smart husband buys his wife fine china so she won't trust him to wash it.

Anybody who claims that marriage is a 50-50 proposition doesn't know the first thing about women or fractions.

I want a husband who is decent, God-fearing, well-educated, smart, sincere, respectful, treats me as an equal, has a great body, and has the same interests in life as me. Now I don't think that's too much to ask of a billionaire, do you?

Getting married is like buying a dishwasher: you'll never need to do it by hand again.

A honeymoon should be like a table: four bare legs and no drawers.

I married Miss Right. I just didn't know her first name was Always.

After 35 years of marriage, a husband said he wanted a divorce. His wife was stunned. 'But John,' she pleaded, 'how could you want to divorce me after all we've been through together? Remember how just after we met, you caught malaria and nearly died, but I looked after you? Then when your family were wiped out in a hurricane, I was there for you. Then when you were falsely accused of armed robbery, I stood by you. Then when you lost £40,000 on the horses, I sympathised. And when that fire destroyed your office, I comforted you. How could you leave me? We've been through so much.' 'That's the problem, Sue. Face it, you're just bad luck.'

The three stages of sex in marriage: tri-weekly; try-weekly; try-weakly.

Before marriage, a man yearns for the woman he loves. After marriage, the Y becomes silent.

After paying for a wedding, all a father has left to give away is the bride.

A woman ran excitedly into the house one morning and yelled to her husband, 'John, pack up your stuff. I just won the lottery!' 'Shall I pack for warm weather or cold?' he said. 'Whatever. Just so long as you're out of the house by noon.'

Courtship is like looking at beautiful photos of flowers in a seed catalogue. Marriage is what actually comes up in your garden.

Why did Adam and Eve have the perfect marriage? He didn't have to listen to her talk about all the other men she could have married, and she didn't have to put up with his mother.

Why do most men die before their wives? They want to.

A marriage counsellor was asking a woman questions about her state of mind. 'Do you wake up grumpy in the morning?' 'No, I let him sleep.'

A couple had a furious row on their 25th wedding anniversary. He was so bitter that he presented her with a gift of a tombstone bearing the inscription: 'Here lies my wife – cold as ever.' In retaliation, she went out the next day and bought him a tombstone with the inscription: 'Here lies my husband – stiff at last.'

A husband is a man with lots of small mouths to feed and one big one to listen to.

Tony: I hear you got married again, Mike.
Mike: Yes, for the fourth time.
Tony: What happened to your first three wives?
Mike: They all died.
Tony: I'm sorry, I didn't know. That's terrible. How did they die?
Mike: The first ate poisonous mushrooms.
Tony: How awful! What about the second?
Mike: She ate poisonous mushrooms.
Tony: Oh no! What about the third? Did she die from poisonous mushrooms too?
Mike: No, she died of a broken neck.
Tony: I see, an accident.
Mike: Not exactly, she wouldn't eat her mushrooms.

He was so henpecked, he had to wash and iron his own apron.

My wife thinks that I'm too nosy. At least that's what she keeps scribbling in her diary.
Drake Sather

Why are married women heavier than single women? Single women come home, see what's in the refrigerator, and go to bed; married women come home, see what's in bed and go to the refrigerator.

A travelling salesman was testifying in divorce proceedings against his wife. His attorney said, 'Please describe the incident that first caused you to entertain suspicions regarding your wife's infidelity.' The salesman answered, 'I'm on the road during the week so naturally when I am home at weekends, I'm particularly attentive to my wife. One Sunday morning we were in the middle of a heavy session of lovemaking when the old lady in the apartment next door pounded on the wall and yelled, 'Can't you at least stop all that racket at the weekend?'

He wears the trousers in his house – right under his apron!

Mrs Czernak appeared before the judge in a divorce action. 'How old are you?' asked the judge. 'Thirty-five,' said Mrs Czernak. The judge noted her greying hair and wrinkled cheeks. 'May I see your birth certificate?' She handed the judge her birth certificate. 'Madam,' he said severely, 'according to this certificate you are not 35 but 50.' 'Your honour,' replied Mrs Czernak, 'the last 15 years I spent with my husband I'm not counting. You call that a life?'

I'm sure my husband would leave home if only he knew how to pack his bag.

I haven't spoken to my wife for three years. I don't like to interrupt her.

I married my wife for her looks – but not the ones she's been giving me lately.

I don't know what all this fuss is about weight. My wife lost two stone swimming last year. I don't know how. I tied them round her neck tight enough. ***Les Dawson***

I put my wife on a pedestal. It makes it easier for her to paint the ceiling.

My wife always lets me have the last word. It's usually 'Yes'.

The only thing my wife doesn't know is why she married me.

The man consulted his priest about getting a divorce. The priest was surprised. 'Why on earth would you want to divorce such a lovely wife? She is soft and gentle and, if I may say so, she is also quite beautiful and nicely proportioned. I really can't see what you have to complain about.' The man took off his shoe. 'See this shoe?' he said, showing it to the priest. 'The leather is soft and gentle. It is a beautiful piece of work and nicely proportioned.' 'Ah,' said the priest, 'a parable.' 'In a way, Father,' replied the man. 'I'm the only one who knows it pinches.'

Has your wife learned to drive yet? Only in an advisory capacity.

What is the penalty for bigamy? Two mothers-in-law.

A woman went to an attorney to ask about a divorce. 'What grounds do you have, madam?' 'About six acres.' 'No, I don't think you quite understand. Let me rephrase the question. Do you have a grudge?' 'No, just a parking space.' 'I'll try again. Does your husband beat you up?' 'No, I always get up at least an hour before he does.' The attorney could see he was fighting a losing battle. 'Madam, are you sure you want a divorce?' 'I'm not the one who wants a divorce,' she said. 'My husband does. He claims we don't communicate.'

Ah, yes, divorce: from the Latin word meaning to rip out a man's genitals through his wallet. ***Robin Williams***

A divorce court judge said to the husband, 'Mr Geraghty, I have reviewed this case very carefully and I've decided to give your wife £800 a week.' 'That's very fair, your honour,' he replied. 'And every now and then I'll try to send her a few quid myself.'

To the horror of the locals, Satan suddenly appeared in the main street of a small town one Sunday morning. Everyone rushed indoors except for one old timer who calmly stayed on his porch reading a book. Satan was furious that this one person should not be afraid of him and went over to challenge him. 'Are you scared of me?' screamed Satan at his most menacing. 'Nope,' said the old timer. 'Aren't you terrified that I'm going to wreak havoc in your nice little community?' 'Nope.' By now steam was coming out of Satan's ears. He raged, 'You do know who I am, don't you?' 'Should do. Been married to your sister for 46 years.'

I met a man who had been married for 66 years. 'Amazing - 66 years!' I said. 'What's the secret to such a long, happy marriage?' 'Well,' he replied, 'It's like this. The man makes all the big decisions and the woman just makes the little decisions.' 'Really?' I responded. 'Does that really work?' 'Oh, yes,' he said proudly. '66 years, and so far, not one big decision!'

A man meets a genie. The genie tells him he can have whatever he wants, provided that his mother-in-law gets double. The man thinks for a moment and then says, 'Okay, give me a million pounds and beat me half to death.'

Quick Quips 2

I took my mother-in-law to Madame Tussaud's Chamber of Horrors, and one of the attendants said, 'Keep her moving, Sir, we're stock-taking.' ***Les Dawson***

By all means marry. If you get a good wife, you'll be happy. If you get a bad one, you'll become a philosopher. ***Socrates***

My mother-in-law had to stop skipping for exercise. It registered seven on the Richter scale. ***Les Dawson***

Long engagements give people the opportunity of finding out each other's character before marriage, which is never advisable.
Oscar Wilde

A coward is a hero with a wife, kids and a mortgage.
Marvin Kitman

A husband is what's left of the lover after the nerve has been extracted. ***Helen Rowland***

A man must marry only a very pretty woman in case he should ever want some other man to take her off his hands. ***Guitry***

Ah, Mozart! He was happily married – but his wife wasn't.
Borge

An archaeologist is the best husband a woman can have; the older she gets, the more interested he is in her.
Agatha Christie

Honolulu – it's got everything. Sand for the children, sun for the wife, sharks for the wife's mother. ***Ken Dodd***

I belong to Bridegrooms Anonymous. Whenever I feel like getting married, they send over a lady in a housecoat and hair curlers to burn my toast for me. ***Dick Martin***

I do not see the EEC as a great love affair. It is more like nine desperate middle-aged couples with failing marriages meeting at a Brussels hotel for a group grope. ***Tynan***

We must respect the other fellow's religion, but only in the sense and to the extent that we respect his theory that his wife is beautiful and his children smart. ***H L Mencken***

I've been asked to say a couple of words about my husband, Fang. How about 'short' and 'cheap'? ***Phyllis Diller***

If you are afraid of loneliness, do not marry. ***Chekhov***

If you never want to see a man again, say, 'I love you, I want to marry you, I want to have children...' – they leave skid marks. ***Rita Rudner***

Jimmy Carter as President is like Truman Capote marrying Dolly Parton. The job is just too big for him. ***Rich Little***

Marriage is a matter of give and take, but so far I haven't been able to find anybody who'll take what I have to give. ***Cass Daley***

Marriages are made in Heaven and consummated on Earth. ***John Lyly***

Men have a much better time of it than women: for one thing, they marry later; for another thing, they die earlier. ***H L Mencken***

Never be unfaithful to a lover, except with your wife.
P J O'Rourke

No man should marry until he has studied anatomy and dissected at least one woman. ***Honoré de Balzac***

Nothing says loving like marrying your cousin! ***Al Bundy***

Perfection is what American women expect to find in their husbands, but English women only hope to find in their butlers.
W Somerset Maugham

Second marriage: the triumph of hope over experience. ***Dr Samuel Johnson***

The days just prior to marriage are like a snappy introduction to a tedious book. ***Wilson Mizner***

The husband who wants a happy marriage should learn to keep his mouth shut and his checkbook open.
Groucho Marx

The most happy marriage I can imagine to myself would be the union of a deaf man to a blind woman. ***S T Coleridge***

There's a way of transferring funds that is even faster than electronic banking. It's called marriage. ***James Holt McGavran***

We in the industry know that behind every successful screenwriter stands a woman. And behind her stands his wife. ***Groucho Marx***

When a man steals your wife, there is no better revenge than to let him keep her. ***Guitry***

A man may be a fool and not know it, but not if he is married. ***H L Mencken***

I love being married. It's so great to find that one special person you want to annoy for the rest of your life. ***Rita Rudner***

Before marriage, a man will lie awake all night thinking about something you said; after marriage, he'll fall asleep before you've finished saying it. ***Helen Rowland***

He marries best who puts it off until it is too late. ***H L Mencken***

One should always be in love – that is one reason why one should never marry. ***Oscar Wilde***

It destroys one's nerves to be amiable every day to the same human being. ***Benjamin Disraeli***

It isn't tying himself to one woman that a man dreads when he thinks of marrying; it's separating himself from all the others. ***Helen Rowland***

Marriage is a very good thing, but I think it's a mistake to make a habit of it. ***W Somerset Maugham***

When a man brings his wife flowers for no reason, there's a reason. ***Molly McGee***

I told my wife that black underwear turns me on, so she didn't wash my shorts for a month. ***Milton Berle***

My wife's an earth sign. I'm a water sign. Together we make mud. ***Henny Youngman***

We're happily married. We wake up in the middle of the night and laugh at each other. ***Bob Hope***

My parents have been married for 50 years. I asked my mother how they did it. She said, "You close your eyes and pretend it's not happening." ***Rita Rudner***

Sex when you're married is like going to a Seven-Eleven. There's not as much variety, but at three in the morning, it's always there. ***Carol Leifer***

We would have broken up except for the children. Who were the children? Well, she and I were. ***Mort Sahl***

Easy-crying widows take new husbands soonest; there's nothing like wet weather for transplanting. ***Oliver Wendell Holmes, Sr***

Sex in marriage is like medicine. Three times a day for the first week. Then once a day for another week. Then once every three or four days until the condition clears up. ***Peter De Vries***

I had my credit card stolen, but I didn't report it because the thief was spending less than my wife did. ***Henny Youngman***

Marrying a man is like buying something you've been admiring for a long time in a shop window. You may love it when you get it home, but it doesn't always go with everything else in the house. ***Jean Kerr***

Many a man in love with a dimple makes the mistake of marrying the whole girl. ***Stephen Leacock***

The trouble with marrying your mistress is that you create a job vacancy.
Sir James Goldsmith

He has decided to take himself a wife, but he hasn't decided yet whose...
Peter De Vries

Whoever perpetrated the mathematical inaccuracy, "Two can live as cheaply as one," has a lot to answer for.
Caren Meyer

I've been in love with the same woman for 41 years. If my wife finds out, she'll kill me. ***Henny Youngman***

It is difficult to tell who gives some couples the most happiness, the minister who marries them or the judge who divorces them.
Mary Wilson Little

Any husband who says, "My wife and I are completely equal partners" is talking about either a law firm or a hand of bridge. ***Bill Cosby***

Marriage is not a man's idea. A woman must have thought of it. Years ago some guy said, "Let me get this straight, honey. I can't sleep with anyone else for the rest of my life, and if things don't work you get to keep half of my stuff? What a great idea."
Bobby Slayton

I hate single bars. Guys come up to me and say, 'Hey cupcake, can I buy you a drink?' I say, "No, but I'll take the three bucks." ***Margaret Smith***

The romance is dead if he drinks champagne from your slipper and chokes on a Dr Scholl's foot pad.
Phyllis Diller

Marriage, as far as I'm concerned, is one of the most wonderful, heart-warming, satisfying experiences a human being can have. I've only been married 17 years, so I haven't seen that side of it yet. ***George Gobel***

When you're in love, it's the most glorious two and a half days of your life. ***Richard Lewis***

A man in love is incomplete until he has married. Then he's finished. ***Zsa Zsa Gabor***

I recently read that love is entirely a matter of chemistry. That must be why my wife treats me like toxic waste. ***David Bissionette***

A woman I know has been married so many times she has rice marks on her face. She has a wash-and-wear bridal gown. ***Henny Youngman***

Marriage is a wonderful invention; but then again, so is a bicycle puncture repair kit. ***Billy Connolly***

Bigamy is the only crime on the books where two rites make a wrong. ***Bob Hope***

Keep your eyes wide open before marriage and half shut afterwards. ***Benjamin Franklin***

Marriage is the deep, deep peace of the double bed after the hurly-burly of the chaise longue. ***Mrs Patrick Campbell***

A bachelor is a man who never makes the same mistake once. ***Ed Wynn***

When a girl marries she exchanges the attentions of many men for the inattention of one. ***Helen Rowland***

I have always thought that every woman should marry, and no man. ***Benjamin Disraeli***

My mother said it was simple to keep a man – you must be a maid in the living room, a cook in the kitchen and a whore in the bedroom. I said I'd hire the other two and take care of the bedroom bit. ***Jerry Hall***

The problem is that God gives men a brain and a penis, and only enough blood to run one at a time. ***Robin Williams***

Not all women give most of their waking thoughts to the problem of pleasing men. Some are married. ***Emma Lee***

I'm the only man who has a marriage licence made out To Whom it May Concern. ***Mickey Rooney***

When you see what some girls marry, you realise how much they must hate to work for a living. ***Helen Rowland***

The quickest way to a man's heart is through his chest. ***Roseanne***

All men are afraid of eyelash curlers. I sleep with one under my pillow instead of a gun. ***Rita Rudner***

I know nothing about sex because I was always married. ***Zsa Zsa Gabor***

No man is an island, but some of us are pretty long peninsulas. ***Ashleigh Brilliant***

On the one hand, we'll never experience childbirth. On the other hand, we can open all our own jars. ***Jeff Green***

What are the three words guaranteed to humiliate men everywhere? 'Hold my purse.'
Francois Morency

When women are depressed, they either eat or go shopping. Men invade another country. ***Elayne Boosler***

Only one man in 1,000 is a leader of men. The other 999 follow women. ***Groucho Marx***

A girl must marry for love, and keep on marrying until she finds it. ***Zsa Zsa Gabor***

Men hate to lose. I once beat my husband at tennis. I asked him, 'Are we going to have sex again?' He said, 'Yes, but not with each other.'
Rita Rudner

Man is the only animal that blushes. Or needs to.
Mark Twain

Men are those creatures with two legs and eight hands.
Jayne Mansfield

Behind every successful man you'll find a woman who has nothing to wear. ***James Stewart***

Behind every successful man stands a proud wife and a surprised mother-in-law.
Brooks Hays

God must love the common man. He made so many of them. ***Abraham Lincoln***

Can you imagine a world without men? No crime and lots of happy, fat women.
Nicole Hollander

I like men to behave like men – strong and childish.
Francoise Sagan

No nice men are good at getting taxis. ***Katherine Whitehorn***

A man is in general better pleased when he has a good dinner upon his table, than when his wife talks Greek.
Samuel Johnson

Giving a man space is like giving a dog a computer. The chances are he will not use it wisely. ***Bette-Jane Raphael***

The male is a domestic animal which, if treated with firmness and kindness, can be trained to do most things.
Jilly Cooper

I require only three things of a man. He must be handsome, ruthless and stupid. ***Dorothy Parker***

I like two kinds of men: domestic and foreign. ***Mae West***

Husbands never become good. They merely become proficient. ***H L Mencken***

I started as a passion and ended as a habit, like all husbands. ***George Bernard Shaw***

A loving wife will do anything for her husband except stop criticising and trying to improve him. ***J B Priestley***

Wives are people who feel they don't dance enough.
Groucho Marx

A woman's place is in the wrong. ***James Thurber***

It is God who makes woman beautiful; it is the Devil who makes her pretty. ***Victor Hugo***

Treat every queen like a whore and every whore like a queen. ***Anthony Quinn***

The only time a woman really succeeds in changing a man is when he's a baby.
Natalie Wood

The more underdeveloped the country, the more overdeveloped the women.
J K Galbraith

Being a woman is a terribly difficult trade, since it consists principally of dealing with men. ***Joseph Conrad***

Woman begins by resisting a man's advances and ends by blocking his retreat. ***Oscar Wilde***

To succeed with the opposite sex, tell her you're impotent. She can't wait to disprove it.
Cary Grant

Being a woman is of special interest only to aspiring male transsexuals. To actual women it is merely a good excuse not to play football.
Fran Lebowitz

When women go wrong, men go right after them. ***Mae West***

I just got back from a pleasure trip. I took my mother-in-law to the airport.
Henny Youngman

The wife's mother said, 'When you're dead, I'll dance on your grave.' I said, 'Good, I'm being buried at sea.'
Les Dawson

My wife has a slight impediment in her speech. Every now and then she stops to breathe. ***Jimmy Durante***

I was married by a judge. I should have asked for a jury.
Groucho Marx

If we take matrimony at its lowest, we regard it as a sort of friendship recognised by the police. ***Robert Louis Stevenson***

What would men be without women? Scarce, sir, mighty scarce. ***Mark Twain***

Happiness is having a large, loving, caring, close-knit family in another city.
George Burns

Marriage is like putting your hand into a bag of snakes in the hope of pulling out an eel. ***Leonardo Di Vinci***

A married man should forget his mistakes; no use two people remembering the same thing. ***Duane Dewel***

The secret of a successful marriage is not to be at home too much. ***Colin Chapman***

In my house I'm the boss, my wife is just the decision maker. ***Woody Allen***

I've had bad luck with both my wives. The first one left me and the second one didn't. ***Patrick Murray***

I wouldn't be caught dead marrying a woman old enough to be my wife.
Tony Curtis

A woman voting for divorce is like a turkey voting for Christmas. ***Alice Glynn***

The appropriate age for marriage is around 18 for girls and 37 for men. ***Aristotle***

Women should be obscene and not heard. ***Groucho Marx***

Whatever women do they must do twice as well as men to be thought half as good. Luckily, this is not difficult.
Charlotte Whitton

A woman is an occasional pleasure but a cigar is always a smoke. ***Groucho Marx***

Wild horses couldn't drag a secret out of a woman. However, women seldom have lunch with wild horses.
Ivern Boyett

Women: can't live with them, can't bury them in the back yard without the neighbours seeing. ***Sean Williamson***

If a woman insists on being called Ms, ask her if it stands for miserable. ***Russell Bell***

Show me a woman who doesn't feel guilt and I'll show you a man. ***Erica Jong***

You know when you put a stick in water and it looks bent? That's why I never take baths. ***Steven Wright***

Men should be like Kleenex - soft, strong and disposable.
Cher

When women kiss it always reminds me of prize fighters shaking hands. ***H L Mencken***

She doesn't understand the concept of Roman numerals. She thought we just fought in world war eleven. ***Joan Rivers***

She looked as if she'd been poured into her clothes and had forgotten to say when.
P G Wodehouse

Women are nothing but machines for producing children. ***Napolean Bonaparte***

If you've got them by the balls, their hearts and minds will follow. ***John Wayne***

I only know that people call me a feminist whenever I express sentiments that differentiate me from a doormat or a prostitute.
Rebecca West

A genius is a man who can rewrap a new shirt and not have any pins left over.
Dino Levi

Give a man a free hand and he'll run it all over you.
Mae West

As long as a woman can look ten years younger than her own daughter, she is perfectly satisfied. ***Oscar Wilde***

Ah, women. They make the highs higher and the lows more frequent.
Friedrich Wilhelm Nietzsche

Men are simple things. They can survive a whole weekend with only three things: beer, boxer shorts and batteries for the remote control.
Diana Jordan

kids

Knock Knock

Knock, Knock! Who's there?
Justin. Justin who? Justin time to let me in!

Knock, Knock! Who's there?
Anna. Anna who? Anna noying habit of yours – locking the door like this!

Knock, Knock! Who's there?
Josie. Josie who? Josie anyone else out here?

Knock, Knock! Who's there?
Paula. Paula who? Paula door open and you'll see!

Knock, Knock! Who's there?
Annette. Annette who? Annette curtain!

Knock, Knock! Who's there?
Angus. Angus who? Angus me coat up and put the kettle on!

Knock, Knock! Who's there?
Homer. Homer who? Homer goodness, I've come to the wrong house!

Knock, Knock! Who's there?
Elvis. Elvis who? Elvis is a turn-up for the books!

Knock, Knock! Who's there?
Alma. Alma who? Alma time seems to be spent on this doorstep!

Knock, Knock! Who's there?
Zeke. Zeke who? Zeke and you will find out!

Knock, Knock! Who's there?
Phil. Phil who? Phil this cup with sugar would you? I've run out!

Knock, Knock! Who's there?
Alex. Alex who? Alex the way you've done the garden!

Knock, Knock! Who's there?
Chas. Chas who? Chas pass the key through the letter box and I'll open the door myself!

Knock, Knock! Who's there?
Mo. Mo who? Mo than you'll ever know!

Knock, Knock! Who's there?
Matt. Matt who? Matt as well settle down, looks like I'm in for a long wait!

Knock, Knock! Who's there?
Dana. Dana who? Dana nice day out here, hurry up and let me in!

Knock, Knock! Who's there?
A Lister. A Lister who? A Lister good reasons why you should open the door!

Knock, Knock! Who's there?
Zeb. Zeb who? Zeb better be a good reason for keeping me waiting out here!

Knock, Knock! Who's there?
Greta. Greta who? Greta friend like that again, and you'll end up with none at all!

Knock, Knock! Who's there?
Will. Will who? Will I have to wait much longer?

Knock, Knock! Who's there?
Woody. Woody who? Woody open the door if we asked him nicely?

Knock, Knock! Who's there?
Kline. Kline who? Kline of you to invite me round!

Knock, Knock! Who's there?
Polly. Polly who? Polly door handle again, I think it's just stiff!

Knock, Knock! Who's there?
Keith. Keith who? Keith your hands where I can see them!

Knock, Knock! Who's there?
Imogen. Imogen who? Imogen you were out here...

Knock, Knock! Who's there?
India. India who? India is some of my stuff and I've come to collect it!

Knock, Knock! Who's there?
Kat. Kat who? Kat you again?

Knock, Knock! Who's there?
Al Gore. Al Gore who? Al Gore to the window so you can see me!

Knock, Knock! Who's there?
Alvin. Alvin who? Alvin your heart – just you vait and see!

Knock, Knock! Who's there?
Tom. Tom who? Tom to the window and have a look!

Knock, Knock! Who's there?
Candy. Candy who? Candy owner of this big red car come and move it off my drive!

Knock Knock

Knock, Knock! Who's there?
Alfie. Alfie who? Alfie good to see you again!

Knock, Knock! Who's there?
Kim. Kim who? Kim just too late to see you!

Knock, Knock! Who's there?
Adair. Adair who? Adair you to guess!

Knock, Knock! Who's there?
Chuck. Chuck who? Chuck the key under the door and I'll let myself in!

Knock, Knock! Who's there?
Khan. Khan who? Khan you give me a lift to school?

Knock, Knock! Who's there?
Mavis. Mavis who? Mavis be the last time you keep me waiting!

Knock, Knock! Who's there?
Darren. Darren who? Darren nother excuse to keep me out here!

Knock, Knock! Who's there?
Luke. Luke who? Luke through the letter box and you'll see!

Knock, Knock! Who's there?
Colin. Colin who? Colin for a chat!

Knock, Knock! Who's there?
Wendy. Wendy who? Wendy you want me to call round again?

Knock, Knock! Who's there?
Tori. Tori who? Tori – I got the wrong address!

Knock, Knock! Who's there?
Trudy. Trudy who? Trudy my work I've come round to collect you!

Knock, Knock! Who's there?
Trish. Trish who? Bless you!

Knock, Knock! Who's there?
Cameron. Cameron who? Cameron say that!

Knock, Knock! Who's there?
Cohen. Cohen who? Cohen to knock just once more, then I'm going away!

Knock, Knock! Who's there?
Kent. Kent who? Kent you stop asking questions and open the door?

Knock, Knock! Who's there?
Alan. Alan who? Alan 'nounce myself once you've opened the door!

Knock, Knock! Who's there?
Penny. Penny who? Penny for the guy, mister?

Knock, Knock! Who's there?
Ahmed. Ahmed who? Ahmed a big mistake coming here, didn't I?

Knock, Knock! Who's there?
Ginger. Ginger who? Ginger hear the doorbell?

Knock, Knock! Who's there?
Courtney. Courtney who? Courtney door – can you open it and let me loose?

Knock, Knock! Who's there?
Isabel. Isabel who? Isabel not working?

Knock, Knock! Who's there?
Guess Simon. Guess Simon who? Guess Simon the wrong doorstep!

Knock, Knock! Who's there?
Wendy. Wendy who? Wendy red, red robin comes bob, bob bobbin' along, along...

Knock, Knock! Who's there?
Amos. Amos who? Amosquito is chasing me – please let me in!

Knock, Knock! Who's there?
Arnie. Arnie who? Arnie ever going to let me in?

Knock, Knock! Who's there?
Ken. Ken who? Ken you come out to play?

Knock, Knock! Who's there?
Sid. Sid who? Sid you'd be ready at three - what's gone wrong?

Knock, Knock! Who's there?
Seymour. Seymour who? Seymour of me by opening the door!

Knock, Knock! Who's there?
Charlie. Charlie who? Charlie you know the sound of my voice by now!

Knock, Knock! Who's there?
Hedda. Hedda who? Hedda nough of this – I'm off!

Knock, Knock! Who's there?
Ivan. Ivan who? Ivan idea you're going to keep me waiting out here!

Knock, Knock! Who's there?
Gin. Gin who? Gin know how cold it is out here?

Knock, Knock! Who's there?
Farmer. Farmer who? Farmer distance your house looks much bigger!

Knock, Knock! Who's there?
Linda. Linda who? Linda hand to get this heavy suitcase up the steps!

Knock, Knock! Who's there?
Tex. Tex who? Tex you ages to open the door!

Knock, Knock! Who's there?
Hardy. Hardy who? Hardy har – fooled you!

Knock, Knock! Who's there?
Yul. Yul who? Yul soon see!

Knock, Knock! Who's there?
Courtney. Courtney who? Courtney good football matches lately?

Knock, Knock! Who's there?
Mary. Mary who? Mary Christmas, ho, ho, ho!

Knock, Knock! Who's there?
Carla. Carla who? Carla taxi, I'm leaving!

Knock, Knock! Who's there?
Giraffe. Giraffe who? Giraffe to ask me that stupid question?

Knock, Knock! Who's there?
Paul. Paul who? Paul the door from your side – it's a bit stiff!

Knock, Knock! Who's there?
Ringo. Ringo who? Ringo, ringo roses...!

Knock, Knock! Who's there?
Mike. Mike who? Mike your mind up!

Knock, Knock! Who's there?
Spock. Spock who? Spock the difference between me and my twin brother!

Knock, Knock! Who's there?
Teacher. Teacher who? Teacher self for a few days – I'm off on my hols!

Knock, Knock! Who's there?
Tessa. Tessa who? Tessa long time for you to open the door!

Knock, Knock! Who's there?
Carl. Carl who? Carl round to my house and I won't keep you waiting!

Knock, Knock! Who's there?
You. You who? Hello!

Knock, Knock! Who's there?
Simon. Simon who? Simon every occasion – you always make me wait!

Knock, Knock! Who's there?
Princess. Princess who? Princess not to come round here any more!

Knock, Knock! Who's there?
Morgan. Morgan who? Morgan you could ever imagine!

Knock, Knock! Who's there?
Jacqueline. Jacqueline who? Jacqueline Hyde!

Knock, Knock! Who's there?
Callista. Callista who? Callista warm reception?

Knock, Knock! Who's there?
Teresa. Teresa who? Teresa jolly good fellow.

Knock, Knock! Who's there?
Mouse. Mouse who? Mouse get a key of my own!

Knock, Knock! Who's there?
Batman. Batman who? You mean there's more than one?

Knock, Knock! Who's there?
Donna. Donna who? Donna knock once more then I'm going home!

Knock, Knock! Who's there?
Egbert. Egbert who? Egbert no bacon!

Knock, Knock! Who's there?
Misty. Misty who? Misty door bell again!

Knock, Knock! Who's there?
Lester. Lester who? Lester worry about!

Knock, Knock! Who's there?
Just Paul. Just Paul who? Just Pauling your leg – it's Steve really!

Knock, Knock! Who's there?
Fitz. Fitz who? Fitz not too much trouble, can you please open the door!

Knock, Knock! Who's there?
Major. Major who? Major mind up to open the door yet?

Knock, Knock! Who's there?
Mandy. Mandy who? Mandy lifeboats!

Knock, Knock! Who's there?
Belle. Belle who? Belle don't work, so I'm having to knock!

Knock, Knock! Who's there?
Alex. Alex who? Alex to knock on doors and run away!

Knock, Knock! Who's there?
Vance. Vance who? Vance more I knock on your door in the dead of night!

Knock, Knock! Who's there?
Yootha. Yootha who? Yootha person with the second-hand cooker for sale?

Knock, Knock! Who's there?
Ozzie. Ozzie who? Ozzie you still have the same front door you did the last time I called!

Knock, Knock! Who's there?
Chester. Chester who? Chester minute – I'm in the wrong street!

Knock, Knock! Who's there?
Carl. Carl who? Carl this a friend greeting – 'cos I don't!

Knock, Knock! Who's there?
Mustapha. Mustapha who? Mustapha good reason to keep me waiting!

Knock, Knock! Who's there?
Willy. Willy who? Willy hurry up and let me in!

Knock, Knock! Who's there?
Posh. Posh who? Posh the door open and you'll see!

Knock, Knock! Who's there?
Baby. Baby who? Baby I shouldn't hab come round wiv dis cold!

Knock, Knock! Who's there?
Fred. Fred who? Fred you'll have to let me in!

Knock, Knock! Who's there?
Russell. Russell who? Russell up a nice hot cup of tea – it's freezing out here!

Knock, Knock! Who's there?
Homer. Homer who? Homer goodness, I can't remember myself!

Knock, Knock! Who's there?
Bart. Bart who? Bart time you opened this door!

Knock, Knock! Who's there?
Denise. Denise who? Denise are cold – let me in!

Knock, Knock! Who's there?
May. May who? May I come in?

Knock, Knock! Who's there?
Doctor. Doctor who? No, Doctor Smith – you sent for me because you have a cold!

Knock, Knock! Who's there?
Lass. Lass who? How long have you been a cowboy?

Knock, Knock! Who's there?
Norbut. Norbut who? Norbut a lad!

Knock, Knock! Who's there?
Giselle. Giselle who? Giselle flowers in there?

Knock, Knock! Who's there?
Will. Will who? Will wait out here until you let us in!

Knock, Knock! Who's there?
Jaffa. Jaffa who? Jaffa keep me waiting?

Knock, Knock! Who's there?
Yul. Yul who? Yuletide greetings, neighbour!

Knock, Knock! Who's there?
Walter. Walter who? Walter strange thing to ask!

Knock, Knock! Who's there?
Wade. Wade who? Wade a minute, I'll just check!

Knock, Knock! Who's there?
Jerome. Jerome who? Jerome at last!

Knock, Knock! Who's there?
Karl. Karl who? Karl again another day!

Knock, Knock! Who's there?
Vince. Vince who? Vince some time since I saw you last!

Knock, Knock! Who's there?
Donna. Donna who? Donna expect you to remember me!

Knock, Knock! Who's there?
Red. Red who? Red your letters – you can have them back now!

Knock, Knock! Who's there?
Jools. Jools who? Jools like these should be worth a lot of money!

Knock, Knock! Who's there?
Pearce. Pearce who? Pearce this balloon with a pin!

Knock, Knock! Who's there?
Whoo ooo oooo ooo. Whoo ooo oooo ooo who? Ah, good, this is the ghosts' club!

Knock, Knock! Who's there?
Fletch. Fletch who? Fletch a bucket of water – your house is on fire!

Knock, Knock! Who's there?
Icing. Icing who? Icing carols – you give me money!

Knock, Knock! Who's there?
Chris. Chris who? Chris packets make a lot of noise in the cinema!

Knock, Knock! Who's there?
Jethro. Jethro who? Jethro this at me?

*Knock, Knock! Who's there?
Vicar. Vicar who? Vicar might have caught something nasty!*

*Knock, Knock! Who's there?
Dan. Dan who? Dan just stand there – let me in!*

*Knock, Knock! Who's there?
Lefty. Lefty who? Lefty home on your own again?*

*Knock, Knock! Who's there?
Yul. Yul who? Yul see when you open the door!*

*Knock, Knock! Who's there?
Arthur. Arthur who? Arthur minute and I'll show you my identification!*

*Knock, Knock! Who's there?
Mickey. Mickey who? Mickey fell down the drain – can you give me a lift?*

*Knock, Knock. Who's there?
Mayor. Mayor who? Mayor come in?*

*Knock, Knock! Who's there?
Butcher. Butcher who? Butcher said I could come and visit you!*

*Knock, Knock! Who's there?
Greengrocer. Greengrocer who? Greengrocer rushes oh!*

*Knock, Knock! Who's there?
Al. Al who? Al huff and I'll puff and blow your house down!*

*Knock, Knock! Who's there?
Howard. Howard who? Howard you know if you won't even open the door?*

*Knock, Knock! Who's there?
Elvis. Elvis who? Elvis is a complete waste of time – I'm off!*

*Knock, Knock! Who's there?
Olly. Olly who? Olly need is love!*

*Knock, Knock. Who's there?
Colin. Colin who? Colin round to see you!*

*Knock, Knock. Who's there?
Lucinda. Lucinda who? Lucinda sky with diamonds...!*

*Knock, Knock! Who's there?
Jester. Jester who? Jester day, all my troubles seemed so far away...!*

*Knock, Knock! Who's there?
Our Tell. Our Tell who? Our Tell you what I want, what I really really want...!*

*Knock, Knock! Who's there?
Honor Claire. Honor Claire who? Honor Claire day, you can see forever...!*

Knock, Knock! Who's there?
Carrie. Carrie who? Carrie your bags to the airport for a fiver?

Knock, Knock! Who's there?
Avon who? Avon to trink your blood!

Knock, Knock! Who's there?
Otto. Otto who? Ottold you not two seconds ago!

Knock, Knock! Who's there?
Carter. Carter who? Carter stray dog – is it yours?

Knock, Knock! Who's there?
Woody. Woody who? Woody lend me a tenner till pay day?

Knock, Knock! Who's there?
Joanna. Joanna who? Joanna have a guess?

Knock, Knock! Who's there?
Wallace. Wallace who? Wallace is a fine how do you do...!

Knock, Knock! Who's there?
Yula. Yula who? Yula pologise for not letting me in straight away when you see who it is!

Knock, Knock! Who's there?
CDs. CDs who? CDs fingers? They're freezing – let me in!

Knock, Knock! Who's there?
Wyatt. Wyatt who? Wyatt you open the door and see?

Knock, Knock! Who's there?
Toyah. Toyah who? Toyah have to ask the same question all the time?

Knock, Knock! Who's there?
Wynn. Wynn who? Wynn de Cleaner!

Knock, Knock! Who's there?
Bea. Bea who? Bea good boy and let me in!

Knock, Knock! Who's there?
Stan. Stan who? Stan in front of your window and you'll see who!

Knock, Knock! Who's there?
Irma. Irma who? Irma little short of time – just open up!

Knock, Knock! Who's there?
Ashley. Ashley who? Bless you!

Knock, Knock! Who's there?
Carrie. Carrie who? Carrie on like this and I'll have frozen to death before I get in!

Knock, Knock! Who's there?
Vidor. Vidor who? Vidor better open soon...!

Knock, Knock. Who's there?
Sara. Sara who? Sara man delivering milk here yesterday – do you think he could deliver some to me too?

Knock, Knock. Who's there?
Cole. Cole who? Cole out here – open up!

Knock, Knock! Who's there?
Mandy. Mandy who? Mandy with tools, if you need any repair work done!

Knock, Knock! Who's there?
Freda. Freda who? Freda jolly good fellow...

Knock, Knock! Who's there?
Piers. Piers who? Piers I've forgotten my key – open up!

Knock, Knock! Who's there?
Holly. Holly who? Holly up and open the door – I'm freezing out here!

Knock, Knock! Who's there?
Alpaca. Alpaca who? Alpaca suitcase and leave you if you don't give me my own key!

Knock, Knock! Who's there?
Tia. Tia who? Tia mount of time I've wasted standing here!

Knock, Knock! Who's there?
Norm. Norm who? Norm more Mr Nice Guy – OPEN THIS DOOR!

Knock, Knock! Who's there?
Alison. Alison who? Alison at the keyhole sometimes!

Knock, Knock! Who's there?
Isiah. Isiah who? Isiah than you – I'm up on the roof!

Knock, Knock! Who's there?
Carib. Carib who? Was it the antlers that gave it away?

Knock, Knock! Who's there?
Jim. Jim who? Jim mind not asking the same old question over and over?

Knock, Knock! Who's there?
Pop. Pop who? Pop down and open this door please!

Knock, Knock! Who's there?
Gladys. Gladys who? Gladys time for lunch!

Knock, Knock! Who's there?
Wilma. Wilma who? Wilma tea be ready soon?

Knock, Knock! Who's there?
Handsome. Handsome who?
Handsome sweets through the letterbox!

Knock, Knock! Who's there?
Olive. Olive who? Olive here, so let me in!

Knock, Knock! Who's there?
Noise. Noise who? Noise to see you!

Knock, Knock! Who's there?
Cows go. Cows go who? No silly, cows go moo!

Knock, Knock! Who's there?
Tish. Tish who? Have you got a cold?

Knock, Knock! Who's there?
Alec. Alec who? Alec sweets and ice-cream!

Knock, Knock! Who's there?
Sarah. Sarah who? Sarah doctor in the house?

Knock, Knock! Who's there?
Aardvark. Aardvark who?
Aardvark a hundred miles for one of your smiles!

Knock, Knock! Who's there?
Aaron. Aaron who? Aaron on the side of caution!

Knock, Knock! Who's there?
Abbott. Abbott who?
Abbott time you answered the door!

Knock, Knock! Who's there?
Abe. Abe who? Abe C D E F G H...!

Knock, Knock! Who's there?
Abyssinia. Abyssinia who?
Abyssinia behind bars one of these days!

Knock, Knock! Who's there?
Ada. Ada who? Ada burger for lunch!

Knock, Knock! Who's there?
Adair. Adair who? Adair once but I'm bald now!

Knock, Knock! Who's there?
Adelia. Adelia who? Adelia the cards and we'll play snap!

Knock, Knock! Who's there?
Adolf. Adolf who? Adolf ball hit me in the mouth!

Knock, Knock Who's there?
Aesop. Aesop who? Aesop I saw a puddy cat!

Knock, Knock! Who's there?
Alaska. Alaska who? Alaska my friend the question then!

Knock, Knock! Who's there?
Aida. Aida who? Aida lot of sweets and now I've got tummy ache!

Knock, Knock! Who's there?
Al. Al who? Al give you a kiss if you open this door!

Knock, Knock! Who's there?
Aladdin. Aladdin who? Aladdin the street wants a word with you!

Knock, Knock! Who's there?
Albee. Albee who? Albee a monkey's uncle!

Knock, Knock! Who's there?
Albert. Albert who? Albert you don't know who this is!

Knock, Knock! Who's there?
Alda. Alda who? Alda time you knew who it was!

Knock, Knock! Who's there?
Aldo. Aldo who? Aldo anywhere with you!

Knock, Knock! Who's there?
Alec. Alec who? Alec-tricity. Isn't that a shock!

Knock, Knock! Who's there?
Alec. Alec who? Alec my lolly!

Knock, Knock! Who's there?
Alex. Alex who? Alex the questions round here!

Knock, Knock! Who's there?
Alfred. Alfred who? Alfred of the dark!

Knock, Knock! Who's there?
Alfred. Alfred who? Alfred the needle if you sew!

Knock, Knock! Who's there?
Allied. Allied who? Allied, so sue me!

Knock, Knock! Who's there?
Almond. Almond who? Almond the side of the law!

Knock, Knock! Who's there?
Alpaca. Alpaca who? Alpaca the trunk, you pack the suitcase!

Knock, Knock! Who's there?
Althea. Althea who? Althea later, alligator!

Knock, Knock! Who's there?
Amahl. Amahl who? Amahl shook up!

Knock, Knock! Who's there?
Amana. Amana who? Amana bad mood!

Knock, Knock! Who's there?
Amazon! Amazon who? Amazon of a gun!

Knock, Knock! Who's there?
Amin. Amin who? Amin thing to do!

Knock, Knock! Who's there?
Ammonia. Ammonia who? Ammonia little kid!

Knock, Knock! Who's there?
Amory. Amory who? Amory Christmas and a Happy New Year!

Knock, Knock! Who's there?
Amos. Amos who? Amosquito just bit me!

Knock, Knock! Who's there?
Amy. Amy who? Amy 'fraid I've forgotten!

Knock, Knock! Who's there?
Anka. Anka who? Anka the ship!

Knock, Knock! Who's there?
Annie. Annie who? Annie one you like!

Knock, Knock! Who's there?
Anthem. Anthem who? You Anthem Devil you!

Knock, Knock! Who's there?
Apple. Apple who? Apple your hair if you don't let me in!

Knock, Knock! Who's there?
Aretha. Aretha who? Aretha flowers!

Knock, Knock! Who's there?
Aries. Aries who? Aries on why I talk this way!

Knock, Knock! Who's there?
Arizona. Arizona who? Arizona room for one of us in this town!

Knock, Knock! Who's there?
Armageddon. Armageddon who? Armageddon getting out of here!

Knock, Knock! Who's there?
Arnold. Arnold who? Arnold friend you haven't seen for years!

Knock, Knock! Who's there?
Athena. Athena who? Athena flying saucer!

Knock, Knock! Who's there?
Austin. Austin who? Austin corrected!

Knock, Knock! Who's there?
Avenue. Avenue who? Avenue heard the good news!

Knock, Knock! Who's there?
Bach. Bach who? Bach of sweets!

Knock, Knock! Who's there?
Bacon. Bacon who? Bacon a cake for your birthday!

Knock, Knock! Who's there?
Bean.Bean who? Bean fishing lately?

Knock, Knock! Who's there?
Beets. Beets who? Beets me!

Knock, Knock! Who's there?
Bella. Bella who? Bella bottom trousers!

Knock, Knock! Who's there?
Ben. Ben who? Ben knocking on this door all morning!

Knock, Knock! Who's there?
Beezer. Beezer who? Beezer black and yellow and make honey!

Knock, Knock! Who's there?
Beirut. Beirut who? Beirut force!

Knock, Knock! Who's there?
Bertha. Bertha who? Bertha-day greetings!

Knock, Knock! Who's there?
Beryl. Beryl who? Beryl of beer!

Knock, Knock! Who's there?
Bolton. Bolton who? Bolton the door!

Knock, Knock! Who's there?
Boo. Boo who? Don't cry it's only a joke!

Knock, Knock! Who's there?
Butch. Butch who? Butch your arms around me!

Knock, Knock! Who's there?
Butcher. Butcher who? Butcher money where your mouth is!

Knock, Knock! Who's there?
Button. Button who? Button in is not polite!

Knock, Knock! Who's there?
Candice. Candice who? Candice get any better!

Knock, Knock! Who's there?
Candy. Candy who? Candy cow jump over the moon?

Knock, Knock! Who's there?
Carmen. Carmen who? Carmen get it!

Knock, Knock! Who's there?
Carrie. Carrie who? Carrie the bags into the house please!

Knock, Knock! Who's there?
Cash. Cash who? I knew you
were nuts!

Knock, Knock! Who's there?
Cassie. Cassie who?
Cassie the wood for the trees!

Knock, Knock! Who's there?
Celeste. Celeste who?
Celeste time I'm going to tell
you this!

Knock, Knock! Who's there?
Cereal. Cereal who? Cereal
pleasure to meet you!

Knock, Knock! Who's there?
Cheese, Cheese who? Cheese a
cute girl!

Knock, Knock! Who's there?
Cher. Cher who? Cher and
share alike!

Knock, Knock! Who's there?
Cherry. Cherry who? Cherry oh,
see you later!

Knock, Knock! Who's there?
Chicken. Chicken who? Chicken
the oven, I can smell burning!

Knock, Knock! Who's there?
Chuck. Chuck who? Chuck and see
if the door is locked!

Knock, Knock! Who's there?
Clare. Clare who? Clare your throat
before you speak!

Knock, Knock! Who's there?
Clarence. Clarence who?
Clarence sale!

Knock, Knock! Who's there?
Colleen. Colleen who? Colleen up
this mess!

Knock, Knock! Who's there?
Custer. Custer who? Custer a penny
to find out!

Knock, Knock! Who's there?
Cy. Cy who? Cy'n on the
bottom line!

Knock, Knock! Who's there?
Dana. Dana who? Dana talk with
your mouth full!

Knock, Knock! Who's there?
Datsun. Datsun who? Datsun
old joke!

Knock, Knock! Who's there?
Dawn. Dawn who? Dawn leave me
out here in the cold!

Knock, Knock! Who's there?
Dolores. Dolores who? Dolores on
the side of the good guys!

Knock, Knock! Who's there? Denise. Denise who? Denise are above your ankles!

Knock, Knock! Who's there? Dewey. Dewey who? Dewey have to keep saying all these jokes!

Knock, Knock! Who's there? Diesel. Diesel who? Diesel teach me to go knocking around on doors!

Knock, Knock! Who's there? Dill. Dill who? Dill we meet again!

Knock, Knock! Who's there? Dimitri. Dimitri who? Dimitri is where the burgers grow!

Knock, Knock! Who's there? Dino. Dino who? Dino the answer!

Knock, Knock! Who's there? Diploma. Diploma who? Diploma to fix the leak!

Knock, Knock! Who's there? Disguise. Disguise who? Disguise the limit!

Knock, Knock! Who's there? Dishes. Dishes who? Dishes a very bad joke!

Knock, Knock! Who's there? Don Juan. Don Juan who? Don Juan to go to school today!

Knock, Knock! Who's there? Donalette. Donalette who? Donalette the bed bugs bite!

Knock, Knock! Who's there? Donkey. Donkey who? Donkey Hotey!

Knock, Knock! Who's there? Doughnut. Doughnut who? Doughnut open until Christmas!

Knock, Knock! Who's there? Douglas. Douglas who? Douglas is broken!

Knock, Knock! Who's there? Dragon. Dragon who? Dragon your feet again!

Knock, Knock! Who's there? Dummy. Dummy who? Dummy a favour and go away!

Knock, Knock! Who's there? Dunce. Dunce who? Dunce-ay another word!

Knock, Knock! Who's there? Dwayne. Dwayne who? Dwayne in Spain falls mainly on the plain!

Knock, Knock! Who's there? Earl. Earl who? Earl be glad to tell you when you open this door!

Knock, Knock! Who's there?
Ears. Ears who? Ears looking at you, kid!

Knock, Knock! Who's there?
Eddie. Eddie who? Eddie body home?

Knock, Knock! Who's there?
Edith. Edith who? Edith, it'll make you feel better!

Knock, Knock! Who's there?
Egg. Egg who? Egg-citing to meet you!

Knock, Knock! Who's there?
Elaine. Elaine who? Elaine of the motorway!

Knock, Knock! Who's there?
Elias! Elias who? Elias a terrible thing!

Knock, Knock! Who's there?
Ella. Ella who? Ella-vator. Doesn't that give you a lift?

Knock, Knock! Who's there?
Ella Man. Ella Man who? Ella Man-tary my dear Watson!

Knock, Knock! Who's there?
Emil. Emil who? Emil for the poor?

Knock, Knock! Who's there?
Emma. Emma who? Emma bit cold out here, can you let me in?

Knock, Knock! Who's there?
Emmett. Emmett who? Emmett your service!

Knock, Knock! Who's there?
Enid. Enid who? Enid some more pocket money!

Knock, Knock! Who's there?
Enoch. Enoch who? Enoch and Enoch but no one answers the door!

Knock, Knock! Who's there?
Ethan. Ethan who? Ethan me out of house and home you are!

Knock, Knock! Who's there?
Essen. Essen who? Essen it fun to listen to these jokes!

Knock, Knock! Who's there?
Esther. Esther who? Esther anything I can do for you!

Knock, Knock! Who's there?
Eunice. Eunice who? Eunice boy, let me in!

School's Out

Why did the maths teacher take a ruler in his car? So he could see how long it took him to get to work in the morning.

What do you shout when Santa Claus does the register? Present!

I thought you were going to play school with me today! I did – I decided to play absent!

Parent: Why have you given my little boy such a bad report – he's as intelligent as the next boy!
Teacher: Yes, but the next boy is an idiot!

Why are you taking that sponge into your lesson? I always find history such an absorbing subject!

Did you hear about the maths teacher who was thrown out of the pizza restaurant – for asking how long his pizza would be?

So, Blenkinsop, you claim to know all your tables – let's hear them then! Dining room table, kitchen table, living room table...

Vicar: Can anyone tell me what Samson did for a living?
Pupil: I think he was a comedian – it says in the Bible that he brought the house down!

Why does your teacher have her hair in a bun? Because she has a face like a burger!

Why do teachers never marry dairy farmers? They are like chalk and cheese!

What do you do if someone faints in a maths exam? Try to bring them 2!

Why do doctors enjoy their schooldays? Because they are good at examinations!

What did the ghostly music teacher play? Haunting melodies!

Why don't vampire teachers like computers? They hate anything new-fangled!

John – what is the plural of baby? Twins!

The maths teacher is feeling run down today. Wow! Did anyone get the number of the car that did it?

What happens to a maths teacher's class when he retires? Before or after you've woken them up?

Teacher: Sally, give me a sentence with the word aroma in it.
Sally: My Uncle Fred is always travelling – he's aroma.

I call my first year class my little treasures – because goodness only knows where they were dug up!

If you multiply 245 by 3456 and divide the answer by 165, then subtract 752, what will you get? The wrong answer, miss!

Give me a sentence with the word politics in it. Our parrot swallowed the alarm clock, and now politics!

In the Bible it tells us that God was a healer. I know that, Sir, because he gave Moses some tablets!

We can't possibly play football out there – the pitch is wet through! I know – the first years have been doing dribbling practice all morning!

Collective nouns:

a NUMBER of maths teachers
a RANGE of cookery teachers
a TEAM of PE teachers
a CONCENTRATION of science teachers
a BAND of music teachers
a FOREST of woodwork teachers
a BANK of economics teachers
a SCHOOL of head teachers

Why do history teachers like fruit cake? Because it's full of dates!

My maths teacher is a real peach! You mean she's pretty? No – I mean she has a heart of stone!

Headteacher: Mr Phelps, do you have any sawdust?
Mr Phelps: No, Head, all my dust is perfectly healthy, thank you!

Why are you always late for school? Because I threw my alarm clock in the bin. Why on earth did you do that? It kept going off when I was still asleep and waking me up!

Blenkinsop, name five things that contain milk. Yoghurt, cheese and three cows!

What's the difference between a train and a teacher? A train says 'choo choo' but a teacher says 'take that gum out of your mouth this instant!'

Why did the scruffy schoolboy finally take a bath? Because he realised that grime doesn't pay!

Blenkinsop – your parents are multi-millionaires, and yet you still smell awful! That's because we're filthy rich, Miss!

Rodrick, how would you address a Dutch man and his twin brother? In double Dutch, Miss!

How do you make a sick insect better? Give it a T, then it will be a stick insect!

Teacher: Clark, have you been an idiot all your life?
Clark: Not yet, Sir!

Why are some snakes really good at maths? They are adders!

What do history teachers do before they get married? They go out on dates!

Why are you scratching yourself, boy? Because no one else knows where I itch!

Who teaches all the boys called Ed? The Ed teacher!

I didn't use a recipe for this casserole – I made it out of my own head ... I thought it tasted of sawdust!

Where do vampire schoolchildren go for field trips? Lake Eerie!

Blenkinsop, where is Turkey? No idea, Sir – we threw ours away after Christmas!

I think our school must be haunted – because teachers keep on going on about the school spirit!

Violin for sale – going cheap, no strings attached!

I'm sorry, Mr Cyclops, I don't think you are suited to teaching – you only have the one pupil!

How many millions of times have I told you, Blenkinsop,to stop exaggerating?

Why did the music teacher ban skeletons from keyboard lessons? Because they have no organs!

This school pie has hairs in it! That's odd – it says rabbit pie on the menu!

Why is that boy locked up in a cage in the corner of the classroom? Oh, he's the teacher's pet!

Please, Miss, I've swallowed my pencil sharpener! You must be choking! No, Miss, I'm perfectly serious!

Inspector: How many teachers work at this school?
Pupil: Very few!

The teacher said that you weren't fit to be with pigs – but I stood up for you! Really? What did you say? I said that you were!

What do you get if you look at a vampire teacher through a telescope? A horrorscope!

How did people react when gas was first used to heat homes? Most people were happy, but one or two were a bit sniffy about it!

How does a maths teacher remove hard wax from his ears? He works it out with a pencil!

You've been playing with that blotting paper the whole lesson – you obviously find it very absorbing!

My Brian is very quick at picking up music – they always send for him when they want to move the school piano!

How did people react when electricity was first discovered? They got a nasty shock!

Why was the teacher chased by a hen? It was after his wages – he said he got paid chicken feed!

What is an alkali? When a drunk tells you something that isn't true!

Why did the music teacher tell his pupil to beat it? He was teaching him to play the bass drum!

What sort of music makes a teacher take his shoes off? Soul music!

What is the first thing teachers at the Frankenstein school do every morning? They go into assembly!

What do you call a satellite that takes secret pictures? An unidentified spying object!

Did you hear about the ex-maths teacher who worked on the stock exchange? He was divided about whether to buy additional shares or take away his profits!

Is the maths teacher in a good mood today? I wouldn't count on it!

What class did the new robot teacher get on his first day? He got all the nuts!

How does the robot teacher get out of school at home time? He makes a bolt for it!

What does the robot teacher's mum do for a living? She's a washer woman!

How can you tell when a robot teacher is going mad? He goes screwy!

I always come out in spots when I'm doing a maths exam. Sounds like a bad case of decimals!

I sprained my ankle and had to miss games for two weeks! Lucky you – our sports teacher never accepts a lame excuse for missing games!

The school dinners here are untouched by human hands – there's a gorilla in the kitchen!

Our school dinners are full of iron – which is probably why they are so difficult to chew!

A School Teacher's Favourite Things:

Book: The Caine Mutiny
Film: Rain Man (because then they cancel games!)
Actor: Michael Caine
Saying: Absence makes the heart grow fonder!

Our school kitchens are spotlessly clean – which is why the food always tastes of soap!

I couldn't do my homework last night because my pen ran out, and I'm not allowed to go out of the house after dark!

Blenkinsop, what is the covering of a tree trunk called? Don't know, Sir! Bark, Blenkinsop, bark! Woof, woof!

It's a good job your name is Mark – because you certainly don't seem able to get any in your exams!

When did early people start wearing clothes? In the Iron Age!

Can anyone tell me which is the longest night of the year? Yes, Miss, a fortnight!

Sir, what would I have to write to get three 'A' levels? Someone else's name at the top of your exam paper!

What happens to children at magic school who misbehave? They are ex-spelled!

Smith – why weren't you here at 8.45 this morning? Because I was held up by that sign outside – it says 'stop children crossing'!

Turn on the TV quick and you'll be able to see our school photograph! Why, are they doing a programme about your school? No, it's Crimewatch!

Where do skinny teachers train? Puny-versity!

Did you hear about the school cleaner who married a history teacher? He was brushing up s ome old dates and he swept her off her feet!

You had better behave in Mr Simkins' music class or you'll find yourself in treble!

How can a school cook also be a history teacher? Easy – if they know more than anyone else about ancient grease!

What qualifications do I need to be a pantomime horse? Three neigh levels!

Smith, how do you feel about HG Wells? No idea, Sir. We get all our water from a tap!

Why did Catherine of Aragon marry Henry VIII? She was told she needed a ruler to help her with her maths exam!

Blenkinsop – why haven't you learned your times table? Because we get the Guardian, Miss!

Where would you find Offa's Dyke? I think you should be asking Offa that question, Miss, not me!

Do you think my son has what it takes to be a pilot? Well, he certainly spends plenty of time with his head in the clouds!

Where do crazy teachers train? Loony-versity!

What happens to old maths teachers? They are taken away!

What happens to old music teachers? They send in a note!

What musical instrument does the school cat play? A mouse organ!

What happens to old history teachers? They reach their best before date!

What happens to old French teachers? One day they realise that un oeuf is enough!

Does your father still help you with your homework? No, Miss, I can get it wrong all on my own now!

Why does this class keep shouting 'Miss, Miss, Miss!' when you know very well that your teacher is a married woman? Because she keeps dodging the stuff we throw at her!

Teacher: Now class, whatever I ask, I want you to all answer at once. How much is 6 plus 4?
Class: At once!

Well, son, how did you find your geography exam? With a map and compass, how else!

Why is the history teacher all dressed up in a suit and tie? No idea – maybe he has an important date!

Blenkinsop, how many times have I told you not to eat sweets in class? Six, Miss! Rather more than six I think, young man. Yes, but that's as far as I can count!

Smith – if I gave you £5 a week for the next six months, what would you have? An insane teacher!

Why did the vampire hate school on Tuesdays? Because that was the day they had stake for school dinners!

Today is flying saucer day in school dinners – because we get unidentified frying objects!

Where do alien teachers train? Moony-versity!

Did you hear about the science teacher who was always playing tricks on people? He was a real particle joker!

Did you hear about the geography teacher who mapped out his career? Or the archaeology teacher whose job was in ruins?

Head: You'll start on a salary of £15,000 and then go up to £20,000 in six months' time.
Teacher: In that case I think I would like to start in six months' time!

Blenkinsop, I think you need glasses! What makes you think that, Sir? You're facing the wrong way!

Lewis – what do you get if you drop a piano down a mineshaft? A flat minor!

Did you hear about the school head who gave a pupil some lines for the first time in his career – it was head line news!

If you want to test the theory about a link between television and violence, try telling your maths teacher that you sat and watched television all night instead of doing your homework!

Sir, have you ever hunted bear? No, Blenkinsop, but I've been fishing in a pair of swimming trunks!

Does anyone know why the Romans built straight roads? Yes, Sir, because they didn't have steering wheels on their chariots!

In your Christmas exam you wrote that there were 25 letters in the alphabet. What were you thinking of? Noel!

What do they have for lunch at monster school? Human beans on toast!

What do you call an assistant head teacher who thinks he's a cowboy? The Deputy Head!

When does Mother Nature need a pencil? When the winter nights start drawing in!

Where does the vampire teacher's girlfriend work? In the class necks to his!

Teacher: I said to draw a cow eating some grass but you've only drawn the cow.
Pupil: Yes, the cow ate all the grass!

What sort of insect plays music? A humbug!

Why are school singing classes like someone locked out of his house? Because neither of them can find the right key!

Sarah, I think your father has been helping you with your homework. No, Miss, he did it all by himself!

School Library New Books:

The Haunted House by Hugo First
The Broken Window by Eva Brickatit
The Filthy Chinese Farmhouse by Who Flung Dung
The Hungry Man by Edna Breakfast

Why did the teacher leave his job? He was head hunted!

Surely you can remember what happened in 1066? It's alright for you, Sir, you were there!

Today we are going to look for the lowest common denomination. Haven't they found that yet? My dad says they were looking for that when he was at school!

Blenkinsop, you deserve 100 lines for this homework. Ah, but it wouldn't be fair on the rest of the class if I always got what I deserved, would it, Sir?

Parent: Do you think my son will make a good Arctic explorer?
Teacher: I would think so, most of his marks are below zero!

Why are maths teachers no good at gardening? Because everything they plant grows square roots!

Did you hear about the maths teacher whose mistakes started to multiply? They took him away in the end!

Now, Roger, if a half-filled barrel of beer fell on someone, how badly hurt would they be? Not at all if it was light ale, Miss!

Did you hear about the two history teachers who met on television? They were on Blind Date!

Susie, how do you make a milk shake? Take it to a scary film, Miss!

Blenkinsop, do you understand how important punctuation is? Yes, Miss, I always make sure I get to school on time!

Mark, how did Moses cut the sea in half? With a see-saw!

Wendy, when do you like school the best? During the school holidays, Sir!

What do Atilla the Hun and Winnie the Pooh have in common? The!

Carol, what is the difference between a policeman and a soldier? You can't dip a policeman into your boiled egg, Sir!

Why are you putting in those ear plugs? I've got to teach form 4B tennis, and they always make such a racket!

Blenkinsop, how can you prove that the Earth is round? I didn't say it was, Sir!

Teacher: You should have been here at 9 o'clock this morning!
Pupil: Why, did something happen?

Where do music teachers train? Tuney-versity!

What is the difference between frog spawn and school pudding? Frog spawn was once warm!

How can you tell if a teacher is in a good mood? Let me know if you ever find out!

Why are you always late for school? It's not my fault, you always ring the bell before I get here!

Why did the teacher make you take the chicken out of the classroom? He said he didn't want anyone to hear fowl language in his lesson!

Howard, which is the largest sea? The Galax-sea!

What is a bunsen burner used for? Setting fire to bunsens, Miss?

Sir, can we do some work on the Iron Age today? Well, I'm not certain. I'm a bit rusty on that period of history!

Smith, how would you hire a horse? Put a brick under each leg?

Blenkinsop, how do you get rid of varnish? Just take out the 'R', Miss!

Smith, where do fish sleep? On a waterbed!

Harry, what does it mean if I say Guten Morgen Herr Dresser? It means you've gone for a haircut!

Sally, what musical instrument do Spanish fishermen play? Cast-a-nets!

Science teacher: Name two liquids that don't freeze.
Pupil: Coffee and tea!

Bill, which is heavier: a full moon or a half moon? A half moon, because a full moon is lighter!

Mary, how did you find the questions in your English exam? Oh, I found the questions easily enough, it's the answers I couldn't find!

Who invented fractions? Henry the Eighth!

Fred, where do most spiders live? Crawley!

Sue, describe crude oil for me. Well, Sir, it is black and sticky and it floats on the surface of water shouting 'knickers'!

Joe, how many seconds are there in a year? Twelve, Miss. January 2nd, February 2nd, March 2nd, April 2nd...

Flora, what is the most important tool we use in mathematics? Multi-pliers!

Teacher: Steven, what's a computer byte?
Steven: I didn't even know they had teeth!

Did you hear about the two history teachers who got married? They liked to sit at home talking about old times!

Where did the metalwork teacher meet his wife? In a bar!

What happened after the wheel was first invented? It caused a revolution!

How do archaeologists get into locked tombs? Do they use a skeleton key, Miss?

Steven, why did Henry the Eighth have so many wives? He liked to chop and change, Miss?

Why did the very first chips not taste very nice? Because they were fried in ancient Greece!

Jane, what do you know about the Dead Sea? I didn't even know it had been poorly, Sir!

William, what is a fungi? A mushroom that likes having a good time!

'John can't come to school today because he has a cold.' 'Who am I speaking to?' 'My father.'

Harry, spell mouse trap. C-A-T.

Where do vampire teachers train? Teacher Draining College!

Billy, what is wombat? It's what you use to play Wom, Miss!

What do you call the teacher who organises all the exams? Mark!

Blenkinsop, I do wish you would pay a little attention. I'm paying as little as I can, Sir!

Fred, how do fleas get from one animal to another? They itch hike!

What do you call a man who keeps on talking when no one is listening? Sir!

John, what is the longest word in the English dictionary? Elastic. How do you work that out? It stretches!

Howard, if I had 12 sausages in one hand, and 15 sausages in the other, how many sausages would I have altogether? No idea, Miss, I'm a vegetarian!

Freda will make a very good astronomer when she leaves school, as she is very good at staring into space for hours on end!

What makes you think that my son Martin is always playing truant? Martin? There's no Martin in this school!

Teacher: You copied from Fred's exam paper, didn't you?
Pupil: How did you know?
Teacher: Fred's paper says 'I don't know' and you've put 'Me neither!'

Philip, why do you always have two plates of food for school dinner? It's important to have a balanced diet, Miss!

Mary, why have you brought that fish into school? Because we will be practising scales in the music lesson!

Jim, why did Robin Hood steal from the rich? Because the poor didn't have anything worth stealing!

Florence, where were most English kings and queens crowned? On the head!

I hope I don't catch you cheating in the maths exam. So do I, Miss!

Father: What did the teacher think of your idea?
Son: She took it like a lamb.
Father: Really? What did she say?
Son: Baa!

Fred, what food do giraffes eat? Neck-tarines!

Robert, why have you been suspended from school? Because the boy next to me was smoking. But if he was smoking, why were you suspended? Because I was the one who set fire to him!

Ian, when was the Forth Bridge constructed? After the first three had fallen down?

Graham, what is a crane? A bird that can lift really heavy weights!

Why did the flea get thrown out of school? He just wasn't up to scratch!

Mandy, do you have to come to school chewing gum? No, Sir, I can stay at home and chew it if you prefer!

Where were traitors beheaded? Just above the shoulders!

Graham, what are net profits? What fishermen have left after paying the crew?

William, how do you make a Mexican chilli? Take him to the South Pole, Miss!

George, you have had a very undistinguished career at this school – have you ever been first in anything? Only the lunch queue, Miss!

How can bats fly without bumping into anything? They use their wing mirrors!

Wilf: My teacher is very musical, you know.
Wilma: Why?
Wilf: He's always fiddling with his beard!

What do you give a sick bird? Tweetment.

How many maths teachers can you get in an empty Mini? Just one – after that it isn't empty any more!

Sarah, give me a sentence with the word 'illegal' in it. My dad took me to the bird hospital the other day and we saw a sick sparrow and an illegal!

William, how fast does light travel? I don't know, Sir. It's already arrived by the time I wake up!

Miriam, what is the hottest planet in our solar system? Mer-Curry!

Time to get up and go to school. I don't want to go – everyone hates me and I get bullied! But you have to go – you're the head teacher!

Teacher: Millie, why did you say that Moses wore a wig?
Millie: Because sometimes he was seen with Aaron, and sometimes without!

Blenkinsop, you could be in the school football team if it wasn't for two things. What are they, Sir? Your feet!

Who was the fastest runner of all time? Adam, because he was first in the human race!

I told my dad I needed an encyclopaedia for school. What did he say? He said I could go on the bus like everyone else!

What is a snake's favourite subject? Hissss-tory!

If I cut a potato in two, I have two halves. If I cut a potato in four, I have four quarters. What do I have if I cut a potato in sixteen? Chips!

How do knights make chain mail? From steel wool.

Pupil: Those eggs look a bit past their best.
School cook: Don't blame me – I only laid the tables!

Why was the glow worm sad? Because her children weren't very bright!

What did the music teacher need a ladder for? Reaching the top notes!

Did you have any problems with your French on your school trip to Paris? No, but the French certainly did!

John, name one use of beech wood. Making deck chairs?

Mary, what do you think a pair of crocodile shoes would cost? That would depend on the size of your crocodile's feet, Miss!

Teacher: What is the coldest place in the world?
Pupil: Chile!

What is easy to get into, but difficult to get out of? Trouble!

Harry, how would you fix a short circuit? Add some more wire to make it longer, Sir?

My mum says that school beef pie is good for you because it's full of iron. That explains why it's so tough then!

What was the blackbird doing in the school library? Looking for bookworms!

Fred, I told you to write 100 lines because your handwriting is so bad, but you have only done 15! Sorry, Miss, but my maths is just as bad as my handwriting!

Where do dim witches go? Spelling classes!

Teacher: Who can tell me where Hadrian's Wall is?
Pupil: I expect it's all round Hadrian's garden Miss!

Why aren't you doing very well in history? Because the teacher keeps asking about things that happened before I was born!

Michael, can you name two inventions that have helped mankind to get up in the world? Yes, Miss – the stepladder and the alarm clock!

Teacher: Well, Fred, how are you getting along with your trampolining lessons?
Fred: Oh, you know, up and down!

What do you call it when the head teacher doesn't tell the truth about nits in his hair? Head lice!

Why was the teacher's hand 11 inches long? Because if it was 12 inches it would be a foot!

What was Richard the Third's middle name? The!

Caroline, how many days of the week start with the letter 'T'? Four: Tuesday, Thursday, today and tomorrow!

Why did the school orchestra have such awful manners? Because it didn't know how to conduct itself.

Teacher: Didn't you hear me call you?
Pupil: But you said not to answer you back!

When a teacher closes his eyes, why should it remind him of an empty classroom? Because there are no pupils to see!

Why were the early days of history called the Dark Ages? Because there were so many knights!

Great news! Teacher says we have a test today come rain or shine. What's so great about that? It's snowing outside!

Art teacher: What colour would you paint the sun and the wind?
Pupil: The sun, rose, and the wind, blew.

The Spanish explorers went round the world in a galleon. How many galleons did they get to the mile?

What kind of lighting did Noah use for the ark? Floodlights!

What was King Arthur's favourite game? Knights and crosses!

Teacher: If I had five apples in my right hand, and six apples in my left hand, what have I got?
Pupil: Very big hands, Miss!

What is a forum? Two-um plus two-um!

What would you get if you crossed a vampire and a teacher? Lots of blood tests!

Where did all the cuts and blood come from? The school went on a trip!

Teacher: Where is your homework?
Pupil: I lost it fighting this kid who said you weren't the best teacher in the school!

Why did the teacher put the lights on? Because the class was so dim!

What's the worst thing you're likely to find in the school cafeteria? The food!

What kind of food do maths teachers eat? Square meals!

Did they play tennis in Ancient Egypt? Yes, the Bible tells how Joseph served in Pharaoh's court!

Teacher: You aren't paying attention to me. Are you having trouble hearing?
Pupil: No, Sir, I'm having trouble listening!

What was the greatest accomplishment of the early Romans? Speaking Latin!

Why did Arthur have a round table? So no one could corner him! Who invented King Arthur's round table? Sir Circumference!

I failed every subject except for algebra. How did you keep from failing that? I didn't take algebra!

Why was the ghost of Anne Boleyn always running after the ghost of Henry VIII? She was trying to get ahead!

What was the first thing Queen Elizabeth did on ascending to the throne? Sit down!

Son: I can't go to school today.
Father: Why not?
Son: I don't feel well.
Father: Where don't you feel well?
Son: In school!

What are the small rivers that run into the Nile? The juve-niles!

Why did the Romans build straight roads? So their soldiers didn't go around the bend!

When a knight in armour was killed in battle, what sign did they put on his grave? Rust in peace!

What English king invented the fireplace? Alfred the Grate!

Teacher: Why is the Mississippi such an unusual river?
Pupil: Because it has four eyes and can't see!

What did you learn in school today? Not enough, I have to go back tomorrow!

Father: I hear you skipped school to play football.
Son: No I didn't, and I have the fish to prove it!

'It's clear,' said the teacher, 'that you haven't studied your geography. What's your excuse?' 'Well, my dad says the world is changing every day. So I decided to wait until it settles down!'

Teacher: When was Rome built?
Pupil: At night.
Teacher: Why did you say that?
Pupil: Because my Dad always says that Rome wasn't built in a day!

What did the Sheriff of Nottingham say when Robin fired at him? That was an arrow escape!

Mother: What was the first thing you learned in class?
Daughter: How to talk without moving my lips!

What did Caesar say to Cleopatra? Toga-ether we can rule the world!

Who designed Noah's ark? An ark-itect!

Why was the headmaster worried? Because there were too many rulers in school!

Where did knights learn to kill dragons? At knight school!

Mother: What did you learn in school today?
Son: How to write.
Mother: What did you write?
Son: I don't know, they haven't taught us how to read yet!

Why did the teacher wear sunglasses? Because his class was so bright!

What are you going to be when you get out of school? An old man!

Teacher: Where is the English Channel?
Pupil: I don't know, my TV doesn't pick it up!

What do history teachers make when they want to get together? Dates!

Whose son was Edward, the Black Prince? Old King Coal!

Where was the Magna Carta signed? At the bottom!

Teacher: This is the third time I've had to tell you off this week, what have you got to say about that?
Pupil: Thank Heavens it's Friday!

How do bees get to school? By school buzz!

Did you hear about the cross-eyed teacher? He couldn't control his pupils!

What was Camelot famous for? Its knight life!

First Roman Soldier: What is the time?
Second Roman Soldier: XX past VII!

Who was the biggest thief in history? Atlas – he held up the whole world!

Teacher: What family does the octopus belong to?
Pupil: Nobody I know!

When were King Arthur's army too tired to fight? When they had lots of sleepless knights!

Teacher: Any five-year-old should be able to solve this one.
Pupil: No wonder I can't do it then, I'm nearly ten!

What happens if you draw on the blackboard when the teacher told you not to? She draws a smack!

Teacher: Why can't you ever answer any of my questions?
Pupil: Well if I could there wouldn't be much point in me being here!

What did the computer do at lunchtime? Had a byte to eat!

My teacher reminds me of history. She's always repeating herself!

Little Monster: I hate my teacher.
Mother Monster: Well, just eat up your salad then dear!

What's a mushroom? The place where they store the school food!

Mother: Why did you just swallow the money I gave you?
Son: Well you did say it was my lunch money!

What kinds of tests do they give witches? Hex-aminations!

Teacher: When do astronauts eat?
Pupil: At launch time!

Why Did The ...?

Why did the doctor take his nose to pieces? He wanted to see what made it run!

Why do pens get sent to prison? To do long sentences!

Why did the ghost get the job? Because he was clearly superior!

Why did the zombie go to the chemist? He wanted something to help stop his coffin!

Why did the two vampire bats get married? Because they were heels over head in love!

Why did the skeleton fall into a hole? It was a grave mistake!

Why did the werewolf start going to the gym? Because he liked the changing rooms!

Why did the shy werewolf hide in a cupboard every full moon? Because he didn't like anyone to see him changing!

Why did the vampire like eating chewy sweets? He liked something to get his teeth into!

Why did the vampire put tomato ketchup on his sandwiches? He was a vegetarian!

Why did the witch take her small book of magic on holiday? The doctor told her to get away for a little spell!

Why did the ghost go the bicycle shop? He needed some new spooks for his front wheel!

Why did the ghoul take so long to finish his newspaper? He wasn't very hungry!

Why did the monster eat a settee and two armchairs? He had developed a suite tooth!

Why did the vampire bats hanging in the church belfry look exactly the same as each other? They were dead ringers!

Why did the idiot apply for a job as a language teacher? Because someone told him he spoke perfect rubbish!

Why did the monster swallow a bag full of pennies? Because he thought the change would do him good!

Why did the skeleton not go to the dance? Because he had no body to go with!

Why did the robot need a manicure? He had rusty nails!

Why did the car driver close his eyes? Because the traffic light was changing!

Why did the farm worker punch the man in a pub? Because he was eating the ploughman's lunch!

Why did the deaf Italian waiter smear pasta sauce on people's ankles? Because he thought they asked for spaghetti below the knees!

Why did the lemon refuse to fight the orange? Because it was yellow!

Why did the doctor write on your foot? He said it was a footnote!

Why did the idiot fall asleep in a bakery? He went there for a long loaf!

Why did the school idiot buy a sea horse? Because he wanted to play water polo!

Why did the crocodile buy his son a camera? Because he was always snapping!

Why did the schoolboy bite the dentist? Because he got on his nerves!

Why did the carpenter go to the doctor? He had a saw hand!

Why did the doctor operate on the man who swallowed a pink biro? He had a cute-pen-inside-is!

Why did the French farmer only keep one chicken? Because in France one egg is un oeuf!

Why did the doll blush? Because she saw the teddy bear!

Why did the farmer feed his pigs sugar and vinegar? Because he wanted sweet and sour pork!

Why did the fly fly? Because the spider spied her!

Why did the man send back his alphabet soup? Because he couldn't find words to describe it!

Why did the idiot drive his car off the side of a mountain? Because someone told him that it was fitted with air brakes!

Why did the cannibal have indigestion? He must have eaten someone who disagreed with him!

Why did the idiot take his windows to the shop? He wanted them measured for new curtains!

Why did the impressionist crash through the ceiling? He was taking off a rocket taking off!

Why did the alien school have no computers? Because someone ate all the apples!

Why did the attendant turn space ships away from the lunar car park? It was a full moon!

Why did the bakers work late? Because they kneaded the dough!

Why did the football manager want to get in touch with the alien? Because he knew where all the shooting stars were!

Why did the boy go to boarding school? Because he was always bored!

Why did the elephant refuse to play cards with his two friends? Because one of them was a lion and the other was a cheetah!

Why did the alien turn the restaurant waiter upside down? Someone told him that you had to tip the waiter!

Why did the idiot come top of the class at school? He was the only one who passed the dope test!

Why did the idiot throw a bucket of water into the wardrobe? Someone told him there was a smoking jacket in there!

Why did the gorilla only eat one computer? Because he couldn't eat another byte!

Why did the man walk around with his umbrella open upside down? He heard that there was going to be some change in the weather!

Why did the landlord of the pub have his cash helmet on? In case anyone started throwing their money around!

Why did the farmer give his chickens a hot water bottle? He wanted them to lay hard boiled eggs!

Why did the idiot make a hole in his umbrella? So that he could tell when it was raining!

Why did the stupid thief fly through the jewellers shop window? He forgot to let go of the brick!

Why did the bodybuilder rub grease onto his muscles at bedtime? He needed to be oily the next morning!

Why did the man with the pony tail go to see his doctor? He was a little hoarse!

Why did the girl have a horse on her head? Because she wanted a pony tail!

Why did the bat miss his bus? Because he hung around too long.

Why did the stupid pilot land his plane on a house? Because the landing lights were on!

Why did the cat put the letter 'M' into the fridge? Because it turns ice into mice!

Why did the stupid witch keep her clothes in the fridge? She liked to have something cool to slip into in the evening.

Why did the snowman call his dog Frost? Because Frost bites!

Why did the monster drink ten litres of anti-freeze? So that he didn't have to buy a winter coat!

Why did the skeleton stay out in the snow all night? He was a numbskull!

Why did the canoeist take a water pistol with him? So he could shoot the rapids!

Why did the teacher wear a life jacket at night? Because she liked sleeping on a waterbed, and couldn't swim!

Why did the farmer plough his field with a steamroller? Because he planned to grow mashed potatoes!

Why did the skunk buy six boxes of paper handkerchiefs? Because he had a stinking cold!

Why did the boy blush when he opened the fridge? He saw the salad dressing!

Why did the mummy leave his tomb after 3000 years? Because he thought he was old enough to leave home!

Why did the two cyclops fight? They could never see eye to eye over anything!

Why did the cannibal feel sick after eating the missionary? Because you can't keep a good man down!

Why did the secretary have the ends of her fingers amputated? So she could write shorthand!

Why did the stupid racing driver make ten pitstops during the race? He was asking for directions!

Why did the man throw his watch out of the window? To see time fly!

Why did the cleaning woman stop cleaning? Because she found grime doesn't pay!

Why did the baker stop making doughnuts? Because he got tired of the hole business!

Why did the cow cross the road? To get to the udder side!

Why did the dinosaur cross the road? Because chickens weren't invented!

Why did the dog cross the road? Because he was barking mad!

Why did the silly kid stand on his head? His feet were tired!

Why did the lazy man want a job in a bakery? So he could loaf around!

Why did the sword swallower swallow an umbrella? He wanted to put something away for a rainy day!

Why did the man take a pencil to bed? To draw the curtains!

Why did the king go to the dentist? To get his teeth crowned!

Why did the snowman stand on the marshmallow? So that he wouldn't fall in the hot chocolate!

Why did the clock get sick? It was run down!

Why did the atoms cross the road? It was time to split!

Why did the cowboy die with his boots on? Because he didn't want to stub his toe when he kicked the bucket!

Why did the scientist install a knocker on his door? He wanted to win the No-bell Prize!

Why did the frog say meow? He was learning a foreign language!

Why did the spider buy a car? So he could take it out for a spin!

Why did the banana go to the hospital? Because he wasn't peeling well.

Why did the one-handed man cross the road? To get to the second hand shop!

Why did the boy throw the butter out of the window? He wanted to see the butterfly!

Why did the orange stop half way down the hill? Because it ran out of juice!

Why did the bus stop? Because it saw the zebra crossing!

Why did the dog jump in the fire? Because he wanted to be a hot-dog!

Why did the cow cross the road? To get to the moovies.

Why did the one-eyed bird cross the road? To get to the Birdseye shop.

Why did the chicken cross the playground? To get to the other slide!

Why did the man stare at the orange juice carton? Because it said concentrate!

Why did the dog go to court? Because he got a barking ticket!

Why did the bubble gum cross the road? Because it was stuck to the chicken's foot!

Why did the toilet paper roll down the hill? Because it wanted to get to the bottom!

Why did the boy take a ladder to school? Because he was in high school!

Why did the reporter walk into the ice cream shop? Because he wanted a scoop!

Why did the student eat his homework? The teacher told him it was a piece of cake!

office

The Business of Laughter

A businessman on his deathbed called his friend and said, 'Bill, I want you to promise me that when I die you will have my remains cremated.' 'And what,' his friend asked, 'do you want me to do with your ashes?' The businessman said, 'Just put them in an envelope and mail them to the Inland Revenue and write on the envelope, "Now you have everything."'

Don't get me wrong, I love the job. It's the work I hate!

The directors decided to award an annual prize of £50 for the best idea of saving the company money. It was won by a young executive who suggested that in future the prize money be reduced to £10.

Corporation: an ingenious device for obtaining individual profit without individual responsibility. ***Ambrose Bierce***

He's got a very important job. He goes to work in a taxi every day. You would too if you were a taxi driver!

I took one of those job assessment tests at work the other day. The report said my aptitudes and abilities were best suited to some form of early retirement.

The Inland Revenue arrived for a surprise audit on a small businessman. 'So everyone here is obviously paid at least the minimum wage?' said the inspector. 'Right,' said the businessman, 'except, of course, for the half-wit.' 'Oh, really,' said the inspector, suddenly taking an interest. 'And what does the half-wit earn?' 'Well,' said the businessman, 'it probably works out at £2 an hour, plus all the cold coffee he can drink and a slice of stale fruitcake at Christmas.' 'I see,' said the inspector. 'Well, if you can just bring the half-wit in here right now so I can have a chat with him.' 'I don't have to bring him in,' said the businessman. 'You're talking to him.'

Employer: In this job we need someone who is responsible.
Applicant: I'm the one you want. On my last job, every time anything went wrong, they said I was responsible.

Top 20 sayings we'd like to see on those office inspirational posters:

1 Rome did not create a great empire by having meetings, they did it by killing all those who opposed them.
2 If you can stay calm while all around you is chaos, then you probably haven't completely understood the seriousness of the situation.
3 Doing a job right the first time gets the job done. Doing the job wrong 14 times gives you job security.
4 Eagles may soar, but weasels don't get sucked into jet engines.
5 Artificial Intelligence is no match for Natural Stupidity.
6 A person who smiles in the face of adversity probably has a scapegoat.
7 Plagiarism saves time.
8 If at first you don't succeed, try management.
9 Never put off until tomorrow what you can avoid altogether.
10 Teamwork means never having to take all the blame yourself.
11 The beatings will continue until morale improves.
12 Never underestimate the power of very stupid people in large groups.
13 We waste time, so you don't have to.
14 Hang in there, retirement is only 50 years away!
15 Go the extra mile. It makes your boss look like an incompetent slacker.
16 A snooze button is a poor substitute for no alarm clock at all.
17 When the going gets tough, the tough take a coffee break.
18 Indecision is the key to flexibility.
19 Succeed in spite of management.
20 Aim Low, Reach Your Goals, Avoid Disappointment.

Lesson One:
An eagle was sitting on a tree resting, doing nothing. A small rabbit saw the eagle and asked him, 'Can I also sit like you and do nothing?' The eagle answered: 'Sure, why not.' So, the rabbit sat on the ground below the eagle and rested. All of a sudden, a fox appeared, jumped on the rabbit and ate it.
Management Lesson: To be sitting and doing nothing, you must be sitting very, very high up.

Lesson Two:
A turkey was chatting with a bull. 'I would love to be able to get to the top of that tree,' sighed the turkey, 'but I haven't got the energy.'
'Well, why don't you nibble on some of my droppings?' replied the bull. 'They're packed with nutrients.'
The turkey pecked at a lump of dung, and found it actually gave him enough strength to reach the lowest branch of the tree. The next day, after eating some more dung, he reached the second branch. Finally after a fourth night, the turkey was proudly perched at the top of the tree. He was promptly spotted by a farmer, who shot him out of the tree.
Management Lesson: Bull shit might get you to the top, but it won't keep you there.

Most of business's great successes are achieved by someone being either clever enough to know it can't be done, or too stupid to realise it can't.

Two shoe sales people were dispatched to a remote African country. In just a few days, their employer received telegrams from each. One read: 'Get me out of here – no one wears shoes.' The other read: 'Send more inventory – no one here owns shoes.'

A successful manager is one who believes in sharing the credit with the man who did the work.

I'm a key man at the Foreign Office. I lock up at night!

First entrepreneur: I've got a great idea. I'm going to open up a bar and grill in the middle of the Sahara desert.
Second entrepreneur: That's a ridiculous idea. You'll be lucky to get more than one customer a month.
First entrepreneur: Maybe, but just think how thirsty he'll be!

Lesson Three:

A little bird was flying south for the winter. It was so cold, the bird froze and fell to the ground into a large field. While he was lying there, a cow came by and dropped some dung on him. As the frozen bird lay there in the pile of cow dung, he began to realise how warm he was. The dung was actually thawing him out! He lay there all warm and happy, and soon began to sing for joy. A passing cat heard the bird singing and came to investigate. Following the sound, the cat discovered the bird under the pile of cow dung, and promptly dug him out and ate him.

Management Lesson:

1 Not everyone who shits on you is your enemy.

2 Not everyone who gets you out of shit is your friend.

3 And when you're in deep shit, it's best to keep your mouth shut!

This ends your two minute management course.

We're a non-profit-making organisation. We don't mean to be, but we are.

Weiss and Stein went into business together and opened up a wholesale men's clothing outlet. Things went well for a year or so, but then the recession came along and they found themselves sitting on 10,000 plaid jackets, which they couldn't sell to save their souls. Just as they were discussing bankruptcy, a fellow came in and introduced himself as a buyer for a big menswear chain in Australia. 'Wouldn't happen to have any plaid jackets, would you?' he asked. 'They're selling like crazy Down Under.' Weiss looked at Stein. 'Maybe we can work something out, if the price is right,' he said coolly to the Aussie. After some tough negotiating, a price was agreed upon and the papers signed. But as he was leaving, their big prospect said, 'Just one thing, mates. I've got to get authorisation from the Home Office for a deal this big. Today's Monday; if you don't get a cable from me by Friday, the deal's final.' For the next four days, Weiss and Stein paced miserably back and forth, sweating blood and wincing every time they heard footsteps outside their door. On Friday the hours crept by, but by four o' clock they figured they were home free – until there was a loud knock on the door. 'Western Union!' a voice called out. As Stein collapsed, white-faced, behind his desk, Weiss dashed to the door. A minute later, he rushed back into the office waving a telegram. 'Great news, Stein,' he cried jubilantly, 'great news! Your mother's dead!'

A mainframe computer on which everyone in the office depended suddenly went down. They tried everything but it still wouldn't work. Finally, they decided to call in a high-powered computer consultant. He arrived, looked at the computer, took out a small hammer and tapped it on the side. Instantly the computer leapt into life. Two days later the office manager received a bill from the consultant for £1,000. Immediately he called the consultant and said, '£1,000 for fixing that computer? You were only here five minutes! I want that bill itemized!' The next day the new bill arrived. It read, 'Tapping computer with hammer: £1. Knowing where to tap: £999.'

The great thing about being in business for yourself is that you get to make all the big decisions, such as will you work 14 hours today or just 12? Seven days this week or just six? And will you develop an ulcer or just collapse from exhaustion?

Work? I love it! I could stand around and watch it all day.

A chicken and a pig were drinking in a bar one night when the chicken said, 'Why don't we go into business together? We could open a ham and egg restaurant.' 'Not so fast,' said the pig. 'For you, it's just a day's work. For me, it's a matter of life and death.'

Thesaurus Update for Office Workers:

TESTICULATING: Waving your arms around and talking bollocks.

BLAMESTORMING: Sitting around in a group, discussing why a deadline was missed or a project failed, and who was responsible.

SEAGULL MANAGER: A manager who flies in, makes a lot of noise, craps on everything and then leaves.

ASSMOSIS: The process by which people seem to absorb success and advancement by sucking up to the boss rather than working hard.

SALMON DAY: The experience of spending an entire day swimming upstream only to get screwed and die.

PRAIRIE DOGGING: When someone yells or drops something loudly in a cube farm, and people's heads pop up over the walls to see what's going on (this also applies to applause from a promotion because there may be cake).

MOUSE POTATO: The online, wired generation's answer to the couch potato.

SITCOMs: Single Income, Two Children, Oppressive Mortgage. What yuppies turn into when they have children and one of them stops working to stay home with the kids or start a 'home business'.

STRESS PUPPY: A person who seems to thrive on being stressed out and whiny.

XEROX SUBSIDY: Euphemism for swiping free photocopies from one's workplace.

PERCUSSIVE MAINTENANCE: The fine art of whacking the crap out of an electronic device to get it to work again.

ADMINISPHERE: The rarefied organisational layers beginning just above the rank and file. Decisions that fall from the adminisphere are often profoundly inappropriate or irrelevant to the problems they were designed to solve. This is often affiliated with the dreaded 'administrivia' (needless paperwork and processes).

404: Someone who's clueless. From the World Wide Web error message '404 Not Found,' meaning that the requested document could not be located.

OHNOSECOND: That minuscule fraction of time in which you realise that you've just made a big mistake (eg. you hit 'reply all').

WOOFies: Well Off Older Folk.

CROP DUSTING: Surreptitiously farting while passing through a cube farm, then enjoying the sounds of dismay and disgust; leads to prairie dogging.

CUBE FARM: An office filled with cubicles.

Hard work never hurt anyone who hired somebody else to do it.

He's a distinguished man of letters. He works for the Post Office.

The boss asked a new employee his name. 'Stuart,' replied the young man. The boss scowled. 'I don't know what kind of namby-pamby place you worked at before, but we don't use first names here. In my view, it breeds familiarity which ultimately leads to a breakdown in authority. So I always call my employees by their last names only – Smith, Jones, Brown etc. They in turn refer to me only as Mr Harvey. Understood? Right. Now that we've got that straight, what's your last name?' 'Darling,' replied the young man. 'My name is Stuart Darling.' 'Okay Stuart, the next thing I want to tell you is ...'

Employee: When will my raise become effective?
Boss: As soon as you do.

What time does your secretary start work? About two hours after she gets here.

A businessman can't win these days. If he does something wrong, he's fined; if he does something right, he's taxed.

Business is what, when you don't have any, you get out of.

An employee went in to see his boss. 'Boss,' he said, 'we're doing some heavy house cleaning at home tomorrow, and my wife needs me to help with clearing stuff out of the attic, the shed and the garage and with scrubbing down all the kitchen cupboards.' 'I'm sorry,' said the boss, 'but we're short-handed at the moment. There's no way I can give you a day off.' 'Thanks, boss,' replied the employee. 'I knew I could rely on you!'

An executive is someone who can take three hours for lunch without hindering production.

A man asked his boss for a raise. 'A raise?' thundered the boss. 'Why should you have a raise? You're never here. Listen. There are 365 days in the year – 366 this year because it's a leap year. The working day is eight hours. That's one-third of the day, so in a year that comes to 122 days. The office is shut on Sundays so that's 52 off, leaving 70. Then you have two weeks' holiday – take off 14, which leaves 56. Then there are four bank holidays, so if you remove them, that leaves 52. The office is closed on Saturdays. There are 52 Saturdays in a year, so you see, you don't do anything at all!

Chairman: Right, let's vote on the recommendation. All those against, raise their hands and say, 'I resign.'

On the first morning in new premises, a young businessman began sorting out his office. He was in the middle of arranging his desk when there was a knock at the door. Eager to imply that he had gone up in the world and that business was brisk, he quickly picked up the phone and called to the person at the door, 'Come in!' A tradesman entered the office, but the young businessman talked into the phone as if he were conducting a meaningful conversation with a client. 'I agree,' he said. 'Yes ... I agree ... Yes ... sure. No problem ... We can fix that ...' After a minute, he broke off from his imaginary conversation and said to the tradesman, 'Can I help you with something?' 'Yes,' he replied. 'I'm here to hook up the phone.'

He's the world's worst businessman. If he was a florist, he'd close on Mother's Day.

Anyone can do any amount of work, provided it isn't the work he is supposed to be doing at that moment.

Robert Benchley

A junior manager, a senior manager and their boss the general manager are on their way to a meeting. On their way through a park, they come across a genie's lamp. They rub the lamp and the genie appears. The genie says, 'Normally, one is granted three wishes. But as you are three, I will allow one wish each.' So the eager senior manager shouted, 'I want the first wish. I want to be in the Bahamas, on a fast boat and have no worries.' Pfuffffff! and he was gone. Now the junior manager could not keep quiet and shouted, 'I want to be in Florida with beautiful girls and plenty of food and cocktails.' Pfuffffff! and he was also gone. The boss calmly said, 'I want these two idiots back in the office after lunch.' So the moral of the story is: Always allow the boss to speak first.

I started this business on a shoestring and after six months I'd tripled my investment. Now I just want to know what to do with the spare shoestring.

A young employee turned to his colleague and said, 'I feel like punching the boss in the face again.' 'Again? Did you say again?' 'Yeah, I felt like punching him in the face once before.'

If this company appoints any more executives, there'll be nobody left to do the work.

Performance evaluation translations:

A KEEN ANALYST: Thoroughly confused.
ACCEPTS NEW JOB ASSIGNMENTS WILLINGLY: Never finishes a job.
ACTIVE SOCIALLY: Drinks heavily.
ALERT TO COMPANY DEVELOPMENTS: An office gossip.
APPROACHES DIFFICULT PROBLEMS WITH LOGIC: Finds someone else to do the job.
AVERAGE: Not too bright.
BRIDGE BUILDER: Likes to compromise.
CHARACTER ABOVE REPROACH: Still one step ahead of the law.
CHARISMATIC: No interest in any opinion but his own.
COMPETENT: Is still able to get work done if supervisor helps.
CONSCIENTIOUS AND CAREFUL: Scared.
CONSULTS WITH CO-WORKERS OFTEN: Indecisive, confused and clueless.
CONSULTS WITH SUPERVISOR OFTEN: Very annoying.
DELEGATES RESPONSIBILITY EFFECTIVELY: Passes the buck well.
DEMONSTRATES QUALITIES OF LEADERSHIP: Has a loud voice.
AGILITY: Dodges and evades superiors well.
DISPLAYS EXCELLENT INTUITIVE JUDGEMENT: Knows when to disappear.
DISPLAYS GREAT DEXTERITY AND ENJOYS JOB: Needs more to do.
EXCELS IN SUSTAINING CONCENTRATION BUT AVOIDS CONFRONTATIONS: Ignores everyone.
EXCELS IN THE EFFECTIVE APPLICATION OF SKILLS: Makes a good cup of coffee.
EXCEPTIONALLY WELL QUALIFIED: Has committed no major blunders to date.
EXPRESSES SELF WELL: Can string two sentences together.
GETS ALONG EXTREMELY WELL WITH SUPERIORS AND SUBORDINATES ALIKE: A coward.
HAPPY: Paid too much.
HARD WORKER: Usually does it the hard way.
IDENTIFIES MAJOR MANAGEMENT PROBLEMS: Complains a lot.
INDIFFERENT TO INSTRUCTION: Knows more than superiors.
INTERNATIONALLY KNOWN: Likes to go to conferences and trade shows in Las Vegas.
IS WELL INFORMED: Knows all office gossip and where all the skeletons are kept.
NOT A DESK PERSON: Did not go to college.

INSPIRES THE COOPERATION OF OTHERS: Gets everyone else to do the work.
IS UNUSUALLY LOYAL: Wanted by no one else.
JUDGEMENT IS USUALLY SOUND: Lucky.
KEEN SENSE OF HUMOUR: Knows lots of dirty jokes.
LISTENS WELL: Has no ideas of his own.
MAINTAINS A HIGH DEGREE OF PARTICIPATION: Comes to work on time.
MAINTAINS PROFESSIONAL ATTITUDE: A snob.
METICULOUS IN ATTENTION TO DETAIL: A nitpicker.
MOVER AND SHAKER: Favours steamroller tactics without regard for other opinions.
OF GREAT VALUE TO THE ORGANISATION: Turns in work on time.
QUICK THINKING: Offers plausible excuses for errors.
REQUIRES WORK-VALUE ATTITUDINAL READJUSTMENT: Lazy and hard-headed.
SHOULD GO FAR: Please.
SLIGHTLY BELOW AVERAGE: Stupid.
SPENDS EXTRA HOURS ON THE JOB: Miserable home life.
STRONG ADHERENCE TO PRINCIPLES: Stubborn.
STERN DISCIPLINARIAN: A real jerk.
STRAIGHTFORWARD: Blunt and insensitive.
TACTFUL IN DEALING WITH SUPERIORS: Knows when to keep mouth shut.
TAKES ADVANTAGE OF EVERY OPPORTUNITY TO PROGRESS: Buys drinks for superiors.
TAKES PRIDE IN WORK: Conceited.
UNLIMITED POTENTIAL: Will stick with us until retirement.
USES ALL AVAILABLE RESOURCES: Takes office supplies home for personal use.
USES RESOURCES WELL: Delegates everything.
USES TIME EFFECTIVELY: Clock-watcher.
VERY CREATIVE: Finds 22 reasons to do anything except original work.
VISIONARY: Cannot handle paperwork or any project that lasts less than a week.
WELL ORGANISED: Does too much busywork.
WILL GO FAR: Relative of management.
WILLING TO TAKE CALCULATED RISKS: Doesn't mind spending someone else's money.
ZEALOUS ATTITUDE: Opinionated.

The businessman decided it was time to give his daughter, a recent business school graduate, a little lecture. 'In business, ethics are very important,' he began. 'Say, for instance, a client comes in and settles his account with a £100 note. After he leaves, you notice a second £100 note stuck to the first one. Immediately you are presented with an ethical dilemma…' The businessman paused for dramatic effect. 'Should you tell your partner?'

Business meetings are important because they are one way of demonstrating how many people the company can operate without.

A man went to his bank manager and said, 'I'd like to start a small business. How do I go about it?' 'Simple,' said the bank manager. 'Buy a big one and wait.'

A businesswoman was explaining her delicate problem to a doctor. She told him she couldn't help passing wind, which was particularly embarrassing for her in board meetings. 'I just can't control myself,' she said. 'The only consolation is that they neither smell nor make a noise. In fact since I've been in your office talking to you, it's happened twice.' The doctor reached for his notebook, scribbled a prescription and handed it to her. 'What, nasal drops?' she said. 'Yes, we'll fix your nose, then we'll have a go at your hearing.'

The Five Golden Rules of Management:

1 Delegating is a sign of weakness. Let someone else do it.
2 Creativity is great, but plagiarism is faster.
3 If God had meant everyone to be a high-flyer, He wouldn't have invented the ground.
4 If at first you do succeed, try to hide your astonishment.
5 If at first you don't succeed, redefine success.

To sell something you have to someone who wants it – that's not business. But to sell something you don't have to someone who doesn't want it – that's business.

Tom had this problem of getting up late in the morning and was always late for work. His boss was mad at him and threatened to fire him if he didn't do something about it. So Tom went to his doctor who gave him a pill and told him to take it before he went to bed. Tom slept well and in fact beat the alarm in the morning by almost two hours. He had a leisurely breakfast and drove cheerfully to work. 'Boss', he said, 'The pill actually worked!' 'That's all well and good,' said the boss, 'but where were you yesterday?'

The two rules for success in business are: 1 Never tell them everything you know...

I used to sell furniture for a living. The trouble was, it was my own. ***Les Dawson***

The banker fell overboard from a friend's sailboat. The friend grabbed a life preserver, held it up, not knowing if the banker could swim, and shouted, 'Can you float alone?' 'Obviously,' the banker replied, 'but this is a hell of a time to talk business.'

A clean tie attracts the soup of the day.

In a small town in the US, there is a rather sizeable factory that hires only married men. Concerned about this, a local woman called on the manager and asked him, 'Why is it you limit your employees to married men? Is it because you think women are weak, dumb, cantankerous or what?' 'Not at all, Ma'am,' the manager replied. 'It is because our employees are used to obeying orders, are accustomed to being shoved around, know how to keep their mouths shut and don't pout when I yell at them.'

A pat on the back is only a few inches from a kick in the pants.

Employee Wanted Ad Translations:

ENERGETIC SELF-STARTER: You'll be working on commission.
ENTRY LEVEL POSITION: We will pay you the lowest wages allowed by law.
FAST LEARNER: You will get no training from us.
FLEXIBLE WORK HOURS: You will frequently work long overtime hours.
GOOD ORGANISATIONAL SKILLS: You'll be handling the filing.
MANAGEMENT TRAINING POSITION: You'll be a salesperson with a wide territory.
MUCH CLIENT CONTACT: You handle the phone or make 'cold calls' on clients.
MUST HAVE RELIABLE TRANSPORTATION: You will be required to break speed limits.
MUST BE ABLE TO LIFT 50 LB: We offer no health insurance or chiropractors.
PLANNING AND COORDINATION: You book the boss's travel arrangements.
QUICK PROBLEM-SOLVER: You will work on projects months behind schedule already.
STRONG COMMUNICATION SKILLS: You will write tons of documentation and letters.

Marketing Concepts

- You see a gorgeous girl at a party. You go up to her and say, 'I am very rich. Marry me!'
  That's Direct Marketing.

- You're at a party with a bunch of friends and see a gorgeous girl. One of your friends goes up to her and pointing at you says, 'He's very rich. Marry him.'
  That's Advertising.

- You see a gorgeous girl at a party. You go up to her and get her telephone number. The next day you call and say, 'Hi, I'm very rich. Marry me.'
  That's Telemarketing.

- You're at a party and see a gorgeous girl. You get up and straighten your tie, you walk up to her and pour her a drink. You open the door for her, pick up her bag after she drops it, offer her a ride, and then say, 'By the way, I'm very rich. Will you marry me?'
  That's Public Relations.

- You're at a party and see a gorgeous girl. She walks up to you and says, 'You are very rich...'
  That's Brand Recognition.

- You see a gorgeous girl at a party. You go up to her and say, 'I'm rich. Marry me.' She gives you a nice hard slap on your face.
  That's Customer Feedback.

- You see a gorgeous girl at a party. You go up to her and say, 'I am very rich. Marry me.' And she introduces you to her husband.
  That's Demand and Supply Gap.

- You see a gorgeous girl at a party. You go up to her and before you say, 'I am very rich. Marry me', she turns to face you – she is your wife!
  That's Competition Eating into Your Market Share.

Keeping a High Profile in an Office

- → Never write a note or memo if you can phone or visit instead; everyone wants to talk whenever you're ready.
- → Don't sit down to talk. The acoustics are better the higher you are, and remember that most people are a bit deaf so speak up louder!
- → Try to talk with at least three people between you and your listener, so that they don't feel left out.
- → The very best place for a conversation is in the corridor, beside someone else's desk. If the corridor is full, try leaning against their cupboard or hanging over their screen.
- → Never warn people of your approach by knocking on their desk or cupboard. People love surprises, especially if they're busy.
- → The best time to disturb someone is when they look thoughtful or are concentrating. It's your duty to give them a break now and again.
- → To make sure that you get regular breaks, never use a 'Do Not Disturb' sign. When other people use them they're only joking.
- → Always hold meetings around a desk. If you book a conference room everyone will think you've got something to hide.
- → If the phone isn't answered after four rings, hang on. Someone will answer it eventually, and they might like a chat, too.
- → Try to whistle, hum or tap your fingers while you work. It is a comfort to others to know that you're still there.

A wealthy investor walked into a bank and said to the bank manager, 'I would like to speak with Mr Reginald Jones, who I understand is a tried and trusted employee of yours.' The banker said, 'Yes, he certainly was trusted. And he will be tried as soon as we catch him.'

Tom was so excited about his promotion to vice president of the company he worked for and kept bragging about it to his wife for weeks on end. Finally, she couldn't take it any longer and told him, 'Listen, it means nothing. They even have a vice president of peas at the grocers!' 'Really?' he said. Not sure if this was true or not, Tom decided to call the grocers. An assistant answered and Tom said, 'Can I please talk to the vice president of peas?' The assistant replied, 'Canned or frozen?'

A businessman was confused about a bill he had received, so he asked his secretary for some mathematical help. 'If I gave you £1,500 minus three per cent, how much would you take off?' The secretary replied, 'Everything but my earrings.'

A man is at work one day when he notices that his co-worker is wearing an earring. This man knows his co-worker to be a somewhat conservative fellow, so naturally he's curious about the sudden change in fashion sense. The man walks up to his co-worker and says, 'I didn't know you were into earrings.' 'Don't make such a big deal, it's only an earring,' he replies sheepishly. Well, I'm curious,' begged the man. 'How long have you been wearing an earring?' 'Er, ever since my wife found it in our bed.'

Fresh out of business school, the young man answered a job vacancy for an accountant. He was being interviewed by a very nervous man who ran a three-man business. 'I need someone with an accounting degree,' the man said. 'But mainly, I'm looking for someone to do my worrying for me.' 'Excuse me?' the young accountant said. 'I worry about a lot of things,' the man said. 'But I don't want to have to worry about money. Your job will be to take all the money worries off my back.' 'I see,' the accountant said. 'And how much does the job pay?' 'I will start you at £85,000.' '£85,000!' the young man exclaimed. 'How can such a small business afford a sum like that?' 'That is your first worry.'

The Six Phases of a Project:

1 Enthusiasm.
2 Disillusionment.
3 Panic and hysteria.
4 Search for the guilty.
5 Punishment of the innocent.
6 Praise and honour for the non-participants.

While the Boss is Away ...

The boss has two secretaries – one for each knee.

The typing pool had a collection for a young man at the office – but they still couldn't afford one.

Joan, who was a rather well-proportioned secretary, spent almost all of her holiday sunbathing on the roof of her hotel. She wore a bathing suit the first day, but on the second, she decided that no one could see her way up there, and she slipped out of it for an overall tan. She'd hardly begun when she heard someone running up the stairs. She was lying on her stomach, so she just pulled a towel over her rear. 'Excuse me, miss,' said the flustered assistant manager of the hotel, out of breath from running up the stairs. 'The Hilton doesn't mind your sunbathing on the roof, but we would very much appreciate your wearing a bathing suit as you did yesterday.' 'What difference does it make?' Joan asked rather calmly. 'No one can see me up here, and besides, I'm covered with a towel.' 'Not exactly,' said the embarrassed man. 'You're lying on the dining room skylight.'

Secretary: I can do 30 words a minute.
Boss: Typing or shorthand?
Secretary: Reading.

He found his secretary sitting in front of two typewriters, working one with her left hand and one with her right. She said, 'I couldn't find the carbon paper.'

The secretary said to her boss, 'You have an appointment at 12.' The boss asked, 'Who is it with?' She said, 'It's the invisible man.' The boss said, 'Tell him I can't see him.'

Boss: You know something, Nugent, it hasn't escaped my notice that every time there's a midweek game on, for some reason you have to take your granny to the doctor's.
Nugent: Good Heavens, you're right, sir. You don't think she's faking it by any chance, do you?

The boss called in his secretary and said, 'Okay, I make the occasional pass at you, but who told you that you could do as you like around the office?' And the secretary said, 'My lawyer.'

I have a spelling checker.
It came with my PC.
It plane lee marks four my revue
Miss steaks aye can knot see.

Eye ran this poem threw it.
Your sure real glad two no.
Its very polished in its weigh,
My checker tolled me sew.

A checker is a blessing.
It freeze yew lodes of thyme.
It helps me right awl stiles two reed,
And aides me when aye rime.

Each frays comes posed up on my screen
Eye trussed too bee a joule.
The checker pours o'er every word
To cheque sum spelling rule.

Bee fore a veiling checkers
Hour spelling mite decline,
And if we're laks oar have a laps,
We wood bee maid too wine.

Butt now bee cause my spelling
Is checked with such grate flare,
There are know faults with in my cite,
Of nun eye am a wear.

Now spelling does not phase me,
It does knot bring a tier.
My pay purrs awl due glad den
With wrapped words fare as hear.

To rite with care is quite a feet
Of witch won should be proud,
And wee mussed dew the best wee can,
Sew flaws are knot aloud.

Sow ewe can sea why aye dew prays
Such soft wear four pea seas,
And why eye brake in two averse
Buy righting want too please.

I don't like drinking too much coffee at work. It makes me toss and turn at my desk all day.

This is the story of four people named Everybody, Somebody, Anybody and Nobody. There was an important job to be done and Everybody was asked to do it. Anybody could have done it, but Nobody did it. Somebody got angry about that, because it was Everybody's job. Everybody thought Anybody could do it, but Nobody realised that Everybody wouldn't do it. Consequently, it wound up that Nobody told Anybody, so Everybody blamed Somebody.

The Ten Ifs of Employment

1 If it rings, put it on hold.
2 If it clunks, call the repairman.
3 If it whistles, ignore it.
4 If it's a friend, stop work and chat.
5 If it's the boss, look busy.
6 If it talks, take notes.
7 If it's handwritten, type it.
8 If it's typed, copy it.
9 If it's copied, file it.
10 If it's Friday, forget it!

I have a perfect attendance record. I haven't missed a tea break in three years.

Boss: You should have been back from lunch at 2 o'clock.
Secretary: I've been having my hair cut.
Boss: In the firm's time?
Secretary: Well, it grows in the firm's time, doesn't it?
Boss: Yes, but it doesn't all grow in the firm's time!
Secretary: Well, I didn't have all of it cut off!

Sexual harassment at work – is it a problem for the self-employed? ***Victoria Wood***

There's nothing wrong with work as long as it doesn't take up too much of your spare time.

Mr Johnson got himself a new secretary. She was young, sweet and very polite. One day while taking dictation, she noticed his fly was open. When leaving the room, she said, 'Mr Johnson, your barracks door is open.' He did not understand her remark, but later on he happened to look down and saw that his zip was open. He decided to have some fun with his secretary. Calling her in, he asked, 'By the way, Miss Jones, when you saw my barracks door was open this morning, did you also notice a soldier standing to attention?' The secretary replied, 'No sir, all I saw was a disabled veteran sitting on two duffel bags.'

Office Arithmetic:

Smart boss + smart employee = profit
Smart boss + dumb employee = production
Dumb boss + smart employee = promotion
Dumb boss + dumb employee = overtime

When the bosses talk about improving productivity, they are never talking about themselves.

Female applicant: Do women get equal pay in this company?
HR manager: Absolutely! We pay all women the same.

The last person who quit or was fired will be the one held responsible for everything that goes wrong – until the next person quits or is fired.

Fred: My secretary's a biblical secretary.
John: A biblical secretary? What's that?
Fred: One who believes in filing things according to the Bible saying 'Seek and ye shall find.'

Don't be irreplaceable: if you can't be replaced, you can't be promoted.

The boss came early in the morning one day and found his manager screwing his secretary. He shouted at him, 'Is this what I pay you for?' The manager replied, 'No, sir, this I do free of charge.'

Eat one live toad first thing in the morning and nothing worse will happen to you for the rest of the day.

Everything can be filed under 'miscellaneous'.

When you take a long time, you're slow.
When your boss takes a long time, he's thorough.

When you don't do it, you're lazy.
When your boss doesn't do it, he's too busy.

When you make a mistake, you're an idiot.
When your boss makes a mistake, he's only human.

When doing something without being told, you're overstepping your authority.
When your boss does the same thing, that's initiative.

Useful expressions for those high stress days:

Don't bother me. I'm living happily ever after.
Do I look like a people person?
This isn't an office. It's purgatory with fluorescent lighting.
I pretend to work. They pretend to pay me.
You! Off my planet!
Therapy is expensive, popping bubble wrap is cheap! You choose.
Practise random acts of intelligence and senseless acts of self-control.
I like cats too. Let's exchange recipes.
Did the aliens forget to remove your anal probe?
Errors have been made. Others will be blamed.
Let me show you how the guards used to do it.
And your cry-baby opinion would be...?
I'm not crazy, I've just been in a very bad mood for 30 years.
Sarcasm is just one more service we offer.
Do they ever shut up on your planet?
I'm just working here till a good fast-food job opens up.
I'm trying to imagine you with a personality.
A cubicle is just a padded cell without a door.
Stress is when you wake up screaming and you realise you haven't fallen asleep yet.
I can't remember if I'm the good twin or the evil one.
How many times do I have to flush before you go away?
I just want revenge. Is that so wrong?
I work 40 hours a week to be this poor.
Can I trade this job for what's behind door #2?
Too many freaks, not enough circuses.
Chaos, panic, and disorder - my work here is done.
Earth is full. Go home.
Is it time for your medication or mine?
Aw, did I step on your poor little bitty ego?
How do I set a laser printer to stun?
I'm not tense, just terribly, terribly alert.
When I want your opinion, I'll give it to you.

Quick Quips 3

The first rule of business is: Do other men for they would do you. ***Charles Dickens***

In the business world, an executive knows something about everything, a technician knows everything about something, and the switchboard operator knows everything. ***Harold Coffin***

By working faithfully eight hours a day, you may eventually get to be a boss and work 12 hours a day. ***Robert Frost***

If you think your boss is stupid, remember you wouldn't have a job if he was smarter. ***Albert Grant***

Any organisation is like a septic tank. The really big chunks rise to the top. ***John Imhoff***

I always arrive late at the office, but I make up for it by leaving early. ***Charles Lamb***

Few great men would have got past personnel. ***Paul Goodman***

His insomnia was so bad, he couldn't sleep during office hours. ***Arthur Baer***

Today's payslip has more deductions than a Sherlock Holmes novel. ***Raymond Cvikota***

To make a long story short, there's nothing like having a boss walk in. ***Doris Lilly***

A memorandum is written not to inform the reader but to protect the writer.
Dean Acheson

If you had to identify in one word the reason why the human race has not achieved and never will achieve its full potential, that word would be 'meetings'. ***Dave Barry***

The longer the title, the less important the job.
George McGovern

Work is the greatest thing in the world, so we should always save some of it for tomorrow. ***Don Herold***

Work is the refuge of people who have nothing better to do. ***Oscar Wilde***

If you break a hundred, watch your golf. If you break eighty, watch your business.
Joey Adams

A conference is a gathering of important people who singly can do nothing, but together can decide that nothing can be done. ***Fred Allen***

Well, we can't stand around here doing nothing, people will think we're workmen.
Spike Milligan

A committee is a group that keeps minutes and loses hours. ***Milton Berle***

A consensus means that everyone agrees to say collectively what no one believes individually. ***Abba Eban***

medical

Doctor, Doctor

Doctor, doctor, I keep thinking I'm a pair of curtains. For Heaven's sake, woman, pull yourself together.

Doctor, doctor, I feel like a pack of cards. I'll deal with you later.

Doctor, doctor, I've only got 59 seconds to live. Wait a minute, please.

Doctor, doctor, I think I've swallowed a pillow. How do you feel? A little down in the mouth.

Doctor, doctor, I can't control my aggression. How long have you had this problem? Who wants to know?

Doctor, doctor, I've swallowed the film from my camera. We'll just have to see what develops.

Doctor, doctor, I'm a manic depressive. Calm down, cheer up, calm down, cheer up, calm down...

Doctor, doctor, I can't pronounce my Fs, Ts or Hs. Well, you can't say fairer than that, then.

Doctor, doctor, I keep thinking I'm a piece of chalk. Get to the end of the cue.

Doctor, doctor, my leg hurts. What can I do? Limp.

Doctor, doctor, my son swallowed a razor blade. Don't panic, I'm coming right away. Have you done anything yet? Yeah, I shaved with an electric razor.

Doctor, doctor, I can't stop singing The Green Green Grass of Home. That's what we doctors call Tom Jones' Syndrome. Oh, really? Is it common? It's not unusual.

Doctor, doctor, I have a split personality. Nurse, bring in another chair.

Doctor, doctor, I keep thinking I'm a clock. Okay, relax. There's no need to get yourself wound up.

Doctor, doctor, I think I'm a bridge. What's come over you? Two cars, a lorry and a coach.

Doctor, doctor, my hair keeps falling out. What can you give me to keep it in? A shoebox. Next.

Doctor, doctor, I think I'm a chicken. How long has this been going on? Ever since I was an egg.

Doctor, doctor, I keep thinking I'm a bell. If the feeling persists, give me a ring.

Doctor, doctor, I have a serious memory problem. I can't remember a thing. How long have you had this problem? What problem?

Doctor, doctor, I get so nervous and frightened during driving tests. Don't worry, you'll pass eventually. But I'm the examiner!

Doctor, doctor, people keep ignoring me. Next!

Doctor, doctor, what's good for excessive wind? A kite.

Doctor, doctor, people tell me I'm a wheelbarrow. Don't let them push you around.

Doctor, doctor, I think I'm shrinking. Well, you'll just have to be a little patient.

Doctor, doctor, I can't stop stealing things. Take these pills for a week and if they don't work, I'll have a colour TV.

Doctor, doctor, I keep talking to myself. That's nothing to worry about. Lots of people mutter to themselves. But I'm a life insurance salesman and I keep selling myself policies I don't want!

Doctors and Nurses

Doctor to patient: I have good news and bad news; the good news is that you are not a hypochondriac.

A doctor prescribed suppositories for a man suffering from constipation but a week later the man returned to the doctor and complained that the treatment wasn't working. 'Have you been taking them regularly?' asked the doctor. 'What do you think I've been doing?' snapped the man. 'Shoving them up my arse?'

A man went to the doctor's with a cucumber in his left ear, a carrot in his right ear and a banana up his nose. 'What's wrong with me?' he asked. 'Simple,' said the doctor. 'You're not eating properly.'

A young medical student approached a patient in bed brandishing a syringe. 'Nothing to worry about,' said the student, 'just a little prick with a needle.' 'Yes, I know you are,' said the patient. 'But what are you going to do?'

So, doctor, do you think I'm going to live? Yes, but I don't advise it!

Doctor examining a woman: You have acute angina.
Woman: Why thank you, Doctor!

An 85-year-old man was having his annual check-up. He boasted to the doctor: 'I've got an 18-year-old bride who is pregnant with my child. How about that eh, doc?' The doctor thought for a moment and said 'Let me tell you a story. I knew a guy who was a keen hunter, but one day he left home in a hurry and accidentally picked up his umbrella instead of his gun. Later that day, he came face to face with a huge grizzly bear. The hunter raised his umbrella, pointed it at the bear and squeezed the handle. And guess what, the bear dropped dead.' 'That's impossible,' said the old man. 'Someone else must have shot that bear.' 'That's kind of what I'm getting at,' said the doctor.

A man wasn't feeling well so he went to the doctor. The doctor asked him what he ate. 'Well, doctor,' said the man, 'for breakfast I have two pool balls – one yellow, one purple. For lunch I have two more pool balls – a blue and a white. And for dinner I have two reds and two blacks.' 'I'm not surprised you're not well,' said the doctor. 'You're not eating enough greens.'

Q. **WHAT HAS THICK GLASSES AND A WET NOSE?**
A. **A SHORT-SIGHTED GYNAECOLOGIST.**

At an out-of-town medical convention which both were attending, a male medic got chatting to a pretty woman. He asked her to dinner and they went to a smart restaurant. Before and after dinner, she made a point of washing her hands. The dinner was a great success and she invited him back to her hotel room. She slipped into the bathroom to wash her hands and then they made love. After sex, she washed her hands again. When she returned, he said, 'I bet you're a surgeon.' 'Yes, I am. How did you know?' she asked. 'Because you're always washing your hands.' She said, 'And I bet you're an anaesthetist.' 'That's right. How did you guess?' 'Because I didn't feel a thing.'

Q. **WHAT IS THE DIFFERENCE BETWEEN GOD AND AN ORTHOPAEDIC SURGEON?**
A. **GOD DOESN'T THINK HE'S AN ORTHOPAEDIC SURGEON.**

A man went to the doctor's complaining of a pain in the stomach. The doctor gave him a thorough examination but could not find anything obviously wrong. The doctor sighed, 'I'm afraid I can't diagnose your complaint. I think it must be drink.' 'All right then,' said the patient. 'I'll come back when you're sober.'

Doctor: We need to get these people to a hospital.
Nurse: What is it, Doctor?
Doctor: It's a big building with lots of doctors inside, but that's not important now!

A woman went to the doctor's. The doctor said, 'You've got tuberculosis.' 'I don't believe you,' said the shocked woman, 'I want a second opinion.' 'Okay,' said the doctor. 'You're ugly as well.'

Patient: My wife is going out of her mind. She spends the whole day blowing smoke rings.
Doctor: There's nothing wrong with that. I like blowing smoke rings myself.
Patient: But my wife doesn't smoke.

Four nurses decided to play a trick on a doctor whom they thought was arrogant. Later, each discussed what they had done. The first nurse said, 'I stuffed cotton wool in his stethoscope so that he couldn't hear.' The second nurse said, 'I let the mercury out of his thermometers and painted them all to read 107 degrees.' The third nurse said, 'I poked holes in all of the condoms he keeps in his desk drawer.' And the fourth nurse fainted.

A woman went to the doctor and told him, 'Every time I sneeze, I have an orgasm.' 'Hmmm. What are you taking for it?' 'Pepper.'

The doctor said to the patient, 'I want you to take your clothes off and stick your tongue out of the window.' 'What will that do?' 'Not much. But I hate my neighbour!'

There's a new medical crisis. Doctors are reporting that many men are having allergic reactions to latex condoms. They say they cause severe swelling. So what's the problem? ***Jay Leno***

Doctor to patient: I've got some bad news and I've got some very bad news.
Patient: You'd better let me have the bad news first.
Doctor: The results of your tests have come back and they say you've only got 24 hours to live.
Patient: Only 24 hours? That's terrible. It's no time at all. What's the very bad news?
Doctor: I've been trying to reach you since yesterday.

The doctor put a stethoscope to the patient's chest. The patient said, 'Doc, how do I stand?' The doctor replied, 'That's what puzzles me.'

An elderly patient went to the doctor. 'I need help, Doctor. Do you remember those voices in my head which I've been complaining about for years?' 'Yes.' 'Well, they've suddenly stopped.' 'That's good. So what's the problem?' 'I think I'm going deaf.'

George was called to the doctor's for a check-up, but the real reason for his recall was to give him some advice. 'How many children have you now, George?' the doctor asked. 'I've got eleven, doctor, at the last count. Not a bad score for a life's work!' George boasted. 'It's about time you thought about your partner,' the doctor scolded. 'Any more children could kill her,' he warned. George's smile left his face as he heeded the warning. 'We won't have any more. If she has any more I'll hang myself.' Time moved on and George's wife confessed that she was pregnant again. When she was out doing the shopping, George fitted a hook into the ceiling and slung a rope over it. Standing on the chair with the rope around his neck, a thought entered his head which made him remove the rope. 'Hold on a bit,' he told himself. 'I might be hanging the wrong man!'

Doctor: So how are your broken ribs coming along?
Patient: Well, I keep getting this stitch in my side.
Doctor: Good, that shows the bones are knitting together.

A woman went to the doctor and complained that she felt constantly exhausted. 'How often do you have sex?' asked the doctor. 'Every Monday, Wednesday and Friday,' replied the woman. 'Well, perhaps you should cut out Wednesdays.' 'I can't – that's the only night I'm home with my husband.'

Doctor to patient: I'm afraid you're dying.
Patient: How long have I got?
Doctor: Ten...
Patient: Ten what? Ten months, ten weeks, ten days...?
Doctor: Ten, nine, eight, seven...

A man rings the doctor in a mad panic. 'Doctor, my wife is pregnant and her contractions are only two minutes apart!' 'Is this her first child?' 'No, you idiot – it's her husband!

A woman phoned the doctor in the middle of the night. 'Doctor, please come over quick. My son has swallowed a condom.' The doctor quickly got dressed but just as he was about to leave, the phone rang again. It was the same woman. 'Don't worry,' she said. 'There's no need to come over after all. My husband just found another one.'

A stockbroker was in hospital. The nurse was taking his temperature. 'What is it now, nurse?' he asked. '102.' 'When it gets to 103, sell!'

A specialist is a doctor with a smaller practice but a bigger home.

Two junior doctors were involved in a fight in the hospital. The senior surgeon had to pull them apart. 'What's all this about?' said the surgeon angrily. 'It's the Inland Revenue inspector in G ward,' said one. 'He's only got two days to live.' 'He had to be told,' said the second doctor. 'I know,' said the first, 'but I wanted to be the one to tell him!'

Doctor, I want to undergo a sex-change operation. From what?

Doctor, can I get a second opinion? Of course you can. Come back tomorrow.

Four surgeons went on a coffee break. The first said, 'I like operating on librarians best because you open them up and everything is in alphabetical order.' The second said, 'I think accountants are the easiest to operate on because everything inside is numbered.' The third said, 'I prefer electricians because everything is colour-coded.' And the fourth said, 'I reckon lawyers are the easiest to operate on because they're heartless, spineless, gutless and their head and their arses are interchangeable.'

Old doctors never die; they just lose their patience.

Doctor: Have you ever been troubled by appendicitis?
Patient: Only when I've tried to spell it.

Doctor, every bone in my body hurts. Well, just be glad you're not a herring!

Doctor, I don't know what's wrong with me but everything hurts. If I touch my shoulder just here, it hurts, and if I touch my leg just here, it hurts, and if I touch my foot just here, it hurts. It sounds to me like you've broken your finger.

Doctor: Your pulse is as steady as a clock.
Patient: Maybe that's because you're feeling my wristwatch!

Eating in a fish restaurant, a diner began to choke on a bone. As his face grew redder and redder, the waiters stood there, not knowing what to do. Finally, another diner rushed over and said, 'I'm a doctor. Let me at him.' The doctor put his arms round the man and suddenly pulled them tight. The bone shot out and the grateful diner turned to the doctor. 'Thank you, thank you,' he said. 'Now tell me, how much do I owe you?' And the doctor said, 'I'll settle for half of what you would have paid me while you were choking.'

Doctor, I get this stabbing pain in my eye every time I have a cup of tea. Try taking the spoon out.

Doctor: I'm afraid you've got a dodgy ticker.
Patient: Thank goodness. I was afraid there might be something wrong with my heart.

Doctor, I think I've broken my neck. Really? Well, keep your chin up.

A man stumbles into a doctor's surgery and says, 'Doctor, my legs keep talking to me!' The doctor says, 'Don't be daft, let me have a listen.' He puts his ear to the man's thigh and it whispers, 'Lend us a tenner.' Amazed, he moves down to the knee and it whispers, 'Give us a fiver.' Astounded, he moves to the calf, which says, 'Give us a quid.' Perplexed, the doctor refers to his medical journal, and finally says, 'Ah, I can see the problem – your leg is broke in three places.'

Doctor: If I find the operation necessary, would you have the money to pay for it?
Patient: If I didn't have the money, would you find the operation necessary?

The doctor didn't stay long with the patient. As he left the house, he told the patient's wife, 'There's nothing wrong with your husband. He just thinks he's sick.' A few days later the doctor rang to check if his diagnosis had been correct. 'How's your husband today?' he asked the wife. 'He's worse,' said the wife. 'Now he thinks he's dead.'

Doctor: That's a nasty cough you've got there. Have you had it before?
Patient: Yes.
Doctor: Well, you've got it again.

Doctor, I'm in great pain with my wooden leg. How can a wooden leg cause you pain? My wife keeps hitting me over the head with it.

I was just going into the doctor's surgery when a nun runs out, screaming at the top of her voice. I said to the doctor: 'So what's with the nun?' The doctor said: 'I just told her she was pregnant.' 'The nun is pregnant?' And the doctor said: 'No, but it certainly cured her hiccups!'

Doctor: I'm afraid I've got bad news for you. You could go at any time.
Patient: But that's good news. I haven't been for six days.

Doctor, I've broken my arm in two places. Don't go back to either of them!

A beautiful woman went to see a gynaecologist. He was so captivated by her beauty that he started behaving in a highly unethical manner, but he just couldn't help himself. First he told her to undress and he started to caress her inner thighs. As he did so, he asked: 'Do you know what I'm doing?' 'Yes,' replied the woman. 'You're checking for any abrasions or skin abnormalities.' 'That's right,' said the gynaecologist. Next he started to fondle her breasts. 'Do you know what I'm doing?' 'Yes,' replied the woman. 'You're checking for lumps.' 'That's right,' he answered. Then he started to have sex with her. 'Do you know what I'm doing now?' he panted. 'Yes,' she replied. 'You're getting herpes.'

Doctor: Did that medicine I gave your uncle straighten him out?
Patient: It certainly did. They buried him yesterday!

Doctor, my son has just swallowed my pen! What shall I do? Use a pencil.

A woman rang the doctor in a panic. 'Doctor, what can I do? My husband has just swallowed a mouse!' The doctor said, 'I'll be right over. But while you're waiting, wave a piece of cheese in front of his mouth.' When the doctor arrived, he discovered the woman waving a mackerel in front of her husband's mouth. 'I said a piece of cheese, not a mackerel!' he cried. And the woman said, 'But I have to get the cat out first!'

Doctor, my irregular heartbeat is bothering me. Don't worry, we'll soon put a stop to it.

A fashionable society doctor received an urgent call and when he arrived and asked what the matter was, the lady of the house said, 'It's the maid. She is in bed and refuses to get up.' 'Perhaps I had better have a few words with her alone,' said the doctor. So he went up the stairs and, entering the room, found the maid in bed as her mistress had said. 'Now,' said the doctor, 'what's the trouble?' 'There's no trouble,' said the maid, 'but I haven't been paid my wages for six weeks, so I am not getting up until I've been paid.' 'Right,' said the doctor, and he started to take off his clothes. 'Here!' cried the maid. 'What are you up to?' 'Nothing,' he replied, 'but just move over. They owe me for a twelvemonth.'

Doctor: The best thing for you to do is to give up drinking, smoking and wild women.
Patient: What's the second best?

Doctor, my hands won't stop shaking. Tell me, do you drink a lot? No, I spill most of it.

A woman went to the doctor's clutching the side of her face. 'What seems to be the problem?' asked the doctor. 'Well,' said the woman, removing her hand, 'it's this pimple on my cheek. There's a small tree growing from it, and tables and chairs, and a picnic basket. What on earth can it be?' 'It's nothing to worry about,' said the doctor. 'It's only a beauty spot.'

Doctor, you've got to help me. Everyone thinks I'm a liar. I find that hard to believe.

Doctor: When you get up in the morning do you have a furry tongue, a pain in the middle of your shoulders and feel terribly depressed?
Patient: Yes, I do.
Doctor: So do I. I wonder what it is.

Tell me, doctor, when my finger heals will I be able to play the piano? Of course you will. That's marvellous, I never could before.

A man went to the doctor. 'It's my penis, doctor,' said the man. 'But when you look at it, you must promise not to laugh.' 'Of course I won't laugh,' said the doctor. 'Now remove your pants, please.' So the man took off his pants. The doctor took one look at his penis and burst out laughing. 'In all my years as a doctor,' he shrieked, 'that is the smallest, tiniest penis I have ever seen! I didn't know it was possible to have one so minute. So tell me what the problem is.' 'It's swollen.'

I went to his evening surgery, I always do. Why's that? Well, I like to give him time for his hands to warm up.

The patient stood nervously in the consulting room of an eminent Harley Street specialist. 'So who did you consult before you came to me?' asked the specialist. 'My local GP.' 'Your GP? They're hopeless. Tell me, what sort of useless advice did he give you?' 'He told me to come and see you.'

Doctor: You've burnt both your ears! How did it happen?
Patient: I was ironing when the telephone rang.
Doctor: But how did you burn both of them?
Patient: Well, just as soon as I put the phone down, it rang again.

The patient, drowsily coming to after his operation, recognized the figure of the surgeon at the end of his bed. 'So how was it?' said the patient. 'Well,' replied the doctor, 'I've got some bad news and some good news. The bad news is that I'm afraid we amputated the wrong leg.' 'Amputated the wrong leg! What sort of good news can there be after you tell me that?' 'Well,' said the surgeon, 'the good news is that your bad leg is getting better.'

Does the doctor still believe in house calls? Certainly. What time can you get to his house?

Doctor: You've got six months to live.
Patient: But what if I can't pay your bill in that time?
Doctor: Then I'll give you another six months.

An army major was visiting sick soldiers in hospital. 'What's your problem, soldier?' he asked. 'Chronic syphilis, Sir.' 'What treatment are they giving you?' 'Five minutes with a wire brush each day.' 'And what's your ambition?' 'To get back to the front, sir.' The major moved on to the next bed. 'And what's your problem, soldier?' 'Chronic diarrhoea, sir.' 'What treatment are they giving you?' 'Five minutes with a wire brush each day.' 'And what's your ambition?' 'To get back to the front, sir.' The major moved to the next bed. 'And what's your problem, soldier?' 'Chronic gum disease, sir.' 'What treatment are they giving you?' 'Five minutes with a wire brush each day.' 'And what's your ambition?' 'To get the wire brush before the other two, sir.'

I'm off to the doctor's. I feel a bit dizzy. Vertigo? No, just round the corner.

Patient: Doctor, I can't sleep at night.
Doctor: Well, I advise you to eat something before you go to bed.
Patient: But two months ago you advised me never to eat anything before going to bed.
Doctor: That was two months ago. Medical science has made enormous strides since then.

The doctor told me to take two tablespoonfuls of Persian cat's milk. How do you get milk from a Persian cat? Take his saucer away.

Doctor: I've decided you're a kleptomaniac.
Patient: You mean I help myself because I can't help myself?

The doctor sat down beside the bed, looked the patient square in the eye and said: 'I'm afraid I've bad news for you. You have only four minutes to live.' 'Four minutes! Is there really nothing you can do for me?' 'Well, I could just about boil you an egg.'

The trouble is, Doctor, I seem to lose my temper very easily these days. I beg your pardon? I told you once, you blithering idiot!

An old man went into hospital for the first time in his life. Toying with the bell cord that had been fastened to his bed, he asked his son, 'What's this thing?' 'It's a bell.' The old man pulled it several times. 'I can't hear it ringing,' he said. 'No,' explained the son, 'it doesn't ring. It turns on a light in the hall for a nurse.' The old man was indignant. 'If the nurse wants a light on in the hall, she can damn well turn it on herself!'

Doctor: Stick your tongue out and say "Aah!"
Patient: Aah!
Doctor: Well, your tongue looks alright, but why the postage stamp?
Patient: So that's where I left it!

Doctor, I'm sick and tired of being sick and tired.

A man walks into the surgery with a duck on his head. The doctor says: 'What can I do for you?' And the duck says: 'I want this wart from my foot removed.'

A woman went to the doctor complaining of feeling lethargic. After a thorough examination, he prescribed the male hormone testosterone for her. Two months later, she returned to the doctor. 'The hormones you've been giving me have really helped,' she said. 'But I'm worried that the dosage is too high because I've started to grow hair in places where I've never grown hair before.' 'That's nothing to worry about,' said the doctor reassuringly. 'A little hair growth is perfectly normal effect of testosterone. Now where exactly has the hair appeared?' 'On my balls.'

The phone rang in the ward and the matron picked it up. The caller said, 'I wonder if you can tell me how your patient Mr Grossmann is.' And the matron said, 'He's getting better all the time. In fact, he'll be ready to leave hospital in a couple of days. Who is this calling?' And the voice said, 'This is Mr Grossman. The doctor won't tell me anything!'

I was having a complete medical examination. The doctor pointed to a jar on the shelf and said, 'I want you to fill that.' I replied, 'What! From here?'

Consultant: Well, you'll be pleased to know that the operation to cure your deafness has been a complete success.
Patient: Pardon?

Before they admitted me to this private hospital, the doctor interviewed me to find out what illness I could afford to have.

Shortly before her fourth marriage, a middle-aged woman went to see her doctor to ask for advice on sex, more particularly on how to do it. The doctor was amazed. He said, 'You've been married three times before - surely you know what you have to do by now?' 'No, that's the point,' said the woman, 'I don't. My first husband was a gynaecologist and all he wanted to do was look at it; my second husband was a psychiatrist and all he wanted to do was talk about it; my third husband worked for the Post Office and he couldn't find it. Now I'm getting married to a lawyer so I'm bound to get screwed sometime!'

She's a lousy nurse. She couldn't even put a dressing on a salad!

Nurse: Look at that operating table - it's ruined!
Doctor: I'm sorry, I must try to learn not to cut so deeply!

They called her Nurse Tonsils – all the doctors wanted to take her out!

An old man went to the doctor's accompanied by his equally aged wife. Since he was deaf, he relied on his wife to act as a sort of interpreter. 'Right,' said the doctor to the old man. 'Take off your shirt, please.' 'What did he say?' asked the old man. 'They want your shirt,' replied the wife. The man took off his shirt which was encrusted with food. Next the doctor said, 'Would you mind removing your socks so that I can examine your feet?' 'What did he say?' boomed the old man. 'I didn't hear a word.' 'They want your socks,' explained the wife. As the old man was removing his smelly socks, the nurse said 'Excuse me, Sir, we need a stool sample and a urine sample.' 'What did she say?' asked the old man. The wife said, 'They want your underpants.'

The things those doctors and nurses get up to at night. Once I heard a nurse tell a doctor to cut it out – and she wasn't talking about an appendix.

A man entered hospital for an appendicitis operation. When he came round afterwards he told the nurse that his throat felt terribly sore. 'Oh,' she said, 'I had better explain. You see, at your operation this morning there were a number of medical students present and when the surgeon had finished they were so impressed that they applauded him; so for an encore he took out your tonsils.'

The consultant was showing the young medical student a set of X-rays. 'As you will observe,' said the consultant, 'one hip seems to be higher than the other. What do you expect to find wrong with the patient?' 'I would expect him to walk with a limp.' 'Good, and so what would you do in the circumstances?' 'I suppose I'd walk with a limp too.'

Doctor: I've some very bad news. You've got cancer and Alzheimer's.
Patient: Well, at least I don't have cancer.

The X-ray specialist married one of his patients. Everybody wondered what he saw in her.

A young man went to see the doctor about his lisp. The doctor told the young man that the lisp was caused by the size of his penis – it was so big that it was pulling his tongue off-centre. 'Can you do anything about it?' asked the young man. 'Well,' said the doctor, 'I could perform an operation to shorten the length of your penis. That should get rid of your lisp.' Two months after the operation, the patient returned to the doctor and complained that while his lisp had gone, his sex life had been ruined. 'I want my penis back,' he demanded. 'Thcrew you,' said the doctor.

My brother's a naval surgeon. Wow, they do specialise these days, don't they?

Nurse: Take off your clothes.
Man: Where shall I put them?
Nurse: On top of mine.

Why do the doctors wear those masks during the operations? So if anything goes wrong, they can't be identified.

Matron: Why are you making that patient jump up and down?
Nurse: Because I've just given him some medicine and I forgot to shake the bottle.

There was a terrible mix-up at the hospital. A man who had been scheduled for a vasectomy was instead given a sex-change operation. When told of the mistake, he was understandably distraught. 'I'll never be able to experience an erection again,' he wailed. The surgeon tried to console him. 'Of course you'll be able to experience an erection – it's just that it will have to be someone else's.'

The same question was put to three different men: 'If you were told by your doctor that you had only one month longer to live, what would you do?' The first man replied, 'I would set about putting my affairs in order, lead a quiet, peaceful life, and prepare for the end.' The next man said, 'I would realize all my assets, have a right good time, and then I wouldn't mind what happened.' The third man merely said, 'I would consult another doctor.'

Doctor to patient: I've got some good news and some bad news. The bad news is that we've got to amputate your legs. The good news is that the guy in the next bed wants to buy your slippers.

A team of Hollywood doctors were working furiously to revive a patient whose heart had stopped in the middle of a quadruple bypass operation. Unfortunately, their efforts were to no avail, and the patient expired on the table. 'Oh doctor,' cried one of the attending nurses, 'what a terrible shame.' 'Hey, lighten up, Peggy,' the head surgeon said reassuringly. 'It's not as though we were making a movie.'

Doctor: Nurse, how is that little boy doing – the one who swallowed all those coins?
Nurse: No change yet.

The doctor pulled the sheet up over the patient's face and turned solemnly to the wife. 'Well, the good news is that he's stable.'

A surgeon was about to perform a haemorrhoidectomy. He summoned the nurse and gave her a list of the instruments he required for the operation. A few minutes later, she brought in a rubber glove, a large jar of Vaseline, a knife and a bottle of beer. The surgeon began the operation. First he picked up the rubber glove and put it on his hand, ensuring that all the wrinkles were smoothed out. Then he held out his hand and the nurse gave him the Vaseline, which he proceeded to smooth over the glove. Then he held out his free hand and the nurse handed him the beer. 'Dammit, nurse!" he said in exasperation. 'I wanted a butt-light!'

At his annual check-up, Bernie was given an excellent bill of health. 'It must run in the family,' commented the doctor. 'How old was your dad when he died?' 'What makes you think he's dead?' asked Bernie. 'He's 90 and still going strong.' 'Aha! And how long did your grandfather live?' 'What makes you think he's dead, doc? He's 106 and getting married to a 22-year-old next week,' Bernie informed him. 'At his age!' exclaimed the doctor. 'Why does he want to marry such a young woman?' 'And what makes you think HE wants to?' ***Henry Youngman***

A small-town doctor routinely performed circumcisions, and got in the habit of saving the foreskins in a jar of formaldehyde. Many years went by, it came time to retire, and the doctor was cleaning out his office when he came across the jar, now completely full. 'Why throw it out?' he reasoned. So he took it to the tailor's shop downstairs with instructions to make whatever he saw fit. Two weeks later the tailor presented him with a beautiful little wallet. 'A wallet! That's all I get after a lifetime of work?' exclaimed the doctor. 'There were hundreds and hundreds of foreskins in that jar!' 'Relax, Doc, just relax,' said the tailor soothingly. 'Rub it for a minute or two and it turns into a suitcase.'

Harry answers the phone, and it's an emergency room doctor. The doctor says, 'Your wife was in a serious car accident, and I have bad news and good news. The bad news is she has lost all use of both arms and both legs, and will need help eating and going to the bathroom for the rest of her life.' Harry says, 'My God. What's the good news?' The doctor says, 'I'm kidding. She's dead!'

What does a gynaecologist do when he gets nostalgic? He looks up an old friend.

Mrs Garwood lived up in the hills and had always been as healthy as a horse, but as old age approached, she began to suffer from some 'female troubles'. Finally, she confessed this to her daughter-in-law, who made an appointment with a gynaecologist in the city and drove her in. A wide-eyed Mrs Garwood lay silent and still as a stone while the doctor examined her. When it was over, she sat up and fixed a beady eye on the physician. 'You seem like such a nice young man,' she said. 'But tell me, does your mother know what you do for a living?'

Did you hear about the gynaecologist who papered the hall through the letterbox?

Doctor: I have some good news and some bad news. Which shall I tell you first?
Patient: Do begin with the bad news, please.
Doctor: All right. Your son has drowned, your daughter is in a coma, your wife has divorced you, your house got blown away, and you have an incurable rare disease.
Patient: Good grief! What's the good news?
Doctor: The good news is that there's no more bad news.

A police officer had just pulled a car over. When the officer walked up to the car, a man rolled down the window and said, 'What's the problem, officer? By the way, I am a doctor.' The officer responded, 'I stopped you for running that red light behind you.' Just then the doctor's wife leaned forward from the passenger seat and said in an obnoxious voice, 'I told him to stop at that light. But did he listen? No. He just kept right on going. Thinks because he's a doctor he can do what he wants.' The doctor turns to his wife and yells 'Shut up!' The officer then continued, 'And just before the light I clocked you going 50 in a 30.' The wife leans forward and again squawks, 'I told him to slow down. But did he listen, no. He never listens to me.' The doctor then looks at his wife and says, 'Hey, didn't I just tell you to shut up?' The officer then looks at the wife and says, 'Does he always talk to you this way?' 'Only when he's been drinking,' she says.

Mrs Fishen walks into a doctor's office and says, 'Doctor, my husband swallowed an alarm clock.' The doctor replies, 'If he swallowed it, why did you come to the office?' She says, 'Because he bit me when I tried to wind it.'

How many doctors does it take to change a light bulb? Depends on whether it has health insurance.

Patient: Doctor, why did the receptionist rush out of the room screaming?
Doctor: When she asked you to strip to the waist ready for my examination she meant you to strip from the neck down, not from the toes up!

A man staggered into the doctor's surgery. He had three knives protruding out of his back, his head was bleeding from a gunshot wound, and his legs had been badly beaten up by a hockey stick. The doctor's receptionist looked up at this pitiful sight and said, 'Do you have an appointment?'

Did you hear about the resourceful proctologist? He always used two fingers, in case his patients wanted a second opinion.

Once I was sick and had to go to an ear, nose and throat man to get well. There are ear doctors, nose doctors, throat doctors, gynae-cologists, proctologists – any place you've got a hole, there's a guy who specialises in your hole. They make an entire career out of that hole. And if the ear doctor, nose doctor, throat doctor, gynaecologist or proctologist can't help you, he sends you to a surgeon. Why? So he can make a new hole!
Alan Prophet

'Doctor, I wish to protest about the spare-part surgery operation you did on me.' 'What's wrong? I gave you another hand when your own was smashed up at your factory.' 'I know. But you gave me a female hand which is very good most of the time – it's only that whenever I go to the toilet it doesn't want to let go.'

I don't understand that nurse. She keeps saying to me: 'How are we today?' and 'Have we eaten this morning?' But when I put my hand on her knee, she slapped our face!

Doctor: How do you feel today?
Patient: With my hands – just like I usually do.

An elderly doctor took a young partner into his practice and said, 'I would like you to accompany me on my visits tomorrow so that you can observe my procedure, which you may care to adopt.' So the next day they set off. The first visit was to a rather plump lady, who was reclining in bed. After introducing his new partner, the old doctor took the patient's temperature but dropped the thermometer which he retrieved from under the bed where it had fallen. As they prepared to depart he said, 'You know, Mrs Goodbody, you would recover much quicker if you didn't eat so many chocolates.' The patient blushed and they left. When they were outside the house, the young doctor asked, 'How did you know about her eating chocolates?' 'Well,' replied the other, 'you saw me stoop down to pick up the thermometer? Under the bed were all the chocolate wrappings.' At the next house a very elegant lady was sitting up in bed in readiness for their visit. So the old doctor said, 'I've brought along my new partner who will attend to you this morning, Mrs Loveday.' Whereupon the young doctor proceeded to take the patient's temperature and he also dropped the thermometer, which fell to the floor. As they were leaving he said, 'You know, Mrs Loveday, you ought not to be taking quite so much interest in church affairs.' When they had left the house, the old doctor asked, 'Why on earth did you say that about the church?' 'Well,' replied the doctor, 'I did the same as you; I dropped the thermometer and when I reached under the bed to pick it up, there was the vicar!'

John: How can I lose 12 pounds of ugly fat?
Doctor: Cut your head off.

A man goes to the doctor and says, 'Doctor, there's a piece of lettuce sticking out of my bottom.' The doctor asks him to drop his trousers and examines him. The man asks, 'Is it serious, doctor?' The doctor replies, 'I'm sorry to tell you, but this is just the tip of the iceberg.'

Doctor: Have you ever had your eyes checked?
Patient: No, Doctor. They've always been brown.

All my doctor does is send me to see other doctors. I don't know if he's really a doctor or a booking agent.

The medical student was accompanying one of the consultants on his hospital rounds. Time after time, the student made a completely wrong diagnosis. 'Have you ever thought about taking up a different career?' asked the consultant. 'One where you would not be fired for frequent misdiagnoses – such as a government economist?'

Patient: Doctor, I think I've got an inferiority complex.
Doctor: Don't be silly. You really are inferior.

Why did the doctor fail as a kidnapper? Because nobody could read the ransom notes.

A man walked into the office of a plastic surgeon and handed over a cheque for £2,000 to the receptionist. 'I think there's some mistake,' said the receptionist. 'Your bill is only £1,000 pounds.' 'I know,' replied the man, 'but the operation was tremendously successful. The surgeon took some skin from my behind - where no one will ever see that it's missing - and grafted it onto my cheek and totally got rid of the large scar I used to have there.' 'So the extra £1,000 is for a job well done?' said the receptionist. 'Not exactly. It's a token of appreciation for all the delight I get every time my mother-in-law kisses my backside and doesn't even know it!'

The London Journal of Medicine reports that nine out of ten doctors agree that one out of ten doctors is an idiot.

The phone rings. The lady of the house answers, 'Hello?' 'Mrs Ward, please.' 'Speaking,' she replies. 'Mrs Ward, this is Doctor Jones at the Medical Testing Laboratory. When your doctor sent your husband's samples to the lab, the samples from another Mr Ward were sent as well, and now we're uncertain as to which ones are your husband's. Frankly, it is either bad or terrible.' 'What do you mean?' Mrs Ward asks. 'Well, one Mr Ward has tested positive for Alzheimer's disease and the other positive for AIDS. We can't tell which your husband's is.' 'That's terrible! Can't we just do the test over?' questions Mrs Ward. 'Normally, yes. But Medicare won't pay for these expensive tests more than once.' 'And? What the hell am I supposed to do now?' she enquires, very upset. 'The people at Medicare recommend that you drop your husband off in the middle of town. If he finds his way home, don't sleep with him.'

Nurse: Can I take your pulse?
Patient: Haven't you got one of your own?

First patient: I see they've brought in another case of diarrhoea.
Second patient: That's good! Anything is better than that awful lemonade they've been giving us.

Late one night a doctor received a telephone call from a man who said urgently, 'Doctor, my mother-in-law is lying at death's door. Can you come round and pull her through?'

Patient: Doctor, you've already said that the operation is very risky. What are my chances of survival?
Doctor: Excellent! The odds against success are 99 to 1, but the surgeon who will be performing the operation on you is looking forward to it as you will be his 100th patient and so you must be a success after all the others.

The patient who had just come round after an operation was recovering in a ward and heard two other patients talking. Said one, 'Some of these surgeons are a bit forgetful. They left a swab in one chap and he had to be opened up again to remove it.' 'Yes,' replied the other. 'I heard that, and there was another patient who had a scalpel left in him.' At that moment the surgeon who had performed the operation on the new patient popped his head round the door and asked, 'Has anyone seen my hat?' and the poor chap fainted.

First student: Why are you saving all those old magazines?
Second student: Because I qualify as a doctor in five years' time and I'll need something suitable for my waiting room.

Doctor, doctor! I'm terribly worried. I keep seeing pink striped crocodiles every time I try to get to sleep! Have you seen a psychiatrist? No – only pink striped crocodiles.

The eminent surgeon was walking through his local churchyard one day when he saw the gravedigger having a rest and drinking from a bottle of beer. 'Hey, you!' called the surgeon. 'How dare you laze about and drink alcohol in the churchyard! Get on with your job, or I shall complain to the vicar!' 'I should have thought you'd be the last person to complain,' said the gravedigger, 'bearing in mind all your blunders I've had to cover up.'

Doctor: Why do you think you've become schizophrenic?
Patient: It was the only way I could think of to prove that two could live as cheaply as one.

'Doctor, I'm worried about my wife. She thinks she's a bird.' 'Well, you had better bring her in to see me.' 'I can't. She's just flown south for the winter.'

A doctor and his wife were sitting in deck chairs on the beach when a beautiful young girl in a very brief bikini jogged towards them. As she came to the doctor she waved at him and said in a huskily sexy voice, 'Hi there!' before continuing on her way. 'Who was that?' demanded the doctor's wife. 'Oh, just someone I met professionally,' replied the doctor. 'Oh, yes?' snorted the wife. 'Whose profession? Yours or hers?'

The doctor had just finished examining a very attractive young girl.
Doctor: Have you been going out with men, Miss Jones?
Miss Jones: Oh no, doctor, never!
Doctor: Are you sure? Bearing in mind that I've now examined the sample you sent, do you still say you've never had anything to do with men?
Miss Jones: Quite sure, Doctor. Can I go now?
Doctor: No.
Miss Jones: Why not?
Doctor: Because, Miss Jones, I'm awaiting the arrival of the Three Wise Men.

A man walked into the chemist's. 'Have you got anything to keep my stomach in?' he asked. The assistant went round the back and brought out a wheelbarrow.

A doctor was fuming when he finally reached his seat at a civic dinner, after breaking away from a woman who sought his advice on a personal health problem. 'Do you think I should send her a bill?' he asked a solicitor who sat next to him. 'Why not?' the solicitor replied. 'You rendered professional service by giving her advice.' 'Thanks,' the physician said, 'I think I'll do that.' When the doctor went to his surgery the next day to send the bill to the woman, he found a letter from the solicitor. It read, 'For legal services, £50.'

'When I stand up I see Donald Duck and Pluto and when I bend suddenly I see Mickey Mouse and Popeye,' said the patient. 'Oh,' said the doctor, 'and how long have you been having these Disney spells?'

Mother: My son can't stop biting nails.
Doctor: How old is your son?
Mother: 15.
Doctor: That's not unusual. Even at his age some people still bite their nails when they're nervous.
Mother: But he bites long nails he's pulled out of the floorboards!

A labourer was working near a guillotine when he bent over a too far and his ear was severed. Man and ear were quickly rushed to the hospital. His injury was cleaned up in one ward, while the ear was prepared for surgery in another. At last he and his ear were ready to be reunited. The ear lay on a tray but the sight of it made the labourer suspicious. 'That's not my ear,' he protested. 'My ear had a cigarette behind it!'

Like Pulling Teeth

A businessman was in Japan to make a presentation to the Toyota motor people. Needless to say, this was an especially important deal, and it was imperative that he make the best possible impression. On the morning of the presentation he awoke to find himself passing gas, in large volumes, with the unpleasant characteristic of sounding like 'Honda'. The man was beside himself. Every few minutes 'Honda', 'Honda' ... Unable to stop this aberrant behaviour, and in desperate need to terminate these odious and rather embarrassing emissions, he sought a physician's aid. After a full examination, the doctor told him that there was nothing inherently wrong with him and that he would just have to wait it out. Being unwilling to accept this state of affairs, he visited a second and then a third doctor, all of whom told him the same thing. Finally, one medic suggested that he visit a dentist. Well, although he could not see how a dentist was going to be of any help, he visited one anyway. Lo and behold, the dentist said, 'Ah, there's the problem.' 'What is it?' the man asked. 'Why you have an abscess,' said the dentist. 'An abscess? How could that be causing my problem?' asked the man. 'That's easy,' replied the dentist. 'Why everyone knows ... abscess makes the fart go Honda.'

Patient: How much to have this tooth pulled?
Dentist: £90.
Patient: £90? For just a few minutes work?
Dentist: I can extract it very slowly if you like.

I said to my dentist, 'Do you promise to pull the tooth, the whole tooth and nothing but the tooth?'

After the dentist finished examining the woman's teeth he says, 'I am sorry to tell you this, but I am going to have to drill a tooth.' The woman says, 'Ooooohhhh, I'd rather have a baby!' To which the dentist replies, 'Make up your mind, I have to adjust the chair.'

My dentist advised me to use striped toothpaste – to make my teeth look longer.

A man went to his dentist because he felt something wrong in his mouth. The dentist examined him and said, 'That new upper plate that I put in six months ago is eroding. What have you been eating?' The man replied, 'All I can think of is that about four months ago, my wife made some asparagus and put some stuff on it that was delicious – Hollandaise sauce. I loved it so much I now put it on everything – meat, toast, fish, vegetables, everything.' 'Well,' said the dentist. 'That's probably the problem. Hollandaise sauce is made with lots of lemon juice, which is highly corrosive. It's eating away at your upper plate. I'll make you a new plate, and this time I'll use chrome.' 'Why chrome?' asked the patient. The dentist replied, 'It's simple. Everyone knows that there's no plate like chrome for the Hollandaise!'

I think my dentist is in trouble. Last week he took out all my gold fillings and put in IOUs.

I'm always amazed to hear of air-crash victims so badly mutilated that they have to be identified by their dental records. What I can't understand is, if they don't know who you are, how do they know who your dentist is? ***Paul Merton***

I see my dentist twice a year – once for each tooth.

He's got so many cavities, he talks with an echo.

I'm changing to a new dentist. The old one got on my nerves.

Nothing gets an old dental bill paid like a new toothache.

Patient: So what's the verdict?
Dentist: Well, your teeth are fine, but your gums have got to come out.

So how did you get on at the dentist's? It was a scream!

So the dentist didn't hurt a bit? Not until I saw the bill.

My dentist said, 'Frankly, I've seen better teeth on a comb.'

Patient: I have yellow teeth. What should I do?
Dentist: Wear a brown tie.

I went to the dentist. He said, 'Say aaah.' I said, 'Why?' He said, 'My dog's died.' ***Tim Vine***

I went to the dentist this morning. Does your tooth still hurt? I don't know – the dentist kept it.

On the Couch

A psychiatrist is called a shrink because that's what he does to your wallet.

Patient: I'm worried that I'm mad. I keep thinking I'm a packet of biscuits.
Psychiatrist: A packet of biscuits? You mean those little square ones with lots of little holes in them?
Patient: That's right!
Psychiatrist: You're not mad...
Patient: Thank goodness!
Psychiatrist: You're crackers!

The funny thing about going to a psychiatrist is that you have to lie down to learn how to stand on your own two feet.

A man goes to a psychiatrist, and tells him, 'Doc, I think I'm obsessed with sex.' 'Well, let's do a few tests,' the doctor says. He draws a square on a piece of paper and asks the man to identify it. The man immediately says, 'Sex.' Next the doctor draws a circle, which the man again identifies as sex. Then the doctor draws a triangle, which, of course, the patient identifies as 'sex'. The doctor puts the drawings away and says to the patient, 'Yes, I do believe you have an obsession with sex.' To which the man replies, 'I'm not the one with the obsession! You're the one drawing all the dirty pictures!'

Patient: Every evening, about seven o' clock, my husband imagines he's a lightbulb.
Psychiatrist: Well, why don't you tell him he isn't?
Patient: What, and eat in the dark?

A psychiatrist is someone who will listen to you as long as you don't make sense.

The psychiatrist told the patient that he was conducting a simple test to monitor normal human responses. 'So,' began the psychiatrist, 'what would happen if I cut off your left ear?' 'I wouldn't be able to hear,' replied the patient. 'And what would happen if I cut off your right ear?' 'I wouldn't be able to see?' 'Why do you say that?' asked the psychiatrist. 'Because my hat would fall down over my eyes.'

The good thing about being a kleptomaniac is that you can always take something for it.

I don't really trust my psychiatrist. First of all, he tells me he doesn't believe in shock therapy. Then he gives me the bill.

A psychiatrist is a mental detective.

A man was convinced he was dead, and nothing, it seemed, could persuade him otherwise. When words failed, his psychiatrist resorted to textbooks and, after three hours of careful argument, backed up by expert testimony, he got the man to agree that dead men don't bleed. 'So now,' said the psychiatrist, 'I will prick your finger with a needle.' He jabbed a needle into the tip of the man's finger, and it started to bleed. 'What does that tell you?' asked the psychiatrist triumphantly. 'That dead men do bleed,' said the man.

He won't go to a shrink. He thinks he's small enough already.

Psychiatrist: Now tell me, do you normally stir your coffee with your right hand?
Patient: Oh, yes.
Psychiatrist: Mmmm, that's odd. Most people use a spoon.

Four psychiatrists were attending an out-of-town conference. Sitting in the hotel lounge one night, they each agreed that it could get pretty tiresome listening to other people's hang-ups all the time. Wouldn't it be nice if someone listened to their complexes and problems for a change? 'Okay,' said one, 'why don't we reveal our innermost feelings now, just between the four of us? I'll go first if you like. My big hang-up is sex. I can't get enough of it, and I have to confess that I frequently seduce my female patients.' The second said, 'My problem is money. I lead an extravagant lifestyle way beyond my means, and to finance this, I regularly overcharge my patients.' The third said, 'My trouble is drugs. I'm a pusher, and I often get my patients to sell drugs for me.' The fourth said, 'My problem is that, no matter how hard I try, I just can't keep a secret.'

I couldn't afford to go to a psychiatrist so I went into group therapy. Instead of couches, we had bunk-beds.

Why is psychoanalysis a lot quicker for men than for women? When it's time to go back to their childhood, men are already there.

Patient: I suppose what makes me different is that I always get my own way. I'm completely selfish. Whatever I want – women, possessions, money, power – I just go out and get, regardless of others.
Psychiatrist: I see. So how long have you had this complaint?
Patient: Who's complaining?

I started going to a psychiatrist when I was slightly cracked – and kept going until I was completely broke.

A man walked into a psychiatrist's office with a pancake on his head, a fried egg on each shoulder and a piece of bacon over each ear. 'What seems to be the problem?' asked the psychiatrist, puzzled. The man said, 'I'm worried about my brother.'

My psychiatrist has helped me a lot. I used to be too afraid to answer the phone. Now I answer it whether it rings or not.

Patient: The trouble is, my husband thinks he's a refrigerator.
Psychiatrist: Well, that's not so bad. It's rather a harmless complex.
Patient: Well, maybe. But he sleeps with his mouth open and the light keeps me awake.

My psychiatrist and I are making real progress. He's taken all my little fears and turned them into one big phobia.

A wife went to a psychiatrist in an attempt to sort out her sex life. For over half an hour, she talked about how unrewarding sex was with her husband, but the psychiatrist was struggling to reach the root of the problem. Then he asked, 'Do you ever watch your husband's face while you're making love?' 'I did once,' she replied. 'And how did he look?' 'Very angry.' 'That's interesting. You say you have only once seen your husband's face during sex? That in itself is unusual. Tell me, what were the circumstances that led you to see his face on the occasion he appeared so angry?' 'He was looking through the window at me.'

Psychiatry is the only business where the customer is always wrong.

Roses are red, violets are blue, I'm a schizophrenic, and so am I.

Patient: I just don't seem to be able to get on with anyone.
Psychiatrist: And why do you think that is?
Patient: How should I know, you moron?

She's so pathologically tidy that her doctor sent her to a psychiatrist. But it was a complete waste of time. She spent the first forty minutes rearranging the couch.

I told my psychiatrist that everyone hates me. He said I was being ridiculous – everyone hasn't met me yet.
Rodney Dangerfield

Patient: My husband has developed this delusion that he is an aeroplane.
Psychiatrist: Have him come in and see me tomorrow.
Patient: I'm afraid he can't come tomorrow. He's appearing in court for flying low over Haywards Heath.

Are you troubled by improper thoughts? Certainly not. I enjoy them!

For years I used to think I was a dog. Then I went to a psychiatrist and he soon put things right. So how are you now? Fine. Feel my nose.

A man had been seeing a psychiatrist for three years in an attempt to cure his fear that there were monsters lurking under his bed. But all the psychiatrist's efforts were in vain and the man was no nearer to being cured. Eventually the man decided that further sessions were a waste of time and money. A few weeks later, the psychiatrist bumped into the man in a bar. The man was looking much happier. 'You look well,' remarked the psychiatrist. 'Yes,' beamed the man. 'That's because I'm cured. After all this time, I can finally go to sleep at night and not worry that there are monsters lurking under my bed.' The psychiatrist was puzzled. 'How have you managed to get cured? Nothing I tried with you seemed to work.' 'I went to see a different doctor,' explained the man. 'He is a behaviourist and he cured me in one session.' 'In one session!' exclaimed the psychiatrist. 'How?' 'It was simple,' said the man. 'He told me to saw off the legs of my bed.'

How much did the psychiatrist charge the elephant? £20 for the session and £200 for the couch.

My son has never been to a psychiatrist. Why? What's wrong with him?

My wife thinks she's the Queen of England. Have you ever told her she isn't? What, and blow my chances of a knighthood?

Patient: My family thinks there's something wrong with me because I love pancakes.
Psychiatrist: But there's nothing wrong with that. I myself love pancakes.
Patient: Really? Then you must come and see me! I've got trunks and trunks full of them!

I had a very friendly psychiatrist. In fact, he was so friendly he used to lie down on the couch with me.

A man bought a hat and afterwards complained that when he put it on he could hear music. He mentioned it to his doctor who, deciding to humour him, gave him the address of a psychiatrist. The man called and explained his trouble, saying that whenever he wore the hat he could hear a tune being played. The psychiatrist took the hat and went into another room and returning in a few moments said, 'Now try it on.' The man did so and exclaimed, 'Wonderful! Music's gone! What did you do?' Said the psychiatrist: 'I merely removed the band!'

Why did the Siamese twins go to a shrink? They were co-dependent.

Nerve is going to a psychiatrist because of a split personality and asking for a group rate.

How many psychiatrists does it take to change a light bulb? One. But the light bulb has to really want to change.

A man thought he was a dog, so he went to see a psychiatrist. 'It's terrible,' said the man. 'I walk around on all fours, I keep barking in the middle of the night and I can't go past a lamp-post any more.' 'Okay,' said the psychiatrist. 'Get on the couch.' The man replied, 'I'm not allowed on the couch.'

How many psychoanalysts does it take to screw in a light bulb? How many do you think it takes?

Q. **WHAT ARE THE DIFFERENCES BETWEEN PSYCHOLOGISTS, PSYCHO-ANALYSTS AND PSYCHIATRISTS?**
A. **PSYCHOLOGISTS BUILD CASTLES IN THE AIR, PSYCHOANALYSTS LIVE IN THEM AND PSYCHIATRISTS COLLECT THE RENT!**

A man went to a psychiatrist and confessed that he had suicidal tendencies. 'I suddenly get the urge to kill myself,' he said. 'I never know when these feelings are going to occur.' 'Hmmm,' said the psychiatrist. 'Under the circumstances, perhaps you'd better pay in advance.'

Then there was the psychiatrist who woke up one morning to find himself under his bed. He decided he was a little potty.

Blessed Are the Sick

I take these tablets. They're not habit forming as long as you take one every day.

A man rushed into the chemist's and said to the assistant: 'Do you have anything that'll stop hiccups?' The assistant leaned over the counter and slapped the man's face. The man said: 'What did you do that for?' The assistant replied: 'Well, you don't have any hiccups now, do you?' And the man said: 'I never did have. I wanted something for my wife. She's out in the car.'

When a doctor doctors a doctor, does the doctor doing the doctoring doctor as the doctor being doctored wants to be doctored or does the doctor doing the doctoring doctor as he wants to doctor?

Doctor: This operation is quite routine and not at all complicated.
Patient: Well, just remember that when you send me the bill!

I knew I was in trouble when the doctor put on his best graveside manner.

A little honey is good for you – until your wife finds out.

An osteopath works his fingers to the bone.

Three old men were talking about their health problems. The 70-year-old said, 'My problem is I wake up every morning at seven and it takes me at least 20 minutes to pee.' The 80-year-old said, 'My problem is I get up at eight and it takes me at least half an hour to have a bowel movement.' The 90-year-old said, 'At seven I pee like a horse, and at eight I crap like a cow.' 'So what's your problem?' asked the others. 'I don't wake up till nine!'

Virus: a Latin word used by doctors and meaning 'Your guess is as good as mine.'

I sent her out to get something for my liver. She came back with a pound of onions.

I take a cold shower every morning – after the rest of my family has taken hot ones.

My health is so bad, my doctor has advised me not to start reading any serials.

My housemaid's knee has been giving me trouble. My wife caught me sitting on it.

A God-fearing man was close to death in hospital, so his family called in the priest. As the priest stood by the bed, the man's condition seemed to deteriorate and he motioned frantically for something to scribble on. The priest handed him a pen and paper and he quickly scribbled a note. No sooner had he finished writing than he died. The priest left the note for three quarters of an hour while the family came to terms with their grief. But as he prepared to leave the hospital, he said, 'I think now would be an appropriate time to read Bill's last note. It was obviously something which meant a lot to him, something he felt the need to say.' The priest opened the piece of paper and read aloud 'Hey, you, you're standing on my oxygen tube.'

You're coughing a lot more easily this morning. I should think so, I've been up all night practising!

I've been in bed all day with a hot-water bottle and a thermometer in my mouth. Well, there's certainly room for both.

Osteopath to woman patient: What's a joint like this doing in a girl like you?

The human body, with proper care, will last a lifetime.

Whenever I get the flu, I go to bed and take a bottle of whisky with me – within three or four hours it's gone. Mind you, I've still got the flu.

'Martha!' shouted frail little Sidney from his bed. 'I'm terribly sick, please call me a vet.' 'A vet?' queried Martha. 'Why do you want a vet and not a doctor?' 'Because,' replied Sidney, 'I work like a horse, live like a dog, and have to sleep with a silly cow!'

The doctor said I could get rid of my cold by drinking a glass of freezing orange juice after a hot bath. Really? And did it work? I don't know. I haven't finished drinking the hot bath yet.

To save money, our local hospital now gets its patients to make their own beds. When you check in, they give you a toolbox and some wood.

I had an operation and the surgeon left a sponge in me. Do you feel any pain? No, but I don't half get thirsty!

A man contracted a terrible disease of the penis in the Far East. Every European doctor he consulted told him that it would have to be amputated. As a desperate last resort, he went to see a doctor in Thailand which was, after all, the country where he had picked up the disease. The Thai doctor examined him closely and announced, 'There is no need to amputate your penis.' 'That's fantastic!' said the man. The Thai doctor continued. 'Any doctor worth his salt can see that it will drop off of its own accord in three weeks.'

Definition of a minor operation: one performed on somebody else.

This patient was so rich he wouldn't accept a local anaesthetic – he insisted on having a foreign one.

The operation was in the nick of time. In another two hours, the patient would have recovered.

They don't allow you to leave this private hospital until you're strong enough to face the accounts department.

I drink to your health when I'm with you, I drink to your health when alone; I drink to your health so often, I've just about wrecked my own!

Nobody is sicker than a man who is sick on his day off.

I haven't recovered from my operation yet. I've still got two more payments to go.

An old lady went to the doctor and asked for birth control pills. 'Why do you want them at your age?' asked the doctor. 'They help me sleep better,' replied the old lady. 'How come?' 'Well, doctor, I put them in my granddaughter's orange juice, and I sleep better at night.'

I reckon old Harry will be in hospital for some time yet. Why, have you seen his doctor? No, I've seen his nurse.

What did they do before they invented X-ray machines? They used to hold up the patient to the light.

You have a cough? Go home, eat a whole box of Ex-Lax, and tomorrow you'll be afraid to cough. ***Pearl Williams***

He has an infinite capacity for faking pains.

My uncle was such a hypochondriac that he insisted on being buried next to a doctor.

The hypochondriac was complaining to his doctor that he was suffering from a fatal liver disease. 'Impossible,' said the doctor. 'You wouldn't be able to tell. With that disease, there's no pain and there's no discomfort.' And the patient said, 'But those are exactly my symptoms!'

Hypochondria is about the only disease she doesn't think she has.

Customer: Do you have some talcum powder?
Pharmacist: Certainly, sir, walk this way.
Customer: If I could walk that way, I wouldn't need the talcum powder.

He's never had a day's illness in his life. He always makes it last a week!

I'm afraid I've got Parkinson's disease – and he's got mine.

I've got this terrible headache. I was putting some toilet water on my hair and the lid fell down.

Hay fever is much achoo about nothing.

I called my acupuncturist and told him I was in terrible pain. He told me to take two safety pins and call him in the morning.

May you live to be as old as your jokes.

A young man woke up one morning to find a strange rash on his penis so he went to the doctor. The doctor gave him some cream to rub in and also advised him that exposing that part of his body to sunlight would help cure the infection. Since it was a nice day, the young man decided to go to a deserted beach and, with no one about, he thought he would follow the doctor's advice by stripping off. He lay on his back for a few minutes, soaking up the sunlight, but was startled to hear voices in the distance. To cover his embarrassment, he quickly dug a hole in the sand, broke off a reed from a plant for breathing purposes, and buried himself. However, because he wanted the infected organ to get as much sunlight as possible, he left it protruding through the sand. The voices turned out to be those of two old women. As they wondered along the beach, they spotted the curious shape sticking up through the sand and began to snigger. One said to the other, 'When I was young, I couldn't get enough of it. As I matured, I was even more desperate for it. When I aged, I even started to pay for it. Now, just my luck, it's growing wild and I'm too old to bend down!'

Q. Which of these doesn't fit in with the rest? AIDS, herpes, gonorrhoea, condominiums.
A. Gonorrhoea, because you can get rid of gonorrhoea.

My brother is a brilliant medical researcher. He's just invented a cure for which there is no known illness.

An old man went to the doctor for his annual check-up. The doctor listened to his heart and announced 'I'm afraid you have a serious heart murmur. Do you smoke at all?' 'No.' 'Do you drink to excess?' 'No.' 'Do you still have a sex life?' 'Yes.' 'Well, I'm sorry to have to tell you, that with this heart murmur, you'll have to give up half your sex life.' 'Which half – the looking or the thinking?'

There are two ways of dealing with the common cold: if you don't treat it, it lasts six or seven days, and if you do treat it, it lasts about a week.

Doctor: You need glasses.
Patient: How do you know?
Doctor: I could tell the moment you walked through that window.

A surgeon of some imprecision
Decided on self-circumcision
A slip of the knife –
'Oh, dear,' said his wife,
'Our sex life will need some revision!'

An elderly couple went to the doctor for their annual check-ups. The old man went in first, and after he was finished, the doctor sent him back out to the waiting room and called in the old woman. The doctor said, 'Before I examine you, I'd like to talk about your husband for a moment. I'm a bit concerned about him. I asked him how he was feeling and he said he had never felt better. He said that when he got up in the morning, he went to the bathroom, opened the door and God turned the light on for him. And when he was done, he shut the door and God turned the light out for him.' 'Oh no,' sighed the wife. 'He's been peeing in the fridge again.'

The latest wonder drug is so powerful, you have to be in perfect health to take it.

We live in a world of increasing medical specialisation. Today four out of five doctors recommend another doctor.

An 83-year-old man went to the doctor's and said: 'Doc, my sex drive is too high. I want it lowered.' The doctor couldn't believe what he was hearing. 'You're 83 and you want your sex drive lowered?' 'That's right,' said the man pointing to his head. 'It's all up here. I want it lowered.'

May you live to be a hundred – and then decide if you want to go on.

May you die in bed aged 97 shot by the jealous husband of a teenage wife.

Casey came home from the doctor looking very worried. His wife said, 'What's the problem?' 'The doctor told me I have to take a pill every day for the rest of my life,' he replied. She said, 'So what? Lots of people have to take a pill every their whole lives.' He said, 'I know, but he only gave me four pills.'

What's the definition of macho? Jogging home from your own vasectomy.

What is the best thing about Alzheimer's? You meet new people every day.

Why do nurses give Viagra to male patients in old folks' homes? To stop them rolling out of bed.

Cousin Arlo died of asbestosis – it took six months to cremate him.

Why do farts smell? So that deaf people can appreciate them too.

A man walked into a crowded doctor's office. As he approached the desk, the receptionist asked, 'Yes, Sir, may we help you?' 'There's something wrong with my dick,' he replied. The receptionist became aggravated and said, 'You shouldn't come into a crowded office and say something like that.' 'Why not? You asked me what was wrong and I told you,' he said. 'We do not use language like that here,' she said. 'Please go outside and come back in and say that there's something wrong with your ear or whatever.' The man walked out, waited several minutes and re-entered. The receptionist smiled smugly and asked, 'Yes?' 'There's something wrong with my ear,' he stated. The receptionist nodded approvingly. 'And what is wrong with your ear, sir?' 'I can't piss out of it,' the man replied.

What is the proper medical term for the circumcision of a rabbit? A hare cut.

A man went for a brain transplant and was offered the choice of two brains – an architect's for £10,000 and a politician's for £100,000. 'Does that mean the politician's brain is much better than the architect's?' asked the man. 'Not exactly,' replied the brain transplant salesman. ' It's just that the politician's has never been used.'

My allergy tests suggest that I may have been intended for life on some other planet.

Sam and John were out cutting wood, and John cut off his arm. Sam wrapped the arm in a plastic bag and took it and John to a surgeon. The surgeon said, 'You're in luck! I'm an expert at re-attaching limbs! Come back in four hours.' So Sam left and when he returned in four hours the surgeon said, 'I got done faster than I expected. John is down at the local pub.' Sam went to the pub and there was John throwing darts. A few weeks later, Sam and John were cutting wood again, and John cut off his leg. Sam put the leg in a plastic bag and took it and John back to the surgeon. The surgeon said, 'Legs are a little tougher. Come back in six hours.' Sam left and when he returned in six hours the surgeon said, 'I finished early. John's down at the soccer field.' Sam went to the soccer field and there was John, kicking goals. A few weeks later, John had a terrible accident and cut off his head. Sam put the head in a plastic bag and took it and the rest of John to the surgeon. The surgeon said, 'Oh dear. Now, heads are really tough. Come back in twelve hours.' So Sam left and when he returned in twelve hours the surgeon said, 'I'm sorry, John died.' Sam said, 'I understand – heads are tough.' The surgeon said, 'Oh, no! The surgery went fine. John suffocated in that plastic bag.'

Anybody who can swallow an aspirin at a drinking fountain deserves to get well.

Do you suffer from arthritis? Of course. What else can you do with it?

If exercise is so good for you, why do athletes have to retire by the age of 35?

What's the best thing about having Alzheimer's disease? You never have to watch reruns on television.

Apparently, this woman's miniature Schnauzer had an infection in its ear. The vet told her that it was due to an ingrown hair and that the best treatment would be to remove the hair with a depilatory cream. The woman went to a pharmacy and asked the pharmacist for assistance in selecting the appropriate product. He went on about how some depilatory creams were better for use on the legs and how some were gentler and better for removing facial hair. Then he said, 'May I ask where you intend to use this?' She replied, 'Well, it's for my Schnauzer.' He said, 'Okay, but you shouldn't ride a bike for two weeks.'

When Chris swallowed a boomerang he returned home from hospital and was re-admitted 98 times.

Quick Quips 4

First the doctor told me the good news: I was going to have a disease named after me. ***Steve Martin***

Death is nature's way of telling you to slow down. ***Dick Sharples***

A psychiatrist is a man who goes to a strip club and watches the audience. ***Merv Stockwood***

No one can feel as helpless as the owner of a sick goldfish. ***Kin Hubbard***

I went to the doctor because I'd swallowed a bottle of sleeping pills. He told me to have a few drinks and get some rest. ***Rodney Dangerfield***

My kid is a born doctor. Nobody can read anything he writes. ***Henny Youngman***

I went to the doctor and said, 'Doctor, every morning when I get up and I look in the mirror, I feel like throwing up. What's wrong with me?' The doctor said, 'I don't know, but your eyesight's perfect.' ***Rodney Dangerfield***

Everything that used to be a sin is now a disease. ***Bill Maher***

I have Bright's disease and he has mine. ***S J Perelman***

I personally stay away from health foods. At my age, I need all the preservatives I can get! ***George Burns***

Doctors are just the same as lawyers; the only difference is that lawyers merely rob you, whereas doctors rob you and kill you too. ***Anton Chekhov***

Physician: one upon whom we set our hopes when ill and our dogs when well.
Ambrose Bierce

I personally stay away from health foods. At my age, I need all the preservatives I can get! ***George Burns***

The only way to keep your health is to eat what you don't want, drink what you don't like and do what you'd rather not. ***Mark Twain***

The best cure for hypochondria is to forget about your own body and get interested in somebody else's. ***Goodman Ace***

The art of medicine consists of amusing the patient while Nature cures the disease.
Voltaire

Attention to health is the greatest hindrance to life.
Plato

One of the first duties of the physician is to educate the masses not to take medicine.
William Osler

After two days in hospital, I took a turn for the nurse.
Rodney Dangerfield

I asked my doctor if I should have a vasectomy. He said let a sleeping dog lie. The last time I had sex my self-winding watch stopped.
Lenny Rush

My doctor has a great stress test. It's called 'The Bill'.
Joey Adams

The thing that bothers me about doctors is they give you an appointment six weeks ahead, then they examine you, then they ask, 'Why did you wait so long to see me?'
Joey Adams

My doctor is wonderful. Once, in 1955, when I couldn't afford an operation, he touched up the X-rays.
Joey Bishop

Medical science has made a lot of progress with new miracle drugs. No matter what illness you have, the doctor can keep you alive long enough for you to pay your bill. ***Joey Adams***

The doctor explained to the heart patient that he would be able to resume his romantic life as soon as he could climb two flights of stairs without becoming winded. The patient listened attentively and said: 'What if I look for a woman who lives on the ground floor?'
Joey Adams

I'd like to be an obstetrician. Look at all the guys you have working for you all the time.
Bert Henry

I went to the doctor. I said: 'Doc, my foot, I can't walk!' He said: 'You'll be walking before the day is out.' He took my car. ***Buddy Hackett***

I'd collapse – but I'm too weak. ***Harry Hershfield***

A psychiatrist is a fellow who asks you a lot of expensive questions your wife asks you for nothing. ***Joey Adams***

A hospital bed is a parked taxi with the meter running.
Groucho Marx

My sister's got asthma. In the middle of an attack she got an obscene phone call. The guy said, 'Did I call you or did you call me?' ***John Mendoza***

There are people who strictly deprive themselves of each and every edible, drinkable and smokable which has in any way acquired a shady reputation. They pay this price for health, and health is all they get for it. ***Mark Twain***

If penicillin is a wonder drug, how come it can't cure bread mould? ***Ron Smith***

Today's hospitals don't kid around. I won't say what happens if you don't pay a bill, but did you ever have your tonsils put back in? ***Joey Adams***

They try to humiliate you in the hospital. They make you pee in a bottle. I hate that. I was in the hospital. The nurse said, 'You have to pee in this bottle.' She left and I filled it with Mountain Dew. She came back and I chugged it. She was puking for days. It's a sick world and I'm a happy guy! ***Larry Reeb***

My aunt, she's had a terrible time. First off she got tonsillitis, followed by appendicitis and pneumonia. After that she got rheumatism, and to top it off they gave her hypodermics and inoculations. I thought she would never get through that spelling bee. ***Judy Canova***

I said, 'Officer, I'm speeding because I'm taking my mom to the hospital. She OD'd onreducing pills.' He said, 'I don't see any woman in the car with you.' I said, 'I'm too late.' ***Emo Philips***

I had general anaesthesia. That's so weird. You go to sleep in one room and then you wake up four hours later in a totally different room. Just like college. ***Ross Shafer***

If I'm ever stuck on a respirator or life support system I would definitely want to be unplugged - but not until I'm down to a size eight. ***Henriette Mantel***

It's a good thing I'm covered by Red, White and Blue Cross. I was operated on at a great hospital – Our Lady of Malpractice. Five years ago they spent three million dollars on a recovery room. It hasn't been used yet. After the operation, the doctor told me, 'Soon, your sex life's gonna be terrific – especially the one in the winter.'
Milton Berle

I don't blame hospitals for trying to keep costs down, but I really think a coin-operated bed pan is going a little too far. ***Joey Adams***

My superiority complex turned out to be an inferiority complex. I said, 'Great, that makes me the least of my problems.' ***Sara B Sirius***

I was in analysis. I was suicidal. As a matter of fact, I would have killed myself, but I was in analysis with a strict Freudian and if you kill yourself they make you pay for the sessions you miss.
Woody Allen

'I wouldn't worry about your son playing with dolls,' the doctor told the middle-aged matron. She said, 'I'm not worried, but his wife is very upset.' ***Joey Adams***

I went to this conference for bulimics and anorexics. It was a nightmare. The bulimics ate the anorexics. It's okay – they were back again ten minutes later. ***Monica Piper***

Right now I'm having amnesia and déjà vu at the same time. I think I've forgotten this before.
Steven Wright

To ward off disease or recover health, man as a rule finds it easier to depend on healers than to attempt the more difficult task of living wisely.
Rene Dubos

Doctors are men who prescribe medicines of which they know little, to cure diseases of which they know less, in human beings of whom they know nothing.
Voltaire

Never go to a doctor whose office plants have died.
Erma Bombeck

Anyone who goes to a psychiatrist ought to have his head examined. ***Sam Goldwyn***

Psychiatrist: a person who pulls habits out of rats.
Dr Douglas Bush

God heals, and the doctor takes the fee. ***Benjamin Franklin***

sport

Leather on Willow

'I have learnt some of white man's magic,' said the tribal chief on returning to his country after a brief stay in England. 'What?' asked his brother. 'First, you must make a smooth piece of ground and get grass to grow on it. Then you carefully tend the grass. After that you place some sticks in the grass and get some men to put on all-white clothes. Two of the men have to carry pieces of wood called 'bats' and another man has to carry a red ball. After a bit of running about between the sticks by two of the men and some throwing of the red ball, it will rain.'

I used to play under the worst captain ever. He always used to put me in to bat in the middle of a hat-trick!

In the 1970s, two dedicated Yorkshiremen were at the match. One discovered that he'd left his wallet at home and his friend offered to go back for it. He returned pale and shaken. 'I've got bad news for thee, Bob. Your wife's run off and left thee, and your house 'as burned to the ground!' 'I've got worse news for thee, lad,' said the other, 'Boycott's out.'

Our wicket-keeper is absolutely hopeless. The only thing he caught all season was a cold.

Although it isn't generally known, there was once an industrial dispute during a test match at the Oval. As a result of it, the batsmen became the first ever union to come out on a non-strike.

Why do they call it a hat-trick? Because it's always peformed by a bowler.

His wife was in full flow: 'Cricket, cricket, cricket – that's all you ever think about. What about us? I bet you can't even tell me what day we were married!' 'Yes I can,' replied the husband. 'It was the day Botham scored 147 against the Australians!'

What happens to a cricketer when his eyesight begins to fail? He applies to be an umpire.

The teacher asked a class to write a brief account of a cricket match. Soon all the children were very engrossed except for one boy who finished his essay in record time. When the teacher saw it, he understood. It read: 'Rain stopped play.'

The captain of a team says to the umpire, 'My players want to know if there is a penalty for thinking.' The Umpire says, 'No.' The captain says, 'Well we think you're an asshole, then.'

Cricket: casting the ball at three straight sticks and defending the same with a fourth. ***Rudyard Kipling***

Jones had taken his wife to a cricket match. She sat through the first innings although plainly bored. In the second innings a batsman gave a tremendous swipe and knocked the ball out of the ground. 'Thank goodness they got rid of it,' she sighed. 'Now we can all go home.'

The two rival cricketers were talking. 'The local team wants me to play for them very badly.' 'Well, you're just the man for the job.'

At the interval, everybody rushed to the bar, where the local publican had thoughtfully provided a case of light ale. Unfortunately, the ale was off and half way through the second innings, everyone was so ill that they abandoned the match. It was a case of bad light stopping play.

The insects were having their annual cricket match. The captain was a grasshopper, who turned to the cricket and said, 'Are you a bowler?' 'Of course,' said the cricket. 'Who ever heard of a cricket bat?'

Sporting Double Entendres

US PGA Commentator: *'One of the reasons Arnie [Arnold Palmer] is playing so well is that, before each tee shot, his wife takes out his balls and kisses them... Oh my God! What have I just said?'*

Metro Radio: *'Julian Dicks is everywhere. It's like they've got eleven Dicks on the field.'*

Harry Carpenter at the Oxford-Cambridge boat race 1977: *'Ah, isn't that nice. The wife of the Cambridge President is kissing the Cox of the Oxford crew.'*

New Zealand Rugby Commentator: *'Andrew Mehrtens loves it when Daryl Gibson comes inside of him.'*

Pat Glenn, weightlifting commentator: *'And this is Gregoriava from Bulgaria. I saw her snatch this morning and it was amazing!'*

Cricket Explained

You have two sides one out in the field and one in. Each man that's in the side that's in goes out and when he's out he comes in and the next man goes in until he's out. When they are all out the side that's out comes in and the side that's been in goes out and tries to get those coming in out. Sometimes you get men still in and not out. When both sides have been in and out including the not outs, that's the end of the game!

A Yorkshireman had emigrated to America, but still used to receive news from home by mail. One day, he got the following telegram: 'Regret father died this morning STOP early hours. Funeral Wednesday STOP Yorkshire two hundred and one for six STOP Boycott not out ninety six.'

What is the difference between a rain barrel and a bad fielder? One catches drops; the other drops catches.

The batsman had been out off the third ball and was back in the pavilion taking an early lunch of fish and chips. 'I don't think much of this batter,' he complained. 'You should talk,' replied the waitress.

Q: **WHICH CRICKET TEAM PLAYS WHILE HALF DRESSED?**
A: **THE VEST INDIES.**

A cricket enthusiast died and went to Hell. After a few days, the Devil came up to him and said, 'What do you feel like doing today? You can have anything you like.' 'Well,' said the cricketer, 'I can think of nothing better than a game of cricket. Can we do that?' 'Certainly,' said the Devil, and off they went to get changed. They arrived at a beautiful pitch, and the batsman in his new gear took up a stance. Nothing happened. 'Come on then,' he said to the Devil, 'bowl the first ball.' 'Ah, that's the Hell of it,' said the Devil. 'We haven't got any balls.'

I bowl so slow that if after I have delivered the ball and don't like the look if it, I can run after it and bring it back.

J M Barrie

The two club members were talking. 'What were the statistical records of the team's tour?' 'Well, as far as we can remember – about 387 gallons of beer and 47 pubs.'

A Different Angle

There's this drunk guy who decides that he wants to go fishing. He packs up all his tackle and sets out in search of a suitable spot. Eventually, he stumbles across a huge area of ice and decides that he'll give it a go. Taking out a saw from his tackle box, he starts to saw a hole. Suddenly, a loud voice booms out at him, 'There's no fish in here.' The drunk looks all around him but can't see anyone. He decides to ignore the voice and carries on sawing. Again, the voice booms out, 'I've told you once, there's no fish in here!' He looks up again but there's still no sign of anyone so he returns to his task. 'Stop it!' shouts the now very angry sounding voice. 'You'd better pack up your stuff and get out of here or there'll be trouble.' 'Who are you?' shouts the drunk guy. 'You don't scare me!' 'Look,' replies the voice, 'I'm the manager of this ice rink!'

Fishing is a jerk on one end of the line waiting for another jerk at the other.

Hey, can't you read? That notice says 'Private – no fishing'. But I wouldn't be so rude as to read a private notice.

Henry's son, David, burst into the house, crying. His mother asked him what the problem was. 'Daddy and I were fishing, and he hooked a giant fish. Really big. Then, while he was reeling it in, the line broke and the fish got away.' 'Now come on, David,' his mother said, 'a big boy like you shouldn't be crying about an accident like that. You should have just laughed it off.' 'But that's just what I did, Mummy.'

Good fishing is just a matter of timing. You have to get there yesterday.

One recent Sunday, a young boy arrived late to his Sunday school class. His teacher knew that the boy was usually very prompt and asked him if anything was wrong. The boy replied no, that he was going to go fishing, but that his dad told him that he needed to go to church instead. The teacher was very impressed and asked the boy if his father had explained to him why it was more important to go to church rather than to go fishing. To which the boy replied, 'Yes, he did. My dad said that he didn't have enough bait for both of us.'

First fisherman: Remember, it's a secret.
Second fisherman: Okay, I won't tell a sole.

Last week I caught a fish so big I nearly dislocated my shoulders just describing it.

A fisherman was fishing a lake that he had never had any luck on, but this day he was catching a fish, it seemed, on every other cast. When he was done for the day, he had caught way too many fish over the limit but he decided he would keep them all even though he would be breaking the law. Half way home the game warden pulled him over and asked to see his fish. When the man showed the warden the fish the warden yelled 'You've caught too many!' The fisherman said calmly, 'Those are not fish out of the lake.' He stated they were his pet fish and that every day he let them go in the lake to feed. The warden, not believing this, said, 'How do you get them back?' The fisherman then explained that he would whistle and they jumped into his boat one by one. Well, the warden, having heard every excuse in the book, said he wanted to see this. So the two of them went out on the lake and stopped in a cove. The warden told him to let the fish go, and cooperating, the man let all his fish go. After a couple of minutes, the warden told him to whistle and get the fish back. Very calmly the fisherman replied, 'What fish?'

Things You Should Never Say at a Strange Tackle Shop

- 'All right, whose going to be a sport and show me their favourite fishing hole?'
- 'Anyone know who owns the red pick-up out front that I just hit?'
- About the shop's merchandise 'Look at all this antique tackle.'
- 'Let me tell you about a fish I once caught...'
- 'What! No high-tech lures? How can you people catch anything?'
- 'You do take travellers' cheques, don't you?'
- 'Your rods look as if they were wrapped at the Lighthouse Project for the Blind.'
- About a picture hung behind the cash register: 'Are those some ugly fish you caught or is that a family portrait?'
- 'I only use imported hooks.'
- 'I need a new rod. Do you have anything in blue to match my reel?'
- When a woman walks into the shop: 'Want to see my lure?'

You've been watching me fish for three hours now. Why don't you try fishing yourself? I couldn't. I haven't got the patience.

The great thing about fishing is that it gives you something to do while you're not doing anything.

Tony and Harold, two avid fisherman and well-known drunks, were out in a boat on their favourite lake one day drowning some worms and polishing off some brews. Suddenly, Tony got what he thought was a nibble. Reeling it in, he found a bottle with a cork in it. Naturally curious, he uncorked the bottle and a large genie appeared. The genie said, 'I'll grant you one wish.' Tony thought for a second and said, 'I wish this whole lake was beer.' His wish came true! The lake was now filled with their favourite brew. Harold looked at Tony in disgust: 'You asshole, now we have to piss in the boat.'

There are two types of fisherman: those who fish for sport and those who catch something.

There's a fine line between fishing and standing on the shore looking like an idiot.

Steven Wright

Hey, you're not allowed to fish here! But I'm not fishing. I'm teaching my worm to swim.

How many fish have you caught so far? Well, when I've caught another, I'll have one.

Two avid fishermen go on a fishing trip. They rent all the equipment: the reels, the rods, the wading suits, the boat, the car, and even a cabin in the woods. They spend a fortune. The first day they go fishing, but they don't catch anything. The same thing happens on the second day and the third day too. It goes on like this until finally, on the last day of their holiday, one of the men catches a fish. As they're driving home they're really depressed. One guy turns to the other and says, 'Do you realise that this one lousy fish we caught cost us £1,500?' The other guy says, 'Wow! It's a good thing we didn't catch any more!'

The Not-so-beautiful Game

My son has the making of a football hooligan: he threw a bottle at the referee yesterday. I wouldn't mind, but he broke the screen.

A keen football fan was about to be a father for the first time. His friend asked, 'What if your wife is having the baby on the same day as the match?' 'No problem, I've just bought a video recorder. So I can watch the birth after the game.'

Why did the chicken run on to the football pitch? Because the referee blew for a fowl.

The elephants were playing the ants at football. It was a close match but when the ants' star player dribbled towards goal, an elephant defender lumbered over towards him, trod on him and killed him. 'What did you do that for?' demanded the referee. 'I didn't mean to kill him,' said the elephant, 'I was just trying to trip him up.'

Striker: I had an open goal – but still I didn't score! I could kick myself!
Manager: I wouldn't bother. You'd probably miss.

A football goalkeeper was walking along the street one day when he heard screams from a nearby building. He looked up to see smoke billowing from a fourth-floor window and a woman leaning out holding a baby. 'Help! Help!' screamed the woman. 'I need someone to catch my baby!' A crowd of onlookers had gathered, but none was confident about catching a baby dropped from such a great height. Then the goalkeeper stepped forward. 'I'm a professional goalkeeper!' he called to the woman. 'I'm renowned for my safe hands. Drop the baby and I will catch it. For me, it will be just like catching a ball.' The woman agreed: 'Okay! When I drop my baby, treat it as if you were catching a ball!' On a count of three, the woman dropped the baby. Everyone held their breath as the goalkeeper lined himself up to catch it. There was a huge sigh of relief, followed by wild cheering as the goalkeeper caught the baby safely in his arms. Then he bounced it twice on the ground and kicked it 50 yards down the street.

For a minute we were in with a great chance. Then the game started.

Burglars recently broke into the Dimchester Rovers ground and stole the entire contents of the trophy room. Police are looking for a man with a blue and white carpet.

Harry: Our captain is a man with polish.
Larry: Only on his boots!

Wife: Football, football, football! That's all you ever think about! If you said you were going to stay at home one Saturday afternoon to help with the housework, I think I'd drop dead from the shock!
Husband: It's no good trying to bribe me, dear.

A friend of mine always books two seats when he goes to watch Chelsea. That's one to sit in and one to throw when the fighting starts.

Snow White arrived home one evening to find her house destroyed by fire. She was doubly worried because she'd left all seven dwarfs asleep inside. As she scrambled among the wreckage, frantically calling their names, suddenly she heard the cry: 'Chelsea for the Cup!' 'Thank goodness,' sobbed Snow White. 'At least Dopey's still alive!'

As far as his team's concerned, he's the eternal optimist. He says they can still get promotion if they win eleven out of their last four games.

He's got one of the least demanding jobs in the country. He's the official scorer for Plymouth Argyle.

A team of mammals was playing a team of insects. The mammals totally dominated the first half and at half-time were leading 39-nil. However, at half-time the insects made a substitution and brought on a centipede. The centipede scored no less than 180 goals and the insects won the game by miles. In the dressing room afterwards, the captain of the mammals was chatting to the insect captain. 'That centipede of yours is terrific,' the captain of the mammals said. 'Why didn't you play him from the start?' 'We'd have liked to,' replied the insect captain, 'but it takes him 45 minutes to get his boots on.'

My local team are so starved of success that they do a lap of honour every time they get a corner.

Sports journalist: Tell me more gossip about the goings-on at Rovers.
Rovers player: I can't. I've already told you more than I've heard myself.

When the manager of a Third Division club started to discuss tactics, some of the team thought he was talking about a new kind of peppermint.

Why did the chicken cross the road? Football managers explain:

Arsene Wenger
From my position in the dug-out I did not see the incident clearly so I cannot really comment. However, I do think that he gets picked on by opposition players and fans who are clearly chickenophobic.

David O'Leary
To be fair, he's just a baby chicken really and crossing the road is just a big exciting adventure for him. He'll enjoy the experience as long as it lasts and learn from it, but I don't seriously expect him to cross it this season.

Sir Alex Ferguson
As far as I'm concerned he crossed the road at least a minute early according to my watch.

George Graham
I want good, solid team chickens who'll cross the road in a straight line when they're told and how they're told. There's no room at this club for a prima donna chicken running around aimlessly – he's not worth it!

Gianluca Vialli
When the fish are down, he'll just be one of the chaps. It doesn't matter to me whether he's an Italian, French or English chicken as long as he's willing to die on the pitch for Chelsea.

Peter Reid
Just cross the f***ing road, you chicken f***!

Glenn Hoddle
The chicken was hit by the lorry when crossing the road because in a previous life it had been a bad chicken.

Brian Clough
If God had wanted chickens to cross roads he'd have put corn in the tarmac. Anyway, I'm more interested in Wild Turkey.

Ron Atkinson
Spotter's badge, Clive. For me, Chicko's popped up at the back stick, little eyebrows, and gone bang! And I'll tell you what – I've got a sneaking feeling that this road's there to be crossed.

Ruud Gullit
I am hoping to see some sexy poultry.

Alex Ferguson calls David Beckham into his office. 'David,' he says, 'I'm worried about your performance the last few games. You've been hopeless, completely off form.' 'Sorry, boss', says David. 'I've not been myself lately. I've got a few problems at home.' 'Oh dear,' says Ferguson, pretending to care. 'What's up? Posh and kids okay?' 'Oh, they're fine,' says David. 'It's just that something's really bugging me and I'm losing sleep and everything. I can't concentrate on my football and it's really messing me up.' 'Whatever's the matter, David?' says Fergie. 'Well, boss,' says David, 'it's pretty serious. You see I'm really stuck on this jigsaw and...' 'A jigsaw?' shouts Alex. 'You're f*****g up every time you play because of a bloody jigsaw?' 'Yeah, boss, but you don't understand, it's really doing my head in,' says David. 'It's really hard and it's this picture of a tiger and it looks really good on the box and I'm sure I've got all the bits and everything but I just can't get it right and it's doing my head in and I even had my hair cut to try and cool my brain down and...' 'David, David, David,' says Ferguson. 'You've got to get a grip. It's affecting our games and nothing is as important as Manchester United's success, other than Roy Keane's wages, obviously.' 'Yeah, boss,' says David, 'but it's this picture of a tiger and it looks really good on the box and I really want to finish it but it's really hard and it's doing my head in and it's this picture ... and it's a tiger and it's hard ... and I can't make the bits fit and, er, it's really hard, er, boss and, er, it's a tiger, er ... on the box ... er ... boss.' Ferguson waits until even Beckham realises he's repeating himself and has got nothing else to say which took a bit longer than usual. 'David,' he says. 'Bring the tiger jigsaw in and let's have a look at it. For Christ's sake, we've got to get you back to playing football.' 'Oh thanks, boss,' says David, 'that'd be really helpful 'cos it's really hard and it's a picture of a tiger and it's doing my head in, that tiger is.' So David brings the jigsaw into Ferguson's office. 'Here it is, boss,' he says, showing Ferguson the picture on the box. 'Look, boss, it's this tiger, right, and it's a really good picture and everything but I just can't do it and it's really hard and it's doing my head in and it's this picture here of a tiger,' says David, emptying all the pieces from the box all over Ferguson's desk. 'David,' sighs Ferguson, 'put the f*****g Frosties back in the box.'

Jerry: That goalie looks very heavy, but they say he's a light eater.
Terry: He is. As soon as it's light he goes and starts eating.

Some flies were playing football in a saucer, using a sugar lump as a ball. One of them said, 'We'll have to do better than this, lads. We're playing in the cup tomorrow.'

It had been a terrible season for Tottenham Hotspur and one of their fans was so depressed that he dressed up in his full Tottenham kit and threw himself into the Thames. When the police retrieved his body, they removed the strip and replaced it with stockings and suspenders. The police told the coroner that they did this 'in order to avoid embarrassing the family'.

I've started watching Luton Town. My doctor said I should avoid any excitement.

A football coach walked into the locker room before a big game, looked over to his star player and said, 'I'm not supposed to let you play since you failed maths, but we really need you in there. So, what I have to do is ask you a maths question, and if you get it right, you can play.' The player agreed, so the coach looked into his eyes intently and asked, 'Okay, now concentrate hard and tell me the answer to this: What is two plus two?' The player thought for a moment and then answered, 'Four?' 'Did you say four?' the coach exclaimed, excited that he had given the right answer. Suddenly, all the other players on the team began screaming, 'Come on coach, give him another chance!'

Q. **WHY DO FOOTBALLERS PLAY ON ARTIFICIAL TURF?**
A. **TO KEEP THEM FROM GRAZING.**

Football Anagrams:

- → Alex Ferguson – Sex organ fuel
- → David Ginola – A livid gonad
- → John McGinlay – Sperm launching joy
- → Andy Gray – Randy Gay
- → Robbie Elliott – Better boil oil
- → Teddy Sheringham – He'd shag dirty men
- → Nathan Blake – An ankle bath
- → Stan Collymore – Measly control
- → Paul Merson – Lump on arse
- → Peter Shilton – Enter hot lips
- → Martin Keown – I'm not wanker
- → Peter Beardsley – Beery plastered
- → Maine Road – I am a drone, A dire moan, No! I am a red
- → Neil Cox – Lexicon
- → Karlheinz Reidle – He killer red Nazi
- → Match Of The Day – They of mad chat
- → George Best – Go get beers
- → Gudni Bergsson – Undressing bog, Guns on bridges
- → Fabrizio Ravanelli – Evil Brazilian afro
- → Gareth Southgate – Treat to huge shag
- → David Lee – Evil Dead
- → Dennis Bergkamp – Pink German beds

What beverage do football players drink? Penal-tea!

Football fans have encyclopaedic memories when it comes to their favourite sport. A friend of mine, for instance, can tell you the nationality of every player in the England squad.

Manchester United have apparently set up a call centre for fans who are troubled by their current form. The number is 0800 10 10 10. Calls charged at peak rate for overseas users. Once again the number is 0800 won nothing won nothing won nothing.

Q: **HOW DOES BECKHAM CHANGE A LIGHTBULB?**
A: **HE HOLDS IT IN THE AIR, AND THE WORLD REVOLVES AROUND HIM.**

Three Liverpool Supporters were in a pub and spotted a United fan at the bar. The first one said he was going to piss him off. He walked over to the United fan and tapped him on the shoulder. 'Hey Manc, I hear your David Beckham is a poof'. 'Really? I didn't know that'. Puzzled, the Scouser walked back to his buddies. 'I told him Beckham was a poof and he didn't care!' 'You just don't know how to set him off, watch and learn'. The second Scouser walked over and tapped the United fan on the shoulder. 'Hey Manc, I hear your David Beckham is a transvestite poof!' 'Oh, Christ I wasn't aware of that, thanks.' Shocked beyond belief, the Scouser went back to his buddies. 'You're right. He's unshakeable!' The third Scouser said, 'No, no, no, I will really piss him off, you just watch.' The Scouser walked over to the United fan tapped him on the shoulder and said, 'Hey Manc, I hear your David Beckham is a Liverpool supporter!' 'Apparently so. Just as your mates said earlier.'

First fan: I wish I'd brought the piano to the stadium.
Second fan: Why would you bring a piano to the football game?
First fan: Because I left the tickets on it.

Our club manager won't stand for any nonsense. Last Saturday he caught a couple of fans climbing over the stadium wall. He was furious. He grabbed them by the collars and said, 'Now you just get back in there and watch the game till it finishes.'

'My wife would make a great goalie,' one man said to his friend. 'I haven't scored for months.'

Who to Blame:

Ball – Striker's scapegoat
Defender – Goalkeeper's scapegoat
Goalkeeper – Defender's scapegoat
Midfielder – Everybody's scapegoat

A rather dim fan arrives at a football match midway through the second half. 'What's the score?' he asks his friend as he settles into his seat. 'Nil-nil,' comes the reply. 'And what was the score at half-time?' he asks.

A bad football team is like an old bra – no cups and little support.

At a local derby between Arsenal and Spurs last season, a spectator suddenly found himself in the thick of dozens of flying bottles. 'There's nothing to worry about, lad,' said the elderly chap standing next to him. 'It's like the bombs during the war. You won't get hit unless the bottle's got your name on it.' 'That's just what I'm worried about,' said the fan. 'My name's Johnny Walker.'

Angry neighbour: Didn't you hear me banging on your wall last night?
Bleary-eyed neighbour: That's all right – we had a bit of a party after the match and we were making quite a lot of noise ourselves.

We've got the best football team in the country – unbeaten and no goals scored against us! How many games have you played? The first one's next Saturday.

In a crucial Cup semi-final a few years ago, the capacity crowd of 30,000 watched a rather diminutive striker get possession of the ball early in the second half. He was immediately tackled by three large defenders, and went down under a pile of thrashing arms and legs. Emerging dazed from the melée a few moments later, he looked round at the crowded stands and gasped, 'How did they all get back in their seats so quickly?'

At the end of the day, football means not having to go to Sainsbury's on Saturday.

Football is a game in which a handful of men run around for one and a half hours watched by millions of people who could really use the exercise.

A great footballer was tragically killed and arriving at Heaven's gates, he came face to face with the angel on duty. 'Is there any reason why you shouldn't be allowed to enter the Kingdom of Heaven?' asked the angel. 'Well,' said the footballer, 'there was one time when I cheated in a major international football game. 'I see,' said the angel, 'tell me about it.' 'Well,' said the footballer, 'I was playing for Wales against France and I used my hand to push the ball past a French defender. The referee didn't see it and I went on to score.' 'And what was the final score?' asked the angel. 'That was the only goal,' said the footballer, 'We won one-nil.' 'Well, that's not too serious. I think we can let you in,' said the angel. 'Oh terrific!' exclaimed the footballer, 'It's been on my mind for years. Thanks a lot, St Peter.' 'That's okay,' said the angel, ushering the footballer in, 'and by the way, it's St Peter's day off today, I'm St David.'

Why are there fouls in football? Same reason there are ducks in cricket.

The local football team was having a dreadful season. They hadn't won a game for twelve weeks and the manager was at the end of his tether. 'Look,' suggested a friend one evening, 'why don't you take the whole squad out for a ten mile run every day?' 'What good will that do?' moaned the manager. 'Well,' replied his friend, 'today's Sunday. By next Saturday they'll be 60 miles away and you won't have to worry about them.'

Humpty Dumpty sat on the wall – so the referee booked him.

'Dad, dad!' cried Philip, as he arrived home one evening. 'I think I've been selected for the school football team!' 'That's good,' said his father. 'But why do you only think you've been selected? Aren't you sure? What position are you playing?' 'Well,' replied Philip, 'it's not been announced officially, but I overheard the football coach tell my teacher that if I was in the team I'd be a great draw-back.'

Sports Roundup 1:

'Barcelona ... a club with a stadium that seats 120,000 people. And they're all here in Newcastle tonight!'
'Ronaldo is always very close to being either onside or offside.'
'We were a little bit outnumbered there, it was two against two.'
'You weigh up the pros and cons and try to put them into chronological order.'
'Robert Lee was able to do some running on his groin for the first time.'
'I never comment on referees and I'm not going to break the habit of a lifetime for that prat.'
'I'm not a believer in luck but I do believe you need it.'
'What will you do when you leave football, Jack? Will you stay in football?'
'Unfortunately, we keep kicking ourselves in the foot.'
'Celtic were at one time nine points ahead, but somewhere along the road, their ship went off the rails.'
'I've got a gut feeling in my stomach...'
'The Uruguayans are losing no time in making a meal around the referee.'

A player was being ticked off by the coach for missing a very easy goal kick. 'All right,' said the player, 'how should I have played the shot?' 'Under an assumed name,' snapped a defender.

What is football? It's been described as a game with 22 players, two linesmen and 20,000 referees.

The Oxford and Cambridge University student teams were due to play when one of the Oxford men had to drop out at short notice. 'Why don't we use Johnson, the head porter at Balliol?' suggested the Oxford captain to the selection committee. 'I've seen him play in a local amateur team and he's a brilliant striker – absolutely unstoppable. We can get him a set of colours and as long as he doesn't speak to anyone, we should be able to get away with it.' The committee thought this might be a little unethical but in desperation they agreed to the plan. They rigged out the Balliol porter and put him on the left wing. He was, as the Oxford captain had said, unstoppable, and they beat Cambridge 9-1, Johnson having scored eight of the goals single-handed. Afterwards in the bar, the Cambridge captain approached Johnson and said sportingly, 'Well done, old boy! A magnificent effort! By the way, what are you studying at Balliol?' The porter thought for a moment, then said brightly, 'Sums!'

Sports Roundup 2:

'The new West Stand casts a giant shadow over the entire pitch, even on a sunny day.'
'I would not say he [David Ginola] is the best left-winger in the Premiership, but there are none better.'
'Johnson has revelled in the 'hole' behind Dwight Yorke...'
'An inch or two either side of the post and that would have been a goal.'
'Both sides have scored a couple of goals, and both sides have conceded a couple of goals.'
'You don't score 64 goals in 86 games at the highest level without being able to score goals.'
'What's it like being in Bethlehem, the place where Christmas began? I suppose it's like seeing Ian Wright at Arsenal...'
'And we all know that in football if you stand still you go backwards...'
'I was saying the other day, how often the most vulnerable area for goalies is between their legs...'
'...an excellent player, but he [Ian Wright] does have a black side.'
'Tottenham are trying tonight to become the first London team to win this Cup. The last team to do so was the 1973 Spurs side.'

Is your goalkeeper getting any better? Not really. Last Saturday he let in five goals in the first ten minutes. He was so fed up when he failed to stop the fifth that he put his head in his hands – and dropped it!

What two things should a footballer never eat before breakfast? Lunch and dinner.

One of the top players in the Premier League was called as a character witness in a matrimonial case and, on being asked his profession, replied, 'I am the greatest footballer in the world!' After the case was over he came in for a good deal of teasing from his team mates. 'How could you stand up in court and say a thing like that?' they asked. 'Well,' he replied, 'you must remember I was under oath.'

Wayne: Why didn't you put a knife and fork on the table for your brother when you laid the table?
Jane: Because mum said that when he's been playing football he eats like a horse.

A match took place recently in Oxford between a local amateur team and a side made up of university tutors and professors. Before the match, the two captains faced each other while the referee flipped the coin to decide who would have choice of ends. The local team won the toss and, as the captain

Sports Roundup 3:

'The lad got over-excited when he saw the whites of the goalpost's eyes.'
'If you can't stand the heat in the dressing room, get out of the kitchen.'
'The lads really ran their socks into the ground.'
'He [Brian Liaudrup] wasn't just facing one defender – he was facing one at the front and one at the back as well.'
'It's now 1-1, an exact reversal of the score on Saturday.'
'...but Arsenal are quick to credit Bergkamp with laying on 75% of their nine goals.'
'We say 'educated left foot'; of course, there are many players with educated right foots.'
'That's twice now he [Terry Phelan] has got between himself and the goal.'
'Mark Hughes at his very best: he loves to feel people right behind him...'
'Gary always weighed up his options, especially when he had no choice.'
'The shot from Laws was precise but wide.'
'The game is balanced in Arsenal's favour.'

shook hands with his opposite number, he said sportingly, 'May the best team win!' The university captain, a professor of English, replied, 'You mean, may the better team win!'

Did you hear about the football captain in a minor league who was offered £1,000 to lose a game? It would have been against his principle to take the money but £1,000 against his principle looked pretty good so he took it.

Mary had a little lamb
Who played in goal a lot.
It let the ball go though its legs
So now it's in the pot.

An amateur team in the west of Ireland played a match against a team from the local monastery. Just before kick-off the visiting team, all of whom were monks, knelt down solemnly on the pitch, put their hands together and indulged in five minutes of silent prayer. The monastery then proceeded to trounce their hosts 9-0. After the match, the home team captain said, 'Well, boys, we've been out-played before but this is the first time we've ever been out-prayed!'

Young footballer: How do I stand for a test trial?
Selector: You don't stand, you grovel.

When is a footballer like a
grandfather clock?
When he's a striker.

Sports Roundup 4:

'We threw our dice into the ring and turned up trumps.'
'And I suppose Spurs are nearer to being out of the FA Cup now than any other time since the first half of this season, when they weren't ever in it anyway.'
'...and he crosses the line with the ball almost mesmerically tied to his foot with a ball of string...'
'I never make predictions and I never will.'
'And there's Ray Clemence looking as cool as ever out in the cold.'
'...and the news from Guadalajara, where the temperature is -5 degrees, is that Falcao is warming up.'
'If history is going to repeat itself I should think we can expect the same thing again.'
'I think that was a moment of cool panic there.'
'Beckenbauer really has gambled all his eggs.'
'Celtic manager Davie Hay still has a fresh pair of legs up his sleeve.'
'You have got to miss them to score sometimes.'
'Tottenham have impressed me. They haven't thrown in the towel even though they have been under the gun.'

It was only the fourth week of the season and United's new goalkeeper had already let in 27 goals. He was having a drink in a pub one night when a man approached him and said, 'I've been watching you play, son, and I think I might be able to help you.' 'Are you a trainer?' said the young goalkeeper hopefully. 'No,' said the stranger, 'I'm an optician.'

When one team scores early in the game, it often takes an early lead. ***Pat Marsde***

'I've been playing football professionally for ten years now. Of course, my father was dead set against my taking up the game at all. In fact he offered me £5,000 not to train.' 'Really? What did you do with the money?'

Their manager, Terry Neil, isn't here today, which suggests he is elsewhere.
Brian Moore

Two boys were playing with a new football on the road outside their house. 'Hey,' shouted their mother, 'where did you get that football?' 'We found it,' replied one of the boys. 'Are you sure it was lost?' asked the mother. 'Yes,' replied the boy, 'we saw some people looking for it.'

Sports Roundup 5:

'Souness gave Fleck a second chance and he grabbed it with both feet.'
'He's very fast and if he gets a yard ahead of himself nobody will catch him.'
'Merseyside derbies usually last 90 minutes and I'm sure today's won't be any different.'
'Many clubs have a question mark in the shape of an axe-head hanging over them.'
'I spent four indifferent years at Goodison Park, but they were great years.'
'Dumbarton player Steve McCahill has limped off with a badly cut forehead.'
'A contract on a piece of paper saying you want to leave is like a piece of paper saying you want to leave.'
'It was that game that put the Everton ship back on the road.'
'And Arsenal now have plenty of time to dictate the last few seconds.'
'Bobby Robson must be thinking of throwing some fresh legs on.'
'What makes this game so delightful is that when both teams get the ball they are attacking their opponent's goal.'

A black and white cat walked across the pitch in front of the team two weeks ago. Since then our luck has been very patchy.

A woman was reading a newspaper one morning and said to her husband, 'Look at this, dear. There's an article here about a man who traded his wife for a season ticket to Arsenal. You wouldn't do a thing like that, would you?' 'Of course I wouldn't!' replied her husband. 'The season's almost over.'

Glen: I had an argument with my sister. I wanted to watch football on TV and she wanted to watch a film.
Ben: What film did you see?

With the very last kick of the game, Bobby McDonald scored with a header.

Alan Parry

A fellow had arranged to take his girlfriend to a local match but unfortunately they were delayed and didn't arrive until nearly half-time. 'What's the score?' the lad asked a bystander. 'Nil-nil,' was the reply. 'Oh, good!' his girlfriend gushed. 'We haven't missed anything!'

Why was the mummy no good at football? He was too wrapped up in himself.

Sports Roundup 6:

'That's football, Mike. Northern Ireland have had several chances and haven't scored but England have had no chances and scored twice, and so they have not been able to improve their 100% record.'
'In terms of the Richter Scale this defeat was a force eight gale.'
'In comparison, there's no comparison.'
'I would also think that the action replay showed it to be worse than it actually was.'
'Mirandinha will have more shots this afternoon than both sides put together.'
'Newcastle, of course, unbeaten in their last five wins.'
'Football's not like an electric light. You can't just flick the switch and change from quick to slow.'
'Certain people are FOR me and certain people are PRO me.'
'I'm going to make a prediction – it could go either way.'
'And with four minutes gone, the score is already 0-0.'
'They have got their feet on the ground and if they stay that way they will go places.'
'I don't think there is anybody bigger or smaller than Maradona.'

Two football fans were up in court for fighting. One fan had bitten off part of the other's ear, and the judge told him he was fined £200. 'But it was self-defence,' he protested. The judge ignored him. 'Fined £200 and bound over to keep the peace for a year,' he pronounced. 'I can't do that,' said the fan. 'I threw it in a dustbin.'

What did the pitch say to the player? I hate it when people treat me like dirt.

And Meade had a hat-trick. He scored two goals.
Richard Whitmore

Boss: I thought you wanted the afternoon off to see your dentist.
Mr Brown: That's right.
Boss: Then how come I saw you leaving the football ground with a friend?
Mr Brown: That was my dentist.

Well, it's Ipswich nil, Liverpool two, and if that's the way the score stays then you've got to fancy Liverpool to win. ***Peter Jones***

First footballer: My girlfriend's really clever. She has brains enough for two.
Second footballer: Then she's obviously the girl for you!

Sports Roundup 7:

'Being naturally right-footed, he doesn't often chance his arm with his left foot.'
'Strangely, in slow motion replay, the ball seemed to hang in the air for even longer.'
'What I said to them at half-time would be unprintable on the radio.'
'If we played like this every week, we wouldn't be so inconsistent.'
'If there weren't such a thing as football, we'd all be frustrated footballers.'
'He's one of those footballers whose brains are in his head.'
'The crowd think that Todd handled the ball – they must have seen something that nobody else did.'
'I can see the carrot at the end of the tunnel.'
'They compare Steve McManaman to Steve Highway and he's nothing like him, but I can see why – it's because he's a bit different.'
'Glenn Hoddle hasn't been the Hoddle we know. Neither has Bryan Robson.'
'There's no way Ryan Giggs is another George Best. He's another Ryan Giggs.'
'I was disappointed to leave Spurs, but quite pleased I did.'

What's the difference between a flea-ridden dog and a bored football spectator? One's going to itch; the other's itching to go.

Bolton are on the crest of a slump. ***Anon***

A footballer was fond of going for long walks to help himself keep fit. 'Every day,' he said to his friend, 'my dog and I go for a tramp in the woods.' 'Does the dog enjoy it too?' asked the friend. 'Yes,' replied the footballer, 'but the tramp's getting a bit fed up.'

What's the best thing to do when a football is in the air? Use your head.

Micky: My brother's away training to be in a football team.
Nicky: Lucky thing! He must be quite grown up now.
Micky: Yes. He wrote the other day saying he'd grown another foot, so my mum is knitting him an extra sock.

A tourist visiting London stopped a man carrying a football and asked, 'How do I get to Wembley?' 'Practise', was the reply.

What did the ball say to the footballer? I get a kick out of you.

Two boys were walking past a house surrounded by a high wall when the owner came out holding a football. 'Is this your ball?' he demanded. 'Er, has it done any damage?' asked the first boy. 'No,' said the householder. 'Then it's ours,' said the second boy.

When can a footballer move as fast as Concorde? When he's inside it.

You couldn't have counted the number of moves Alan Ball made ... I counted four and possibly five. ***John Motson***

First footballer: That ointment the doctor gave me to rub on my knee makes my hands smart.
Second footballer: Then why don't you rub some into your head?

When Harry retired from the team he said he was going to work in a bank. 'Why do you want to do that?' asked Larry. 'I've heard there's money in it,' replied Harry.

Old Butterfingers had let five goals through in the first half. 'Can you lend me 10p?' he asked the captain. 'I want to phone a friend.' 'Here's 20p,' said the captain. 'Phone all your friends.'

Two fans were discussing their packed lunches. 'What have you got?' asked the first. 'Tongue sandwiches,' was the reply. 'Ugh, I couldn't eat something that had come out of an animal's mouth,' said the first. 'What have you got then?' asked the second. 'Egg sandwiches,' was the reply.

What was the star player awarded when he missed a penalty? A constellation prize.

I am a firm believer that if you score one goal, the other team have to score two to win. ***Howard Wilkinson***

What can light up a dull evening? A football match.

Manager: This dressing room is disgusting! It hasn't been cleaned for a month!
Cleaner: Don't blame me. I've only been here for a fortnight.

A man was up in court for trying to set fire to Chelsea's grandstand. When questioned by the judge he said he had a burning interest in football.

Ian Rush unleashed his left foot and it hit the back of the net. ***Mike England***

Why do Moscow Dynamos play such a fast game? Because they're always rush'n'.

It was a warm day for football and the striker kept missing his shots. At half-time he said, 'What couldn't I do with a long, cold drink.' His captain looked at him thoughtfully. 'Kick it?' he asked.

Why did the potato go to the match? So it could root for the home team.

First player: Why is your arm in a sling?
Second player: I get all the breaks.

How do ghost footballers keep fit? With regular exorcise.

Captain: Why are you late for training?
Player: I sprained my ankle.
Captain: That's a lame excuse.

It will be a shame if either side lose. And that applies to both sides. ***Jock Brown***

United had been playing badly and their manager hired a hall in which to hold a press conference. Afterwards, Bill said to Gill, 'Did you notice how the manager's voice filled the hall?' 'Yes,' she replied. 'And did you notice how many people left to make room for it?'

The architect was showing the team round the new stadium. 'I think you'll find it's flawless,' he said proudly. 'What do we walk on then?' asked one of the players.

Harry: Every night I dream about football – of running down the pitch, passing the ball, avoiding tackles...
Larry: Don't you ever dream about girls?
Harry: What? And miss a chance at goal?

It was a good match, which could have gone either way and very nearly did.
aim Sherwin

When is a footballer like a baby? When he dribbles.

When is a kick like a boat? When it's a punt.

A father asked his son what he'd like for Christmas. 'I've got my eye on that special football in the sports shop window,' replied the lad. 'The £50 one?' asked his dad. 'That's right,' replied his son. 'You'd better keep your eye on it then – because it's unlikely your boot will ever kick it,' said his dad firmly.

Mum: Was there a fight at the match? You've lost your front teeth.
Tommy: No, I haven't. They're in my pocket.

Two fleas were leaving a football match when it started to rain. 'Shall we walk?' asked the first flea. 'No,' said the second, 'let's take a dog.'

He had an eternity to play that ball, but he took too long over it. ***Martin Tyler***

First player: Why do you call the team captain Camera?
Second player: Because he's always snapping at me.

Why can't horses play football? Because they've got two left feet.

How does an octopus go onto a football pitch? Well armed.

The great goalkeeper Jim 'Big Hands' O'Reilly was walking down the street. 'I recognise that man,' said Ken. 'But what's his name?' 'That's Big Hands,' replied Ben. 'Oh, really?' 'No, O'Reilly.'

Which football manager is found in the greengrocer's? Terry Vegetables.

Why was Cinderella thrown out of the football team? Because she kept running away from the ball.

There was a young player from
Tottenham,
His manners he'd gone and
forgotten'em.
One day at the doc's,
He took off his socks,
Because he complained he felt
hot in 'em.

There was a young striker from
Clyde,
Who hated his eggs boiled or
fried.
When asked to say why,
'It's just because I
Am a poacher by trade,' he
replied.

A striker from somewhere in
Kent,
Took free kicks which dipped
and then bent.
In a match on the telly,
He gave one some welly,
And the keeper the wrong way
he sent.

There once was a footballing
cat,
Who played in a black bowler
hat.
When he ran down the wing,
He could not see a thing,
You can guess what the crowd
thought of that!

A team of footballers from
Stroud,
Had supporters who shouted
too loud.
When all ceased their din,
Goals just rocketed in,
So now they're a much quieter
crowd.

A football pitch groundsman
from Leeds,
Went and swallowed a packet
of seeds.
In less than an hour,
His head was in flower,
And his feet were all covered in
weeds.

A player who turned out for
Dover,
Had no shirt, so he wore a
pullover.
But the thing was too long,
And he put it on wrong,
So that all he could do was fall
over.

There was a young striker from
Reading,
Who bumped his brow on a
door at a wedding.
It made his head swell,
But he said 'Just as well,
'Cos now I'll improve on my
heading.'

Why did the footballer put his head in the fireplace? He wanted to sleep like a log.

Everything in our favour was against us. ***Danny Blanchflower***

What do you call a noisy soccer fan? A foot-bawler.

Why do people play football? For kicks.

Dad: Your school report is terrible. You've come bottom out of 30 in every subject. You're even bottom in football, and that's your favourite.
Son: It could be worse.
Dad: How?
Son: I'd be bottom out of 50 if I were in John's class – it's bigger.

Nearly all the Brazilian players are wearing yellow shirts. It's a fabulous kaleidoscope of colour.
John Motson

Weedy Willie was rather underweight and was told by his doctor that he'd be a better football player if he put on a few pounds. 'Tell you what,' said the doctor, 'eat a plum. If you swallow it whole you'll gain a stone.'

Titles in the Football Club Library:

Embarrassing Moments on the Pitch by Lucy Lastic
Twenty-five Years in Goal by Annie Versary
Willie Win by Betty Wont
Let the Game Begin by Sally Forth
The Unhappy Fan by Mona Lott
The Poor Striker by Miss D Goal
Why I Gave Up Football by Arthur Itis
Keep Trying Until the Final Whistle by Percy Vere
Heading the Ball by I C Starrs
We'll Win the Cup by R U Sure
Pre-Match Night Nerves by Eliza Wake
Keep Your Subs Handy by Justin Case
Training Hard by Xavier Strength
Buying Good Players by Ivor Fortune
The New Player by Izzy Anygood
Great Shot! by Major Runn
Advertising the Match by Bill Poster
Half-time Drinks by R E Volting

Ben: I hear that new player's father is an optician.
Len: Is that why he keeps making such a spectacle of himself?

What's the difference between the Prince of Wales and a throw-in? One's heir to the throne; the other's thrown in the air.

What position did Cinderella play in the football team? Sweeper.

A footballer had been hit very hard on his knee, which had swollen up . 'If it gets any bigger I won't be able to get my shorts on,' he told the doctor. 'Don't worry, I'll write you a prescription,' said the doctor. 'What for?' 'A skirt.'

Why is football like fresh milk? It strengthens the calves.

What do you do if you're too hot at a football match? Sit next to a fan.

Millie: Did you hear the football club was burgled – but all they took were the soap and towels from the players' dressing room.
Willie: The dirty crooks!

What happened when a herd of cows had a football match? There was udder chaos.

What can a footballer never make right? His left foot.

How do you hire a professional footballer? Stand him on a chair.

What happened to the snowman who left the football team? He just drifted around.

Jim: How should I have kicked that ball?
Tim: Under an assumed name.

What team is good in an omelette? Best ham.

Why did the thief who broke into the football club and stole all the entrance money take a shower before he left? So he could make a clean getaway.

Mrs Green: My husband's found a hobby he can stick to at last.
Mrs White: What's that?
Mrs Green: He spends all evening glued to the football on TV.

What wears out football boots but has no feet. The ground.

Why did the footballer put corn in his boots? He had pigeon toes.

Why did the manager have his pitch flooded? He wanted to bring on his sub.

Did you hear about the footballer who threw away his boots because he thought they were sticking out their tongues at him?

Park keeper: Why are you boys playing football in the trees?
Boys: Because the sign says 'No ball games on the grass.'

How did the Japanese football millionaire make all his money? He had a yen for that kind of thing.

Where can a fan stop for a drink when he's driving to the match? At a T-junction.

Old Harry had been retired from the game for many years, but he still liked to tell people how good he'd once been. 'They still remember me, you know,' he said. 'Only yesterday, when I was at the players' entrance, there were lots of press photographers queuing to take my picture.' 'Really?' said a disbelieving listener. 'Yes. And if you don't believe me, ask Eric Cantona – he was standing next to me.'

What do you call a press photographer taking pictures of the match? A flash guy.

First footballer: Girls whisper that they love me.
Second footballer: Well, they'd never admit it out loud!

First footballer: How did you manage to break your leg?
Second footballer: See those steps down to the car park?
First footballer: Yes.
Second footballer: I didn't.

What was wrong with the footballer whose nose ran and feet smelt? He was built upside down.

Did you hear the story of the peacock who played football? It was a beautiful tail.

What's the easiest way to find a broken bottle on the football pitch? Play in your bare feet.

Giles: What's a football made of?
Miles: Pig's hide.
Giles: Why do they hide?
Miles: No – the pig's outside.
Giles: Then bring him in. Any friend of yours is a friend of mine.

What's the difference between a gutter and a poor goalie? One catches drops; the other drops catches.

Bob: I can't find my football boots, and I've looked everywhere for them.
Teacher: Are you sure these aren't yours? They're the only pair left.
Bob: Quite sure. Mine had snow on them.

When is a footballer in hospital with a broken leg a contradiction? When he's an impatient patient.

What's higher than an Italian football captain? His cap.

One day when United were playing, the referee didn't turn up, so the captain asked if there was anyone among the spectators with refereeing experience. A man stepped forward. 'Have you refereed before?' asked the captain. 'Certainly,' said the man. 'And if you don't believe me, ask my three friends here.' 'I'm sorry,' said the captain. 'But I don't think we can use you.' 'Why not?' 'You can't be a real referee because no real referee has three friends.'

Who's in goal when the ghost team plays football? The ghoulie, of course!

What belongs to a footballer but is used more by other people? His name.

How can a footballer make more of his money? If he folds up a note he'll find it in creases.

Policeman: I'm sorry but I'm going to have to lock you up for the night.
Unruly fan: What's the charge?
Policeman: There's no charge, it's all part of the service.

Darren: Did you hear about the footballer who ate little bits of metal all day?
Sharon: No.
Darren: It was his staple diet.

Who runs out on the pitch when a player is injured and says, 'Miaow'? The first-aid kit.

A man realised that his new neighbour was a famous footballer player. 'I've seen you on TV, on and off,' he said. 'And how do you like me?' asked the player. 'Off,' replied his neighbour.

Andy: Do you have holes in your football shorts?
Bertie: No.
Andy: Then how do you get them on?

When do a footballer's swimming trunks go ding dong? When he wrings them out.

What did the football sock say to the football boot? 'Well, I'll be darned!'

Father: You mustn't fight – you must learn to give and take.
Dennis: I did. I gave Danny a black eye and took his football!

Why did the conceited player throw a bucket of water on the pitch when he made his debut? He wanted to make a big splash.

What runs around all day and lies at night with its tongue hanging out? A football boot.

Older brother: Have you got your football boots on yet?
Young brother: Yes, all but one.

Why are a pair of much-worn football boots like a taxi driver? They both drive you away.

A group of neighbours was organising a village friendly match followed by a picnic and realised they'd forgotten to invite the eccentric old lady who lived on the green. So they sent a child to invite her. 'It's no use now,' said the old lady, 'I've already prayed for rain.'

Traffic warden: Why did you park your car there?
Football fan: Because the notice says, 'Fine for parking'.

The team kept losing, but the captain shrugged off their run of bad luck. 'After all, what's defeat?' 'What you're supposed to kick the ball with,' answered one of the players.

What's the cheapest time to phone a footballer? When he's out!

Angry neighbour: I'll teach you to kick footballs into my greenhouse!
Naughty boy: I wish you would – I keep missing!

Why was the snowman no good playing in the big match? He got cold feet.

What happens if you wrap your sandwiches in your favourite comic when you go to football practice? You get crumby jokes!

First footballer: Do you think it will rain for the match this afternoon?
Second footballer: That depends on the weather, doesn't it?

Why did the bald footballer throw away his keys? He'd lost all his locks.

Mother: Why are you taking the baby's bib out with you, Tommy? I thought you were going to football practice?
Tommy: Yes, but the coach said we'd be dribbling this week.

A few more clean sheets and Sven's problems on and off the field would disappear.
Brian O'Keefe

Why is a football crowd learning to sing like a person opening a tin of sardines? They both have trouble with the key.

First footballer: When's your birthday?
Second footballer: 2 June.
First footballer: Which year?
Second footballer: Every year.

What does a footballer do if he splits his sides laughing? Runs until he gets a stitch.

Mother to muddy, footballing daughter: You're pretty dirty, Bobbie.
Bobbie: I'm even prettier clean.

A fan driving at 120 mph so he wouldn't arrive late at the match was stopped by the police. 'Oh dear,' he said, 'was I driving too fast?' 'No, sir,' said the officer. 'Flying too low.'

How can you make a tall footballer short? Ask him to lend you all his money.

Donny: I've never refereed a football match before. Do I have to run after the ball?
Ronnie: No, after the match.

Old football players never die, they just go on dribbling.

Referee: I didn't come here to be insulted!
Disgruntled fan: Where do you usually go?

I used to be a half-back for Huddersfield Town. I tore the tickets in two and gave them half back.

Billie: That new striker's a man who's going places?
Willie: And the sooner the better!

What happened when the boy footballer married a girl footballer? People said it was a perfect match.

A Good Walk Spoiled

A young man went for a round of golf with a girl he liked from work. Beforehand, he slipped into the professional's shop and bought a couple of golf balls which he put in his pocket. When he met the girl on the first tee, she couldn't help noticing the bulge in his pocket. 'It's only golf balls,' he explained. 'Oh, I'm sorry,' she replied. 'Is it something like tennis elbow?'

Give me my golf clubs, fresh air and a beautiful partner, and you can keep my golf clubs and fresh air. ***Jack Benny***

You can always tell the golfer who's winning. He's the one who keeps telling his opponent that it's only a game.

Two golfers went to see the professional at their club. 'Can you give me any tips?' asked one of the men as he stood on the practice ground. The professional said, 'You're standing too close to the ball.' The man's partner added, '... After you've hit it.'

A golf nut met the Pope on a trip to Rome. 'Your Holiness,' he said, 'I'm crazy about golf. I play every day of the year. But tell me, is there a golf course in Heaven?' 'I'm not sure,' said the Pope. 'I'll have to ask God.' A few days later, the man bumped into the Pope again. 'Any news from God about the golf course in Heaven?' he asked. 'Oh, yes,' replied the Pope. 'Apparently there is a beautiful course in Heaven with velvet-smooth greens and lush fairways. The bad news is you have a tee time for tomorrow morning.'

I've advised my friend to seek psychological help. He treats golf as if it were a game!

My neighbour was crying because her husband had left her for the sixth time. I consoled her, 'Don't be unhappy, he'll be back.' 'Not this time,' she sobbed. 'He's taken his golf clubs.'
Joey Adams

'I'd move Heaven and earth to break 100,' puffed the rookie golfer as he thrashed away at the ball in deep rough. 'Try Heaven,' advised his playing partner. 'I think you've already moved enough earth.'

He plays a fair game of golf – if you watch him.

Phil and Dave went for a game of golf one Saturday afternoon, but Phil was under strict instructions from his wife to be back by four o'clock because she wanted him to take her shopping. Four o'clock passed, so did five o'clock and six o'clock. Eventually Phil arrived home at seven. 'Where on earth have you been?' she screamed. 'Honey,' said Phil, 'a terrible thing happened. We made it to the first green when Dave dropped dead of a heart attack.' The wife felt guilty. 'That's awful,' she said. 'You're telling me,' said Phil. 'The rest of the round it was hit the ball, drag Dave, hit the ball, drag Dave...'

Golf got its name because all the other four-letter words were taken.

Four married guys went away on a golfing weekend. On the second fairway, they began discussing the problems they'd had getting permission from their wives. The first said, 'I had no end of trouble getting away. I had to promise my wife I'll paint the whole house next weekend.' The second said, 'It was no easier for me. I've had to promise my wife I'll go shopping with her next weekend.' The third said, 'I know what you mean. I've promised my wife she can have a new fitted kitchen.' The fourth guy said, 'It was no problem for me. I just set my alarm for 5.30 this morning. When it went off, I gave my wife a nudge and said "Golf course or intercourse?" And she said "Don't forget your sweater."'

Golfer: Okay, Caddie, can you count?
Caddie: Certainly, Sir.
Golfer: And can you add up?
Caddie: Of course.
Golfer: So what is four plus five plus three?
Caddie: Nine, sir.
Golfer: Come on, you'll do.

His doctor told him to play 36 holes a day, so he went out and bought a harmonica.

'Why don't you play golf with Jim any more?' the wife asked her husband. 'Would you play with someone who moves his ball to a better lie when no one is looking, who deliberately coughs half-way through his opponent's back-swing and who lies about his handicap?' 'Well, no,' said the wife. 'Neither will Jim.'

He's hopeless. He's the only golfer I know who shouts 'Fore!' when he putts.

After a long day on the course, an exasperated golfer turned to his caddie and said, 'You must be the worst caddie in the world.' 'I don't think so,' replied the caddie. 'That would be too much of a coincidence.'

I love golf. I live golf. I dream golf. If only I could play golf!

The only shots you can be dead sure of are those you've had already. ***Byron Nelson***

A preacher was an avid golfer and couldn't help sneaking off to play a round one Sunday. An angel watching him from above was furious and told God, 'Look at that preacher down there, abandoning his duties to play golf on a Sunday. He should be punished.' God agreed and promised to act. A few minutes later, the preacher hit a superb hole-in-one on a 350-yard hole. The angel rounded on God: 'I thought you were going to punish him! Instead he's just hit a perfect hole-in-one.' God smiled: 'Think about it - who can he tell?'

Last week I missed a spectacular hole-in-one – by only five strokes.

A keen golfer stood trial for killing his wife. After initially denying the offence, he finally broke down in court and admitted his guilt. 'How did you kill her?' asked the judge. 'With three strokes of a five iron.' 'Three strokes?' queried the judge. 'Yes. On the first two, I lifted my head.'

Finding his ball in the deep rough, a golfer took an almighty swing, but struck nothing more than a divot. He swung again, missed the ball again and got another big chunk of turf. Just then, two ants climbed on to the ball, saying, 'Let's get up here before we get killed!'

Golfer: I've never played this badly before.
Caddie: You've played before?

A golfer was poised over his tee shot for ages. 'For goodness sake, hurry up!' said his partner. 'But my wife is watching from the clubhouse. I want to make this a perfect shot.' 'Forget it– you'll never hit her from here!'

A golfer came home in a foul mood. 'I only hit two good balls today,' he moaned, 'and that was when I stood on a rake!'

A man had been stranded on a desert island for ten years and in that time hadn't seen another living person. Then one day, to his amazement, a gorgeous blonde stepped out of the sea wearing a wet suit and scuba diving gear. She walked over to him and started caressing his beard. 'How long is it since you last had a cigarette?' she asked. 'Ten years,' he gasped. She slowly unzipped a waterproof pocket on her left sleeve and produced a packet of cigarettes and a box of matches. He lit the cigarette and sighed, 'I've been desperate for a cigarette. This is fantastic.' When he had finished the first cigarette, she said, 'And how long is it since you last tasted whisky?' 'Ten years,' he replied. And she slowly unzipped the waterproof pocket on her right sleeve and brought out a bottle of whisky. 'This is great,' he said, drinking half of the bottle. 'I'd forgotten how good whisky tasted.' Then she began to unzip the long fastening at the front of her wet suit and purred seductively, 'And how long has it been since you had some real fun?' The man could hardly believe his luck. 'Don't tell me you've got a set of golf clubs in there!'

He couldn't help cheating at golf. One day, when he got a hole-in-one, he wrote a zero on his card.

A husband and wife were both keen golfers. The wife was feeling neglected and wanted to know how much he loved her. 'If I were to die tomorrow,' she said, 'and you remarried, would you give your new wife my jewellery?' 'What an awful thing to ask!' exclaimed the husband. 'But no, of course not.' 'And would you give her any of my clothes?' 'No, honey, of course not.' 'What about my golf clubs?' 'No. She's left-handed.'

I think that I shall never see
A hazard rougher than a tree
A tree o'er which my ball must fly
If on the green it is to lie.

A tree that stands that green to guard
And makes the shot extremely hard
A tree whose leafy arms extend
To kill the six-iron shot I send.

A tree that stands in silence there
While angry golfers rave and swear.
Irons were made for fools like me
Who cannot ever miss a tree.

I'm hitting the woods just great, but I'm having a terrible time getting out of them. ***Harry Tofcano***

A man came home from a game of golf to be greeted by his young son. 'Daddy, daddy!' he cried. 'Did you win?' 'Well,' explained the father, 'in golf it doesn't matter so much if you win. But I tell you one thing – I got to hit the ball more times than anybody else.'

After a whirlwind romance, a couple were on their honeymoon when the guy announced, 'Honey, I have a confession to make. I'm a golf nut. I play every weekend in the summer. You'll hardly see me.' The wife took a deep breath and said, 'And I have a confession to make too. I'm a hooker.' 'That's no big deal,' said the husband. 'Just keep your head down and your left arm straight.'

Man: My doctor has advised me to give up golf.
Friend: Why? Did he examine your heart?
Man: No. He had a look at my score card.

Standing on the first tee, a golfer said to his playing partner, 'Why don't you try this ball - you can't lose it.' 'What do you mean, you can't lose it?' 'It's a special ball. If you hit into the woods, it beeps. If you hit it in water, it sends up bubbles. If it lands in deep rough, it emits a plume of smoke.' 'Wow! That's fantastic. Where did you get it?' 'I found it.'

My wife claims that her golf is improving because today she hit the ball in one.

An employee went for a game of golf with his boss who owned a small white poodle. The dog always used to accompany its master on the course and every time the boss hit a good drive or sank a long putt, the poodle stood on its hind legs and applauded with its two front paws. The employee was amazed. 'What happens,' he asked, 'if you land in a bunker or miss a short putt?' 'Oh,' said the boss, 'the dog turns somersaults.' 'How many?' The boss replied, 'Depends on how hard I kick him up the butt.'

Golfer (very keen to improve his game): Do you notice any improvement in me today, caddie?
Caddie: Yes, sir. You've had a haircut.

Bill walked into his place of work wearing a heavy head bandage and knew that he'd have some explaining to do about his accident when confronted by the boss. 'I got it playing golf,' he explained. 'My word!' said his boss. 'It must have been some size of golf ball that hit you to make that sort of a mess!' 'It wasn't a golf ball that did it, it was a club,' he explained further. 'Sit down,' said the boss. 'This sounds interesting.' Bill sat down gingerly, trying not to make any unnecessary movement with his head and the story began to unfold. 'I was playing a round of golf with my friend,' he went on, 'when my ball veered from the direction I had hit it and ended up in an adjoining field where cows where grazing. When I got there a lady golfer from another group was also busy looking for her lost ball. I found mine without any trouble, then I noticed that one of the cows kept giving a violent twitch of its tail. Lifting the tail I noticed a golf ball stuck in the cleavage beneath the cow's tail. Giving a whistle and a shout I beckoned the lady across. She looked puzzled at first, and then I raised the cow's tail. "This looks like yours," I said. It was then that she walloped me with her golf club.'

My golf is definitely improving. I'm missing the ball much closer than I used to.

Andrew came rushing into the clubhouse in a state of great agitation. 'I've just sliced the ball into a tree but it rebounded and went into the road where it hit the rider of a motorbike who fell off his bike and then a lorry ran into him, causing its load of onions to spill all over the road which has caused more cars to crash and there are bodies and smashed vehicles all over the place. What can I do?' The club president thought deeply for a moment and then suggested, 'Take it a bit easier on the back-swing in future.'

Golf is not and has never been a fair game. ***Jack Nicklaus***

Notice in golf club: Members are requested not to pick up lost balls until they have stopped running.

Golfer: This is a terrible golf course. I've never played on a worse one.
Caddie: But this isn't the course! We left that more than an hour ago.

Jesus and Moses went golfing, and were about even until they reached the 15th hole, a par five. Both balls landed about 20 ft from the edge of a little pond that stood between them and the hole. Moses took out a five-wood and landed his ball in excellent position. Jesus took out a five-iron. 'Hang on, hang on,' cautioned Moses. 'Use a wood - you'll never make it.' 'If Arnold Palmer can make that shot with a five-iron, so can I,' said Jesus. His ball landed in the middle of the lake. Moses parted the waters, retrieved the ball, and sighed when he saw Jesus still holding the five-iron. 'If Arnold Palmer can make that shot with a five-iron, so can I,' maintained Jesus. Again Moses had to part the waters to retrieve the ball. By this time there were a number of people waiting to play through, and Moses said firmly, 'Listen, Jesus. I'm not fetching the ball another time. Use a wood.' Jesus, however, still insisted. 'If Arnold Palmer can make that shot with a five-iron, so can I.' Splash! Moses shook his head. 'I told you, I'm not budging. Get it yourself.' So Jesus walked off across the water to where the ball had landed. At this, the onlookers gaped in astonishment. One came over to Moses and stammered, 'I can't believe my eyes - the guy must think he's Jesus Christ!' In response, Moses shook his head gloomily. 'He is Jesus Christ. He thinks he's Arnold Palmer.'

Ten things in golf that sound dirty:

1 Look at the size of his putter.

2 Oh, damn, my shaft's all bent.

3 You really whacked the hell out of that sucker.

4 After 18 holes I can barely walk.

5 My hands are so sweaty I can't get a good grip.

6 Lift your head and spread your legs.

7 You have a nice stroke, but your follow through leaves a lot to be desired.

8 Just turn your back and drop it.

9 Hold up, I've got to wash my balls.

10 Damn, I missed the hole again.

A man takes a gorilla out golfing. At the first tee, the gorilla says, 'So what am I supposed to do?' And the man says, 'You see that little round green area about 400 yards away? You've got to hit the ball on to that.' So the gorilla grabs a club and whacks the ball and it goes screaming down the fairway and lands on the green. Then the man drives his ball and travels about 150 yards. He takes a second shot and then a third shot and finally his ball arrives on the green just near the gorilla's ball. The gorilla says, 'What do I do now?' And the man says, 'You hit the ball into that little cup.' And the gorilla says, 'Why didn't you tell me that back there?'

What's the difference between a golf ball and a woman's G-spot? A man will spend half an hour looking for a golf ball.

I think I fail just a bit less than everyone else.

Jack Nicklaus

I was playing golf with a friend the other day and, just as we were about to tee off, a funeral procession went by. My friend put his club down, took off his cap and bowed his head as the cortege passed us. I said, 'That was a very decent gesture.' And he said, 'It was the least I could do. She was a damned good wife to me.'

Sunday is the day all of us bow our heads. Some are praying and some are putting.

The avid golfer was out on the course with his wife one day. He played a shot on the fifth that sliced so badly it ended up in the gardener's equipment shed. Looking in the door, the couple saw the ball sitting right in the middle of the room. 'Look,' volunteered the golfer's wife. 'If I hold open the door, you can play a shot from here to the green.' This struck the golfer as an interesting challenge, but, alas, the ball missed the open door and struck his wife on the temple, killing her instantly. Many years later, the widower was playing with a friend when he hit the exact same slice. The two of them walked into the shed, and, sure enough, there sat the ball in the centre of the room. 'I tell you what,' said the friend. 'If I hold the door open, I bet you can get the ball back onto the green.' 'Oh no,' said the golfer, shaking his head. 'I tried that once before and it took me seven shots to get out.'

The harder you work, the luckier you get. ***Gary Player***

Golfer: Caddie, will you please stop looking at your watch all the time? It's very distracting.
Caddie: It's not my watch, sir, it's my compass.

Old Harry is dead. And to think that he was going to play golf with us tomorrow. It's awful! It's tragic! But wait a minute - maybe we can get Bob to fill in for him!

Is it a sin to play golf on a Sunday? No, but the way you play it any day is a crime.

Tom sits in the clubhouse bar thinking about his next extra marital affair. Deep in thought about the subject, he absentmindedly starts thinking aloud. 'Not worth it,' he muttered. 'Never as good as you hoped. Expensive and above all drives the wife berserk.' A friend who was sitting close by at the time and overheard Tom's words leaned across and said, 'Come on, Tom, you knew what to expect when you took up golf.'

My doctor has told me I can't play golf. So he's played with you too, has he?

Golfer: So, what's my score?
Caddie: Fifteen, Sir.
Golfer: Fifteen, eh? Not bad! Let's try the second hole.

My wife says if I don't give up golf she'll leave me. That's bad luck. I know, I'm really going to miss her.

Well, caddie, how do you like my game? It's terrific, sir. Mind you, I still prefer golf.

One of the nicest things about golf is that you can play it for years and years. There were these two old friends who'd been playing together since they were kids, every Saturday morning and Sunday afternoon. Lester was 82 and his friend Ralph was 81. One day, on the eighth tee, Lester suddenly gave up. He turned to his pal and said, 'Ralphie, old boy, I'm afraid I'm gonna have to quit. I just can't see anymore. I hit the ball, but I don't know where it goes.' Ralph said to him, 'You can't quit. We've been playing together all these years. It wouldn't be the same without you.' 'But what can I do?' asked Lester. 'You just leave it up to me. You go ahead and hit, and I'll keep my eye on it,' said Ralph. So Lester teed up and let it fly. They stood silently for a few seconds. Then Lester said, 'Well, Ralph, that sounded pretty good. Did you see where it went?' 'Of course I did!' said Ralph. Lester said, 'Well, where did it go?' Ralph thought for a few seconds and said, 'I forgot.' ***Bob Kaliban***

The secret of good golf is to hit the ball hard, straight and not too often.

There are two guys out on the course that come up on a couple of ladies playing slow. One of the guys walks up towards the ladies to ask if they can play through. About half way there he turns around and comes back and says to his friend, 'I can't go up there and talk to them, that is my wife and my mistress.' So his friend replies, 'I'll go up and ask them.' When he is half way there he turns around and comes back and states to his friend, 'Small world.'

Golf is a game in which you yell 'fore', shoot six and write down five. ***Paul Harvey***

I don't play golf. Personally, I think there's something psychologically wrong with any game in which the person who gets to hit the ball the most is the loser.

What do you call a woman who can suck a golf ball through 50 ft of garden hose? Darling.

Husband and wife were playing in the mixed foursomes. He hit a great drive down the middle – she sliced the second shot into a copse of trees. Unfazed, he played a brilliant recovery shot, which went onto the green a metre from the pin. She poked at the putt and sent it 5 m beyond the pin. He lined up the long putt and sank it. To his wife he said, 'We'll have to do better. That was a bogey five.' 'Don't blame me,' she snapped, 'I only took two of them.'

One of the quickest ways to meet new people is to pick up the wrong ball on a golf course.

The golf swing is like sex. You can't be thinking about the mechanics of the act while you are performing. ***Dave Hill***

One fine day, Jim and Bob are out golfing. Jim slices his ball deep into a wooded ravine. He grabs his eight-iron and proceeds down the embankment into the ravine in search of his ball. The brush is quite thick, but Jim searches diligently and suddenly he spots something shiny. As he gets closer, he realises that the shiny object is in fact an eight-iron in the hands of a skeleton lying near an old golf ball. Jim calls out to his golfing partner in an agitated voice, 'Hey Bob, come here, I got trouble down here.' Bob comes running over to the edge of the ravine and calls out, 'What's the matter Jim?' Jim shouts back, 'Throw me my seven-iron! You can't get out of here with an eight-iron.'

Why do businessmen play golf? So they can dress up like pimps.

Mike and Bob had just finished the first nine and it was obvious that Mike was having a bad day. 'Blimey Mike, you're just not your old self today, what's the matter?' asked Bob. Mike, looking pretty glum, said, 'I think Mabel's dead.' 'That's terrible,' said Bob. 'You think your wife is dead. Aren't you sure?' 'Well,' responded Mike, 'the sex is the same, but the dishes are piling up.'

Two golfers are at the first tee. Golfer one: 'Hey, guess what! I got a set of golf clubs for my wife!'' Golfer two: 'Great trade!''

The greatest liar in the world is the golfer who claims he plays the game for merely exercise. ***Tommy Bolt***

What's the difference between a Ford and a golf ball? You can drive a golf ball 200 yards.

Q: **THESE DAYS, WHAT DO YOU NEED TO SHOOT TO WIN A PROFESSIONAL GOLF TOURNAMENT?**
A: **TIGER WOODS.**

Golf is the hardest game in the world to play, and the easiest to cheat at. ***Dave Hill***

There are three golfers, Bob, Max and Ted, who are looking for a fourth. Bob mentions that his friend George is a pretty good golfer, so they decide to invite him for the following Saturday. 'Sure, I'd love to play,' says George, 'but I may be about ten minutes late, so wait for me.' So Saturday rolls around. Bob, Max and Ted arrive promptly at 9am and find George already waiting for them. He plays right-handed and beats them all. Quite pleased with their new fourth, they ask him if he'd like to play again the following Saturday. 'Yeah, sounds great,' says George. 'But I maybe about ten minutes late, so wait for me.' The following Saturday, again, all four golfers show up on time, but this time George plays left-handed and beats them all. As they're getting ready to leave, George says, 'See you next Saturday, but I may be about ten minutes late, so wait for me.' Every week, George is right on time and plays great with whichever hand he decides to use. And every week, he departs with the same message. After a couple of months, Ted is pretty tired of this routine, so he says, 'Wait a minute, George. Every week you say you may be about ten minutes late, but you're right on time. You beat us either left-handed or right-handed. What's the story?' 'Well,' George says, 'I'm kind of superstitious. When I get up in the morning, I look at my wife. If she's sleeping on her left side, I play left-handed, and if she's sleeping on her right side, I play right-handed.' 'So what do you do if she's sleeping on her back?' Bob asks. 'Well... that's when I'm about ten minutes late.'

Competitive golf is played mainly on a five-and-a-half-inch course, the space between your ears. ***Bobby Jones***

There's no game like golf: you go out with three friends, play 18 holes and return with three enemies.

One day a sailor and a priest go golfing. It's like any day, the sailor goes up to hit his ball and it flies off course and he says, 'Oh damn it, I missed.' The priest stands up and says, 'Don't say that or God will punish you.' Then the priest hits the ball perfect shot, so they hop in a cart and drive to their balls. The sailor gets out and hits his ball further off course and says, 'Oh damn it, I missed.'

The priest promptly says, 'Don't say that or God will punish you.' They go for one last shot before the priest wins. The sailor hits his ball and misses again. 'Oh damn it, not again.' The priest says, 'Don't say that or God will punish you.' Then all of a sudden a thunder cloud comes in and a lightening bolt strikes the priest dead and a deep rumbling voice says, 'Oh damn it, I missed.'

Putts get real difficult the day they hand out the money.
Lee Trevino

Golf is a game in which the slowest people in the world are those in front of you, and the fastest are those behind.

A hack golfer spends a day at a plush country club, playing golf and enjoying the luxury of a complimentary caddie. Being a hack golfer, he plays poorly all day. Round about the 18th hole, he spots a lake off to the left of the fairway. He looks at the caddie and says, 'I've played so poorly all day, I think I'm going to go drown myself in that lake.' The caddie looks back at him and says, 'I don't think you could keep your head down that long.'

Golf: a five-mile walk punctuated with disappointments.

I'm in the woods so much I can tell you which plants are edible. ***Lee Trevino***

A man walks into confessional and says, 'Forgive me, Father, for I have sinned.' The priest replies, 'What is it that brings you here?' 'Well Father,' says the man, 'I used the f-word over the weekend.' 'Oh, is that all? Say five Hail Marys and may the Lord be with you.' The man replies, 'But I really need to talk.' 'Let's have it then,' the priest says, as he leans back on the bench. 'You see, Father, I was playing golf this weekend and on the first tee I was lining up my drive and proceeded to hit a horrendous slice into the trees.' 'And that's when you cursed aloud?' the priest queried. 'No, not yet. As luck would have it, I found my ball and had a clear shot to the green from a nice lie when all of a sudden, a squirrel scampered out of some bushes, picked up my ball by its teeth and darted up a tree.' 'That must have been when you cursed?' 'No, because just as the squirrel had climbed to the top of the tree, a bird swooped out of the skies and grabbed the squirrel. The bird flew out the trees and back out over the green. Then the squirrel dropped my ball from its mouth, landing five inches from the cup!' 'And that's when you cursed aloud,' the priest said assuredly. 'No, no.' The priest interjected, 'Don't tell me you missed the f*****g putt!'

The laws of golfing

1 No matter how bad your last shot was, the worst is yet to come. This law does not expire on the 18th hole, since it has the supernatural tendency to extend over the course of a tournament, a summer and, eventually, a lifetime.
2 Your best round of golf will be followed almost immediately by your worst round ever. The probability of the latter increases with the number of people you tell about the former.
3 Brand new golf balls are water-magnetic. Though this cannot be proven in the lab, it is a known fact that the more expensive the golf ball, the greater its attraction to water.
4 Golf balls never bounce off trees back into play. If one does, the tree is breaking a law of the universe and should be cut down.
5 No matter what causes a golfer to muff a shot, all his playing partners must solemnly chant 'You looked up,' or invoke the wrath of the universe.
6 The higher a golfer's handicap, the more qualified he deems himself as an instructor.
7 Every par-three hole in the world has a secret desire to humiliate golfers. The shorter the hole, the greater its desire.
8 Topping a three-iron is the most painful torture known to man.
9 Palm trees eat golf balls.
10 Sand is alive. If it isn't, how do you explain the way it works against you?
11 Golf carts always run out of juice at the farthest point from the clubhouse.
12 A golfer hitting into your group will always be bigger than anyone in your group. Likewise, a group you accidentally hit into will consist of a football player, a professional wrestler, a convicted murderer and an IRS agent – or some similar combination.
13 All three-woods are demon-possessed.
14 Golf balls from the same 'sleeve' tend to follow one another, particularly out of bounds or into the water (see Law 3).
15 A severe slice is a thing of awesome power and beauty.
16 'Nice lag' can usually be translated to 'lousy putt.' Similarly, 'tough break' can usually be translated 'you missed an easy one, sucker.'

17 The person you would most hate to lose to will always be the one who beats you.
18 The last three holes of a round will automatically adjust your score to what it really should be.
19 Golf should be given up at least twice per month.
20 All vows taken on a golf course shall be valid only until the sunset of the same day.

I'm not saying my golf game went bad, but if I grew tomatoes they would have come up sliced. ***Lee Trevino***

The secret of good golf is to hit the ball hard, straight and not too often.

A golf club walks into a local bar and asks the barman for a pint of beer. The barman refuses to serve him. 'Why not?' asks the golf club. 'You'll be driving later,' replies the barman.

'That can't be my ball, caddie. It looks far too old,' said the player looking at a ball deep in the trees. 'It's a long time since we started, sir.'

Four men were out golfing. 'These hills are getting steeper as the years go by,' one complained. 'The sand traps seem to be bigger than I remember them too,' said the third senior. After hearing enough from his senior buddies, the oldest and the wisest of the four of them, at 87 years old, piped up and said, 'Just be thankful we're still on the right side of the grass!'

Golf was once a rich man's sport, but now it has millions of poor players.

A pretty terrible golfer was playing a round of golf for which he had hired a caddie. The round proved to be somewhat tortuous for the caddie to watch and he was getting a bit exasperated by the poor play of his employer. At one point the ball lay about 180 yards from the green and as the golfer sized up his situation, he asked his caddie, 'Do you think I can get there with a five-iron?' And the caddie replied, 'Eventually.'

Q. **WHY DOES A GOLFER WEAR TWO PAIRS OF PANTS?**
A. **IN CASE HE GETS A HOLE-IN-ONE.**

A golfer is in a competitive match with a friend, who is ahead by a couple of strokes. The golfer says to himself, 'I'd give anything to sink this next putt.' A stranger walks up to him and whispers, 'Would you give up a fourth of your sex life?' The golfer thinks the man is crazy and that his answer will be meaningless but also that perhaps this is a good omen and will put him in the right frame of mind to make the difficult putt and says, 'Okay.' He sinks the putt. Two holes later he mumbles to himself, 'Boy, if I could only get an eagle on this hole.' The same stranger moves to his side and says, 'Would it be worth another fourth of your sex life?' The golfer shrugs and says, 'Sure.' And he makes an eagle. Down to the final hole. The golfer needs yet another eagle to win. Though he says nothing, the stranger moves to his side and says, 'Would you be willing to give up the rest of your sex life to win this match?' The golfer says, 'Certainly,' and makes the eagle. As the golfer walks to the clubhouse, the stranger walks alongside and says, 'You know, I've really not been fair with you because you don't know who I am. I'm the Devil and from now on you will have no sex life.' 'Nice to meet you,' says the golfer. 'My name's Father O'Malley.'

In primitive society, when native tribes beat the ground with clubs and yelled, it was called witchcraft; today, in civilized society, it is called golf.

I play in the low eighties. If it's any hotter than that, I won't play. ***Joe E Lewis***

An amateur golfer is one who addresses the ball twice: once before swinging, and once again after swinging.

Golf is a game whose aim is to hit a very small ball into an even smaller hole, with weapons singularly ill-designed for the purpose.
Winston Churchill

A husband takes his wife to play her first game of golf. Of course, the wife promptly hacked her first shot right through the window of the biggest house adjacent to the course. The husband cringed, 'I warned you to be careful! Now we'll have to go up there, find the owner, apologize and see how much your lousy drive is going to cost us.' So the couple walked up to the house and knocked on the door. A warm voice said, 'Come on in.' When they opened the door, they saw the damage that was done - glass was all over the place, and a broken antique bottle was lying on its side near the pieces of window glass. A man reclining on the couch asked, 'Are you the people who broke my window?' 'Uh... yeah, sir. We're really sorry about that,' the husband replied. 'Oh, no apology is necessary... Actually I want to thank you. You see, I'm a genie, and I've been trapped in that bottle for a thousand years. Now that you've released me, I'm allowed to grant three wishes. I'll give you each one wish, but if you don't mind, I'll keep the last one for myself.' 'Wow, that's great!' the husband said. He pondered a moment and blurted out, 'I'd like a million pounds a year for the rest of my life.' 'No problem,' said the genie. 'You've got it, it's the least I can do. And I'll guarantee you a long, healthy life!' 'And now you, young lady, what do you want?' the genie asked. 'I'd like to own a gorgeous home complete with servants in every country in the world,' she said. 'Consider it done,' the genie said. 'And your homes will always be safe from fire, burglary and natural disasters!' 'And now,' the couple asked in unison, 'what's your wish, genie?' 'Well, since I've been trapped in that bottle, and haven't been with a woman in more than 1,000 years, my wish is to have sex with your wife.' The husband looked at his wife and said, 'Darling, you know we both now have a fortune, and all those houses. What do you think?' She mulled it over for a few moments and said, 'You know, you're right. Considering our good fortune, I guess I wouldn't mind, but what about you, sweetheart?' 'You know I love you,' said the husband. 'I'd do the same for you!' So the genie and the woman went upstairs where they spent the rest of the afternoon enjoying each other. The genie was insatiable. After about three hours of non-stop sex, the genie rolled over and looked directly into her eyes and asked, 'How old are you and your husband?' 'Why, we're both 35,' she responded breathlessly. 'No kidding,' he said. 'Thirty-five years old and both of you still believe in genies?'

Golf is an expensive way of playing marbles. ***G K Chesterton***

Many a golfer prefers a golf cart to a caddie because the cart cannot count, criticise or laugh.

The club grouch was unhappy about everything: the food, the assessments, the parking, the other members. The first time he hit a hole-in-one he complained, "Damn it, just when I needed the putting practice!" ***Joey Adams***

Golf is a game where the ball lies poorly, and the players well.

Bill and his wife Sally died and went to Heaven together. They were met at the gates by an angel whose job it was to show them round the place. 'Right!' said the angel. 'Over here, we have our very own golf course.' 'Wow! It's beautiful! Can we play it now?' they both asked. 'Sure,' said the angel. So the couple began playing. It was the most beautiful course they had ever seen. Everything was perfect - the fairways, the greens, even the roughs. The more they played, the more the woman beamed with happiness, but she noticed her husband was becoming disheartened and angry. Sally confronted her husband about what was wrong. She said, 'I can't understand why you're not happy. We're in Heaven! We're together! We're playing on the most beautiful and perfect golf course ever! What's wrong with you?' Bill replied, 'If you hadn't fed us those damn bran muffins, we'd have been here years ago!'

Real golfers don't miss putts, they get robbed.

If you watch a game, it's fun. If you play it, it's recreation. If you work at it, it's golf. ***Bob Hope***

I attended a golf convention in London over the winter and was somewhat interested in the result of one particular study performed on golfers; specifically late afternoon league golfers. This study indicated that the single gentlemen who play in these leagues are 'skinnier' than the married ones. The reason for this phenomenon was quite simple when we finally found the answer. The single golfer goes out and plays his round of golf, has a 'refreshment' at the 19th hole, goes home and goes to his refrigerator. He finds nothing decent there, so he goes to bed. The married golfer goes out and plays his round of golf, has a 'refreshment' at the 19th hole, goes home and goes to bed, finds nothing decent there, so he goes to his refrigerator.

Golf is a game where guts and blind devotion will always net you absolutely nothing but an ulcer. ***Tommy Bolt***

The schoolteacher was taking her first golfing lesson. 'Is the word spelt p-u-t or p-u-t-t?' she asked the instructor. 'P-u-t-t is correct,' he replied. 'Put means to place a thing where you want it. Putt means merely a vain attempt to do the same thing.'

What's the difference between a bad golfer and a bad skydiver? A bad golfer goes: WHACK ...'Damn!' A bad Skydiver goes: 'Damn!'... WHACK.

Q. **WHAT DO YOU CALL A BLONDE GOLFER WITH AN IQ OF 125?**
A. **A FOURSOME.**

A worm living underneath a golf course decided to check out the weather early one morning. Meanwhile, above the ground, a lady golfer had been caught short and was forced to squat in the long grass for a pee. She urinated just as the worm stuck its head above ground. The worm got soaked and quickly dived back beneath the soil. It said to its friend, 'Not only is it raining, but it's raining so hard the birds are building their nests upside down!'

The fun you get from golf is in direct ratio to the effort you don't put into it. ***Bob Allen***

A golfer has one advantage over a fisherman. He doesn't have to produce anything to prove his story.

The other day I broke 70. That's a lot of clubs.

Henry Youngman

I only play golf on days that have a 'd' in them.

When I'm on a golf course and it starts to rain and lightning, I hold up my one-iron, 'cause I know even God can't hit a one-iron. ***Lee Trevino***

Top Ten Reasons Why Golf is Better than Sex:

10 You have a hoice of public or private courses.

9 Lessons are available.

8 If you're good you can turn pro and do it full time.

7 You can clean balls at every hole.

6 You have a choice of wood, aluminium or graphite.

5 The fewer strokes the better.

4 If you lose a ball, you still have two left.

3 Threesomes and foursomes happen all the time.

2 You can pick the size of your shaft.

1 Every hole is well groomed and manicured.

politics

Left and Right

A politician running for office was outraged at certain remarks which had been made about him in the local newspaper. Incensed, he barged into the editorial room of the paper and shouted, 'You are printing lies about me, and you know it!' 'Relax,' said the editor calmly. 'What on God's green earth would you do if we told the truth about you?'

Political speeches are like a steer: a point here, a point there, and a lot of bull in between.

Concluding a powerful and impassioned speech enumerating his many splendid qualities, the candidate finally asked if anyone had any questions. 'Yes, Sir,' called out a voice from the crowd. 'Who else is running?'

If you've got 'em by the balls, their hearts and minds will follow. ***Sign in the White House office of Charles Colson***

I hear that the Democrats are considering changing their emblem from a donkey to a condom because a condom stands for inflation, halts production, discourages cooperation, protects a bunch of dicks, and gives one a sense of security whilst screwing others.

How many prime ministers does it take to change a light bulb? None. They'll only promise change.

A farmer was out working in his field one day when a carload of politicians came flying by. They were going too fast for the curve and turned over in the ditch. Later, the sheriff stopped by and asked the farmer if he had seen the car. 'Yes,' replied the farmer. 'Where are they?' asked the sheriff. 'Over there,' replied the farmer, pointing to the ditch filled with fresh dirt. 'You buried them?' asked the sheriff, 'Were they still alive?' Replied the farmer, 'They said they were, but you know how those people lie.'

The prime minister tells us she has given the French President a piece of her mind – not a gift I would receive with alacrity. ***Dennis Healey***

How to speak about women and remain politically correct:

She is not a BABE or a CHICK– she is a BREASTED AMERICAN.
She is not a SCREAMER or a MOANER – she is VOCALLY APPRECIATIVE.
She is not EASY – she is HORIZONTALLY ACCESSIBLE.
She has not BEEN AROUND – she is a PREVIOUSLY ENJOYED COMPANION.
She does not GET YOU EXCITED – she causes TEMPORARY BLOOD DISPLACEMENT.
She is not an AIRHEAD – she is REALITY IMPAIRED.
She does not have MAJOR LEAGUE HOOTERS – she is PECTORALLY SUPERIOR.
She is not a TWO-BIT WHORE – she is a LOW-COST PROVIDER.
She is not OLD – she is CHRONOLOGICALLY GIFTED.
She is not OVERWEIGHT – she is GRAVITY ENHANCED.
She is not a BAD COOK – she is MICROWAVE COMPATIBLE.
She does not have a RICH DADDY – she is a RECIPIENT OF PARENTAL ASSET INFUSION.
She is not a BLEACHED BLONDE – she is PEROXIDE DEPENDENT.
She does not GET DRUNK – she becomes VERBALLY DYSLEXIC.
She is not a BAD DRIVER – she is AUTOMOTIVELY CHALLENGED.
She does not PUT ON WEIGHT – she is a METABOLIC UNDERACHIEVER.
She is not FRIGID – she is THERMALLY INCOMPATIBLE.
She is not DUMB – she is a DETOUR OFF THE INFORMATION HIGHWAY.
She does not get PMS – she becomes HORMONALLY HOMICIDAL.
She does not have a KILLER BODY – she is TERMINALLY ATTRACTIVE.
She does not have a MOUSTACHE – she is IN TOUCH WITH HER MASCULINE SIDE.
She does not WEAR TOO MUCH MAKE-UP – she is COSMETICALLY OVERSATURATED.
She is not TOO SKINNY – she is SKELETALLY PROMINENT.
She does not have SEXY LIPS – she is COLLAGEN DEPENDENT.
She is not having a BAD HAIR DAY – she is suffering from REBELLIOUS FOLLICLE SYNDROME.
She is not HOOKED ON SOAP OPERAS – she is MELODRAMATICALLY FIXATED.

I believe that Ronald Reagan can make this country what it once was – an Arctic region covered with ice. ***Steve Martin***

Capitalism works better than it sounds, while socialism sounds better than it works. ***Richard Nixon***

I'm not politically correct – I still say 'black'. 'Cause 'African American' doesn't give you no bonus. It doesn't make your life any easier. You don't see black people standing around saying, 'Oh, yeah, African American, mmm-hmm-hmm; man, I tell you, this beats the hell out of being black. We should have made the switch years ago.' ***Wanda Sykes-Hall***

A candidate was addressing an election meeting: 'When my party comes to power, workers' wages will be doubled.' A woman shouted out, 'And what about the tarts and prostitutes who defile our streets?' The candidate replied, 'When my party comes to power, they will be driven underground.' And a voice from the back shouted, 'There you go again, favouring the bloody miners.'

He says he's the man to get the country moving. He's right! If he gets in, I'm moving!

Franklin D Roosevelt: He had every quality that morons esteem in their heroes. He was the first American to reach the real depths of vulgar stupidity. ***H L Mencken***

He tells us that he's standing on his record – that's one way of making sure we can't see it.

She [Mrs Thatcher] is very democratic. She'll talk down to anyone. ***Austin Mitchell***

His popularity has hit rock bottom. Even if he ran unopposed, he'd lose.

In the Cabinet you can say what you like about the Prime Minister. But God help you if you say what you don't like.

How to speak about men and remain politically correct:

He is not a MALE CHAUVINIST PIG – he has SWINE EMPATHY.
He does not GET LOST ALL THE TIME – he INVESTIGATES ALTERNATIVE DESTINATIONS.
He is not a CRADLE SNATCHER – he prefers GENERATIONALLY DIFFERENTIAL RELATIONSHIPS.
He is not AFRAID OF COMMITMENT – he is MONOGAMOUSLY CHALLENGED.
He does not have a BEER GUT – he has developed a LIQUID GRAIN STORAGE FACILITY.
He does not EAT LIKE A PIG – he suffers from REVERSE BULIMIA.
He is not STUPID – he suffers from MINIMAL CRANIAL DEVELOPMENT.
He is not DISHONEST – he is ETHICALLY DISORIENTED.
He is not SHORT – he is ANATOMICALLY COMPACT.
He is not LAZY – he is ENERGETICALLY DECLINED.
He is not a PSYCHOPATH – he is SOCIALLY MISALIGNED.
He is not GOING BALD – he is in FOLLICLE REGRESSION.
He is not UNSOPHISTICATED – he is SOCIALLY MALFORMED.
He is not IMPOTENT – he is PROCREATIONALLY DISABLED.
He does not FART AND BELCH – he is GASTRONOMICALLY EXPRESSIVE.
He is not QUIET – he is a CONVERSATIONAL MINIMALIST.
He does not FALL DOWN DRUNK – he becomes ACCIDENTALLY HORIZONTAL.
He does not behave like a TOTAL ARSE – he develops a case of RECTAL-CRANIAL INVERSION.
He does not have a DIRTY MIND – he has INTROSPECTIVE PORNOGRAPHIC MOMENTS.
He is not WEIRD – he is BEHAVIOURALLY DIFFERENT.
He does not SNORE – he is NASALLY REPETITIVE.
He is not IGNORANT – he is FACTUALLY UNENCUMBERED.
He does not HOG THE BLANKETS – he is THERMALLY UNAPPRECIATIVE.

Many people today vote Conservative because their fathers voted Conservative. On the other hand, many people today vote Labour because their fathers voted Conservative.

Clement Attlee: He is a sheep in sheep's clothing. ***Winston Churchill's view of the mild-mannered English prime minister***

It's said that every new president of the United States should carry with him three envelopes. At the end of his first year in office, when the going is usually rough, he should open the first envelope. Inside he will find a note that reads, 'Blame the previous administration!'
At the end of the second year, if things don't get any better, he should open the second envelope. Inside he will find a note that reads, 'Blame Congress!'
And at the end of the third year, if things still haven't got any better, he should open the third envelope. Inside he will find a note that reads, 'Prepare three envelopes!'

I admire the straightforward way in which my opponent dodges the issues.

I bear no ill will to my opponent. He did what any despicable little rat would do in the circumstances.

I don't support any organised party. I vote Conservative.

Bill Clinton is the Willy Loman of Generation X, a travelling salesman who has the loyalty of a lizard with his tail broken off and the midnight tastes of a man who'd double date with the Rev Jimmy Swaggart. ***Hunter S Thompson***

I vow to keep the promises I made during the election campaign - in a small filing cabinet in the basement of Number Ten.

A cannibal was walking through the jungle and came upon a restaurant opened by a fellow cannibal. Feeling somewhat hungry he sat down and looked over the menu:
Broiled Missionary: £10.00
Fried Explorer: £15.00
Baked Politician: £100.00.
The cannibal called the waiter over and asked, 'Why such a price difference for the politician?' The cook replied 'Have you ever tried to clean one of them?'

The only president who didn't blame the previous administration for all his troubles was George Washington.

I wouldn't call him a cheap politician. He's costing this country a fortune!

Spiro T Agnew: Agnew reminds me of the kind of guy who would make a crank call to the Russians on the hot line. ***Dick Gregory***

I've got lots of friends in politics. They're the best that money can buy.

Based on what you know about him in history books, what do you think Abraham Lincoln would be doing if he were alive today? 1. Writing his memoirs of the Civil War. 2. Advising the President. 3. Desperately clawing at the inside of his coffin.

David Letterman

At the very heart of British government there is a luxuriant and voluntary exclusion of talent.

Brian Chapman

In crime, they say take the money and run. In politics, they say run, then take the money.

Thomas Jefferson Green: He has all the characteristics of a dog except loyalty. ***Sam Houston***

If you have half a mind to read their manifesto, that's all you'll need.

Within hours of the death of the sitting MP, an ambitious young hopeful rang the local party agent. 'I hope you don't mind me ringing at this time,' he said, 'but I was wondering whether I might take the place of the deceased…' 'I hadn't really thought about it,' replied the agent, 'but if the undertaker doesn't mind, then neither will I.'

Looking at the two candidates, it makes you grateful only one of them can get elected.

She [Mrs Thatcher] cannot see an institution without hitting it with her handbag.

Julian Critchley

Not a very responsible politician? I was responsible for losing the last election, wasn't I?

Of course our party is looking up. It has to. It's flat on its back!

Stanley Baldwin: Baldwin occasionally stumbles over the truth, but he always hastily picks himself up and hurries on as if nothing had happened. ***Winston Churchill***

Please support me in my ambition to get the country back on its knees.

Politicians are people who put in their place people who put them in their place.

Things are really tough for the prime minister at the moment. I popped into a pub near Downing Street the other night and there he was, propped up against the bar, telling the barman, 'My country doesn't understand me.'

Socialism is when the state owns everything; capitalism is when your bank does.

Calvin Coolidge: I do wish he did not look as if he had been weaned on a pickle.
Alice Roosevelt Longworth

Politics is the art of the passable.

Joseph Chamberlain: Dangerous as an enemy, untrustworthy as a friend, but fatal as a colleague.
Sir Hercules Robinson

The French elections: the Socialists stand accused of staying in Toulon and deserving Toulouse.

James G Blaine: No man in our annals has filled so large a space and left it so empty.
Charles E Russell

The hotel is expecting a political convention. They're putting their Gideon Bibles on chains.

Harold Wilson: He is going round the country stirring up apathy. ***William Whitelaw***

There are two sides to every question – and a good politician takes both.

When I was a kid I was told anyone could become prime minister. I'm beginning to believe it.

My father was a Socialist, my grandfather was a Socialist and that's why I'm a Socialist. But that's no argument. What if your father was a swindler and your grandfather was a swindler? Would that make you a swindler? No, that would make me a Conservative.

Jimmy Carter: Sometimes when I look at all my children, I say to myself, 'Lillian, you should have stayed a virgin.' ***Lillian Carter***

There are two lunatics living in Westminster who think they're the prime minister. And one of them's right!

Hillary Clinton: A raisin-eyed, carrot-nosed, twig-armed, straw-stuffed mannequin trundled on a go-kart by the mentally bereft powerbrokers of the Democratic Party.
Camille Paglia

You always know when the middle classes have joined the revolutionaries: the Molotov cocktails have olives in them.

To err is human; to blame it on someone else is politics.

In the Bob Hope Golf Classic the participation of President Gerald Ford was more than enough to remind you that the nuclear button was at one stage at the disposal of a man who might have either pressed it by mistake or else pressed it deliberately to obtain room service. ***Clive James***

What an unstable country! They have so many coups and revolutions that the Cabinet meets in a revolving door.

Sir Winston Churchill: He would kill his own mother just so that he could use her skin to make a drum to beat his own praises.
David Lloyd George

What we need is more people giving up politics – but staying in office.

A liberal is a man who has enemies left and right.

A priest walked into a barber shop in Washington, DC. After getting his hair cut, he asked how much it would be. The barber said, 'No charge. I consider it a service to the Lord.' The next morning the barber arrived for work to find twelve prayer books and a thank you note from the priest at the front door. Later that day, a police officer walked into the same barber shop. After getting his hair cut, he asked how much it would be. The barber said, 'No charge. I consider it a service to the community.' The next morning the barber arrived for work to find twelve doughnuts and a thank you note from the police officer at the front door. Then a senator walked into the barber shop. After getting his hair cut, he asked how much it would be. The barber said, 'No charge. I consider it a service to the nation.' The next morning the barber arrived for work to find twelve senators at the front door.

Tony Blair: The great prime ministers, those who leave a mark on history, are those who make the political weather and not those who skilfully avoid its storms and shelter from its downpours.

Lord Jenkins

Do you think voters today are apathetic? Who cares?

Why spend good money having your family tree traced? Go into politics and your opponents will do it for you.

Neville Chamberlain: Listening to a speech by Chamberlain is like paying a visit to Woolworth's; everything it its place and nothing above sixpence.

Winston Churchill

I'd join your party if it wasn't so full of self-serving hypocrites. Oh, there's always room for one more.

I'm thinking of standing for the town council. Yes, but do you think they'll stand for you?

Jimmy Carter needs Billy like Van Gogh needs stereo. ***Johnny Carson, on the president's brother Billy***

Sometimes I think war is God's way of teaching us geography. ***Paul Rodriguez***

Margaret Thatcher: Atilla the Hen. ***Clement Freud***

How to Speak About Teenagers and Remain Politically Correct:

His bedroom is not CLUTTERED – it is PASSAGE RESTRICTIVE
His homework isn't MISSING – it's having an OUT-OF-NOTEBOOK EXPERIENCE
He is not SLEEPING IN CLASS – he is RATIONING CONSCIOUSNESS
He has not got a DETENTION AT SCHOOL – he is merely one of the EXIT DELAYED

I made so much money betting on the Labour Party that I became a Conservative!

Bill Clinton: The prince of sleaze. ***Jerry Brown***

She believes in the two-party system: one in the evening and one a bit later.

Richard Nixon: Richard Nixon means never having to say you're sorry. ***Wilfred Sheed***

Collective noun: a CHARM of politicians.

Isn't capitalism wonderful? Under what other system could the ordinary man in the street owe so much?

Randolph Churchill: A typical triumph of modern science to find the only part of Randolph that was not malignant and remove it. ***Evelyn Waugh, after Churchill had a lung removed and it proved to be benign***

Under capitalism, it's dog eat dog. Under communism, it's just the opposite.

Ken Livingstone: Ken Livingstone suffers from the politician's most debilitating disease: the need to see his picture in the papers every day. ***Lord Hattersley***

Joseph McCarthy: Joseph McCarthy is the only major politician in the country who can be labelled 'liar' without fear of libel. ***Joseph Alsop***

Why do communists drink such horrible tea? Because all proper tea is theft.

Dwight D Eisenhower: As an intellectual, he bestowed upon the games of golf and bridge all the enthusiasm and perseverance that he withheld from his books and ideas. ***Emmet John Hughes***

Capitalism is the exploitation of one man by another. And communism? Communism is the opposite.

Michael Dukakis: He is the stealth candidate ... His campaign jets from place to place, but no issues show up on the radar screen.
George Bush

In the nudist colony for communists, two old men are sitting on the porch. One turns to the other and says, 'I say, have you read Marx?' And the other says, 'Yes – think it's these wicker chairs.'

A Conservative is someone who believes that nothing should be done for the first time.

Edward Livingstone: He was a man of splendid abilities but utterly corrupt. Like rotten mackerel by moonlight, he shines and stinks. ***John Randolph***

A Conservative is someone who admires radicals a century after they're dead.

The Conservative Party stands for progress, change and innovation. But not yet.

Henry Kissinger: When Kissinger can get the Nobel Peace Prize, what is there left for satire? ***Tom Lehrer***

Democracy is a state of mind in which every man is as good as every other man, provided he really is.

If you're in the peanut business, you learn to think small. ***Eugene McCarthy.***

When a little boy desperately needed £100 to buy a present, his mother suggested that he pray for it. So he wrote to God asking for the money. The Post Office intercepted the letter and forwarded it to the prime minister, who was so touched by the request that he instructed his secretary to send the boy £5. On receiving the money, the boy wrote back: 'Dear God. Thank you very much for sending me the money. I noticed that you had to send it through Downing Street. As usual, those thieving bastards deducted £95.'

The great thing about living in a democracy is that you can say what you think without thinking.

Stephen A Douglas: His argument is as thin as the homeopathic soup that was made by boiling the shadow of a pigeon that had been starved to death.
Abraham Lincoln

If the economy is really bouncing back, why are our customers' cheques doing the same?

Sir Stafford Cripps: He has a brilliant mind until it is made up. ***Margot Asquith***

Don't forget, economists have accurately forecast nine out of the last five recessions.

Benjamin Disraeli: A self-made man who worships his creator. ***John Bright***

Prosperity is something that businessmen create for politicians to take the credit for.

Millard Fillmore: At a time when we needed a strong man, what we got was a man who swayed with the slightest breeze. ***Harry S Truman***

The economy is now on a solid foundation – it's on the rocks!

Gerald Ford: Richard Nixon impeached himself. He gave us Gerald Ford as his revenge.
Bella Abzug

Andrew Jackson: A barbarian who could not write a sentence of grammar and could hardly spell his own name. ***John Quincy Adams***

If you think there's too much government now, just think what it would be like if we got as much as we're paying for.

Anthony Eden: He is not only a bore, but he bores for England. ***Malcolm Muggeridge***

Just tell me one thing: why is there only one Monopolies Commission?

William F Buckley Jr: Looks and sounds like Hitler, but without the charm. ***Gore Vidal***

Standing at the top of Whitehall, a visitor to London asked a policeman, 'Can you tell me which side the Foreign Office is on?' And the policeman replied, 'Ours, I think.'

John Foster Dulles: Foster Dulles is the only case I know of a bull who carries a china shop with him. ***Winston Churchill***

Charles de Gaulle: He is like a female llama surprised in her bath. ***Winston Churchill***

Lady Astor to Winston Churchill: Winston, if I were married to you, I'd put poison in your coffee. *Churchill:* Nancy, if you were my wife, I'd drink it.

Calvin Coolidge's perpetual expression was of smelling something burning on the stove. ***Sherwin L Cook***

Parliament is a place where a man gets up to speak, says nothing and nobody listens and then everyone disagrees.

Thomas E Dewey: You really have to get to know Dewey to dislike him. ***Robert A Taft***

How long does a US congressman serve? Until he gets caught.

Theodore Roosevelt: His idea of getting hold of the right end of the stick is to snatch it from the hands of somebody who is using it effectively, and to hit him over the head with it. ***George Bernard Shaw***

Why don't politicians like golf? Because it's too much like their work: trapped in one bad lie after another.

[Nixon] told us he was going to take crime off the streets. He did. He took it into the White House. ***Ralph Abernathy***

Diplomat – an ex-politician who has mastered the art of holding his tongue.

Gerald Ford was unknown throughout America. Now he's unknown throughout the world. ***Anon***

Politician – someone who divides his time between running for office and running for cover.

George Bush doesn't have the manhood to apologise. ***Walter Mondale***

On the manhood thing, I'll put mine up against his any time. ***Bush's reply***

Before Al Gore was American Vice President – in fact, even before he became involved in politics – he spent some time as a drummer for a small band playing in local clubs. He was, in fact, quite a good drummer, and he developed quite a reputation for his impressive drum solos. Some of his routines were incredible for their mathematical precision. They became known as the Al-Gore-rhythms.

Michael Foot: A kind of walking obituary for the Labour Party. ***Chris Patten***

The Rt Hon Bessie Braddock, MP, to Winston Churchill: Winston, you're drunk.
Churchill: And Madam, you're ugly. Tomorrow morning, however, I shall be sober.

Sir Geoffrey Howe: Being attacked in the House by him is like being savaged by a dead sheep. ***Denis Healey***

Gerry Ford is a nice guy, but he played too much football with his helmet off. ***Lyndon B Johnson***

A little boy goes to his dad and asks, 'What is politics?' Dad says, 'Well son, let me try to explain it this way: I'm the breadwinner of the family, so let's call me Capitalism. Your Mum, she's the administrator of the money, so we'll call her the Government. We're here to take care of your needs, so we'll call you the people. The nanny, we'll consider her the Working Class. And your baby brother, we'll call him the Future. Now, think about that and see if that makes sense.' So the little boy goes off to bed thinking about what dad had said. Later that night, he hears his baby brother crying, so he gets up to check on him. He finds that the baby has severely soiled his diaper. So the little boy goes to his parents' room and finds his mother sound asleep. Not wanting to wake her, he goes to the nanny's room. Finding the door locked, he peeks in the keyhole and sees his father in bed with the nanny. He gives up and goes back to bed. The next morning, the little boy says to his father, 'Dad, I think I understand the concept of politics now.' The father says, 'Good son, tell me in your own words what you think politics is all about.' The little boy replies, 'Well, while Capitalism is screwing the Working Class, the Government is sound asleep, the People are being ignored and the Future is in deep shit.'

You've got to be careful quoting Ronald Reagan because when you quote him accurately it's called mudslinging. ***Walter Mondale***

George Bush was out jogging one morning along the parkway when he tripped, fell over the bridge railing and landed in the creek below. Before the Secret Service guys could get to him, three kids who were fishing pulled him out of the water. He was so grateful he offered the kids whatever they wanted. The first kid said, 'I sure would like to go to Disneyland.' George said, 'No problem. I'll take you there on Air Force One.' The second kid said, 'I really need a new pair of Nike Air Jordan's.' George said, 'I'll get them for you and even have Michael sign them!' The third kid said, 'I want a motorised wheelchair with a built-in TV and stereo headset!' George Bush is a little perplexed by this and says, 'But you don't look like you are injured.' The kid says, 'But I will be after my dad finds out I saved your ass from drowning!'

Sir Robert Peel: The Right Honourable Gentleman's smile is like the silver fittings on a coffin. ***Benjamin Disraeli***

Earl of Sandwich: I do not know whether you will die on the gallows or of the pox.
John Wilkes: My Lord, that will depend on whether I embrace your principles or your mistress.

Hubert Humphrey: He talks so fast that listening to him is like trying to read Playboy magazine with your wife turning the pages.
Barry Goldwater

Bill and Hillary were going down a back road and stopped at a petrol station. As the worker was filling up their car, he said to Hillary, 'I went to high school with you.' She recognised him and agreed with him. Later as they were driving down the road Bill said, 'If you had married him, you wouldn't be married to the president.' Hillary said, 'Oh yes I would – he would be president.'

Lord John Russell: If a traveller were informed that such a man was leader of the House of Commons, he may well begin to comprehend how the Egyptians worshipped an insect.
Benjamin Disraeli

Two terrorists are chatting. One of them opens his wallet and flips through pictures. 'You see, this is my oldest. He's a martyr. Here's my second son. He's a martyr, too.' The second terrorist says, gently, 'Ah, they blow up so fast, don't they?'

President Bush has said that he does not need approval from the UN to wage war, and I'm thinking, well, hell, he didn't need the approval of the American voters to become president, either.
David Letterman

Richard Rush: Never was ability so much below mediocrity so well rewarded: no, not even when Caligula's horse was made a consul.
John Randolph

Thomas Jefferson founded the Democratic Party; Franklin Roosevelt dumbfounded it. ***Dewey Short***

Adolf Hitler: He is inconsequent and voluble, ill-poised, insecure. He is the very prototype of the little man. ***Dorothy Thompson***

Jean Lesage: The only person I know who can strut sitting down. ***John Diefenbaker***

William Ewart Gladstone: A misfortune is if Gladstone fell into the Thames; a calamity would be if someone pulled him out. ***Benjamin Disraeli***

Warren G Harding: He has a bungalow mind. ***Woodrew Wilson***

Gary Hart: Hart is Kennedy typed on the eighth carbon. ***Lance Morrow***

Edward Heath: A shiver looking for a spine to run up. ***Harold Wilson***

MAKE THE PIE HIGHER
by George W Bush

I think we all agree, the past is over.
This is still a dangerous world.
It's a world of madmen and uncertainty
And potential mental losses.
Rarely is the question asked
'Is our children learning?'
Will the highways of the internet become more few?
How many hands have I shaked?
They misunderestimate me.
I am a pit bull on the pant leg of opportunity.
I know that the human being and the fish can coexist.
Families is where our nation finds hope,
Where our wings take dream.
Put food on your family!
Knock down the tollbooth!
Vulcanize Society!
Make the pie higher!
Make the pie higher!

This is a poem made up entirely of actual quotes from George W Bush. The quotes have been arranged only for aesthetic purposes by Washington Post writer Richard Thompson.

White House Wit

Trying to stop suiciders – which we're doing a pretty good job of on occasion – is difficult to do. And what the Iraqis are going to have to eventually do is convince those who are conducting suicides who are not inspired by Al Qaeda, for example, to realise there's a peaceful tomorrow. ***George W Bush, Washington, DC, 24 May 2006***

I would say the best moment of all was when I caught a 7.5 lb largemouth bass in my lake. ***George W Bush, on his best moment in office, interview with the German newspaper Bild am Sonntag, 7 May 2006***

If people want to get to know me better, they've got to know my parents and the values my parents instilled in me, and the fact that I was raised in west Texas, in the middle of the desert, a long way away from anywhere, hardly. There's a certain set of values you learn in that experience. ***George W Bush, Washington, DC, 5 May 2006***

You never know what your history is going to be like until long after you're gone. ***George W Bush, Washington, DC, 5 May 2006***

The point now is how do we work together to achieve important goals. And one such goal is a democracy in Germany. ***George W Bush, Washington, DC, 5 May 2006***

That's George Washington, the first president, of course. The interesting thing about him is that I read three – three or four books about him last year. Isn't that interesting? ***George W Bush, while showing German newspaper reporter Kai Diekmann the Oval Office, Washington, DC, 5 May 2006***

That's called 'A Charge To Keep', based upon a religious hymn. The hymn talks about serving God. The president's job is never to promote a religion. ***George W Bush, showing German newspaper reporter Kai Diekmann the Oval Office, Washington, DC, 5 May 2006***

I was not pleased that Hamas has refused to announce its desire to destroy Israel. ***George W Bush, Washington, DC, 4 May 2006***

I can look you in the eye and tell you I feel I've tried to solve the problem diplomatically to the max, and would have committed troops both in Afghanistan and Iraq knowing what I know today. ***George W Bush, Irvine, California, 24 April 2006***

I'm the decider, and I decide what is best. And what's best is for Don Rumsfeld to remain as the Secretary of Defense. ***George W Bush, Washington, DC, 18 April 2006***

I strongly believe what we're doing is the right thing. If I didn't believe it – I'm going to repeat what I said before – I'd pull the troops out, nor if I believed we could win, I would pull the troops out. ***George W Bush, Charlotte, NC, 6 April 2006***

I believe that a prosperous, democratic Pakistan will be a steadfast partner for America, a peaceful neighbour for India, and a force for freedom and moderation in the Arab world. ***George W Bush, mistakenly identifying Pakistan as an Arab country, Islamabad, Pakistan, 3 March 2006***

No question that the enemy has tried to spread sectarian violence. They use violence as a tool to do that. ***George W Bush, Washington, DC, 22 March 2006***

If the Iranians were to have a nuclear weapon they could proliferate. ***George W Bush, Washington DC, 21 March 2006***

And so I'm for medical liability at the federal level. ***George W Bush, on medical liability reform, Washington, DC, 10 March 2006***

People don't need to worry about security. This deal wouldn't go forward if we were concerned about the security for the United States of America. ***George W Bush, on the deal to hand over US port security to a company operated by the United Arab Emirates, Washington, DC, 23 February 2006***

I think it's really important for this great state of baseball to reach out to people of all walks of life to make sure that the sport is inclusive. The best way to do it is to convince little kids how to – the beauty of playing baseball. ***George W Bush, Washington, DC, 13 February 2006***

I like my buddies from west Texas. I liked them when I was young, I liked them then I was middle-aged, I liked them before I was president, and I like them during president, and I like them after president. ***George W Bush, Nashville, Tennessee, 1 February 2006***

He was a state sponsor of terror. In other words, the government had declared, 'You are a state sponsor of terror.' ***George W Bush, on Saddam Hussein, Manhattan, Kan., 23 January 2006***

I'll be glad to talk about ranching, but I haven't seen the movie. I've heard about it. I hope you go – you know – I hope you go back to the ranch and the farm is what I'm about to say. ***George W Bush, after being asked whether he's seen Brokeback Mountain, Manhattan, Kan., 23 January 2006***

It's a heck of a place to bring your family. ***George W Bush, on New Orleans, New Orleans, La., 12 January 2006***

As you can possibly see, I have an injury myself – not here at the hospital, but in combat with a cedar. I eventually won. The cedar gave me a little scratch. As a matter of fact, the Colonel asked if I needed first aid when she first saw me. I was able to avoid any major surgical operations here, but thanks for your compassion, Colonel. ***George W Bush, after visiting with wounded veterans from the Amputee Care Center of Brooke Army Medical Center, San Antonio, Texas, 1 January 2006***

You took an oath to defend our flag and our freedom, and you kept that oath under seas and under fire. ***George W Bush, addressing war veterans, Washington, DC, 10 January 2006***

As a matter of fact, I know relations between our governments is good. ***George W Bush, on US-South Korean relations, Washington DC, 8 November 2005***

It's a myth to think I don't know what's going on. It's a myth to think that I'm not aware that there's opinions that don't agree with mine, because I'm fully aware of that. ***George W Bush, Philadelphia, Pa., 12 December 2005***

I mean, there was a serious international effort to say to Saddam Hussein, 'You're a threat.' And the 9/11 attacks extenuated that threat, as far as I am concerned.
George W Bush, Philadelphia, 12 December 2005

Those who enter the country illegally violate the law.
George W Bush, Tucson, Ariz., 28 November 2005

Wow! Brazil is big. ***George W Bush, after being shown a map of Brazil by Brazilian president Luiz Inacio Lula da Silva, Brasilia, Brazil, 6 November 2005***

Bin Laden says his own role is to tell Muslims, quote, 'What is good for them and what is not.' ***George W Bush, Washington DC, 6 October 2005***

I think if you know what you believe, it makes it a lot easier to answer questions. I can't answer your question.
George W Bush, Reynoldsburg, Ohio, 4 October 2000

More and more of our imports are coming from overseas. ***George W Bush, NPR's Morning Edition, 26 September 2000***

Well, I think if you say you're going to do something and don't do it, that's trustworthiness.
George W Bush, CNN online chat, 30 August 2000

I understand small business growth. I was one. ***George W Bush, New York Daily News, 2000***

We cannot let terriers and rogue nations hold this nation hostile or hold our allies hostile. ***George W Bush, Des Moines, Iowa, 21 August 2000***

If most of the tax breaks go to wealthy people it's because most of the people who pay taxes are wealthy. ***George W Bush***

The mission must be to fight and win war and therefore to prevent war from happening in the first place. ***George W Bush***

I think we need not only to eliminate the tollbooth to the middle class, I think we should knock down the tollbooth. ***George W Bush, Nashua, NH, as quoted by Gail Collins in the New York Times, 1 February 2000***

It's clearly a budget. It's got a lot of numbers in it. ***George W Bush, Reuters, 5 May 2000***

The most important job is not to be governor, or first lady in my case. ***George W Bush, Pella, Iowa, as quoted by the San Antonio Express-News, 30 January 2000***

What I am against is quotas. I am against hard quotas, quotas they basically delineate based upon whatever. However they delineate, quotas, I think vulcanize society. So I don't know how that fits into what everybody else is saying, their relative positions, but that's my position. ***Molly Ivins, the San Francisco Chronicle, 21 January 2000***

This campaign not only hears the voices of the entrepreneurs and the farmers and the entre-preneurs, we hear the voices of those struggling to get head. ***George W Bush, Des Moines, Iowa, 21 August 2000***

And, you know, hopefully, condoms will work, but it hasn't worked. ***George W Bush, Meet the Press, 21 November 1999***

His new website, www.georgewbush.com, states that the No 3 priority of the campaign is 'Putting Education First.' ***Al Kamen, Washington Post, 19 July 2000***

The only thing that I can tell you is that every case I have reviewed I have been comfortable with the innocence or guilt of the person that I've looked at. I do not believe we've put a guilty ... I mean innocent person to death in the state of Texas. ***All Things Considered, NPR, 16 June 2000***

At one of these governors' conferences, George W Bush turns to me and says: What are they talking about? I said, 'I don't know.' He said, 'You don't know anything, do you?' And I said, 'Not one thing.' Bush said, 'Neither do I.' And we kind of high-fived. ***Govenor Gary Johnson of New Mexico, Los Angeles Times, 31 May 2000***

It's a time of sorrow and sadness when we lose a loss of life. ***George W Bush, Washington, DC, 21 December 2004***

They can get in line like those who have been here legally and have been working to become a citizenship in a legal manner. ***George W Bush, on immigrant workers, Washington, DC, 20 December 2004***

And so during these holiday seasons, we thank our blessings. ***George W Bush, Fort Belvoir, Va., 10 December 2004***

Justice ought to be fair. ***George W Bush, speaking at the White House Economic Conference, Washington, DC, 15 December 2004***

The president and I also reaffirmed our determination to fight terror, to bring drug trafficking to bear, to bring justice to those who pollute our youth. ***George W Bush, speaking with Chilean President Ricardo Lagos, Santiago, Chile, 21 November 2004***

We thought we were protected forever from trade policy or terrorist attacks because oceans protected us. ***George W Bush, speaking to business leaders at APEC Summit, Santiago, Chile, 20 November 2004***

I always jest to people, the Oval Office is the kind of place where people stand outside, they're getting ready to come in and tell me what for, and they walk in and get overwhelmed in the atmosphere, and they say, 'Man, you're looking pretty.' ***George W Bush, Washington, DC, 4 November 2004***

I have a record in office, as well. And all Americans have seen that record. September the 4th, 2001, I stood in the ruins of the Twin Towers. It's a day I will never forget. ***George W Bush, Marlton, New Jersey, 18 October 2004***

After standing on the stage, after the debates, I made it very plain, we will not have an all-volunteer army. And yet, this week – we will have an all-volunteer army! ***George W Bush, Daytona Beach, Fla., 2004***

I hear there's rumours on the Internets that we're going to have a draft. ***George W Bush, second presidential debate, St Louis, Mo., 8 October 2004***

The truth of that matter is, if you listen carefully, Saddam would still be in power if he were the president of the United States, and the world would be a lot better off. ***George W Bush, second presidential debate, St Louis, Mo., 8 October 2004***

When a drug comes in from Canada, I wanna make sure it cures ya, not kill ya... I've got an obligation to make sure our government does everything we can to protect you. And one – my worry is that it looks like it's from Canada, and it might be from a third world. ***George W Bush, second presidential debate, St Louis, Mo., 8 October 2004***

We all thought there was weapons there, Robin. My opponent thought there was weapons there. ***George W Bush, second presidential debate, St Louis, Mo., 8 October 2004***

Let me see where to start here. First, the National Journal named Senator Kennedy the most liberal senator of all. ***George W Bush, referring to Senator Kerry, second presidential debate, St Louis, Mo., 8 October 2004***

I own a timber company? That's news to me. Need some wood? ***George W Bush, second presidential debate, St Louis, Mo., 8 October 2004***

Give me a chance to be your president and America will be safer and stronger and better. ***Still-President George W Bush, Marquette, Michigan, 13 July 2004***

Another example would be the Dred Scott case, which is where judges, years ago, said that the Constitution allowed slavery because of personal property rights. That's a personal opinion. That's not what the constitution says. The constitution of the United States says we're all – you know, it doesn't say that. It doesn't speak to the equality of America.
George W Bush, second presidential debate, St Louis, Mo., 8 October 2004

The enemy understands a free Iraq will be a major defeat in their ideology of hatred. That's why they're fighting so vociferously.
George W Bush, first presidential debate, Coral Gables, Fla., 30 September 2004

I think it's very important for the American President to mean what he says. That's why I understand that the enemy could misread what I say. That's why I try to be as clearly I can. ***George W Bush, Washington, DC, 23 September 2004***

I saw a poll that said the right track/wrong track in Iraq was better than here in America. It's pretty darn strong. I mean, the people see a better future. ***George W Bush, Washington, DC, 23 September 2004***

I'm not the expert on how the Iraqi people think, because I live in America, where it's nice and safe and secure. ***George W Bush, Washington, DC, 23 September 2004***

The CIA laid out several scenarios and said life could be lousy, life could be okay, life could be better, and they were just guessing as to what the conditions might be like.
George W Bush, New York City, 2004

Free societies are hopeful societies. And free societies will be allies against these hateful few who have no conscience, who kill at the whim of a hat. ***George W Bush, Washington, DC, 17 September 2004***

Too many good docs are getting out of the business. Too many OB-GYNs aren't able to practise their love with women all across this country. ***George W Bush, Poplar Bluff, Mo., 6 September 2004***

We will make sure our troops have all that is necessary to complete their missions. That's why I went to the Congress last September and proposed fundamental – supplemental funding, which is money for armour and body parts and ammunition and fuel. ***George W Bush, Erie, Pa., 4 September 2004***

Had we to do it over again, we would look at the consequences of catastrophic success, being so successful so fast that an enemy that should have surrendered or been done in escaped and lived to fight another day. ***George W Bush, telling Time magazine that he underestimated the Iraqi resistance***

They've seen me make decisions, they've seen me under trying times, they've seen me weep, they've seen me laugh, they've seen me hug. And they know who I am, and I believe they're comfortable with the fact that they know I'm not going to shift principles or shift positions based upon polls and focus groups. ***George W Bush, interview with USA Today, 27 August 2004***

I hope you leave here and walk out and say, 'What did he say?' ***George W Bush, Beaverton, Oregon, 13 August 2004***

So community colleges are accessible, they're available, they're affordable, and their curriculums don't get stuck. In other words, if there's a need for a certain kind of worker, I presume your curriculums evolved over time. ***George W Bush, Niceville, Fla., 10 August 2004***

Let me put it to you bluntly. In a changing world, we want more people to have control over your own life. ***George W Bush, Annandale, Va, 9 August 2004***

As you know, we don't have relationships with Iran. I mean, that's – ever since the late '70s, we have no contacts with them, and we've totally sanctioned them. In other words, there's no sanctions – you can't – we're out of sanctions.' ***George W Bush, Annandale, Va, 9 August 2004***

Tribal sovereignty means that; it's sovereign. I mean, you're a – you've been given sovereignty, and you're viewed as a sovereign entity. And therefore the relationship between the federal government and tribes is one between sovereign entities. ***George W Bush, speaking to minority journalists, Washington, DC, 6 August 2004***

We actually misnamed the war on terror. It ought to be the Struggle Against Ideological Extremists Who Do Not Believe in Free Societies Who Happen to Use Terror as a Weapon to Try to Shake the Conscience of the Free World. ***George W Bush, 2004***

I cut the taxes on everybody. I didn't cut them. The Congress cut them. I asked them to cut them. ***George W Bush, Washington, DC, 6 August 2004***

I wish I wasn't the war president. Who in the heck wants to be a war president? I don't. ***George W Bush, Washington, DC, 6 August 2004***

Our enemies are innovative and resourceful, and so are we. They never stop thinking about new ways to harm our country and our people, and neither do we. ***George W Bush, Washington, DC, 5 August 2004***

We stand for things. ***George W Bush, Davenport, Iowa, 5 August 2004***

I mean, if you've ever been a governor of a state, you understand the vast potential of broadband technology, you understand how hard it is to make sure that physics, for example, is taught in every classroom in the state. It's difficult to do. It's, like, cost-prohibitive. ***George W Bush, Washington, DC, 24 June 2004***

I don't know why you're talking about Sweden. They're the neutral one. They don't have an army. ***George W Bush, during an Oval Office meeting with Rep. Tom Lantos, as reported by the New York Times***

I want to thank my friend, Senator Bill Frist, for joining us today. You're doing a heck of a job. You cut your teeth here, right? That's where you started practising? That's good. He married a Texas girl, I want you to know. Karyn is with us. A west Texas girl, just like me. ***George W Bush, Nashville, Tenn., 27 May 2004***

I'm honoured to shake the hand of a brave Iraqi citizen who had his hand cut off by Saddam Hussein. ***George W Bush, Washington, DC, 25 May 2004***

Like you, I have been disgraced about what I've seen on TV that took place in prison. ***George W Bush, Parkersburg, West Virginia, 13 May 2004***

Iraqis are sick of foreign people coming in their country and trying to destabilise their country. ***George W Bush, interview with Al Arabiya Television, 5 May 2004***

My job is to, like, think beyond the immediate. ***George W Bush, Washington, DC, 21 April 2004***

This has been tough weeks in that country. ***George W Bush, Washington, DC, 13 April 2004***

Coalition forces have encountered serious violence in some areas of Iraq. Our military commanders report that this violence is being insticated by three groups. ***George W Bush, Washington, DC, 13 April 2004***

One of the most meaningful things that's happened to me since I've been the governor – the president – governor – president. Oops. Ex-governor. I went to Bethesda Naval Hospital to give a fellow a Purple Heart, and at the same moment I watched him – get a Purple Heart for action in Iraq – and at that same – right after I gave him the Purple Heart, he was sworn in as a citizen of the United States – a Mexican citizen, now a United States citizen. ***George W Bush, Washington, DC, 9 January 2004***

Obviously, I pray every day there's less casualty. ***George W Bush, Fort Hood, Texas, 11 April 2004***

And if you're interested in the quality of education and you're paying attention to what you hear at Laclede, why don't you volunteer? Why don't you mentor a child how to read? ***George W Bush, St Louis, Mo., 5 January 2004***

So thank you for reminding me about the importance of being a good mom and a great volunteer as well. ***George W Bush, St Louis, Mos., 5 January 2004***

I want to remind you all that in order to fight and win the war, it requires an expenditure of money that is commiserate with keeping a promise to our troops to make sure that they're well-paid, well-trained, well-equipped. ***George W Bush, Washington, DC, 2003***

See, without the tax relief package, there would have been a deficit, but there wouldn't have been the commiserate – not 'commiserate' – the kick to our economy that occurred as a result of the tax relief. ***George W Bush, Washington, DC, 15 December 2003***

The Iraqis need to be very much involved. They were the people that was brutalised by this man. ***George W Bush, Washington, DC, 15 December 2003***

The best way to find these terrorists who hide in holes is to get people coming forth to describe the location of the hole, is to give clues and data. ***George W Bush, Washington, DC, 15 December 2003***

Justice was being delivered to a man who defied that gift

from the Almighty to the people of Iraq. ***George W Bush, Washington, DC, 15 December 2003***

This very week in 1989, there were protests in East Berlin and in Leipzig. By the end of that year, every communist dictatorship in Central America had collapsed. ***George W Bush, Washington, DC, 6 November 2003***

America stands for liberty, for the pursuit of happiness, and for the unalienalienable right of life. ***George W Bush, Washington, DC, 3 November 2003***

The ambassador and the general were briefing me on the – the vast majority of Iraqis want to live in a peaceful, free world. And we will find these people and we will bring them to justice. ***George W Bush, Washington, DC, 27 October 2003***

Whether they be Christian, Jew, or Muslim, or Hindu, people have heard the universal call to love a neighbour just like they'd like to be called themselves. ***George W Bush, Washington, DC, 8 October 2003***

See, free nations are peaceful nations. Free nations don't attack each other. Free nations don't develop weapons of mass destruction. ***George W Bush, Milwaukee, Wis., 3 October 2003***

Washington is a town where there's all kinds of allegations. You've heard much of the allegations. And if people have got solid information, please come forward with it. And that would be people inside the information who are the so-called anonymous sources, or people outside the information – outside the administration. ***George W Bush, Chicago, 30 September 2003***

We've had leaks out of the administrative branch, had leaks out of the legislative branch, and out of the executive branch and the legislative branch, and I've spoken out consistently against them, and I want to know who the leakers are. ***George W Bush, Chicago, 30 September 2003***

I glance at the headlines just to kind of get a flavour for what's moving. I rarely read the stories, and get briefed by people who are probably read the news themselves. ***George W Bush, Washington, DC, 21 September 2003***

As Luce reminded me, he said, without data, without facts, without information, the discussions about public education mean that a person is just another opinion. ***George W Bush, Jacksonville, Florida, 9 September 2003***

I'm a follower of American politics. ***George W Bush, Crawford, Texas, 8 August 2003***

That's just the nature of democracy. Sometimes pure politics enters into the rhetoric. ***George W Bush, Crawford, Texas, 8 August 2003***

We had a good Cabinet meeting, talked about a lot of issues. Secretary of State and Defense brought us up to date about our desires to spread freedom and peace around the world. ***George W Bush, Washington, DC, 1 August 2003***

And the other lesson is that there are people who can't stand what America stands for, and desire to conflict great harm on the American people. ***George W Bush, Pittsburgh, Pennsylvania, 28 July 2003***

Security is the essential roadblock to achieving the road map to peace. ***George W Bush, Washington, DC, 25 July 2003***

Our country puts $1 billion a year up to help feed the hungry. And we're by far the most generous nation in the world when it comes to that, and I'm proud to report that. This isn't a contest of who's the most generous. I'm just telling you as an aside. We're generous. We shouldn't be bragging about it. But we are. We're very generous. ***George W Bush, Washington, DC, 16 July 2003***

It's very interesting when you think about it, the slaves who left here to go to America, because of their steadfast and their religion and their belief in freedom, helped change America. ***George W Bush, Dakar, Senegal, 8 July 2003***

My answer is bring them on. ***George W Bush, on Iraqi insurgents attacking US forces, Washington, DC, 3 July 2003***

You've also got to measure in order to begin to effect change that's just more – when there's more than talk, there's just actual – a paradigm shift. ***George W Bush, Washington, DC, 1 July 2003***

I urge the leaders in Europe and around the world to take swift, decisive action against terror groups such as Hamas, to cut off their funding, and to support – cut funding and support, as the United States has done. ***George W Bush, Washington, DC, 25 June 2003***

Iran would be dangerous if they have a nuclear weapon. ***George W Bush, Washington, DC, 18 June 2003***

Now, there are some who would like to rewrite history – revisionist historians is what I like to call them. ***George W Bush, Elizabeth, NJ, 16 June 2003***

I am determined to keep the process on the road to peace. ***George W Bush, Washington, DC, 10 June 2003***

We are making steadfast progress. ***George W Bush, Washington, DC, 9 June 2003***

I'm the master of low expectations. ***George W Bush, aboard Air Force One, 4 June 2003***

The war on terror involves Saddam Hussein because of the nature of Saddam Hussein, the history of Saddam Hussein, and his willingness to terrorise himself. ***George W Bush, Grand Rapids, Mich., 29 January 2003***

I'm also not very analytical. You know I don't spend a lot of time thinking about myself, about why I do things. ***George W Bush, aboard Air Force One, 4 June 2003***

When Iraq is liberated, you will be treated, tried and persecuted as a war criminal. ***George W Bush, Washington, DC, 22 January 2003***

One year ago today, the time for excuse-making has come to an end. ***George W Bush, Washington, DC, 8 January 2003***

You see, the Senate wants to take away some of the powers of the administrative branch. ***George W Bush, Washington, DC, 19 September 2002***

The goals for this country are peace in the world. And the goals for this country are a compassionate American for every single citizen. That compassion is found in the hearts and souls of the American citizens.
George W Bush, Washington, DC, 19 December 2002

I think the American people – I hope the American – I don't think, let me – I hope the American people trust me.
George W Bush, Washington, DC, 18 December 2002

There's only one person who hugs the mothers and the widows, the wives and the kids upon the death of their loved one. Others hug but having committed the troops, I've got an additional responsibility to hug and that's me and I know what it's like. ***George W Bush, 2002***

In other words, I don't think people ought to be compelled to make the decision which they think is best for their family. ***George W Bush, on smallpox vaccinations, Washington, DC, 11 December 2002***

You believe in the Almighty, and I believe in the Almighty. That's why we'll be great partners. ***George W Bush, to Turkish Prime Minister Recap Tayyip Erdogan, Washington, DC, 10 December 2002***

Sometimes, Washington is one of these towns where the person – people who think they've got the sharp elbow is the most effective person.
George W Bush, New Orleans, 3 December 2002

There's no cave deep enough for America, or dark enough to hide. ***George W Bush, Oklahoma City, 29 August 2002***

The law I sign today directs new funds and new focus to the task of collecting vital intelligence on terrorist threats and on weapons of mass production.
George W Bush, Washington, DC, 27 November 2002

Haven't we already given money to rich people? Why are we going to do it again?
George W Bush, to economic advisers discussing a second round of tax cuts, as quoted by Paul O'Neil, Washington, DC, 26 November 2002

I need to be able to move the right people to the right place at the right time to protect you, and I'm not going to accept a lousy bill out of the United Nations Senate.
George W Bush, South Bend, Ind., 31 October 2002

I'm the commander – see, I don't need to explain – I do not need to explain why I say things. That's the interesting thing about being president.
George W Bush, as quoted in Bob Woodward's Bush at War

I know something about being a government. And you've got a good one.
George W Bush, campaigning for Governor Mike Huckabee, Bentonville, Ark., 4 November 2002

These people don't have tanks. They don't have ships. They hide in caves. They send suiciders out. ***George W Bush, speaking about terrorists, Portsmouth, NH, 1 November 2002***

John Thune has got a common-sense vision for good forest policy. I look forward to working with him in the United Nations Senate to preserve these national heritages. ***George W Bush, Aberdeen, SD, 31 October 2002***

Any time we've got any kind of inkling that somebody is thinking about doing something to an American and something to our homeland, you've just got to know we're moving on it, to protect the United Nations Constitution, and at the same time, we're protecting you. ***George W Bush, Aberdeen, SD, 31 October 2002***

I was proud the other day when both Republicans and Democrats stood with me in the Rose Garden to announce their support for a clear statement of purpose: you disarm, or we will. ***George W Bush, speaking about Saddam Hussein, Manchester, NH, 5 October 2002***

We need an energy bill that encourages consumption. ***George W Bush, Trenton, NJ, 23 September 2002***

Let me tell you my thoughts about tax relief. When your economy is kind of ooching along, it's important to let people have more of their own money. ***George W Bush, Boston, 4 October 2002***

People say, how can I help on this war against terror? How can I fight evil? You can do so by mentoring a child; by going into a shut-in's house and say I love you. ***George W Bush, Washington, DC, 19 September 2002***

There's an old saying in Tennessee – I know it's in Texas, probably in Tennessee – that says, fool me once, shame on – shame on you. Fool me – you can't get fooled again. ***George W Bush, Nashville, Tenn., 17 September 2002***

See, we love – we love freedom. That's what they

didn't understand. They hate things; we love things. They act out of hatred; we don't seek revenge, we seek justice out of love. ***George W Bush, Oklahoma City, 29 August 2002***

President Musharraf, he's still tight with us on the war against terror, and that's what I appreciate. He's a – he understands that we've got to keep Al Qaeda on the run, and that by keeping him on the run, it's more likely we will bring him to justice. ***George W Bush, Ruch, Ore., 22 August 2002***

I'm a patient man. And when I say I'm a patient man, I mean I'm a patient man. Nothing he [Saddam Hussein] has done has convinced me – I'm confident the Secretary of Defense – that he is the kind of fellow that is willing to forgo weapons of mass destruction, is willing to be a peaceful neighbour, that is – will honour the people – the Iraqi people of all stripes, will – values human life. He hasn't convinced me, nor has he convinced my administration. ***George W Bush, Crawford, Texas, 21 August 2002***

I'm thrilled to be here in the bread basket of America because it gives me a chance to remind our fellow citizens that we have an advantage here in America – we can feed ourselves. ***George W Bush, Stockton, Calif., 23 August 2002***

The federal government and the state government must not fear programs who change lives, but must welcome those faith-based programs for the embetterment of mankind. ***George W Bush, Stockton, Calif., 23 August 2002***

I promise you I will listen to what has been said here, even though I wasn't here. ***George W Bush, speaking at the President's Economic Forum in Waco, Texas, 13 August 2002***

There may be some tough times here in America. But this country has gone through tough times before, and we're going to do it again. ***George W Bush, Waco, Texas, 13 August 2002***

The trial lawyers are very politically powerful... But here in Texas we took them on and got some good medical – medical malpractice. ***George W Bush, Waco, Texas, 13 August 2002***

I firmly believe the death tax is good for people from all walks of life all throughout our society. ***George W Bush, Waco, Texas, 13 August 2002***

I love the idea of a school in which people come to get educated and stay in the state in which they're educated. ***George W Bush, Milwaukee, Wis., 14 August 2002***

The problem with the French is that they don't have a word for entrepreneur. ***George W Bush, discussing the decline of the French economy with British Prime Minister Tony Blair***

There was no malfeance involved. This was an honest disagreement about accounting procedures... There was no malfeance, no attempt to hide anything. ***George W Bush, White House press conference, Washington, DC, 2002***

I also understand how tender the free enterprise system can be. ***George W Bush, White House press conference, Washington, DC, 8 July 2002***

Over 75 per cent of white Americans own their home, and less than 50 per cent of Hispanos and African Americans don't own their home. And that's a gap, that's a home ownership gap. And we've got to do something about it. ***George W Bush, Cleveland, Ohio, 1 July 2002***

I just want you to know that, when we talk about war, we're really talking about peace. ***George W Bush, 18 June 2002***

I'd rather have them sacrificing on behalf of our nation than, you know, endless hours of testimony on congressional hill. ***George W Bush, Fort Meade, Maryland, 4 June 2002***

We're working with Chancellor Schröder on what's called 10-plus-10-over-10: $10 billion from the U.S.,$10 billion from other members of the G7 over a 10-year period, to help Russia securitize the dismantling – the dismantled nuclear warheads. ***George W Bush, Berlin, Germany, 23 May 2002***

We hold dear what our Declaration of Independence says, that all have got uninalienable rights, endowed by a Creator. ***George W Bush, to community and religious leaders in Moscow, 24 May 2002***

And one of the things we've got to make sure that we do is anything. ***George W Bush, discussing the Middle East after meeting with Israeli Prime Minister Ariel Sharon, Washington, DC, 7 May 2002***

After all, a week ago, there were – Yasser Arafat was boarded up in his building in

Ramallah, a building full of, evidently, German peace protestors and all kinds of people. They're now out. He's now free to show leadership, to lead the world. ***George W Bush, Washington, DC, 2 May 2002***

The public education system in America is one of the most important foundations of our democracy. After all, it is where children from all over America learn to be responsible citizens, and learn to have the skills necessary to take advantage of our fantastic opportunistic society. ***George W Bush, 1 May 2002***

Do you have blacks, too? ***George W Bush, to Brazilian President Fernando Cardoso, 8 November 2001, as reported in 28 April 2002 Estado Sao Pauloan column by Fernando Pedreira, a close friend of President Cardoso***

This foreign policy stuff is a little frustrating. ***George W Bush, as quoted by the New York Daily News, 23 April 2002***

It would be a mistake for the United States Senate to allow any kind of human cloning to come out of that chamber. ***George W Bush, Washington, DC, 10 April 2002***

And so, in my State of the – my State of the Union – or state – my speech to the nation, whatever you want to call it, speech to the nation – I asked Americans to give 4,000 years – 4,000 hours over the next – the rest of your life – of service to America. That's what I asked – 4,000 hours. ***George W Bush, Bridgeport, Conn., 9 April 2002***

We've got pockets of persistent poverty in our society, which I refuse to declare defeat – I mean, I refuse to allow them to continue on. And so one of the things that we're trying to do is to encourage a faith-based initiative to spread its wings all across America, to be able to capture this great compassionate spirit. ***George W Bush, O'Fallon, Mo., 18 March 2002***

My mom often used to say, 'The trouble with W' - although she didn't put that to words. ***George W Bush, Washington, DC, 3 April 2002***

Sometimes when I sleep at night I think of Dr Seuss's Hop on Pop. ***George W Bush, in a speech about childhood education, Washington, DC, 2 April 2002***

We've tripled the amount of money – I believe it's from $50 million up to $195 million available. ***George W Bush, Lima, Peru, 23 March 2002***

Laura and I will thank them from the bottom of my heart. ***George W Bush, Alexandria, Virginia, 20 March 2002***

I understand that the unrest in the Middle East creates unrest throughout the region. ***George W Bush, Washington, DC, 13 March 2002***

There's nothing more deep than recognising Israel's right to exist. That's the most deep thought of all ... I can't think of anything more deep than that right. ***George W Bush, Washington, DC, 13 March 2002***

I am here to make an announcement that this Thursday, ticket counters and airplanes will fly out of Ronald Reagan Airport. ***George W Bush, Washington, DC, 3 October 2001***

They didn't think we were a nation that could conceivably sacrifice for something greater than our self; that we were soft, that we were so self-absorbed and so materialistic that we wouldn't defend anything we believed in. My, were they wrong. They just were reading the wrong magazine or watching the wrong Springer show. ***George W Bush, Washington, DC, 12 March 2002***

My trip to Asia begins here in Japan for an important reason. It begins here because for a century and a half now, America and Japan have formed one of the great and enduring alliances of modern times. From that alliance has come an era of peace in the Pacific. ***George W Bush, who apparently forgot about a little something called WW II, Tokyo, 18 February 2002***

Ann and I will carry out this equivocal message to the world: Markets must be open. ***George W Bush, at the swearing-in ceremony for Secretary of Agriculture Ann Veneman, 2 March 2001***

You know, I was campaigning in Chicago and somebody asked me, is there ever any time where the budget might have to go into deficit? I said only if we were at war or had a national emergency or were in recession. Little did I realise we'd get the trifecta. ***George W Bush, Charlotte, North Carolina, 27 February 2002***

I couldn't imagine somebody like Osama bin Laden understanding the joy of Hanukkah. ***George W Bush, at a White House Menorah lighting ceremony, Washington, DC, 10 December 2001***

He [Japanese Prime Minister Junichiro Koizumi] said I want to make it very clear to you exactly what I intend to do and he talked about non-performing loans, the devaluation issue and regulatory reform and he placed equal emphasis on all three. ***George W Bush, who had meant to say 'the deflation issue' rather than 'the devaluation issue,' and accidentally sent the Japanese Yen tumbling, Tokyo, 18 February 2002***

I've been to war. I've raised twins. If I had a choice, I'd rather go to war. ***George W Bush, Charleston, West Virginia, 27 January 2002***

Not over my dead body will they raise your taxes. ***George W Bush, Ontario, California, 5 January 2002***

The United States and Russia are in the midst of transformationed relationship that will yield peace and progress. ***George W Bush, Washington, DC, 13 November 2001***

I want to thank you for taking time out of your day to come and witness my hanging. ***George W Bush, at the dedication of his portrait, Austin, Texas, 4 January 2002***

But all in all, it's been a fabulous year for Laura and me. ***George W Bush, summing up his first year in office, Washington, DC, 20 December 2001***

We need to counter the shockwave of the evildoer by having individual rate cuts accelerated and by thinking about tax rebates. ***George W Bush, Washington, DC, 4 October 2001***

The folks who conducted to act on our country on September 11th made a big mistake. They underestimated America. They underestimated our resolve, our determination, our love for freedom. They misunderestimated the fact that we love a neighbour in need. They misunderestimated the compassion of our country. I think they misunderestimated the will and determination of the Commander-in-Chief, too. ***George W Bush, Washington, DC, 26 September 2001***

We are fully committed to working with both sides to bring the level of terror down to an acceptable level for both. ***George W Bush, after a meeting with congressional leaders, Washington, DC, 2 October 2001***

The suicide bombings have increased. There's too many of them. ***George W Bush, Albuquerque, NM, 15 August 2001***

Border relations between Canada and Mexico have never been better. ***George W Bush, in a press conference with Canadian Prime Minister Jean Chretien, 24 September 2001***

When I take action, I'm not going to fire a $2 million missile at a $10 empty tent and hit a camel in the butt. It's going to be decisive. ***George W. Bush, Washington, D.C. 19 September 2001***

When I was a kid I remember that they used to put out there in the Old West a wanted poster. It said, 'Wanted: Dead or Alive'. ***George W Bush, Washington, DC, 18 September 2001***

A dictatorship would be a heck of a lot easier, there's no question about it. ***George W Bush, 27 July 2001***

I'm confident we can work with Congress to come up with an economic stimulus package that will send a clear signal to the risk takers and capital formators of our country. ***George W Bush, Washington, DC, 17 September 2001***

Arbolist ... Look up the word. I don't know, maybe I made it up. Anyway, it's an arbo-tree-ist, somebody who knows about trees. ***George W Bush, as quoted in USA Today, 21 August 2001***

One of the interesting initiatives we've taken in Washington, DC, is we've got these vampire-busting devices. A vampire is a – a cell deal you can plug in the wall to charge your cell phone. ***George W Bush, Denver, 14 August 2001***

There's a lot of people in the Middle East who are desirous to get into the Mitchell process. And – but first things first. The – these terrorist acts and, you know, the responses have got to end in order for us to get the framework – the groundwork – not framework, the groundwork to discuss a framework for peace, to lay the – all right. ***George W Bush, referring to former Senator George Mitchell's report on Middle East peace, Crawford, Texas, 13 August 2001***

My administration has been calling upon all the leaders in the – in the Middle East to do everything they can to stop the violence, to tell the different parties involved that peace will never happen. ***George W Bush, Crawford, Texas, 13 August 2001***

He married, like me, above his head. ***George W Bush, on US Ambassador to Canada, Paul Cellucci, Quebec City, 22 April 2001***

You saw the president yesterday. I thought he was very forward-leaning, as they say in diplomatic nuanced circles. ***George W Bush, referring to his meeting with Russian President Vladimir Putin, 23 July 2001***

I know what I believe. I will continue to articulate what I believe and what I believe – I believe what I believe is right. ***George W Bush, in Rome, 22 July 2001***

It is white. ***George W Bush, asked by a child in Britain what the White House was like, 19 July 2001***

I can't tell you what it's like to be in Europe, for example, to be talking about the greatness of America. But the true greatness of America are the people. ***George W Bush, Washington, DC, 2 July 2001***

It's my honor to speak to you as the leader of your country. And the great thing about America is you don't have to listen unless you want to. ***George W Bush, speaking to recently sworn in immigrants on Ellis Island, 10 July 2001***

Well, it's an unimaginable honour to be the president during the Fourth of July of this country. It means what these words say, for starters. The great inalienable rights of our country. We're blessed with such values in America. And I – it's – I'm a proud man to be the nation based upon such wonderful values. ***George W Bush, visiting the Jefferson Memorial, Washington, DC, 2 July 2001***

You know, sometimes when you study history, you get stuck in the past. ***George W Bush, on what he told Russian President Vladimir Putin, as quoted in the Wall Street Journal, 25 June 2001***

It's negative to think about blowing each other up. That's not a positive thought. That's a Cold War thought. That's a thought when people were enemies with each other. ***George W Bush, as quoted in the Wall Street Journal, 25 June 2001***

I'm sure you can imagine it's an unimaginable honour to live here. ***George W Bush, addressing agricultural leaders at the White House, 18 June 2001***

I want to thank you for coming to the White House to give me an opportunity to urge you to work with these five senators and three congressmen, to work hard to get this trade promotion authority moving. The power that be, well most of the power that be, sits right here. ***George W Bush, Washington, DC, 18 June 2001***

I looked the man in the eye. I found him to be very straightforward and trustworthy ... I was able to get a sense of his soul. ***George W Bush, after meeting Russian President Vladimir Putin, 16 June 2001***

We spent a lot of time talking about Africa, as we should. Africa is a nation that suffers from incredible disease. ***George W Bush, at a news conference in Europe, 14 June 2001***

So on behalf of a well-oiled unit of people who came together to serve something greater than themselves, congratulations. ***George W Bush, in remarks to the University of Nebraska women's volleyball team, the 2001 national champions, 31 May 2001***

It's amazing I won. I was running against peace, prosperity, and incumbency. ***George W Bush, speaking to Swedish Prime Minister Goran Perrson, unaware that a live television camera was still rolling, 14 June 2001***

I haven't had a chance to talk, but I'm confident we'll get a bill that I can live with if we don't. ***George W Bush, referring to the McCain-Kennedy patients' bill of rights, 13 June 2001***

Russia is no longer our enemy and therefore we shouldn't be locked into a Cold War mentality that says we keep the peace by blowing each other up. In my attitude, that's old, that's tired, that's stale. ***George W Bush, Des Moines, Iowa, 8 June 2001***

Anyway, I'm so thankful, and so gracious – I'm gracious that my brother Jeb is concerned about the hemisphere as well. ***George W Bush, 4 June 2001***

It's important for young men and women who look at the Nebraska champs to understand that quality of life is more than just blocking shots. ***George W Bush, in remarks to the University of Nebraska women's volleyball team, the 2001 national champions, 31 May 2001***

If a person doesn't have the capacity that we all want that person to have, I suspect hope is in the far distant future, if at all. ***George W Bush, 22 May 2001***

There's no question that the minute I got elected, the storm clouds on the horizon were getting nearly directly overhead. ***George W Bush, 11 May 2001***

For every fatal shooting, there were roughly three non-fatal shootings. And, folks, this is unacceptable in America. It's just unacceptable. And we're going to do something about it. ***George W Bush, Philadelphia, Penn., 14 May 2001***

But I also made it clear to Vladimir Putin that it's important to think beyond the old days of when we had the concept that if we blew each other up, the world would be safe. ***George W Bush, 1 May 2001***

First, we would not accept a treaty that would not have been ratified, nor a treaty that I thought made sense for the country. ***George W Bush, on the Kyoto accord, 24 April 2001***

It is time to set aside the old partisan bickering and finger-pointing and name-calling that comes from freeing parents to make different choices for their children. ***George W Bush, on 'parental empowerment in education,' 12 April 2001***

It's very important for folks to understand that when there's more trade, there's more commerce. ***George W Bush, at the Summit of the Americas in Quebec City, 21 April 2001***

We must have the attitude that every child in America – regardless of where they're raised or how they're born – can learn. ***George W Bush, New Britain, Conn., 18 April 2001***

This administration is doing everything we can to end the stalemate in an efficient way. We're making the right decisions to bring the solution to an end. ***George W Bush, Washington, DC 10 April 2001***

I think we're making progress. We understand where the power of this country lay. It lays in the hearts and souls of Americans. It must lay in our pocketbooks. It lays in the willingness for people to work hard. But as importantly, it lays in the fact that we've got citizens from all walks of life, all political parties, that are willing to say, I want to love my neighbour. I want to make somebody's life just a little bit better. ***George W Bush, 11 April 2001***

We want to develop defenses that are capable of defending ourselves and defenses capable of defending others. ***George W Bush, White House press conference, Washington, DC, 29 March 2001***

It would be helpful if we opened up ANWR [Arctic National Wildlife Refuge]. I think it's a mistake not to. And I would urge you all to travel up there and take a look at it, and you can make the determination as to how beautiful that country is. ***George W Bush, White House press conference, 29 March 2001***

I've coined new words, like, misunderstanding and Hispanically. ***George W Bush, speaking at the Radio & Television Correspondents dinner, 29 March 2001***

We'll be a great country where the fabrics are made up of groups and loving centres. ***George W Bush, Kalamazoo, Michigan, 27 March 2001***

But the true threats to stability and peace are these nations that are not very transparent, that hide behind the - that don't let people in to take a look and see what they're up to. They're very kind of authoritarian regimes. The true threat is whether or not one of these people decide, peak of anger, try to hold us hostage, ourselves; the Israelis, for example, to whom we'll defend, offer our defences; the South Koreans. ***George W Bush, in a media roundtable discussion, 13 March 2001***

A lot of times in the rhetoric, people forget the facts. And the facts are that thousands of small businesses – Hispanically-owned or otherwise – pay taxes at the highest marginal rate. ***George W Bush, speaking to the Hispanic Chamber of Commerce, 19 March 2001***

My plan plays down an unprecedented amount of our national debt. ***George W Bush, in his budget address to Congress, 27 February 2001***

I do think we need for a troop to be able to house his family. That's an important part of building morale in the military. ***George W Bush, speaking at Tyndall Air Force Base in Florida, 12 March 2001***

I suspect that had my dad not been president, he'd be asking the same questions: How'd your meeting go with so-and-so? ... How did you feel when you stood up in front of the people for the State of the Union Address – state of the budget address, whatever you call it. ***George W Bush, in an interview with the Washington Post, 9 March 2001***

I have said that the sanction regime is like Swiss cheese – that meant that they weren't very effective. ***George W Bush, during a White House press conference, 22 February 2001***

We both use Colgate toothpaste. ***George W Bush, on what he had in common with Tony Blair, Camp David, Maryland, 23 February 2001***

You teach a child to read, and he or her will be able to pass a literacy test. ***George W Bush, 21 February 2001***

My plan reduces the national debt, and fast. So fast, in fact, that economists worry that we're going to run out of debt to retire. ***George W Bush, radio address, 24 February 2001***

Home is important. It's important to have a home. ***George W Bush, Crawford, Texas, 18 February 2001***

It's good to see so many friends here in the Rose Garden. This is our first event in this beautiful spot, and it's appropriate we talk about policy that will affect people's lives in a positive way in such a beautiful, beautiful part of our national – really, our national park system, my guess is you would want to call it. ***George W Bush, 8 February 2001***

We're concerned about AIDS inside our White House – make no mistake about it. ***George W Bush, 7 February 2001***

There's no such thing as legacies. At least, there is a legacy, but I'll never see it. ***George W Bush, speaking to Catholic leaders at the White House, 31 January 2001***

I am mindful not only of preserving executive powers for myself, but for predecessors as well. ***George W Bush, Washington, DC, 29 January 2001***

I appreciate that question because I, in the state of Texas, had heard a lot of discussion about a faith-based initiative eroding the important bridge between church and state. ***George W Bush, speaking to reporters, Washington, DC, 29 January 2001***

Then I went for a run with the other dog and just walked. And I started thinking about a lot of things. I was able to – I can't remember what it was. Oh, the inaugural speech, started thinking through that. ***George W Bush, in a pre-inaugural interview with US News & World Report***

Redefining the role of the United States from enablers to keep the peace to enablers to keep the peace from peacekeepers is going to be an assignment. ***George W Bush, 14 January 2001***

My pro-life position is I believe there's life. It's not necessarily based in religion. I think there's a life there, therefore the notion of life, liberty, and the pursuit of happiness. ***George W Bush, as quoted in the San Francisco Chronicle, 23 January 2001***

I'm hopeful. I know there is a lot of ambition in Washington, obviously. But I hope the ambitious realise that they are more likely to succeed with success as opposed to failure.
George W Bush, 18 January 2001

I do remain confident in Linda. She'll make a fine labour secretary. From what I've read in the press accounts, she's perfectly qualified. ***George W Bush, commenting on Linda Chavez, 8 January 2001***

I want everybody to hear loud and clear that I'm going to be the president of everybody. ***George W Bush, Washington, DC, 18 January 2001***

The California crunch really is the result of not enough power-generating plants and then not enough power to power the power of generating plants. ***George W Bush, 14 January 2001***

If he's – the inference is that somehow he thinks slavery is a – is a noble institution I would – I would strongly reject that assumption – that John Ashcroft is a open-minded, inclusive person. ***George W Bush, 14 January 2001***

I want it to be said that the Bush administration was a results-oriented administration, because I believe the results of focusing our attention and energy on teaching children to read and having an education system that's responsive to the child and to the parents, as opposed to mired in a system that refuses to change, will make America what we want it to be – a more literate country and a hopefuller country. ***George W Bush, 11 January 2001***

I think it's very important for world leaders to understand that when a new administration comes in, the new administration will be running the foreign policy. ***George W Bush, interview with USA Today, 12 January 2001***

It'll be hard to articulate. ***George W Bush, anticipating how he'd feel upon assuming the presidency, January 2001***

It's about past seven in the evening here so we're actually in different time lines. ***George W Bush, congratulating newly elected Philippine President Gloria Macapagal Arroyo, Washington, DC, January 2001***

I mean, these good folks are revolutionising how businesses conduct their business. And, like them, I am very optimistic about our position in the world and about its influence on the United States. We're concerned about the short-term economic news, but long-term I'm optimistic. And so, I hope investors, you know – secondly, I hope investors hold investments for periods of time – that I've always found the best investments are those that you salt away based on economics. ***George W Bush, Austin, Texas, 4 January 2001***

The person who runs FEMA is someone who must have the trust of the president. Because the person who runs FEMA is the first voice, often times, of someone whose life has been turned upside down hears from. ***George W Bush, Austin, Texas, 4 January 2001***

History is Bunk

A group of American tourists were visiting Runnymede and the tour guide was explaining its significance. 'This is where the Magna Carta was signed,' he told them. 'When was that?' came a voice from the crowd. The guide replied, '1215.' 'Goddammit,' said the voice, 'We missed it by 20 minutes!'

It's amazing how much we can learn from history – and how little we have.

Queen Anne: Anne when in good humour was meekly stupid, and when in bad humour was sulkily stupid. ***Thomas Macaulay***

It's no wonder the Red Indians got fed up with the early settlers - always paying their bills before six o' clock in the morning.

Back in the Middle Ages, there was a travelling show that toured throughout Europe. It was famous across the whole continent for its fabulous and death-defying shows. The show was named 'The Show of Tension', because of the daring nature of most of the stunts, and thus the performers and other staff associated with the show gained the nickname 'Tensions'. Sadly, the shows didn't survive the poverty that swept Europe in the Middle Ages. As people got poorer, they couldn't afford to spend money on frivolous things like a travelling show. And thus was born the expression 'unable to pay a tension'...

King George III: George the Third, Ought never to have occurred. One can only wonder, At so grotesque a blunder. ***E Clerihew Bentley***

One of my American ancestors was killed because he wouldn't pay a buccaneer. And we think corn is expensive today!

King Edward VIII: He had hidden shallows. ***Clive James***

When you hear two different eyewitness accounts of the same traffic accident, you begin to worry about history.

Student: What were the main effects of the French Revolution?
Professor: I think it's a little too early to say.

King Edward VII: Bertie seemed to display a deep-seated repugnance to every form of mental exertion.
Lytton Strachey

In the early 1900s, the President of America went to visit Russia. Of course, Russia was still ruled by the Czar back then, and the American president was warmly welcomed by the whole Russian royal household. As the two leaders and their entourages were dining one day in one of the huge dining rooms in the palace, the Americans were telling the Russians about some of the great things in their country. One of the topics of conversation was the Grand Canyon in Colorado. Of course, the Americans were quite boastful about this being the largest canyon in the world, when suddenly, from the head of the table, the Czar stood up and made an announcement. 'In Russia,' he said, 'we have a canyon even bigger than your Grand Canyon!' Now, no one was going to stand up and contradict the Czar, but of course no one believed him either. Finally, the American president stood up, and said 'Okay. Let's see this canyon then.' So an expedition was organised. Of course, their destination was way out in the remote wilderness, and they only had horses to travel with, so the going was slow. But eventually, after several weeks' gruelling journey, they finally arrived at where the canyon was supposed to be. But there wasn't one. Not even a little one. And then it dawned on everyone – he had been using Czar chasm to make them look stupid.

Queen Elizabeth I: Oh dearest Queen, I've never seen, A face more like a soup-tureen.
Anon

My family's records go back at least eight centuries. How about yours? Ours were lost in the Flood!

King Henry VIII: A pig, an ass, a dunghill, the spawn of an adder, a basilisk, a lying buffoon, a mad fool with a frothy mouth. ***Martin Luther***

Old kings never die; they just get throne away.

Back in the days of the Roman Empire, the famous emperor Nero instituted a new game. The players would take those little disks you set your glass on in order to protect the furniture, and see who could get the most distance rolling them across the floor. They were the first roller coasters. Back in those days, the disks were made of iron, and they would bet on whose disk would roll the farthest. They called them ferrous wheels.

Napoleon III of France: His mind is like an extinct sulphur pit giving out the smell of rotten eggs.

Thomas Carlyle

It was terrible weather on the King's coronation day. I guess it was the reigny day he had been saving up for?

King Philip II of Spain: I cannot find it in me to fear a man who took ten years a-learning his alphabet.

Queen Elizabeth I

In the days of yore, a knight was on his way to do something terribly important, riding his horse into the ground to get to his destination as fast as possible. After being ridden too hard for too long, his horse became lame, and seeing a small town ahead he headed straight for the stables there. 'I must have a horse!' he cried. 'The life of the King depends upon it!' The stablekeeper shook his head. 'I have no horses,' he said. 'They have all been taken in the service of your King.' 'You must have something – a pony, a donkey, a mule, anything at all?' the knight asked. 'Nothing... unless... no, I couldn't.' The knight's eyes lit up. 'Tell me!' The stablekeeper led the knight into the stable. Inside was a dog, but it was no ordinary dog. This dog was a giant, almost as large as the horse the knight was riding. But it is also the filthiest, shaggiest, smelliest, mangiest dog that the knight has ever seen. Swallowing hard, the knight said, 'I'll take it. Where is the saddle?' The stablekeeper walked over to a saddle near the dog and started gasping for breath, holding the walls to keep himself upright. 'I can't do it,' he told the knight. 'You must give me the dog!' cried the knight. 'Why can't you?' The stablekeeper said, 'I just couldn't send a knight out on a dog like this.'

Queen Victoria: Nowadays, a parlour maid as ignorant as Queen Victoria was when she came to the throne, would be classed as mentally defective.

George Bernard Shaw

Nostalgia – living life in the past lane.

King William IV: The King blew his nose twice, and wiped the royal perspiration repeatedly from a face which is probably the largest uncivilised spot in England.
Oliver Wendell Holmes

Queen Victoria was visiting a town in Northern England to open a new hospital. The town mayor made an announcement that in honour of the occasion, the town would name a road after the Queen. The first road that was suggested was a residential road, and the suggested name was 'Victoria Mews'. Sadly, the Queen didn't like the idea of giving her name to that road. As she said, 'We are happy to be a city-centre street, but we are not a Mews!'

Duchess of Windsor: The people are used to looking up to their King's representatives – the Duchess of Windsor is looked upon as the lowest of the low. ***The Queen Mother***

Teacher: How was the Roman Empire cut in half?
Pupil: With a pair of Caesars!

Leonardo da Vinci: He bores me. He ought to have stuck to his flying machines.
Auguste Renoir

A tour group stopped at the Tower of London, and were given the chance to try out some of the ancient armour. Two men - one from Prague and another from Athens - took up the opportunity. One donned a slightly damaged suit of plate armour and the other chain-mail, while the rest of the group crowded around. But in the full suits, the onlookers couldn't tell one from the other. 'Is that the Czech wearing the plate armour?' asked one tourist. 'No,' replied another, 'The Greek has the broken plate, and the Czech is in the mail.'

Leonardo da Vinci did everything, and did nothing very well. ***Marie Bashkirtseff***

Wish I had been born 1,000 years ago! Why is that? Just think of all the history that I wouldn't have to learn!

This is a compilation of alleged student bloopers collected by teachers:

1 Ancient Egypt was inhabited by mummies and they all wrote in hydraulics. They lived in the Sarah Dessert and travelled by Camelot. The climate of the Sarah is such that the inhabitants have to live elsewhere.
2 The Bible is full of interesting caricatures. In the first book of the Bible, Guinessis, Adam and Eve were created from an apple tree. One of their children, Cain, asked, 'Am I my brother's son?'
3 Moses led the Hebrew slaves to the Red Sea, where they made unleavened bread which is bread made without any ingredients. Moses went up on Mount Cyanide to get the ten commandments. He died before he ever reached Canada.
4 Solomom had three hundred wives and seven hundred porcupines.
5 The Greeks were a highly sculptured people, and without them we wouldn't have history. The Greeks also had myths. A myth is a female moth.
6 Actually, Homer was not written by Homer but by another man of that name. Socrates was a famous Greek teacher who went around giving people advice. They killed him. Socrates died from an overdose of wedlock. After his death, his career suffered a dramatic decline.
7 In the Olympic Games, Greeks ran races, jumped, hurled the biscuits, and threw the java.
8 Eventually, the Romans conquered the Greeks. History calls people Romans because they never stayed in one place for very long.
9 Julius Caesar extinguished himself on the battlefields of Gaul. The Ides of March murdered him because they thought he was going to be made king. Dying, he gasped out 'Tee hee, Brutus.'
10 Nero was a cruel tyranny who would torture his subjects by playing the fiddle to them.
11 Joan of Arc was burnt to a steak and was cannonized by Bernard Shaw. Finally Magna Carta provided that no man should be hanged twice for the same offence.
12 In miDevil times most people were alliterate. The greatest writer of the futile ages was Chaucer, who wrote many poems and verses and also wrote literature.
13 Another story was William Tell, who shot an arrow through an

apple while standing on his son's head.
14. Queen Elizabeth was the 'Virgin Queen.' As a queen she was a success. When she exposed herself before her troops they all shouted 'hurrah.'
15 It was an age of great inventions and discoveries. Gutenberg invented removable type and the Bible. Another important invention was the circulation of blood. Sir Walter Raleigh is a historical figure because he invented cigarettes and started smoking. And Sir Francis Drake circumcised the world with a 100 foot clipper.
16 The greatest writer of the Renaissance was William Shakespeare. He was born in the year 1564, supposedly on his birthday. He never made much money and is famous only because of his plays. He wrote tragedies, comedies, and hysterectomies, all in Islamic pentameter. Romeo and Juliet are an example of a heroic couplet. Romeo's last wish was to be laid by Juliet.
17 Writing at the same time as Shakespeare was Miguel Cervantes. He wrote 'Donkey Hote'. The next great author was John Milton. Milton wrote 'Paradise Lost'. Then his wife died and he wrote 'Paradise Regained.'
18 During the Renaissance, America began. Christopher Columbus was a great navigator who discovered America while cursing about the Atlantic. His ships were called the Nina, the Pinta, and the Santa Fe. Later, the Pilgrims crossed the ocean, and this was called Pilgrim's Progress. The winter of 1620 was a hard one for the settlers. Many people died and many babies were born. Captain John Smith was responsible for all this. One of the causes of the Revolutionary War was the English put tacks in their tea. Also, the colonists would send their parcels through the post without stamps. Finally the colonists won the War and no longer had to pay for taxis. Delegates from the original 13 states formed the Contented Congress. Thomas Jefferson, a Virgin, and Benjamin Franklin were two singers of the Declaration of Independence. Franklin discovered electricity by rubbing two cats backwards and declared, 'A horse divided against itself cannot stand.' Franklin died in 1790 and is still dead. Soon the Constitution of the United States was adopted to secure domestic hostility. Under the constitution the people enjoyed the right to keep bare arms.

19 Abraham Lincoln became America's greatest Precedent. Lincoln's mother died in infancy, and he was born in a log cabin which he built with his own hands. Abraham Lincoln freed the slaves by signing the Emasculation Proclamation. On the night of 14 April 1865, Lincoln went to the theatre and got shot in his seat by one of the actors in a moving picture show. The believed assinator was John Wilkes Booth, a supposedly insane actor. This ruined Booth's career.

20 Meanwhile in Europe, the enlightenment was a reasonable time. Voltaire invented electricity and also wrote a book called Candy.

21 Gravity was invented by Issac Walton. It is chiefly noticeable in the autumn when the apples are falling off the trees.

22 Johann Bach wrote a great many musical compositions and had a large number of children. In between he practiced on an old spinster which he kept up in his attic. Bach died from 1750 to the present. Bach was the most famous composer in the world and so was Handel. Handel was half German, half Italian and half English. He was very large.

23 Beethoven wrote music even though he was deaf. He was so deaf he wrote loud music. He took long walks in the forest even when everyone was calling for him. Beethoven expired in 1827 and later died for this.

24 The French Revolution was accomplished before it happened and catapulted into Napoleon. Napoleon wanted an heir to inherit his power, but since Josephine was a baroness, she couldn't have any children.

The sun never set on the British Empire because the British Empire is in the East and the sun sets in the West.

25 Queen Victoria was the longest queen. She sat on a thorn for 63 years. She was a moral woman who practised virtue. Her death was the final event which ended her reign.

26 The nineteenth century was a time of a great many thoughts and inventions. People stopped reproducing by hand and started reproducing by machine. The invention of the steamboat caused a network of rivers to spring up. Cyrus McCormick invented the McCormick raper, which did the work of a hundred men.

If Friar Tuck, while attending divinity school, had gotten PhDs in both comparative theologies and Greek philosophy, would he then have graduated as a really deep, fat friar...?

It's little known that William Shakespeare, as well as writing, also enjoyed a good game of rugby in his spare time. So, the team is assembled for practice one Saturday afternoon. It's the middle of winter, and even for England, it's cold and wet. The pitch is a muddy swamp, and the players decide that they simply can't play in these conditions. So they go to the clubhouse for a bit, but they very quickly get bored. And then one of the players has a bright idea. 'Why don't we all go over to William's house?' Shakespeare is doubtful, but they persuade him, and pretty soon, the whole squad is relaxing in his living room. Well, they're rugby players, and true to the stereotype, they all quickly get drunk, and of course, they come up with the even better idea - having their rugby practice in the house ('Well, it's a big house, after all'). William has also been drinking, so he's easy to persuade this time, and after moving some furniture out of the way, they get down to the serious business of practising their sport. Meanwhile, not far away, the King has just had a great idea for a play, and dispatches a messenger to summon his favourite playwright. Well, the messenger arrives at the house, and he can hear this enormous commotion from inside, with shouting and crashes, and he thinks that William Shakespeare must be getting attacked. He braces himself, and crashes through the front door... and lands directly in the path of two groups of large hairy rugby players. The messenger is pinned to the floor for a while, and he can't move. He does manage to free himself momentarily, before getting trapped again, up against a wall. Finally, he escapes, and returns to the palace as quickly as his mangled body will allow. The King takes one look at him, and gasps. 'What happened to you?' he asks. 'I think,' said the messenger, 'that I got caught between a ruck and a bard's place.'

An unemployed jester is nobody's fool.

Once, long ago, a King summoned all his provincial rulers to his castle. He was in a rather belligerent mood, and wanted to scare them into giving him extra taxes. Unknown to him, they met in secret on the way, and decided that they should agree to pay the extra, but they would at first pretend to refuse, so they could try to bargain down the actual amount extra they would have to pay. They arrived at the King's castle, and gathered in the audience chamber. The King made his demands, and as agreed, they started to refuse. Unfortunately, they hadn't realised just how belligerent the King's mood was - as soon as they started to refuse, he got angry, and ordered his guards to kill them on the spot. More than half of them were slain before they even realised what was happening, and the others had to do some very quick grovelling to survive. After everything had settled down, those who remained explained to the King their plan, and the King was filled with remorse for his hasty actions. The moral of the story? Don't hatchet your counts before they chicken.

The Romans didn't find algebra very challenging, because X was always 10.

When they asked George Washington for his ID, he just took out a quarter.

Stephen Wright

Before he became a writer, William Shakespeare used to sell Swiss cheese. He gave up the job because people kept complaining about his cheese. They would say to him 'No holes, bard.'

Sign in an ancient Egyptian funeral parlour: 'Satisfaction guaranteed, or your mummy back.'

A new young monk arrives at the monastery. He is assigned to help the other monks in copying the old canons and laws of the church by hand. He notices, however, that all of the monks are copying from copies, not from the original manuscript. So the new monk goes to the head abbot to question this, pointing out that if someone made even a small error in the first copy, it would never be picked up. In fact, that error would be continued in all of the subsequent copies. The head monk says, 'We have been copying from the copies for centuries, but you make a good point, my son.' So he goes down into the dark caves underneath the monastery where the original manuscript is held as archives in a locked vault that hasn't been opened for hundreds of years. Hours go by and nobody sees the old abbot. The young monk gets worried and goes downstairs to look for him. He sees him banging his head against the wall, and wailing, 'We forgot the 'R', We forgot the 'R'!' His forehead is all bloody and bruised and he is crying uncontrollably. The young monk asks the old abbot, 'What's wrong, father?' With a choking voice, the old abbot replies, 'The word is celebrate. The word is celebRate.'

On revisionist history: What was sliced bread the greatest thing since?

Quick Quips 5

Politics is the art of looking for trouble, finding it everywhere, diagnosing it incorrectly, and applying the wrong remedies. ***Groucho Marx***

If anybody comes up to you and says, 'My kid is a conservative, why is that?' you say, 'Remember in the sixties when we told you if you kept using drugs your kids would be mutants?' ***Mort Sahl***

There were four million people in the Colonies, and we had Jefferson and Paine and Franklin. Now we have 240 million and we have Bush and Quayle. What can you draw from this? Darwin was wrong. ***Mort Sahl***

All the problems we face in the United States today can be traced to an unenlightened immigration policy on the part of the American Indian. ***Pat Paulsen***

Voting in this election is like trying to decide which street mime to stop and watch. ***A Whitney Brown***

The man with the best job in the country is the vice president. All he has to do is get up every morning and say, 'How's the president?' ***Will Rogers***

LBJ always told the truth, except when his lips moved. ***Red Buttons***

State legislators are merely politicians whose darkest secret prohibits them from running for higher office.
Marc Price

Diplomacy is the art of saying 'Nice doggie' until you can find a rock. ***Will Rogers***

Ninety-eight per cent of the adults in this country are decent, hard-working Americans. It's the other lousy two per cent that get all the publicity. But then – we elected them. ***Lily Tomlin***

Democrats are better lovers than Republicans. You've never heard of a good piece of elephant, have you?
Milton Berle

A fanatic is one who can't change his mind and won't change the subject.
Winston Churchill

As far as the men who are running for president are concerned, they aren't even people I would date.
Nora Ephron

Being in politics is like being a football coach. You have to be smart enough to understand the game and dumb enough to think it's important. ***Eugene McCarthy***

Any party which takes credit for the rain must not be surprised if its opponents blame it for the drought.
Dwight W Morrow

Generosity is part of my character, and I therefore hasten to assure this government that I will never make an allegation of dishonesty against it whenever a simple explanation of stupidity would suffice. ***Leslie Lever***

Conservative: a statesman who is enamoured of existing evils, as distinguished from the Liberal, who wishes to replace them with others. ***Ambrose Bierce***

Do not criticise your government when out of the country. Never cease to do so when at home. ***Winston Churchill***

I have learned that one of the most important rules of politics is poise – which means looking like an owl after you've behaved like a jackass. ***Ronald Reagan***

I never dared be radical when young, for fear it would make me conservative when old. ***Robert Frost***

I sometimes marvel at the extraordinary docility with which Americans submit to speeches. ***Adlai Stevenson***

I never vote for anyone. I always vote against. ***W C Fields***

I once said cynically of a politician, 'He'll double-cross that bridge when he comes to it.' ***Oscar Levant***

I seldom think of politics more than 18 hours a day. ***Lyndon B Johnson***

In order to become the master, the politician poses as the servant. ***Charles de Gaulle***

My opponent has a problem. He won't get elected unless things get worse – and things won't get worse unless he's elected. ***George Bush***

Congress consists of one-third, more or less, scoundrels; two-thirds, more or less, idiots; and three-thirds, more or less, poltroons. ***H L Mencken***

No party is as bad as its leaders. ***Will Rogers***

Politics is supposed to be the second oldest profession. I have come to realise that it bears a very close resemblance to the first.
Ronald Reagan

Politics: a strife of interests masquerading as a conflict of principles. The conduct of public affairs for private advantage. ***Ambrose Bierce***

The middle of the road is all of the usable surface. The extremes, right and left, are in the gutters.
Dwight D Eisenhower

The House of Lords must be the only institution in the world which is kept efficient by the persistent absenteeism of most of its members. ***Herbert Samuel***

The politician is an acrobat. He keeps his balance by saying the opposite of what he does. ***Maurice Barres***

Too bad 90 per cent of politicians give the other 10 per cent a bad reputation.
Henry Kissinger

There is but one way for a newspaperman to look at a politician, and that is down.
Frank H Simonds

It could probably be shown by facts and figures that there is no distinctly native American criminal class except Congress. ***Mark Twain***

Senate office hours are from twelve to one with an hour off for lunch. ***George S Kaufman***

Democracy is a form of government by popular ignorance. ***Elbert Hubbard***

There are two periods when Congress does no business: one is before the holidays, and the other after.
George D. Prentice

Communism doesn't really starve or execute that many people. Mainly it just bores them to death. ***P J O'Rourke***

Democracy is a form of religion. It is the worship of the jackals by the jackasses.
H L Mencken

Democracy gives every man the right to be his own oppressor. ***James Russell Lowell***

One-fifth of the people are against everything all the time. ***Robert F Kennedy***

A politician is a man who approaches every question with an open mouth.
Adlai Stevenson

Economists are people who see something work in practice and wonder if it would work in theory.
Ronald Reagan

Give me a one-handed economist! All my economists say, 'On the one hand ... on the other.'
Harry S Truman

I learned in business that you had to be very careful when you told somebody that's working for you to do something, because the chances were very high he'd do it. In government, you don't have to worry about that. ***George Shultz***

Reading about one's failings in the daily papers is one of the privileges of high office in this free country of ours.
Nelson A Rockefeller

Never believe anything until it has been officially denied.
Claud Cockburn

Democracy: a government of bullies tempered by editors.
Ralph Waldo Emerson

The other night I dreamed that I was addressing the House of Lords. Then I woke up and by God I was.
Duke of Devonshire

The constitution provides for every accidental contingency in the Executive – except a vacancy in the mind of the president. ***John Sherman***

Liberal: a power worshipper without the power.
George Orwell

Too bad all the people who know how to run the country are busy driving cabs and cutting hair. ***George Burns***

A liberal will hang you from a lower branch. ***Adlai Stevenson***

Liberals have invented whole college majors – Psychology, Sociology, Women's Studies – to prove that nothing is anybody's fault. ***P J O'Rourke***

As usual, the Liberals offer a mixture of sound and original ideas. Unfortunately, none of the sound ideas is original and none of the original ideas is sound. ***Harold Macmillan***

Winston [Churchill] has devoted the best years of his life to preparing his impromptu speeches. ***F E Smith***

If presidents don't do it to their wives, they do it to their country. ***Mel Brooks***

Nothing is so admirable in politics as a short memory.
J K Galbraith

Now I know what a statesman is; he's a dead politician. We need more statesmen. ***Bob Edwards***

Americans have different ways of saying things. They say 'elevator', we say 'lift', they say 'president', we say "stupid psychopathic git". ***Alexi Sayle***

Show me where Stalin is buried and I'll show you a Communist plot. ***Edgar Bergen***

Politicians make strange bedfellows, but they all share the same bunk. ***Edgar A Shoaff***

A political war is one in which everyone shoots from the lip. ***Raymond Moley***

If the Republicans stop telling lies about us, we will stop telling the truth about them. ***Adlai Stevenson***

A radical is a man with both feet planted firmly in the air. ***Franklin D Roosevelt***

A liberal is one who is too broadminded to take his own side in a quarrel. ***Robert Frost***

A conservative is a man who is too cowardly to fight and too fat to run. ***Elbert Hubbard***

A conservative is a man who thinks and sits, mostly sits. ***Woodrow Wilson***

Being president is like being a jackass in a hailstorm. There's nothing to do but stand there and take it. ***Lyndon B Johnson***

Fleas can be taught nearly anything that a congressman can. ***Mark Twain***

I have often wanted to drown my troubles, but I can't get my wife to go swimming.
Jimmy Carter

I have orders to be awakened at any time in the case of a national emergency, even if I'm in a cabinet meeting.
Ronald Reagan

If you don't drink, when you wake up in the morning, that's the best you're gonna feel all day. ***Martin Mull***

If I had stood unopposed at the last election, I would still have come second. ***John Major***

I envy people who drink – at least they know what to blame everything on.
Oscar Levant

History is a set of lies agreed upon. ***Napoleon Bonaparte***

Though God cannot alter the past, historians can.
Samuel Butler

One reason I don't drink is that I want to know when I'm having a good time. ***Nancy Astor***

An alcoholic is someone you don't like who drinks as much as you do. ***Dylan Thomas***

I have no interest in sailing around the world. Not that there is any lack of requests for me to do so. ***Edward Heath***

The whole world is about three drinks behind.
Humphrey Bogart

I wish Stanley Baldwin no ill, but it would have been much better if he had never lived.
Winston Churchill

What contemptible scoundrel stole the cork from my lunch? ***W C Fields***

The Labour Party has lost the last four elections. If they lose another, they get to keep the Liberal Party. ***Clive Anderson***

If the word 'No' was removed from the English language, Ian Paisley would be speechless. ***John Hume***

I am extraordinarily patient, provided I get my own way in the end. ***Margaret Thatcher***

The Labour Party's election manifesto is the longest suicide note in history. ***Greg Knight***

At every crisis the Kaiser crumpled. In defeat he fled; in revolution he abdicated; in exile he remarried. ***Winston Churchill***

Democracy is being allowed to vote for the candidate you dislike least. ***Robert Byrne***

Democracy means simply the bludgeoning of the people by the people for the people. ***Oscar Wilde***

We'd all like to vote for the best man but he's never a candidate. ***Kin Hubbard***

Anybody who enjoys being in the House of Commons probably needs psychiatric help. ***Ken Livingstone***

An ideal form of government is democracy tempered with assassination. ***Voltaire***

When you say you agree to a thing in principle you mean that you have not the slightest intention of carrying it out in practice. ***Otto Von Bismark***

drink

This One's On Me

One night Judge O'Brien tottered into his house very late and very drunk indeed, so gone that he managed to throw up all over himself. In the morning he sheepishly told his wife that a drunk sitting next to him on the train home had managed to vomit all over him. The judge managed to make it into the courthouse, where it occurred to him that his story might not have been very convincing to his wife. Inspired, he called home and said, 'Honey, you won't believe this, but I just had the drunk who threw up on me last night show up in court, and I gave him 30 days.' 'Give him 60 days,' said the judge's wife. 'He shat in your pants, too.'

Alcohol is good for you. My grandfather proved it. He drank two quarts of booze every mature day of his life and lived to the age of 103. I was at the cremation; that fire would not go out.

Dave Astor

How many drunks does it take to change a lightbulb? Two. One to hold the bulb and the other to drink until the room spins.

Two drinking buddies made a night of it. As they closed the last bar in town, one admitted to the other, 'God, I hate getting in at this hour. All I want to do is take my shoes off and crawl into bed, but Marge always wakes up and nags the shit out of me for what seems like hours.' 'Sneaking's not the way to do it,' said his buddy conspiratorially as they staggered arm in arm down the pavement. 'Try slamming the front door, stomping upstairs, and yelling, "Hey baby, let's do it!" My wife always pretends she's sound asleep.'

On the chest of a barmaid in Sale,
Were tattooed the prices of ale,
And on her behind,
For the sake of the blind,
Was the same information in Braille.

What's the difference between an alcoholic and a drunk? A drunk doesn't have to go to meetings.

A wife was in bed with her lover when she heard her husband's key in the door. 'Stay where you are,' she said. 'He's so drunk he won't even notice you're in bed with me.' Sure enough, the husband lurched into bed none the wiser, but a few minutes later, through a drunken haze, he saw six feet sticking out at the end of the bed. He turned to his wife. 'Hey, there are six feet in this bed. There should only be four. What's going on?' 'Nonsense,' said the wife. 'You're so drunk you miscounted. Get out of bed and try again. You can see better from over there.' The husband climbed out of bed and counted. 'One, two, three, four. You're right, you know.'

Let's get out of these wet clothes and into a dry martini. ***Robert Benchley; also attributed to Alexander Woollcott***

A drunk staggered into a church and ended up in the confession booth. After a few moments, the priest said, 'What do you need my son?' The drunk asked, 'Is there any paper on your side?'

Absinthe makes the heart grow fonder.

The Ten Stages of Drunkenness:

1 Witty and charming
2 Rich and famous
3 Benevolent
4 Clairvoyant
5 Fuck dinner
6 Patriotic
7 Crank up the Enola Gay
8 Witty and charming Part Two
9 Invisible
10 Bulletproof

WARNING: The consumption of alcohol may leave you wondering what the hell happened to your bra and panties.

I never consume alcohol. You see, I don't think it's right to drink in front of my children. And when I'm away from my children, I don't need to drink.

WARNING: The consumption of alcohol may create the illusion that you are tougher, smarter, faster and better looking than most people.

My uncle was feeling under the weather so he went to the doctor for a check-up. They found the problem. There was a small amount of blood in his alcoholic system.

The Board of Health has proposed that warning signs be placed on all alcohol bottles to tip off drinkers about the possible peril of drinking a pint or two of any alcoholic beverage.

1 WARNING: Consumption of alcohol may cause you to wake up with breath that could knock a buzzard off a reeking dead animal that is one hundred yards away.
2 WARNING: Consumption of alcohol is a major factor in dancing like an idiot.
3 WARNING: Consumption of alcohol may cause you to tell the same boring story over and over again until your friends want to assault you.
4 WARNING: Consumption of alcohol may cause you to thay shings like thish.
5 WARNING: Consumption of alcohol may cause you to tell the boss what you really think of him.
6 WARNING: Consumption of alcohol is the leading cause of inexplicable rug burn on the forehead.
7 WARNING: Consumption of alcohol may create the illusion that you are tougher, handsomer and smarter than some really, really big guy named Psycho Bob.

He drinks so much, when you dance with him you can hear him slosh.

Drunk: Take me to 150, Church Lane.
Taxi driver: You're already at 150, Church Lane.
Drunk: All right, but next time don't drive so damned fast!

A short-sighted good Samaritan was on his way home one evening when he met a drunk slumped in the doorway of a block of flats. 'Do you live here?" asked the Samaritan, peering through his thick glasses. 'Yeah,' said the drunk, 'on the second floor.' 'Would you like me to take you upstairs?' 'Thanks.' The Samaritan gingerly led the drunk up to the second floor but decided that he didn't really want to face the wrath of an angry wife. So he opened the first door he came to and pushed the drunk through it. Having done his good deed for the day, he went back downstairs where, to his surprise, he found another drunk. This man also said he lived on the second floor, so the Samaritan led him slowly up the stairs, pushed him through the same door and went back down the stairs with the intention of completing his journey home. But when he got to the bottom of the stairs, he found yet another drunk who said he lived on the second floor. So the Samaritan guided him up the stairs, pushed him through the same door and went back downstairs. Once again a drunk was standing there, leaning against the wall and looking decidedly worse for wear. But before the Samaritan could do anything, the drunk staggered over to a passing police officer and said, 'Officer, protect me from this man. He keeps taking me upstairs and throwing me down the elevator shaft!'

This guy's not an ordinary, garden-variety drunk. Far from it. Last year he donated his body to science, and he's preserving it in alcohol until they can use it.

A friend of mine drank so much on a trip around Europe that when he got to Italy he was the only one in the party who couldn't see anything wrong with the Tower of Pisa. And he was so drunk when he came back that they had to pay duty on him to get him through Customs.

Why do elephants drink?
It helps them forget.

Her: What do you mean by coming home half drunk?
Him: It's not my fault I ran out of money!

I took her home from the party. I placed her head on my shoulder. Someone else was carrying her feet.

One day, Adam's teacher told the class that everyone must find out a moral for the next day's class. One boy came in and said, 'Don't count your chickens before they hatch.' The second boy said, 'Don't judge a book by it's cover.' Then Adam came in with a broken jaw and black eyes and said, 'I asked my Uncle Johnny for a moral and he told me to shut up. I told him he had to help me because it was homework.' The teacher said, 'What is the moral, Johnny?' 'Don't mess with Uncle Johnny when he's drinking!''

Our lager,
Which art in barrels,
Hollowed be thy drink.
I will be drunk,
At home as in the tavern.
Give us this day our foamy
head,
And forgive us our spillages,
As we forgive those who
spill against us.
And lead us not into
incarceration,
But deliver us from
hangovers.
For thine is the beer, the
bitter and the lager,
Forever and ever,
Barmen.

I walked into a bar the other day and ordered a double. The barman brought out a guy who looked just like me.

Phil Harris sees a psychiatrist once a week to make him stop drinking – and it works. Every Wednesday between five and six he doesn't drink.

Joe E Lewis

He may have had a little too much to drink last night. Two hours after the bar closed he was still out in the car park, doing his imitation of a speed bump.

A drunk was staggering home with a pint of booze in his back pocket when he slipped and fell heavily. Struggling to his feet, he felt something wet running down his leg. 'Please, God,' he implored, 'let that be blood!'

For the perfect pick-me-up, take the juice from a bottle of whisky.

After four martinis my husband turns into a disgusting beast, and after the fifth I pass out altogether.

What do American beer and a rowing boat have in common? They're both close to water.

Reasons to allow drinking at work:

1 It's an incentive to show up.
2 It reduces stress.
3 It leads to more honest communications.
4 It reduces complaints about low pay.
5 It cuts down on time off because you can work with a hangover.
6 Employees tell management what they think, not what management wants to hear.
7 It helps save on heating costs in the winter.
8 It encourages carpooling.
9 Increases job satisfaction because if you have a bad job you don't care.
10 It eliminates holidays because people would rather come to work.
11 It makes fellow employees look better.
12 It makes the cafeteria food taste better.
13 Bosses are more likely to hand out raises when they are wasted.
14 If someone does something stupid on the job, it will be quickly forgotten.

I drink to steady my nerves. Last night I got so steady I couldn't move.

I'd rather have a bottle in front of me than a frontal lobotomy.

A man who has obviously had a little too much to drink staggers into an Alcoholics Anonymous meeting and is met at the door by a member who says, 'So, you've obviously come here to join.' 'No,' says the man, 'I've come here to resign!'

I know I'm drunk when I feel sophisticated but can't pronounce it.

I wouldn't call him a steady drinker – his hands shake too much.

I had 18 bottles of whisky in my cellar and was told by my sister to empty the contents of each and every bottle down the sink, or else. I said I would and proceeded with the unpleasant task. I withdrew the cork from the first bottle and poured the contents down the sink with the exception of one glass, which I drank. I then withdrew the cork from the second bottle and did likewise with it, with the exception of one glass, which I drank. I then withdrew the cork from the third bottle and poured the whisky down the sink which I drank. I pulled the cork from the fourth bottle down the sink and poured the bottle down the glass, which I drank. I pulled the bottle from the cork of the next and drank one sink out of it, and threw the rest down the glass. I pulled the sink out of the next glass and poured the cork down the bottle. Then I corked the sink with the glass, bottled the drink and drank the pour. When I had everything emptied, I steadied the house with one hand, counted the glasses, corks, bottles, and sinks with the other, which were 29, and as the houses came by I counted them again, and finally I had all the houses in one bottle, which I drank. I'm not under tha affluence of incohol as some tinkle peep I am. I'm not half as thunk as you might drink. I fool so feelish I don't know who is me, and the drunker I stand here, the longer I get.

You're not drunk if you can lie on the floor without holding on. ***Dean Martin***

I am sparkling; you are unusually talkative; he is drunk.

What is the difference between a dog and a fox? About five drinks.

Every time I get drunk I see rabbits with red spots. Have you seen your doctor? No, just rabbits with red spots.

How many brewers does it take to change a lightbulb? About one-third less than for a regular bulb.

Policeman: And where do you think you might be going at this time of night, Sir?
Drunk: To a lecture, Officer.
Policeman: And tell me, Sir, who on earth would be giving a lecture at this time of night?
Drunk: My wife.

I've decided I've got to stop drinking. I don't think I'm an alcoholic yet, but I am beginning to see the writing on the floor.

Sometimes when I reflect back on all the wine I drink I feel shamed. Then I look into the glass and think about the workers in the vineyards and all of their hopes and dreams. If I didn't drink this wine, they might be out of work and their dreams would be shattered. Then I say to myself, 'It is better that I drink this wine and let their dreams come true than be selfish and worry about my liver.' *Jack Handy*

He couldn't make both ends meet because he made one end drink.

Frankly, I'd rather have a case of the measles than a case of this wine.

Two friends arrived home after spending the night in several bars. The first one took the key from his pocket and tried unsuccessfully to put it into the lock. After several failed attempts, his friend said, 'Do you want me to try and steady your hand?' 'No, my hand's okay. You try and hold the house!'

A drunk is someone who goes into a bar optimistically and comes out misty optically.

WARNING: The consumption of alcohol may cause pregnancy.

He's very particular about what he drinks. It has to be liquid.

I don't drink to be sociable. I drink to get drunk.

As always, my husband went out fit as a fiddle and came home tight as a drum.

I've invented a new cocktail called a Card Table. When you've had a couple, your legs fold up right under you.

Reasons Why Beer is Better than Cucumbers:
Beer bottles don't get sprayed with pesticides.
Beer bottles don't shrivel up and grow mouldy if you leave them in the fridge for a month.
Beer is always in season.
Beer removes unsightly flab and wrinkles (on the person you're looking at, if you drink enough).
Eating cucumbers to forget doesn't work.

Reasons Why Cucumbers are Better than Beer:
You can't get drunk, no matter how many you eat.
They won't give you a hangover.
They have fewer calories.
Your wife won't complain about you sitting around all day watching TV and eating cucumbers.
You can grow your own without buying lots of equipment.
Your wife won't complain that your breath stinks of cucumbers.
You can eat as many as you like, and drive home later.
You can open a cucumber using only your teeth.
It won't shatter if you drop it on the ground.
You can shake it up, and it won't explode when you bite it.

Dignity is the one thing that alcohol doesn't preserve.

WARNING: The consumption of alcohol may lead you to think people are laughing with you.

I've just joined the AAAA. It's for people who've being driven to drink.

Do you know, in this town there are more than 300 pubs. And I'm proud to say that I haven't been in one of them. I forget which one it is, but there's one of them I definitely haven't been in.

Our new pub has got three barmaids – two for serving and one for listening.

The woman opened her front door to find her husband's boss standing there. He said, 'Polly - can I come in? I've got some terrible news, I'm afraid.' 'Is it about Jack?' The boss said, 'I'm afraid so. There's been a terrible accident down at the brewery. Jack fell into a vat of beer and drowned.' 'Oh, no, my poor Jack! That's terrible. But tell me, did he at least go quickly?' 'I'm afraid not,' said the boss. 'In fact, he got out three times to have a pee.'

1-star hangover
No pain. No real feeling of illness. You slept in your own bed and when you woke up there were no traffic cones in there with you. You are still able to function relatively well on the energy stored up from all those vodka Redbulls. However, you can drink ten bottles of water and still feel as parched as the Sahara.

2-star hangover
No pain, but something is definitely amiss. You may look okay but you have the attention span and mental capacity of a stapler. The coffee you hug to try and remain focused is only exacerbating your rumbling gut, which is craving a full English breakfast. Although you have a nice demeanour about the office, you are costing your employer valuable money because all you really can handle is some light filing.

3-star hangover
Slight headache. Stomach feels crap. You are definitely a space cadet and not so productive. Any time a girl or lad walks by you gag because the perfume/aftershave reminds you of the random gin shots you did with your friends after the bouncer kicked you out at 1.45am. Life would be better if you were in your bed with a dozen doughnuts and a litre of coke watching daytime TV. You've had four cups of coffee and a gallon of water yet you haven't peed once.

4-star hangover
You have lost the will to live. Your head is throbbing and you can't speak too quickly or else you might spew. Your boss has already lambasted you for being late and has given you a lecture for reeking of booze. You wore nice clothes, but you smell of socks, and you can't hide the fact that you missed an oh-so crucial spot shaving. Your teeth have their own individual sweaters. You would give a week's pay for one of the following – home time, a doughnut and somewhere to be alone, or a time machine so you could go back and not have gone out the night before.

5-star hangover
You have a second heartbeat in your head, which is annoying the employee who sits next to you. Vodka vapour is seeping out of every pore and making you dizzy. You still have toothpaste crust in the corners of your mouth from brushing your teeth. Your body has

lost the ability to generate saliva, so your tongue is suffocating you. Your boss doesn't even get mad at you and your co-workers think that your dog just died because you look so pathetic. You should have called in sick because all you can manage to do is breathe – very gently.

6-star hangover

You arrive home. Sleep comes instantly. You get about two hours' sleep until the noises inside your head wake you up. You notice that your bed has been cleared for take off and is flying relentlessly around the room. No matter what you do you now, you're going to chuck. After walking along the skirting boards on alternating walls knocking off all the pictures, you find the toilet. If you are lucky you will remember to lift the lid before you spontaneously explode and wake the whole house up with your impersonation of walrus mating calls. You sit there on the floor in your undies, cuddling the only friend in the world you have left (the toilet), randomly continuing to make the walrus noises, spitting and farting. Help usually comes at this stage, even if it is short lived. Tears stream down your face and your abdomen hurts. Help now turns into abuse and he/she usually goes back to bed, leaving you there in the dark. With your stomach totally empty, your spontaneous eruptions have died back to 15-minute intervals, but your body won't relent. You are convinced that you are starting to turn yourself inside out and swear that you saw your tonsils shoot out of your mouth on the last occasion. It is now dawn and you pass your disgusted partner getting up for the day as you try to climb into bed. She/he abuses you again for trying to get into bed with lumpy bits of dried vomit in your hair. You reluctantly accept their advice and have a shower in exchange for them driving you to the hospital. Work is not an option. The whole day is spent trying to avoid anything that might make you sick again, like moving. You vow never to touch a drop again and who knows, for the next two or three hours at least you might even succeed.

Okay, now hands up all those who have never had a 6-star hangover.

Thought so!

A drinker rolled home late on a Friday night and, as he walked in, he found his wife with her hand outstretched. She said, 'Okay, hand over your pay packet!' With a guilty look on his face, he pulled it out of his pocket, handed it to her and said, 'It's not all there. I spent half of it on something for the house.' And she said, 'Oh, that was nice. What was it?' And he said, 'A round of drinks!'

And anyway, I've got all day sober to Sunday up in.

When we drink, we get drunk. When we get drunk, we fall asleep. When we fall asleep, we commit no sin. When we commit no sin, we go to Heaven. Sooooo, let's all get drunk, and go to Heaven.

Brian O'Rourke

A new priest at his first mass was so nervous he could hardly speak. After mass he asked the monsignor how he had done. The monsignor replied, 'When I am worried about getting nervous on the pulpit, I put a glass of vodka next to the water glass. If I start to get nervous, I take a sip.' So next Sunday he took the monsignor's advice. At the beginning of the sermon, he got nervous and took a drink. He proceeded to talk up a storm. Upon his return to his office after the mass, he found this note on the door:

1) Sip the vodka, don't gulp.
2) There are ten commandments, not twelve.
3) There are twelve disciples, not ten.
4) Jesus was consecrated, not constipated.
5) Jacob wagered his donkey, he did not bet his ass.
6) We do not refer to Jesus Christ as the late JC.
7) The Father, Son, and Holy Ghost are not referred to as Daddy, Junior and the Spook.
8) David slew Goliath, he did not kick the shit out of him.
9) When David was hit by a rock and was knocked off his donkey, don't say he was stoned off his ass.
10) We do not refer to the cross as the 'Big T'.
11) When Jesus broke the bread at the last supper he said, 'Take this and eat it for it is my body.' He did not say 'Eat me.'
12) The Virgin Mary is not called 'Mary with the Cherry.'
13) The recommended grace before a meal is not: Rub-A-Dub-Dub thanks for the grub, Yeah God.
14) Next Sunday there will be a taffy-pulling contest at St Peter's not a peter-pulling contest at St Taffy's.

My uncle used to go round drinking champagne from ladies' slippers. He wound up with athlete's tongue.

The police said I was drunk but I don't think that's fair. It's just the way I react to an excess of alcohol. I've ruined my health by drinking to everyone else's.

WARNING: The consumption of alcohol may cause you to tell your friends over and over again that you love them.

The beer is so flat at this pub they serve it on a plate.

WARNING: The consumption of alcohol may cause you to think you can sing.

There's a local bar that employs only midget waiters – to make the drinks look bigger.

WARNING: The consumption of alcohol may make you think you can logically converse with members of the opposite sex without spitting.

There's nothing wrong with drinking like a fish as long as you drink what a fish drinks.

They say that liquor improves with age and I think they're right. The older I get, the more I like it.

A man is in bed with his wife when there is a rat-a-tat-tat on the door. He rolls over and looks at his clock, and it's half past three in the morning. 'I'm not getting out of bed at this time,' he thinks and rolls over. Then, a louder knock follows. 'Aren't you going to answer that?' says his wife. So he drags himself out of bed, and goes downstairs. He opens the door and there is man standing at the door. It didn't take the homeowner long to realise the man is drunk. 'Hi there,' slurs the stranger, 'Can you give me a push?' 'No, get lost, it's half past three. I was in bed,' says the man and slams the door. He goes back up to bed and tells his wife what happened and she says, 'Dave, that wasn't very nice of you. Remember that night we broke down in the pouring rain on the way to pick the kids up from the babysitter and you had to knock on that man's house to get us started again? What would have happened if he'd told us to get lost?' 'But the guy was drunk,' says Dave. 'It doesn't matter,' says the wife. 'He needs our help and it would be the Christian thing to help him.' So Dave gets out of bed again, gets dressed, and goes downstairs. He opens the door, and not being able to see the stranger anywhere he shouts, 'Hey, do you still want a push?' and he hears a voice cry out, 'Yeah, please.' So, still being unable to see the stranger he shouts, 'Where are you?' And the stranger replies, 'I'm over here, on your swing.'

Do you drink? No. Then hold this bottle while I tie my shoelaces.

Do you know a way you could sell more beer? No, how could I sell more beer? Just fill the glasses properly.

Me, drunk? But I've only had tee martoonies!

I've invented this marvellous new tonic wine containing iron, glucose and rum. The iron gives you strength, the glucose gives you energy, and the rum? The rum gives you ideas of what to do with all that strength and energy.

I fell down the stairs with two pints of whisky. Heavens, did you spill any? No, I managed to keep my mouth shut.

Vicar: Drunk again, eh?
Drinker: Really? So am I.

My wife drives me to drink. You're lucky, I have to walk!

This brandy is 100 years old. Really? It tastes just like new!

Where's the nearest boozer? You're talking to him.

Whisky is slow poison. I'm in no hurry.

Why do you call your local the Stradivarius? Because it's a vile inn.

Doctor: Do you drink to excess? Patient: I'll drink to anything!

Temperate temperance is best; intemperate temperance injures the cause of temperance. ***Mark Twain***

Alcoholics have one thing in common with arthritics – they're always stiff in one joint or another.

WARNING: The consumption of alcohol may make you think you are whispering when you are not.

His problem is he doesn't just drink to excess, he drinks to anything.

If you're rich you're an alcoholic, if you're poor you're just a drunk.

'Ere, Barman!

A woman in a bar says that she wants to have plastic surgery to enlarge her breasts. Her husband tells her, 'Hey, you don't need surgery to do that. I know how to do it without surgery.' The lady asks, 'How do I do it without surgery?' 'Just rub toilet paper between them.' Startled, the lady asks, 'How does that make them bigger?' 'I don't know, but it worked for your ass.'

An old cowboy sat down at the bar and ordered a drink. As he sat sipping it, a young woman sat down next to him. She turned to him and asked, 'Are you a real cowboy?' He replied, 'Well, I've spent my whole life breaking colts, working cows, going to rodeos, fixing fences, pulling calves, bailing hay, doctoring calves, cleaning my barn, fixing flats, working on tractors and feeding my dogs, so I guess I am a cowboy.' She said, 'I'm a lesbian. I spend my whole day thinking about women. As soon as I get up in the morning, I think about women. When I shower, I think about women. When I watch TV, I think about women. I even think about women when I eat. It seems that everything makes me think of women.' The two sat sipping in silence. A little while later, a man sat down on the other side of the old cowboy and asked, 'Are you a real cowboy?' He replied, 'I always thought I was, but I just found out I'm a lesbian.'

A guy at a bar was eyeing up a girl wearing the tightest trousers he'd ever seen. Finally, curiosity got the better of him and he asked, 'Tell me, how do you get into those trousers?' 'Well,' she replied, 'you could start by buying me a drink.'

A drunk staggered into a bar and sat himself down next to a priest. The drunk had lipstick on his collar, booze on his breath and a half bottle of gin sticking out of his pocket. His clothes were heavily stained. He started reading a newspaper and then turned to the priest and said, 'What causes arthritis?' The priest, who was clearly uncomfortable in his presence, responded testily, 'It's caused by loose living, too much alcohol, seeking the company of cheap women, and having a general contempt for one's fellow man!' 'Well, I'll be damned,' muttered the drunk. The priest immediately began to feel guilty about his outburst. 'I'm sorry I came on a bit strong just then. How long have you had arthritis?' 'I don't have it, Father,' said the drunk. 'I was just reading here that the Pope does.'

A man walked into a bar and sat down beside a woman. Suddenly her glass eye popped out and he caught it. She thanked him and asked him if he would join her for breakfast the next day. He agreed and got her address. The next day he went to her house and had a lovely breakfast. He asked, 'Do you treat all men like this?' She smiled and said, 'Just the ones who catch my eye.'

A man brings a bodiless head into a bar. The head asks the barman for a drink and after he is finished - POOF! - a torso appears. So the head asks for another drink and after it finishes - POOF! - arms come out of the torso. So the head asks the barman for another drink and when he's finished - POOF! - legs appear. So the head is thinking, 'Hey, this stuff is great!' and so it asks the barman for one more drink for the road and - POOF! - his whole body disappears. The barman turns to him and says, 'You should have quit while you were a head.'

A man walks into a bar with three little ducks and sits each of them on a stool. He looks up at the barman and says, 'Could you mind my ducks while I go use the phone?' The barman is puzzled, but he doesn't see a problem and agrees to look after the three little ducks. When the owner of the ducks leaves, the barman says to the first duck, 'What's your name?' The duck says, ''My name is Huey.'' And the barman, an affable fellow, especially around ducks, says, 'Hello Huey, how has your day been?' 'My day's been great,' answers the duck, 'I've been slipping in and out of puddles all day.' Satisfied, the barman moves to the next duck and asks the same questions. The second duck replies, 'My name is Dewey and I've had a great day; I've been slipping in and out of puddles all day.' The barman says, ''That sounds nice.' With this, the barman moved to the third duck and thinks to himself about the first two ducks' responses, then says to the third duck, 'Don't tell me - your name's Louie and you've been slipping in and out of puddles all day too.' To which the duck replies, 'No. My name's Puddles, and I've had a pig of a day.'

A guy walks into a bar and sees a dog playing poker. The guy is amazed. 'Barman, is that a real dog playing poker?' the guy asks. 'Yep, real as can be,' the barman replies. 'Well is he any good?' the guy asks. 'Nah, every time he has a good hand he wags his tail.'

A drunk is sitting at a bar when a woman stands behind him and raises her arm really high to get the barman's attention. She has very hairy armpits. The drunk sees this and yells at the barman, 'Get the ballerina a drink.' She gets her drink and goes away. Later she returns and raises her arm again. The drunk sees her and yells to the barman, 'Get the ballerina another drink.' She gets her drink and goes away again. The barman asks the drunk how he knows that she is a ballerina given that she is a stranger and has never been in the bar before. The drunk replies, 'She's got to be a ballerina if she can lift her leg that high.'

This guy in a bar notices a woman, always alone, who comes in on a fairly regular basis. After the second week, he makes his move. 'No, thank you,' she says politely. 'This may sound rather odd in this day and age, but I'm keeping myself pure until I meet the man I love.' 'That must be rather difficult,' the man replies. 'Oh, I don't mind too much,' she says. 'But my husband's pretty upset.'

A man walks into a bar and orders a 12-year-old scotch. The barman, believing that the customer will not be able to tell the difference, pours him a shot of the cheap three-year-old house scotch that has been poured into an empty bottle of the good stuff. The man takes a sip and spits the scotch out on the bar and says to the barman, 'This is the cheapest three-year-old scotch you can buy. I'm not paying for it. Now, give me a good 12-year-old scotch.' The barman, now feeling a bit of a challenge, pours him a scotch of much better quality, six-year-old scotch. The man takes a sip and spits it out on the bar. 'This is only six-year-old scotch. I won't pay for this, and I insist on a good, 12-year-old scotch.' The barman finally relents and serves the man his best quality, 12-year-old scotch. An old drunk from the end of the bar, who has witnessed the entire episode, walks down to the finicky scotch drinker and sets a glass down in front of him and asks, 'What do you think of this?' The scotch expert takes a sip, and in disgust, violently spits out the liquid yelling, 'Why, this tastes like piss!' The old drunk replies, 'That's right, now tell me how old I am.'

A blind man walked into a bar with his guide dog. He picked up the dog and swung it around and around over his head. The barman ran up and asked, 'What the hell are you doing?' The blind man replied, 'Just looking around.'

Three mice were sitting at a bar talking about how tough they were. The first mouse slams a shot and says, 'I play with mousetraps for fun. I'll run into one on purpose and as it is closing on me, I grab the bar and bench press it 20 to 30 times.' And, with that, he slams another shot. The second mouse slams a shot and says, 'That's nothing. I take those poison bait tablets, cut them up and snort them, just for the hell of it.' And, with that, he slams another shot. The third mouse slams a shot, gets up, and walks away. The first two mice look at each other, then turn to the third mouse and ask, 'Where the hell are you going?' The third mouse stops and replies, 'I'm going home to screw the cat.'

There are two pieces of tarmac sitting by the side of the bar, and they are having a drinking contest, to see which one is the hardest. After twelve shots of vodka, both pieces of tarmac are still unfazed, when suddenly the door opens and a green piece of tarmac walks in. Upon seeing the green piece of tarmac, one piece of tarmac runs straight for the bathroom. An hour later, he ventures out and discovers that the green piece of tarmac has left. The other piece of tarmac asks why he ran off, to which he replies 'Haven't you heard about him? He's a CYCLE-PATH!'

Two men walked into a bar. You would think at least one of them would have ducked.

The Lone Ranger and Tonto were at the bar drinking when in walks a cowboy who yells, 'Who's white horse is that outside?' The Lone Ranger finishes off his whisky, slams down the glass, turns around and says, 'It's my horse. Why do you want to know?' The cowboy looks at him and says, 'Well, your horse is standing out there in the sun and he don't look too good.' The Lone Ranger and Tonto run outside and they see that Silver is in bad shape, suffering from heat exhaustion. The Lone Ranger moves him into the shade and gets a bucket of water. He then pours some of the water over the horse and gives the rest to him to drink. It is then he notices that there isn't a breeze, so he asks Tonto if he would start running around Silver to get some air flowing and perhaps cool him down. Being a faithful friend, Tonto starts running around Silver. The Lone Ranger stands there for a while, then realises there is not much more he can do, so he goes back into the bar and orders another whisky. After a while a cowboy walks in and says, 'Who's white horse is that outside?' Slowly the Lone Ranger turns around and says, 'That is my horse, what's wrong with him now?' 'Nothing,' replies the cowboy, 'I just wanted to let you know that you left your injun running.'

A cowboy rode into town and stopped at the saloon for a drink. Unfortunately, the locals always had a habit of picking on newcomers. When he left the bar some time later, he realised that his horse had been stolen. The cowboy rushed back into the bar, handily flipped his gun into the air, caught it above his head without even looking, and then fired a shot into the ceiling. 'Who stole my horse?' he yelled with surprising forcefulness. No one answered. 'I'm gonna have another beer and if my horse ain't back outside by the time I'm finished, I'm gonna do what I did back in Texas. And let me tell you, I don't wanna have to do what I did back in Texas!' Some of the locals shifted restlessly. The cowboy had another beer, then walked outside to find his horse was back. So, he saddled up and prepared to ride out of town. The barman wandered out of the bar and said, 'Say partner, what happened in Texas anyway?' The cowboy turned back and said, 'I had to walk home.'

A neutron walks into a bar. 'I'd like a beer,' he says. The barman promptly serves up a beer. 'How much will that be?' asks the neutron. 'For you?' replies the barman, 'no charge.'

A guy walks into a bar with his pet monkey. He orders a drink and while he's drinking, the monkey starts jumping all over the place. It grabs some olives off the bar and eats them, then grabs some sliced limes and eats them, then jumps up on the pool table, grabs the cue ball, sticks it in his mouth and swallows it whole. The barman screams at the guy, 'Did you see what your monkey just did?' The guy says, 'No, what?' 'He just ate the cue ball off my pool table - whole!' says the barman. 'Yeah, that doesn't surprise me,' replies the patron. 'He eats everything in sight, the little twerp. I'll pay for the cue ball and stuff.' He finishes his drink, pays his bill and leaves. Two weeks later he's in the bar again, and he still has his monkey with him. He orders a drink and the monkey starts running around the bar again. While the man is drinking, the monkey finds a maraschino cherry on the bar. He grabs it, sticks it up his butt, pulls it out, and eats it. The barman is disgusted. 'Did you see what your monkey did?' 'Now what?' asks the patron. 'Well, he stuck a maraschino cherry up his butt, then pulled it out and ate it!' says the barman. 'Yeah, that doesn't surprise me,' replies the patron. 'He still eats everything in sight, but ever since he ate that damn cue ball he measures everything first!'

The Taco Bell Chihuahua, a Doberman and a Bulldog are in a bar having a drink when a great-looking female Collie comes up to them and says, 'Whoever can say liver and cheese in a sentence can have me.' So the Doberman says, 'I love liver and cheese.' The Collie replies, 'That's not good enough.' The Bulldog says, 'I hate liver and cheese.' She says, 'That's not creative enough.' Finally, the Chihuahua says, 'Liver alone ... cheese mine.'

A man in his hospital bed keeps ringing for the nurse because he has to take a dump really badly. He can't hold it any more and finally messes in his bed.

Desperate to clean it up and avoid embarrassment, he pulls the sheet off the bed, wads it up, and tosses it out the window. Joe, the local inebriate, is on his way to his favourite haunt when this sheet happens to land right on his head. He staggers into the bar and the barman, taking one look and a getting a whiff of the brown stuff, says, 'Joe, you smell awful!' Joe says, 'You would too, if you just beat the shit out of a ghost!'

One night, a guy walked into a bar and asked the barman for a drink. Then he asked for another. After a couple more drinks, the barman got worried. 'What's the matter?' he asked the guy. 'My wife and I got into a fight,' explained the guy, 'and she vowed not to talk to me for 31 days.' He took another drink, and said, 'And tonight is the last night.'

A man walks into a bar and asks the barman, 'If I show you a really good trick, will you give me a free drink?' The barman considers it, then agrees. The man reaches into his pocket and pulls out a tiny rat. He reaches into his other pocket and pulls out a tiny piano. The rat stretches, cracks his knuckles, and proceeds to play the blues. After the man finished his drink, he asked the barman, 'If I show you an even better trick, will you give me free drinks for the rest of the evening?' The barman agrees, thinking that no trick could possibly be better than the first. The man reaches into his pocket and pulls out a tiny rat. He reaches into his other pocket and pulls out a tiny piano. The rat stretches, cracks his knuckles, and proceeds to play the blues. The man then reaches into another pocket and pulls out a small bullfrog who begins to sing along with the rat's music. While the man is enjoying his beverages, a stranger confronts him and offers him £100,000 for the bullfrog. 'Sorry,' the man replies, 'he's not for sale.' The stranger increases the offer to £250,000 cash up front. 'No,' he insists, 'he's not for sale.' The stranger again increases the offer, this time to £500,000 cash. The man finally agrees, and turns the frog over to the stranger in exchange for the money. 'Are you insane?' the barman demanded. 'That frog could have been worth millions to you, and you let him go for a mere £500,000!' 'Don't worry about it,' the man answered. 'The frog was really nothing special. You see, it's the rat that's a ventriloquist.'

The barman was dumbfounded when a gorilla came in and asked for a martini, but he couldn't think of any reason not to serve the beast. He was even more amazed to find the gorilla coolly holding out a ten-pound note when he returned with the drink. As he walked over to the cash register, he decided to try something. He rang up the sale, headed back to the animal, and handed it a pound change. The gorilla didn't say anything, he just sat there sipping his Martini. Finally the barman couldn't take it any more. 'You know,' he offered, 'we don't get too many gorillas in here.' And the gorilla replied, 'At nine quid a drink, I'm not surprised.'

A seriously drunk man walked into a bar and, after staring for some time at the only woman in there, walked over to her and kissed her. She jumped up and slapped him hard. He immediately apologised and explained, 'I'm sorry. I thought you were my wife. You look exactly like her.' 'Why you worthless, insufferable, wretched, no good drunk!' she screamed. 'Funny,' he muttered, 'you even sound exactly like her.'

A skeleton walked into a bar and said, 'I'll have a Budweiser and a mop, please.'

Two guys were in a bar, and they were both watching the television when the news came on. It showed a man on a bridge who was about to jump, obviously suicidal. 'Bet you £10 he'll jump,' said the first guy. 'Bet you £10 he won't,' said the second guy. Then, the man on the television closed his eyes and threw himself off the bridge. The second guy handed the first guy the money. 'I can't take your money,' said the first guy. 'I cheated you. The same story was on the five o'clock news.' 'No, no. Take it,' said the second guy. 'I saw the five o'clock news too. I just didn't think the guy was dumb enough to jump again!'

A circus owner walked into a bar to see everyone crowded around a table watching a little show. On the table was an upside down pot with a duck tap dancing on it. The circus owner was so impressed that he offered to buy the duck from its owner. After some wheeling and dealing, they settled for £10,000 for the duck and the pot. Three days later the circus owner runs back to the bar in anger, 'Your duck is a rip off! I put him on the pot before a whole audience, and he didn't dance a single step!' 'So?' asked the duck's former owner, 'did you remember to light the candle under the pot?'

A seal walks into a bar and asks the barman for a drink. The barman asks the seal, 'What's your pleasure?' The seal replies, 'Anything but Canadian Club.'

A man walks into a bar, and as he makes his way to the counter, he stops and talks to everyone in the bar. As he finishes with each group of people, they all get up and leave and go and stand outside the window, looking in. Finally, the bar is empty except for this man and the barman. The man walks up to the counter, and says to the barman, 'I bet you £1,000 that I can spray beer from my mouth into a shot glass from 30 ft away, and not get any outside the glass.' The barman thinks that this guy is a nutcase, but he wants his £1,000, so he agrees. The barman gets out a shot glass, paces off 30 ft, and the contest begins. The man sprays beer all over the bar. He doesn't even touch the shot glass. When he finishes, the barman looks at him and says, 'Well, I guess you owe me £1,000, huh?' The man answers, 'Yeah, but I bet all of those people outside the window £500 a piece that I could come in here and spray beer all over the bar.'

A man goes into a bar and seats himself on a stool. The barman looks at him and says, 'What'll it be?' The man says, 'Set me up with seven whisky shots and make them doubles.' The barman does this and watches the man slug one down, then the next, then the next, and so on, until all seven are gone almost as quickly as they were served. Staring in disbelief, the barman asks why he's doing all this drinking. 'You'd drink them this fast too if you had what I have.' The barman hastily asks, 'What do you have?' The man replies, 'A quid.'

A man goes to a bar with his dog and asks for a drink. The barman says, 'You can't bring that dog in here.' The guy, without missing a beat, says, 'This is my seeing-eye dog.' 'Oh,' the barman says, 'I'm sorry. Here, the first one's on me.' The man takes his drink and goes to a table near the door. Another man walks into the bar with a Chihuahua. The first man sees him, stops him and says, 'You can't bring that dog in here unless you tell him it's a seeing-eye dog.' The second man graciously thanks the first man and continues to the bar. He asks for a drink. The barman says, 'Hey, you can't bring that dog in here.'
The second man replies, 'This is my seeing-eye dog.' The barman says, 'No, I don't think so. They do not have Chihuahuas as seeing-eye dogs.' The man pauses for a half-second and replies, 'What? They gave me a Chihuahua?'

Three vampires walk into a bar and sit down at a table. The waitress comes over and asks the first vampire what he would like. The first vampire responds, 'I vould like some blood.' The waitress turns to the second vampire and asks what he would like. The vampire responds, 'I vould like some blood.' The waitress turns to the third vampire and asks what he would like. The vampire responds, 'I vould like some plasma.' The waitress looks up and says, 'Let me see if I have this order correct. You want two bloods and a blood light?'

There's a man sitting at a bar just looking at his drink. He stays like that for half an hour. Then, a big trouble-making lorry driver steps next to him, takes the drink from the man, and downs it in one. The poor man starts crying.

The lorry driver says, 'Oh come on, I was just joking. Here, I'll buy you another drink. I just can't stand seeing a man crying.' 'No, it's not that,' says the man. 'It's just that this is the worst day of my life. First, I fall asleep, and I'm late to my office. My boss, in an outrage, fires me. When I leave the building to my car, I find out it was stolen. The police say they can do nothing. I get a taxi to return home and when I leave it, I remember I left my wallet and credit cards there. The taxi driver just drives away. I go home and when I get there, I find my wife sleeping with the gardener. I leave home and come to this bar. And when I was thinking about putting an end to my life, you show up and drink my poison.'

The barman asks the man sitting at the bar, 'What'll you have?' The man answers, 'A scotch, please.' The barman hands him the drink, and says 'That'll be £5,' to which the guy replies, 'What are you talking about? I don't owe you anything for this.' A lawyer, sitting nearby and overhearing the conversation, then says to the barman, 'You know, he's got you there. In the original offer, which constitutes a binding contract upon acceptance, there was no stipulation of remuneration.' The barman was not impressed, but says to the guy, 'Okay, you beat me for a drink. But don't ever let me catch you in here again.' The next day, the same guy walks into the bar. Barman says, 'What the hell are you doing in here? I can't believe you've got the audacity to come back!' The guy says, 'What are you talking about? I've never been in this place in my life!' The barman replies, 'I'm very sorry, but this is uncanny. You must have a double.'

A brain walks into a bar and says, 'I'll have a pint of beer please.' The barman looks at him and says 'Sorry, I can't serve you.' 'Why not?' asks the brain. 'You're already out of your head.'

A man went into a bar in a high rise. He saw another man take a pill, take a drink, walk to the window and jump out. He flew around for a minute and zipped back into the bar. As the amazed newcomer watched, the man repeated this twice more. Finally, the man asked if he could have a pill. The flier said it was his last one. The man offered £500 to no avail, so he made a final offer of £1,000, saying that it was all he had on him. The flier reluctantly gave in, took the cash, surrendered the pill, and turned back to the bar. The man took the pill, took a drink, went to the window, and jumped out, only to fall to his death. The barman walked over to the flier at the bar and, wiping a glass, said, 'You sure are mean when you're drunk, Superman.'

A regular at Bob's Bar came in one evening sporting a matched pair of swollen black eyes that appeared extremely painful. 'Whoa, Sam!' said the barman. 'Who gave those beauties to you?' 'Nobody gave them to me,' said Sam. 'I had to fight like crazy for both of them.'

A construction worker walks into a bar. He's a rather large, menacing guy. He orders a beer, chugs it back, and bellows, 'All you guys on this side of the bar are a bunch of idiots!' A sudden silence descends. After a moment he asks 'Anyone got a problem with that?' The silence lengthens. He then chugs back another beer and growls, 'And all you guys on the other side of the bar are all scum!' Once again, the bar is silent. He looks around belligerently and roars, 'Anyone got a problem with that?' A lone man gets up from his stool unsteadily and starts to walk towards the man. 'You got a problem, buddy?' 'Oh no,' says the man. 'I'm just on the wrong side of the bar.'

A fellow decides to take off early from work and go drinking. He stays until the bar closes at three in the morning, at which time he is extremely drunk. After leaving the bar, he returns home on foot. When he enters his house, he doesn't want to wake anyone, so he takes off his shoes and starts tip-toeing up the stairs. Halfway up the stairs though, he falls over backwards and lands flat on his back. That wouldn't have been so bad, except that he had a couple of empty pint bottles in his back pockets, and they broke; the broken glass carved up his back terribly. Yet, he was so drunk that he didn't know he was hurt. A few minutes later, as he was undressing, he noticed blood, so he checked himself out in the mirror, and, sure enough, his behind was cut really badly. He then repaired the damage as best he could under the circumstances, and went to bed. The next morning, his head was hurting, his back was hurting, and he was hunkering under the covers trying to think up some good story, when his wife came into the bedroom. 'Well, you really tried one on last night,' she said. 'Where'd you go?' 'I worked late,' he said, 'and I stopped off for a couple of beers.' 'A couple of beers? That's a laugh,' she replied. 'You were completely plastered. Where did you go?' 'What makes you so sure I got drunk last night, anyway?' 'Well,' she replied, 'my first big clue was when I got up this morning and found a whole load of plasters stuck to the mirror.'

A man walks into a bar and orders a beer. He takes his first sip and sets it down. While he is looking around the bar, a monkey swings down and steals the pint of beer from him before he is able to stop it. The man asks the barman who owns the monkey. The barman tells him it belongs to the piano player. The man walks over to the piano player and says, 'Do you know your monkey stole my beer?' The pianist replies, 'No, but if you hum it, I'll play it.'

A man walked in to a bar after a long day at work. As he began to drink his beer, he heard a voice say seductively, 'You've got great hair!' The man looked around but couldn't see where the voice was coming from, so he went back to his beer. A minute later, he heard the same soft voice say, 'You're a handsome man!' The man looked around, but still couldn't see where the voice was coming from. When he went back to his beer, the voice said again, 'What a stud you are!' The man was so baffled by this that he asked the barman what was going on. The barman said, 'Oh, that'll be the nuts – they're complimentary.'

Two cartons of yoghurt walk into a bar. The barman, who was a tub of cottage cheese, says to them, 'We don't serve your kind in here.' One of the yoghurt cartons says back to him, 'Why not? We're cultured individuals.'

A man stumbles up to the only other patron in a bar and asks if he could buy him a drink. 'Why, of course,' comes the reply. The first man then asks: 'Where are you from?' 'I'm from Ireland,' replies the second man. The first man responds: 'You don't say, I'm from Ireland too! Let's have another round to Ireland.' 'Of course,' replies the second man. 'I'm curious,' the first man then says. 'Where in Ireland are you from?' 'Dublin,' comes the reply. 'I can't believe it,' says the first man. 'I'm from Dublin too! Let's have another drink to Dublin.' 'Of course,' replies the second man. Curiosity again strikes and the first man asks: 'What school did you go to?' 'St Mary's,' replies the second man, 'I graduated in '62.' 'This is unbelievable!' the first man says. 'I went to St Mary's and graduated in '62, too!' Around that time, in comes one of the regulars and sits down at the bar. 'What's been going on?' he asks the barman. 'Nothing much,' replies the barman. 'The O'Kinly twins are drunk again.'

Celine Dion walked into a bar. 'Why the long face?' said the barman.

A number twelve walks into a bar and asks the barman for a pint of beer. 'Sorry, I can't serve you,' states the barman. 'Why not?' asks the number twelve angrily. 'You're under 18,' replies the barman.

A customer walked into a bar and started dialling numbers on his hand as if it were a phone. The barman looked at him warily. 'Look,' warned the barman, 'I don't know what you're up to, but this is a tough neighbourhood and I don't want any trouble.' The customer said, 'I'm not out to cause trouble, I promise. Let me explain. I'm very hi-tech and I had a phone installed in my hand because I got tired of carrying around my mobile.' The barman looked at him as if he were a crank. 'I don't believe a word of it.'

'Okay,' said the customer, 'I'll prove it to you.' And he pressed the digits on his hand, held his wrist up to his ear and began conducting a conversation. Then he gave his hand to the barman and, to the barman's amazement, he could hear a voice coming through the hand. 'That's incredible,' said the barman at the end of the call. 'I was able to talk to someone through your hand.' 'It's ingenious,' said the customer. 'It means I can keep in touch with my broker, my wife, anyone, without needing a conventional phone. By the way, where is the men's room?' The barman directed him down the corridor to the toilets but began to get a bit worried when the customer hadn't returned 20 minutes later. Knowing of the reputation of the neighbourhood, he thought he'd better go and check that he was all right. On opening the door, he found the customer spread-eagled against the wall, with his pants down and a roll of toilet paper rammed up his behind. 'Oh God,' exclaimed the barman. 'Did they rob you? Are you hurt?' 'No, I'm fine,' answered the customer. 'I'm just waiting for a fax.'

A stranger rushed into a bar and ordered a double whisky. 'Tell me,' he asked the barman agitatedly, 'how high does a penguin grow?' 'Oh, about so high,' replied the barman, placing his hand 2ft from the floor. 'Are you sure?' said the stranger. 'Positive,' said the barman. 'Damn, I guess I just ran over a nun!'

A smartly dressed man entered a plush bar and took a seat. The barman came over and asked, 'What can I get you to drink, Sir?' 'Nothing, thank you,' replied the man. 'I tried alcohol once but I didn't like it, and I haven't drunk since.' The barman was a little perplexed but being a friendly, outgoing sort, he pulled out some cigarettes from his pocket, flipped the top of the pack and offered one to the man. But the man refused, saying, 'I tried smoking once, didn't like it, and I have never smoked since. Look, actually, I wouldn't be in here at all, except that I'm waiting for my son.' To which the barman replied, 'Your only child, I presume?'

A termite walked into a bar and said, 'Is the bar tender here?'

A snail slid into a bar and ordered a beer. The barman said, 'Get out, you're a snail.' And he picked up the snail, threw him out of the door and across the street. Eleven months later, while collecting glasses, the barman felt a tap at his ankle. The snail said, 'What the hell did you do that for?'

A man was sitting quietly at the bar when the barman presented him with a riddle. 'My mother had a child. It wasn't my brother, and it wasn't my sister. Who was it?' The man thought for a minute but then gave up. 'It was me, you idiot!' exclaimed the barman triumphantly. The man thought it was a good trick and decided to play it on his wife when he got home. He announced, 'My mother had a child. It wasn't my brother, and it wasn't my sister. Who was it?' His wife looked at him blankly and gave up. 'It was Sid at the Wagon and Horses, you idiot!'

A guy walked into a bar. The barman said, 'You've got a steering wheel down your pants.' 'Yeah, I know,' said the guy. 'It's driving me nuts!'

A little pig walked into a bar, ordered a drink and asked where the toilet was. 'Just along the corridor,' said the barman. Then a second little pig walked into the bar, ordered a drink and asked where the toilet was. 'Just along the corridor,' said the barman. Then a third little pig walked into the bar and ordered a drink. The barman said, 'I suppose you want to use the toilet too?' 'No, I'm the little pig that goes wee wee wee wee all the way home.'

A man went into a bar and ordered a succession of Martinis. After each one, he removed the olive and put it into a jar. After two hours, the barman felt compelled to ask, 'Why do you keep doing that?' 'Because,' slurred the man, 'my wife sent me out for a jar of olives.'

A man spent six hours in a bar before rolling home to his wife blind drunk. 'Where have you been?' she demanded. 'I've been to this amazing bar,' he slurred, rocking on his feet. 'It's called the Golden Saloon and everything there is golden. At the front there are two huge golden doors, the floors are golden and even the urinals are golden.' 'What rubbish,' snapped the wife. 'I don't believe a word of it.' 'Here,' said the husband, rummaging in his pocket for a piece of paper. 'Ring this number if you don't believe me.' So the following day she phoned the number on the slip of paper. 'Is this the Golden Saloon?' she asked. 'It is,' replied the barman. 'Tell me,' said the wife, 'do you have two huge golden doors at the front of the building?' 'Sure do,' said the barman. 'And do you have golden floors?' 'Yup.' 'What about golden urinals?' There was a long pause and then the wife heard the barman yell, 'Hey, Duke, I think I got a lead on the guy that pissed in your saxophone last night!'

A man walked into a bar with a piece of tarmac under his arm. He said, 'I'll have a beer please, and one for the road.'

A grasshopper walked into a bar. The barman said, 'Hey, we have a drink named after you.' The grasshopper said, 'You have a drink named Marlon?'

A man was sitting outside a bar, enjoying a quiet drink when a nun came up and started lecturing him on the evils of alcohol. 'How do you know alcohol is evil?' said the man. 'Have you ever tasted it?' 'Of course not,' answered the nun. 'Then let me buy you a drink and, afterwards, if you still believe that it's evil, I promise I'll never touch another drop.' 'But I can't possibly be seen to be drinking,' said the nun. 'Right. Well, I'll get the barman to put it in a teacup for you.' The man went inside and asked for a beer and a vodka. 'And would you mind putting the vodka in a teacup?' 'Oh no,' said the barman. 'It's not that bloody nun again, is it?'

A sherrif walked into a bar and said, 'Has anyone seen Brown Paper Jake? He wears a brown paper hat, a brown paper waistcoat, a brown paper shirt, brown paper boots, paper pants and a brown paper jacket?' The barman said, 'What's he wanted for?' 'Rustlin'.'

A man had spent all day drinking in a bar. By ten o' clock at night, he was blind drunk but still wanted more. However, he had run out of money. 'I must have another drink,' he told the barman, 'can't you put it on the slate?' 'You know the rules,' replied the barman. 'No slate. But I'll tell you what, it's a quiet night in here and I fancy a bit of fun. So how about a deal? I'll let you have three more drinks on the house if you perform three tasks.' 'Sure,' said the drunk. 'What do you want me to do?' 'First, I want you to go up to the burly bouncer on the door and knock him out cold; then I want you to pull a loose tooth belonging to Satan, the bulldog in the back room. Finally, I want you to have sex with the town run-around who's sitting alone at the end of the bar.' 'No problem,' said the drunk, levering himself off the stool. He staggered over to the bouncer and, taking him by surprise, felled him with a single blow. The barman was amazed and pointed to the back room where the bulldog was waiting. The drunk lurched through the door to the back room and the barman waited to hear the commotion. Any second, he expected to see the drunk rush out, hotly pursued by Satan. Instead there was silence. Then after a few minutes the dog started barking. Five minutes later, the drunk emerged with a satisfied grin. 'Right,' he said, 'now where's the run-around with the loose tooth?'

A little man walked into a bar and slipped on a pile of dog poo by the door. Moments later, a burly biker came in and slipped on it as well. The little man said, 'I just did that.' So the biker hit him.

Late at night, a drunk was on his knees beneath a street light, evidently looking for something. A passer-by, being a good Samaritan, offered to help. 'What is it you have lost?' he asked. 'My watch,' replied the drunk. 'It fell off when I tripped over the pavement.' The passer-by joined in the search but after a quarter of an hour, there was still no sign of the watch. 'Where exactly did you trip?' asked the passer-by. 'About half a mile up the street,' replied the drunk. 'Then why are you looking for your watch here if you lost it half a mile up the street?' The drunk said, 'Because the light's a lot better here.'

A guy walked into a bar with a giraffe. They both drank so much that the giraffe passed out on the floor. There was no way the guy could get the giraffe back on its feet so he decided to go home and collect it in the morning. As he headed for the door, the barman called out, 'Hey, you can't leave that lyin' there.' The guy said, 'That's not a lion – it's a giraffe.'

A drunk was eyeing up a woman in a bar. He said to the barman, 'I really fancy that woman. If I buy her a drink, will you send it over to her and say it's from me?' The barman replied, 'I ought to warn you she's a hooker. She'll do what you want for money.' So the drunk ambled over to the woman and asked, 'Is it true you're a hooker?' 'Yes,' she said. 'I do it for money. I'll do anything for £200.' The drunk pulled out £200 from his wallet, handed it to her and said, 'Paint my house.'

A young stockbroker was unwinding in a bar after a hard week's work and was in the mood for a bit of fun and so he announced, 'If anyone can drink 20 pints of Guinness, I'll give them £150.' The barman lined up the 20 pints, but there were no immediate takers. Without saying a word, one man got off his stool, popped out, came back a few minutes later and declared that he could drink all 20. And to everyone's amazement, he did. The stockbroker handed over the money and asked the man where he had nipped out to. 'Well,' he said, 'first I had to go to the bar next door to make sure I could do it!'

A guy walked into a bar with a dog under his arm and bet anyone present £100 that his dog could talk. The barman took up the challenge. The owner looked at the dog and asked, 'What is on the top of this building to prevent the rain coming in?' The dog answered, 'Roof.' 'Are you kidding?' said the barman, 'I'm not falling for that.' 'Okay,' said the dog owner. 'How about double or quits? I'll ask him another question. Who was the greatest baseball player of all time?' The dog answered, 'Roof.' 'Right, that's it,' said the barman, and he threw them both out into the street. As they bounced off the pavement, the dog looked at the owner and said, 'DiMaggio?'

A guy went into a bar and ordered a double shot of bourbon. He downed it, reached in his pocket and pulled out a photo. After staring at the picture for a few moments, he put it away and ordered another double. When he had finished that drink, he pulled out the photo again, looked at it for a moment, put it back and ordered another double. He repeated this procedure for the next hour. Finally the barman's curiosity got the better of him. 'Excuse me,' he said, 'but after each drink, why do you keep taking out that picture and staring at it?' 'It's a picture of my wife,' explained the customer, 'and when she starts to look good, I'm going home.'

A jump lead walks into a bar. And the barman says, 'Okay, I'll serve you, but don't start anything.'

A piece of string walked into a bar and asked for a Budweiser. 'I'm afraid we don't serve pieces of string,' said the barman. Dejected, the piece of string went outside, back-combed his hair and went back in to the bar. The barman eyed him suspiciously. 'Are you that same piece of string that was in a few moments ago?' 'No, I'm a frayed knot.'

One night a man walks into a bar with a pig. The barman, being the observant sort, noticed right off that the pig had a wooden leg. He goes over to the man and asks about it. The man says, 'For a beer I'll tell you all about this very special pig.' The barman figures it's got to be a good story and so he gives the man a beer. The man begins, 'Let me tell you about this pig. He is one special pig. One night, about a year ago, my house caught fire. This pig broke out of his pen, came into the house, dragged my two littlest children out of the house, woke me and my wife and then guided us out of the house. This pig saved my life and my family's lives.' The barman, impressed but still wondering about the leg, says, 'Well, that's great. But why does he have a wooden leg?' The man says, 'For another beer, I'll tell you about this very special pig.' The barman, hooked, gives him another beer. The man says, 'Out behind my house there is a small lake. I was out sailing on it when the boat capsized. I cracked my head on the boom and couldn't swim. This pig broke out of his pen, swam out to me and dragged me to shore. He then went into the house and got my wife to come out. She gave me mouth-to-mouth resuscitation. This pig saved my life.' The barman, fascinated, but getting a little impatient, says, 'That's really terrific, but why the wooden leg?' The man says, 'For another beer...' The barman gives him another beer. The man says, 'Let me tell you about this pig. He is one special pig. Last week during a tornado I was on my way to the basement when I stepped on a rake and knocked myself out. This pig broke out of his pen and dragged me into the basement. He saved my life.' The barman, figuring this has got to be the last story, says, 'Wow, that is one special pig. He saved you from a fire, from a tornado, and from drowning. But why does he have a wooden leg?' To which the man replies, 'Well, sir, with a pig this special, you don't eat it all at once.'

A man in a nice suit goes to a bar. He says, 'Barman, give me a triple Jack Daniels.' He gives him a triple Jack Daniels, and he belts it down. He has five more in a row, belts them all down, passes out dead drunk, and someone kicks him in the ass. The next night, he walks into the bar and says, 'Barman, give me a triple Jack Daniels.' He gives him a triple Jack Daniels, and he belts it down. He has five more in a row, belts them all down, passes out dead drunk, and someone in the bar kicks him in the ass. The next night, he walks into the bar and says, 'Barman, give me a triple tequila.' The barman says, 'I thought you drank Jack Daniels?' He says, 'Not any more. Jack Daniels makes my ass hurt.'

A patron is sitting at a bar, and from out of an old suitcase he takes out a tiny piano and a little man about a foot tall. The little man sits down at the piano and starts playing beautifully. A fellow sitting next to the patron at the bar looks on in sheer amazement. 'That's unbelievable! Where on earth did you get him?' says the fellow. 'Well, I have this magic lamp here that was given to me by a genie.' 'Could I try it?' asks the fellow. 'Sure, be my guest.' The fellow rubs the lamp, and out comes a handsome genie. 'For what do you wish?' asks the genie. 'I'd like a million bucks,' says the fellow. Suddenly, the room is filled with a million quacking ducks. 'I asked for a million BUCKS, not DUCKS!' the fellow says to the patron. 'I know,' said the patron. 'The genie is a little hard of hearing. You don't really think I asked for a twelve-inch pianist, do you?'

Two hamburgers walk into a bar. The barman said, 'Sorry, we don't serve food.'

A man with no arms walked into a bar and asked for a beer. The barman shoved the foaming glass in front of him. 'Look,' said the customer, 'I have no arms - would you please hold the glass up to my mouth?' 'Sure,' said the barman, and he did. 'Now,' said the customer, 'I wonder if you'd be so kind as to get my handkerchief out of my pocket and wipe the foam off my mouth?' 'Certainly.' And it was done. 'If,' said the armless man, 'you'd reach in my right-hand pocket, you'll find the money for the beer.' The barman got it. 'You've been very kind,' said the customer. 'Just one thing more. Where's the men's room?' 'Out the door,' said the barman, 'turn left, walk two streets away, and there's one in the petrol station on the corner.'

An Englishman, an Irishman and a Scotsman

An Englishman, an Irishman and a Scotsman were in a pub, talking about their sons. 'My son was born on St George's Day,' commented the Englishman. 'So we obviously decided to call him George.' 'That's a real coincidence,' remarked the Scot. 'My son was born on St Andrew's Day, so obviously we decided to call him Andrew.' 'That's incredible, what a coincidence,' said the Irishman. 'Exactly the same thing happened with my son Pancake.'

Five Englishmen boarded a train just behind five Scots, who, as a group, had only purchased one ticket. Just before the conductor came through, all the Scots piled into the toilet stall at the back of the car. As the conductor passed the stall, he knocked and called, 'Tickets, please!' and one of the Scots slid a ticket under the door. It was punched, pushed back under the door, and when it was safe all the Scots came out and took their seats. The Englishmen were tremendously impressed by the Scots' ingenuity. On the trip back, the five Englishmen decided to try this themselves and purchased only one ticket. They noticed that, oddly, the Scots had not purchased any tickets this time. Anyway, again, just before the conductor came through, the Scots piled into one of the toilet stalls, the Englishmen into the other. Then one of the Scots leaned out, knocked on the Englishmen's stall and called 'Tickets, please!' When the ticket slid out, he picked it up and quickly closed the door.

An Englishman, roused by a Scot's scorn of his race, protested that he was born an Englishman and hoped to die an Englishman. 'Man,' scoffed the Scot, 'have you no ambition?'

A Scotsman, an Englishman and Claudia Schiffer were sitting together in a train carriage going through Wales. Suddenly the train went through a tunnel and as it was an old-style train, there were no lights in the carriages and it went completely dark. There was this kissing noise and the sound of a really loud slap. When the train came out of the tunnel, Claudia Schiffer and the Scotsman were sitting as if nothing had happened and the Englishman had his hand against his face, as he had been slapped. The Englishman was thinking, 'The Scottish fella must have kissed Claudia Schiffer and she missed him and slapped me instead.' Claudia Schiffer was thinking, 'The English fella must have tried to kiss me and actually kissed the Scotsman and got slapped for it.' And the Scotsman was thinking, 'This is great. The next time the train goes through a tunnel I'll make that kissing noise and slap that English b**tard again!'

One day an Englishman, a Scotsman, and an Irishman walked into a pub together. They each bought a pint of Guinness. Just as they were about to enjoy their creamy beverage, three flies landed in each of their pints, and got stuck in the thick head. The Englishman pushed his beer away in disgust. The Scotsman fished the fly out of his beer, and continued drinking it, as if nothing had happened. The Irishman, too, picked the fly out of his drink, held it out over the beer, and started yelling, 'SPIT IT OUT, SPIT IT OUT, YOU BAS**RD!'

They say an Englishman laughs three times at a joke. The first time when everybody gets it, the second a week later when he thinks he gets it, the third time a month later when somebody explains it to him.

Two Irishmen in London looking for work are strolling down Oxford Street. Suddenly, Paddy turns to his pal and says, 'Michael, will you look at that shop over there. I thought London was supposed to be expensive, but that shop is as cheap as chips!' 'You're right, Paddy, so you are. I can't believe it. Suits £10, Shirts £4, Trousers £5. I think that we should buy the lot and take them back to Ireland. We would make a tidy profit selling them in Dublin, so we would.' 'Michael, that is as good an idea as you'll ever have, but I'm pretty sure you'd have to pay taxes and duty on things like that. The shopkeeper will never let us have them if he thinks we want to export them and make our fortune.' 'Paddy, I've got an idea! You can do the best English accent. You go in there and do the talking and I'll just stand behind you and say nothing. He'll never guess we're Irish.' 'Okay Michael,' agrees Paddy, 'I'll do the talking, you just look English.' So the two visitors go into the shop, where Paddy is greeted politely by the owner. Paddy then proceeds to do his best Warren Mitchell impression. 'Awwright Guvnor, I'll 'ave 20 of yer Whistle 'n Flutes, 20 Dickie Dirts and 20 pairs of strides. And if yer don't mind I'll be paying with the 380 Pictures of the Queen in me Sky Rocket.' The owner smiles, takes a look at Michael as well, then says to Paddy, 'You're Irish, aren't you?' Quite bemused, Paddy replies, 'Oh, bejabbers, if that ain't me best English accent! How in God's name did you know we were Irish?' The shopkeeper replies, 'This is a dry cleaners'.

A guy walks into a bar with an octopus. He sits the octopus down on a stool and tells everyone in the bar that this is a very talented octopus. 'He can play any musical instrument in the world.' Everyone in the bar laughs at the man, calling him an idiot. So he says that he will wager £50 to anyone who has an instrument that the octopus can't play. A guy walks up with a guitar and sets it beside the octopus. Immediately the octopus picks up the guitar and starts playing better than Jimi Hendrix. The guitar man pays up his £50. Another guy walks up with a trumpet. This time the octopus plays the trumpet better than Louis Armstrong. The guy pays up his £50. Then a Scotsman walks up with some bagpipes. He puts them down and the octopus fumbles with them for a minute and then sits down with a confused look. 'Ha Ha!' the Scot says. 'Ye canny play it, can ye?' The octopus looks up at him and says, 'Play it? I'm going to f**k it as soon as I figure out how to get its pyjamas off.'

Concerning bagpipes: the Irish invented them and gave them to the Scots as a joke. The Scots haven't seen the joke yet.

An Englishman and an Irishman are driving head on, at night, on a twisty, dark road. Both are driving too fast for the conditions and collide on a sharp bend in the road. To their amazement, they are unscathed, though their cars are both destroyed. In celebration of their luck, both agree to put aside their dislike for the other from that moment on. At this point, the Irishman goes to the boot and fetches a twelve-year-old bottle of Jameson whisky. He hands the bottle to the Englishman, who exclaims, ''May the English and the Irish live together forever, in peace and harmony.' The Englishman then tips the bottle and lashes half of it down. Still flabbergasted over the whole thing, he goes to hand the bottle to the Irishman, who replies, 'No thanks, I'll just wait till the police get here.'

Two Irishmen met in a pub and discussed the illness of a third. 'Poor Michael Hogan! Faith, I'm afraid he's goin' to die.' 'Sure, an' why would he be dyin'?' asked the other. 'Ah, he's gotten so thin. You're thin enough, and I'm thin – but by my soul, Michael Hogan is thinner than both of us put together.'

An Irishman walks into a pub. The barman asks him, 'What'll you have?' The man says, 'Give me three pints of Guinness, please.' So the barman brings him three pints and the man proceeds to alternately sip one, then the other, then the third until they're gone. He then orders three more. The barman says, 'Sir, I know you like them cold. You don't have to order three at a time. I can keep an eye on it and when you get low I'll bring you a fresh cold one.' The man says, 'You don't understand. I have two brothers, one in Australia and one in the States. We made a vow to each other that every Saturday night we'd still drink together. So right now, my brothers have three Guinness stouts too, and we're drinking together.' The barman thought that was a wonderful tradition. Every week the man came in and ordered three drinks. Then one week he came in and ordered only two. He drank them and then ordered two more. The barman said to him, 'I know what your tradition is, and I'd just like to say that I'm sorry that one of your brothers died.' The man said, 'Oh, me brothers are fine – I just quit drinking.'

'What do Irish people do about Irishman jokes?' I was asked. 'They tell Kerryman jokes,' I replied. 'Well, what about the Kerrymen then, what do they do about Kerryman jokes?' 'They put them into books and sell them to Englishmen,' I said.

An Englishman, a Scotsman and an Irishman were at the fair and about to go on the helter-skelter when an old crone steps in front of them. 'This is a magic ride,' she says. 'You will land in whatever you shout out on the way down.' 'I'm game for this,' says the Scotsman and slides down the helter-skelter shouting 'GOLD!' at the top of his voice. Sure enough, when he hit the bottom he found himself surrounded by thousands of pounds worth of gold coins. The Englishman goes next and shouts 'SILVER!' at the top of his voice. At the bottom he lands in more silver coinage than he can carry. The Irishman goes last and, launching himself from the top of the slide, shouts 'WEEEEEEE!'

Why do they make Irishman jokes so simple? So Englishmen can understand them!

An Englishman asked an Irishman to show him the biggest building in an Irish town. 'There it is now,' said the Irishman. 'Isn't it a fine structure entirely?' 'Is that your biggest building?' asked the Englishman. 'Why back in England we have buildings over a hundred times the size of that!' 'I'm not surprised,' said the Irishman. 'That's the local lunatic asylum.'

An Englishman, Scotsman and an Irishman are on a plane together when it begins to dive-bomb, sending them to certain death. In order to escape, the plane has to lose lots of weight quickly to allow it to continue to fly. They decide that each man has to throw out a possession. 'I'll throw out a rose, 'cos there's lots of them in my country,' says the Englishman. 'I'll throw out a thistle, 'cos there's lots of them in my country,' says the Scotsman. 'I'll throw out a bomb, 'cos' there's lots of them in my country,' says the Irishman. Luckily, their plan works and they survive, and they each go home to their families. As the Englishman comes home, he sees his dad weeping and says, 'Dad! Dad! Why are you crying?' To which his dad replies, 'A rose fell out the sky and the thorns slit your mother's throat!' As the Scotsman comes home, he sees his dad weeping and says, 'Dad! Dad! Why are you crying?' To which his dad replies, 'A thistle fell from the sky and the prickles blinded your mother!' As the Irishman comes home, he sees his dad laughing and says, 'Dad! Dad! Why are you laughing?' To which his dad replies, 'I farted and next door's house blew up!'

An Englishman, an Irishman and a Scotsman were standing looking at a prize cow in a field. The Englishman says, 'Look at that fine English cow.' The Irishman disagreed, saying, 'No, it's an Irish cow.' The Scotsman thought for a moment and then clinched the argument. 'No, it's a Scottish cow – it's got bagpipes underneath!'

Three guys, one Irish, one English and one Scottish, are walking along the beach one day. They come across a lantern and a genie pops out of it. 'I'll give you each one wish - that's three wishes in total,' says the genie. The Irish guy says, 'I am a fisherman, my Dad's a fisherman, his Dad was a fisherman and my son will be one too. I want all the oceans full of fish for all eternity.' So, with a blink of the genie's eye, 'Alkazoom!' – and the oceans are teeming with fish. The English guy is amazed, so he says, 'I want a wall around England, protecting her, so that nothing will get in for all eternity.' Again, with a blink of the genie's eye, 'Alkazoom!' – there's a huge wall around England. The Scot asks, 'I'm very curious. Please tell me more about this wall.' The genie explains, 'Well, it's about 150 ft high, 50 ft thick, protecting England so that nothing can get in or out.' The Scot says, 'Ach, fill it up with water.'

An Englishman, Scotsman and a Welshman walk into a bar. And the barman says, 'Is this some kind of joke?'

There was an Englishman, an Irishman and a Scotsman swimming in the sea one day, when they were captured by pirates. The captain said to them, 'You're getting locked up in a dungeon for 50 years, but I'll give you something to go in with.' The Englishman says he wants to go in with booze, so he goes in with his booze. The Scotsman says he wants some women, so he goes in with his women. Finally, the Irishman wants to go in with cigarettes, so he goes in with his cigarettes. Then 50 years later, the Englishman comes out of his dungeon pissed, the Scotsman comes out with his women and kids, and the Irishman comes out and says, 'Got a light?'

Quick Quips 6

When I read about the evils of drinking, I gave up reading. ***Henry Youngman***

One more drink and I'd be under the host. ***Dorothy Parker***

A woman drove me to drink and I never even had the courtesy to thank her. ***W C Fields***

Without question, the greatest invention in the history of mankind is beer. Oh, I grant you that the wheel was also a fine invention, but the wheel does not go nearly as well with pizza. ***Dave Barry***

Work is the curse of the drinking class. ***Oscar Wilde***

Actually, it only takes one drink to get me loaded. Trouble is, I can't remember if it's the thirteenth or fourteenth. ***George Burns***

I drink to forget I drink. ***Joe E Lewis***

I once shook hands with Pat Boone and my whole right side sobered up. ***Dean Martin***

During one of my treks through Afghanistan, we lost our corkscrew and were compelled to live on food and water for several days. ***W C Fields***

Time is never wasted when you're wasted all the time. ***Catherine Zandonella***

I'm not saying he's a world champion drinker, but he'd got an entry in the Record Book of Guinnesses.
Frederick Oliver

Drinking provides a beautiful excuse to pursue the one activity that truly gives me pleasure: hooking up with fat hairy girls. ***Ross Levy***

Always do sober what you said you'd do drunk. That will teach you to keep your mouth shut. ***Ernest Hemingway***

The problem with some people is that when they aren't drunk, they're sober.
William Butler Yeats

An intelligent man is sometimes forced to be drunk to spend time with his fools. ***Ernest Hemingway***

No animal ever invented anything as bad as drunkenness – or as good as drink. ***G K Chesterton***

Abstainer: a weak person who yields to the temptation of denying himself a pleasure.
Ambrose Bierce

Reality is an illusion that occurs due to lack of alcohol.
Anon

Beauty lies in the hands of the beer holder. ***Anon***

Life is a waste of time, time is a waste of life, so get wasted all of the time and have the time of your life.
Michelle Mastrolacasa

24 hours in a day, 24 beers in a case. Coincidence?
Stephen Wright

You can't be a real country unless you have a beer and an airline. It helps if you have some kind of a football team, or some nuclear weapons, but at the very least you need a beer. ***Frank Zappa***

Always remember that I have taken more out of alcohol than alcohol has taken out of me. ***Winston Churchill***

He was a wise man who invented beer. ***Plato***

Beer is proof that God loves us and wants us to be happy. ***Benjamin Franklin***

Why is Australian beer served cold? So you can tell it from urine. ***David Moulton***

The problem with the world is that everyone is a few drinks behind. ***Humphrey Bogart***

If you ever reach total enlightenment while drinking beer, I bet it makes beer shoot out your nose. ***Deep Thought, Jack Handy***

Give me a woman who loves beer and I will conquer the world. ***Kaiser Wilhelm***

I would kill everyone in this room for a drop of sweet beer. ***Homer Simpson***

I drink to make other people interesting. ***George Jean Nathan***

All right, brain, I don't like you and you don't like me – so let's just do this and I'll get back to killing you with beer. ***Homer Simpson***

death

Funereal Laughter

Minutes before her husband's funeral, a widow took one last look at his body. To her horror, she saw that he was wearing a brown suit, whereas she had issued strict instructions to the undertaker that she wanted him buried in a blue suit. She sought out the undertaker and demanded that the suit be changed. At first, he tried to tell her that it was too late but when he could see that she wasn't going to back down, he ordered the mortician to wheel the coffin away. A few minutes later, just as the funeral was about to start, the coffin was wheeled back in and, incredibly, the corpse was now wearing a blue suit. The widow was delighted and, after the service, praised the undertaker for his swift work. 'Oh, it was nothing,' he said. 'It so happened there was another body in the back room and he was already dressed in a blue suit so all we had to do was switch heads.'

A man had his wife cremated. As smoke came out, he said to his friend, 'That's the first time I ever saw her hot.'

Man: I want you to bury my wife.
Undertaker: But I buried your wife last year.
Man: Yes, but I remarried.
Undertaker: Oh, congratulations, Sir.

The chief problem about death, incidentally, is the fear that there may be no afterlife – a depressing thought, particularly for those who have bothered to shave. Also, there is the fear that there is an afterlife but no one will know where it's being held.

Woody Allen

The businesswoman ordered a fancy floral arrangement for the grand opening of her new outlet, and she was furious when it arrived adorned with a ribbon, which read 'May You Rest in Peace'. Apologising profusely, the florist finally got her to calm down with the reminder that in some funeral home stood an arrangement bearing the words 'Good Luck in Your New Location'.

Funeral director: A guy who tries to look sad at a £10,000 funeral.

When old Mr O'Leary died, an elaborate wake was planned. In preparation, Mrs O'Leary called the undertaker aside for a private little talk. 'Please be sure to secure his toupee to his head very securely. No one but I knew he was bald,' she confided, 'and he'd never rest in peace if anyone found out at this point. But our friends are sure to hold his hands and touch his head before they're through paying their last respects.' 'Rest assured, Mrs O'Leary,' comforted the undertaker. 'I'll fix it so that toupee will never come off.' Sure enough, the day of the wake the old timers were giving O'Leary's corpse quite a going-over, but the toupee stayed firmly in place. At the end of the day, a delighted Mrs O'Leary offered the undertaker an extra £100 for handling the matter so professionally. 'Oh, I couldn't possibly accept your money,' protested the undertaker. 'After all, what's a few nails?'

My grandfather's funeral has cost us £5,000 so far – we buried him in a rented suit.

My sister is going out with an undertaker. She's sure he only wants her for her body.

There was once a fellow named Clyde,
Who went to a funeral and cried.
When asked who was dead,
He stammered and said,
'I don't know, I just came for the ride.'

My uncle created the solar-powered funeral home. He's got basic solar technology, big solar panels on the roof, the sun beats down, it heats up the panels. Trouble is, he can't cremate, he can only poach. ***Heywood Banks***

My uncle was a chain smoker. They buried him in a flip-top coffin.

A lawyer attended the funeral of a rich man. A friend, arriving late, took a seat beside him and whispered, 'How far has the service gone?' The lawyer nodded toward the clergyman in the pulpit and whispered back, 'He just opened for the defence.'

Ways To Be Offensive At A Funeral:

- → Tell the widow she looks horny in black.
- → Take bets on how long it takes a body to decompose.
- → Drive behind the hearse and keep honking your horn.
- → Tell the undertaker your dog died and ask if you can sneak him into the coffin.
- → Put a hard-boiled egg in the mouth of the deceased.
- → Punch the body and tell people he hit you first.
- → Goose the widow as she bends over to throw dirt on to the coffin.
- → Ask someone to take a Polaroid of you shaking hands with the deceased.
- → Go around telling people that you've seen the will and that they're not in it.
- → Listen to your Walkman at the graveside.
- → Tell the widow that you're the deceased's secret gay lover.
- → Put a whoopee cushion on the widow's chair.
- → Use the deceased's tongue to lick a postage stamp.
- → Take a flower from the wreath as a button hole.
- → Attend the funeral wearing a clown's costume.
- → Whenever the widow cries, blow a raspberry every time she wipes her nose.
- → Toss a handful of cooked rice on to the deceased, screaming 'Maggots, maggots!' then pretend to faint.
- → Tell the widow that the deceased's last wish was that she make love to you.
- → Slip plastic vampire teeth into the deceased's mouth.

Our local undertaker is having a special sale this week. For just £5 extra, you can take a friend.

There's a funeral procession with two hearses, and behind the two hearses is a guy with a vicious dog and behind him about a hundred guys. As they're all passing through town a guy steps off the curb and asks the guy with the dog what's going on. 'My dog killed my wife and my mother-in-law,' was the answer. 'Can I borrow the dog?' the guy asks. 'Get in line.' ***Henny Youngman***

A stone mason was approached to prepare a headstone for a well known member of the local community. There was little time but the stone was to be in place for an official unveiling to be held in front of visiting dignitaries and members of the press. The mason accepted the order and set about his task. The evening before the unveiling, the stone was erected with suitable solemnity and duly covered from prying eyes. An official, checking that all was well, peered at the inscription in the fading light. He was horrified to discover that the mason had missed a letter from the final line of text. Contacting the mason, he babbled, 'You've missed an 'e' off the last line! What will we do?' The mason was unperturbed and assured the official that he would attend the site in the morning and add the errant letter. All apparently went well and, even as the procession was approaching the cemetery, the last chips of stone flew off the end of the busy chisel. The ceremony complete, the stone was unveiled and all the world was delighted to read the final script: 'E God, she was thin.'

Remember, all men are cremated equal.

A husband and wife walked up to view the body of his mother-in-law at the funeral. As he began to weep, his wife slapped him and said, 'Why are you crying, you never liked my mother anyway!' The husband replied, 'I know, I thought I saw her move!'

Did you hear about the undertaker who buried someone in the wrong place and was sacked for the grave mistake?

Three smiling corpses are lying in a morgue in Arkansas, and a detective goes into the coroner's to find the causes of death. The coroner points to the first dead man. 'This is Cletus,' he says. 'He died of shock after winning $20 million on the lottery.' He then moves on to the second smiling corpse. 'This is Bo,' the coroner says with a grin. 'He died while doing 'it' with Trudy-May.' Finally he moves on to the last smiling corpse. 'This is Roscoe,' says the coroner. 'He died after being struck by lightning.' 'Well,' says the detective, 'Why in hell was the fool smiling?' 'Oh,' says the coroner. 'He thought he was having his picture taken.'

The man who first said, 'You can't take it with you,' must have been thinking about the cost of funerals.

A cardiologist died and was given an elaborate funeral. A huge heart covered in flowers stood behind the casket during the service. Following the eulogy, the heart opened, and the casket rolled inside. The heart then closed, sealing the doctor in the beautiful heart forever. At that point, one of the mourners burst into laughter. When all eyes stared at him, he said, 'I'm sorry, I was just thinking of my own funeral. I'm a gynaecologist.' And that's when the proctologist fainted.

There are two things we're sure of, death and taxes. Now, if only we could get them in that order!

The town founder had passed away and the whole town turned out, as did his family, who arrived from all over the globe. This threw the mortuary into an uproar. They had some employees doing two or three jobs and others switching jobs to get everything done. After the chapel services, all the members of the funeral party piled into the different cars for the drive to the cemetery. The procession was very long, and one group of family members, not knowing their way, decided to ask the driver how much further it would be. The patriarch tapped the driver on the shoulder, and said, 'Pardon me...' The driver let out a scream and turned with a grimace of horror to see who had tapped him. In doing so, he drove the car into the ditch and through a farmer's fence, almost overturning it. After calming everyone down, the driver explained, 'I'm so sorry for what happened, but you see, I usually drive the hearse.'

Did you hear about the do-it-yourself funeral? They just loosen the earth and you sink down by yourself.

How can they tell?

Dorothy Parker, on being informed of the demise of President Calvin Coolidge

The old man had died. A wonderful funeral was in progress and the country vicar talked at length of the good traits of the deceased – what an honest man he was, and what a loving husband and kind father. Finally, the widow leaned over and whispered to one of her children, 'Go up there and take a look in the coffin and see if that's your father, will you?'

Why do you want to be buried at sea? Because my wife says she wants to dance on my grave.

A funeral service is being held for a woman who has just passed away. At the end of the service, the pallbearers are carrying the casket out when they accidentally bump into a wall, jarring the casket. They hear a faint moan. They open the casket and find that the woman is actually alive. She lives for ten more years and then dies. A ceremony is again held and at the end of the service the pallbearers are again carrying out the casket. As they are walking, the husband cries out, 'Watch out for the wall!'

I was so sorry to hear you buried your mother last week. Well, we had to, you know, she was dead.

John and Patrick were passing through the cemetery when Patrick paused to read a particularly ornate headstone. 'It says here,' he read aloud, 'here lies an honest man and a lawyer.' Turning to John with a puzzled expression, Patrick asked, 'Now why would they bury two men together like that?'

One time I had to go to a funeral at 6am. I shouldn't have been there. I'm not a mourning person.

Jones 'The Box', the local funeral director, and his trusted assistant were called to a remote Welsh hill farm in the depths of a bad winter to collect the body of Evan, the deceased farmer. Failing to break through the snowdrifts on the lower slopes, Jones, fuelled by a sense of duty, instructed his aide to unload the coffin. Attaching ropes to the handles, together they pushed on through the worsening weather, towing the coffin behind. At the farm, they placed the defunct Evan in the coffin and set off to haul him back to the vehicle. Disaster struck when Jones lost his footing on the windblown hillside and fell backward onto the coffin lid. Evan, in the box, and Jones on top, set off at great speed down the hill, pursued frantically by the assistant. Together, the three arrived at the outer wall of the village pub with a resounding thud. 'Well,' said Jones, a pragmatist at the best of times, brushing himself down and looking not a little shaken, 'if Evan is so determined to call in for a last pint, who are we to disagree then?' And there they stayed until the storm subsided. Jones 'The Box' inside and Evan, outside, in his box.

I want to die the same way my grandfather did, peacefully in his sleep. Not like his passengers, who were screaming and shouting to the end...

Her husband having passed away, Alice, ever a thrifty Scot, called on the local carpenter and arranged to have a coffin made up from old packing cases. She next visited the draper, MacDougal, and asked for a length of material, suitable for sewing into a shroud. When the gentleman stated his price, Alice threw up her hands in horror. 'Why, I can buy a similar cloth down the road for half that amount,' she said. 'Och, aye, that you can,' replied MacDougal. 'But the stuff is so poor quality that it'll wear through at the knees within a week...'

The brash and successful young businessman returned to his small hometown for a family funeral. Rapidly bored with family gossip, he wandered off and eventually found himself at the town cemetery. Working in the bottom of a new grave was the ancient town gravedigger. 'Hey!' called the young man, 'Is that you, Tom?' Pausing in his labours to peer up at the fresh young face above, the old man wiped the sweat from his brow before responding. 'Ayup, surely is.' 'Amazing,' muttered the youngster to himself. 'How old are you anyway, Tom?' Unperturbed by the rude arrogance of the youth, old Tom pondered the question before squinting up to the daylight again. 'Oh, must be all of 75 by now,' he said happily. Turning on his heel and striding off the businessman threw back over his shoulder, 'Hardly seems worth your while climbing back out of that one then, does it?'

At an atheist funeral: Here lies an atheist, all dressed up and nowhere to go.

Pearly Gates

A minister dies and is waiting in line at the Pearly Gates. Ahead of him is a guy who is dressed in sunglasses, a loud shirt, leather jacket and jeans. St Peter addresses this guy. 'Who are you, so that I may know whether or not to admit you to the Kingdom of Heaven?' The guy replies, 'I'm Joe, taxi driver, of Noo Yawk City.' St Peter consults his list. He smiles and says to the taxi driver, 'Take this silken robe and golden staff and enter the Kingdom of Heaven.' The taxi driver goes into Heaven with his robe and staff. Now it's the minister's turn. He stands erect and booms out, 'I am Joseph, rector of St Mary's for the last 43 years.' St Peter consults his list and says to him, 'Take this cotton robe and wooden staff and enter the Kingdom of Heaven.' 'Just a minute,' says the minister. 'That man was a taxi driver, and he gets a silken robe and golden staff. How can this be?' 'Up here, we work by results,' says St Peter. 'While you preached, people slept; while he drove, people prayed.'

A Catholic, a Jew and an Episcopalian are lined up at the Pearly Gates. The Catholic asks to get in and St Peter says, 'Nope, sorry.' 'Why not?' says the Catholic, 'I've been good.' 'Well, you ate meat on a Friday in Lent, so I can't let you in.' The Jew walks up and again St Peter says no. The Jew wants an explanation so St Peter replies, 'There was that time you ate pork – sorry, you have to go to the other place.' Then the Episcopalian goes up and asks to be let in and St Peter again says no. 'Why not?' asks the Episcopalian. 'What did I do wrong?' 'Well,' says St Peter, 'you once ate your entrée with the salad fork.'

Three fellows die and are transported to the Pearly Gates, where St Peter explains that admission depends on a quick quiz, a mere formality. 'I'm just going to ask each of you a single question,' he explains, turning to the first guy. 'What, please, is Easter?' 'That's easy. Easter is when you celebrate the Pilgrims' landing. You buy a turkey...' 'Sorry,' interrupts St Peter briskly, 'you're out.' And he asks the second man, 'What can you tell me about Easter?' 'No problem,' the fellow responds promptly. 'That's when we commemorate Jesus' birth by going shopping, decorating a tree...' 'No, no, no,' St Peter bursts out, and turns in exasperation to the last guy. 'I don't suppose you know anything about Easter?' 'Certainly I do. See, Christ was crucified, and He died, and they took the body down from the cross and wrapped it in a shroud and put it in a cave and rolled this big stone across the entrance...' 'Hang on a sec,' interrupts St Peter excitedly, beckoning the other two over. 'Listen. We've got someone here who actually knows his stuff.' 'And after three days they roll the stone away,' continues the third guy confidently, 'and if He sees His shadow, there's going to be six more weeks of winter.'

There was once a nobleman who died at the age of 65 and then proceeded to Heaven. At the Pearly Gates, he was met by St Peter who asked him whether he wanted to go to Heaven or Hell. He could take a tour of both and decide for himself. First, he was taken to Heaven. There he was shown people praying and, in general, leading an austere kind of existence. Then he was taken on a grand tour of Hell where he saw people were drinking and having a good time, lots of good-looking women and a lot of merrymaking. When he was taken back to St Peter, he asked to be put in Hell. Suddenly, a huge servant from Hell pulled him gruffly by the arm and took him to Hell. But he was shocked to see that everywhere people were being tortured. There were vats of boiling oil and lots of strange-looking Devilish creatures. He exclaimed to the attendant, 'This is not what I was shown a little while ago.' To this the attendant laughed and replied, 'Oh, that was our demo model!'

A man died and went up to Heaven, where he was greeted by St Peter. 'And who are you?' asked St Peter. 'My name is Steven Richards.' And what did you do for a living?' asked St Peter. 'I was unemployed.' 'Unemployed, hmmm?' mused St Peter. 'And have you ever done anything good in your life?' 'As a matter of fact, I have. I was walking along the street once and I saw a group of bikers who were threatening to beat up a defenceless girl. So I rushed to her rescue, pulled the ringleader off by his hair, kicked him hard where it hurts and told him and his gang to clear off.' 'That's highly commendable,' said St Peter flicking through the man's file, 'but I can't see any report of this incident. When did it happen?' 'About five minutes ago.'

A nun, Sister Margaret, went to Heaven, only to be told by St Peter that there was a waiting list. 'Go home and relax,' suggested St Peter. 'Give me a call in a week and I'll let you know whether your accommodation is ready.' The following week she phoned up and said, 'Peter, this is Margaret. I have a confession to make: I had my first ever cigarette yesterday. Will it affect my chances of getting into Heaven?' 'I'm sure it won't,' said St Peter. 'But your room isn't ready yet. Call me in a week.' A week later, she called again. 'Peter, this is Margaret. I have a confession to make: I had my first ever alcoholic drink yesterday. Will it affect my chances of getting into Heaven?' 'I'm sure it won't,' said St Peter. 'But your room still isn't ready. Call me in three days.' Three days later, she rings again. 'Peter, this is Margaret. I have a confession to make: last night I kissed a man for the first time. Do you think it will wreck my chances of getting into Heaven?' 'I shouldn't think so,' said St Peter. 'But give me a ring tomorrow. By then I'll have checked it out with the boss man and I'll know about your accommodation.' The next day, she phoned again. 'Pete, this is Meg, forget about the room.'

Everybody on Earth died and went to Heaven. On their arrival, God announced that he wanted the men to form two lines - one for all those who had dominated their women on Earth, the other for all the men who had been dominated by their women. Then he told all the women to go with St Peter. When God turned around, he saw that the men had indeed formed two lines. The line of men who had been dominated by their women stretched back 80 miles whereas the line of men who had dominated their women consisted of just one person. God was furious. 'You men should be ashamed of yourselves for having been so weak,' he boomed. 'Only one of my sons has been strong. He is the only one of whom I am truly proud.' God addressed the man standing alone. 'Tell me, my son, how did you manage to be the only one in this line?' 'I'm not sure,' replied the man meekly. 'My wife told me to stand here!'

St Peter became aware of a man pacing up and down outside the Pearly Gates. 'Can I help you?' he asked the man. The man looked at his watch impatiently. 'No, it's okay, I won't be long,' the man replied. Five minutes later, St Peter looked out again and saw that the man still seemed agitated about something. 'What is it?' asked St Peter. The man stopped his pacing. 'Look,' he said, 'you know I'm dead; I know I'm dead. So will someone please tell the cardiac arrest team?'

St Peter had gone on holiday, leaving God in charge of the Pearly Gates. One day an engineer arrived at the gates but God, who wasn't used to the procedure, took one look at him and said, 'You're in the wrong place.' Dejected, the engineer caught the escalator down to Hell where he received a warm welcome from the Devil. But after a week, the engineer decided that Hell was too hot and uncomfortable so he arranged with the Devil for a few improvements to be made. The engineer said, 'How about if

I fix it for water to be piped in, air conditioning to be installed and a few swimming pools to be built?' 'Sounds great,' said the Devil, and within three weeks Hell was transformed into a tropical paradise. Not long after, God called the Devil for one of their regular chats. 'How's things down there?' chortled God. 'Pretty hot, huh?' 'As a matter of fact, no,' said the Devil. 'It's fantastic. We've got an engineer down here who has worked wonders. We've got air conditioning, swimming pools, the lot.' 'What!' boomed God. 'That's a mistake, the engineer was supposed to be up here.' 'Too bad,' said the Devil, 'we're keeping him.' 'That's what you think,' stormed God. 'I want that engineer. I'm going to sue.' The Devil gave a supremely confident smile and replied, 'Yeah? Where are you going to get a lawyer?'

St Peter stood at the Pearly Gates, waiting for the incoming. He saw Jesus walking by and caught his attention. 'Jesus, could you mind the gate while I go do an errand?' 'Sure,' replied Jesus. 'What do I have to do?' 'Just find out about the people who arrive. Ask about their background, their family and their lives. Then decide if they deserve entry into Heaven.' 'Sounds easy enough. Okay.' So Jesus waited at the gates while St Peter went off on his errand. The first person to approach the gates was a wrinkled old man. Jesus summoned him to the examination table and sat across from him. Jesus peered at the old man and asked, 'What did you do for a living?' The old man replied, 'I was a carpenter.' Jesus remembered his own earthly existence and leaned forward. 'Did you have any family?' he asked. 'Yes, I had a son, but I lost him.' Jesus leaned forward some more. 'You lost your son? Can you tell me about him?' 'Well, he had holes in his hands and feet.' Jesus leaned forward even more and whispered, 'Father?' The old man leaned forward and whispered, 'Pinocchio?'

A young man dies and goes to Heaven, where he finds he is third in line at the Pearly Gates. St Peter is taking a much needed break, so an angel is admitting the newly arrived to Heaven. The angel tells the three new arrivals that because so many drug dealers and other criminals have managed to sneak into Heaven that St Peter must now be a little stricter with the screening process. Each person is required to state his former occupation and tell his or her yearly salary. The first man in line says, 'I was an actor, and I earned £1,000,000 last year.' The angel says, 'Okay, you may enter.' He turns to the woman in line and asks her about her life. She states, 'I earned £150,000 as a solicitor.' The angel thinks for a moment and then lets her in, too. He turns to the third one in line and asks, 'What have you done with your life?' The man replies, 'I earned £8,000 last year... 'Oh,' the angel interrupts. 'What did you teach?'

Jake, Johnny and Billy died and went to Heaven. 'Welcome,' St Peter said. 'You'll be very happy here if you just obey our rule: never step on a duck. If you step on a duck, the duck quacks, they all start quacking and it makes a terrible racket.' That sounded simple enough until they passed the Pearly Gates and found thousands of ducks everywhere. Jake stepped on one right away. The ducks quacked, making an unholy racket, and St Peter came up to Jake bringing with him a ferocious-looking Amazon woman. 'I warned you if you broke the rule you'd be punished,' St Peter said. Then he chained the Amazon woman to Jake for eternity. Several hours later, Johnny stepped on a duck. The duck quacked, they all quacked, and St Peter stepped up to Johnny with an angry-looking, shrewish woman. 'As your punishment,' St Peter told Johnny, 'you'll be chained to this woman for eternity.' Billy was extremely careful not to step on a duck. Several months went by. Then St Peter came up to him with a gorgeous blonde and chained her to Billy, uniting them for all time. 'Wow!' exclaimed Billy. 'I wonder what I did to deserve this?' 'I don't know about you,' said the beautiful woman, 'but I stepped on a duck.'

Three married couples – one Jewish, one Irish, one American – all died on the same day and arrived at Heaven. St Peter was waiting at the gates to take down their names. After telling St Peter about all the good works he had done, the Jew told him that his wife's name was Penny. 'I'm sorry,' said St Peter, 'but I can't admit anyone with a name connected to money.' Next up was the Irishman. He too told St Peter of his many charitable works and said that his wife's name was Brandy. 'I'm sorry,' said St Peter, 'but I can't admit anyone with a name linked to alcohol.' Hearing all this, the American guy turned to his wife and said, 'Fanny, I think we may have a problem.'

A successful female executive stood before the Pearly Gates, facing St Peter himself. 'Strange,' mused St Peter. 'We've never had an executive make it this far before. I'm not sure what to do with you. While I think it over, I'll let you experience a day here and a day in Hell.' So the female executive spent an entire day lounging on clouds, playing the harp and having intelligent civilised discussions with great philosophers. Her 24 hours passed quickly and she was then transported to Hell where the Devil took her to a beautiful country club where she found many of her old friends, dressed to the nines, drinking, joking, laughing and having a great time. They talked about old times, played golf, had steak and lobster, drank champagne and danced till dawn. Before she knew it, her 24 hours were up and she was back at the Pearly Gates. St Peter said, 'I've considered your placement, and decided I'll just let you choose where you wish to spend eternity.' She thought only briefly before she replied, 'Well, Heaven was nice, but, no offence, I had a great time in Hell.' And back down she went. But this time she found herself in a desolate wasteland covered with garbage. Her friends were still there, but now they were dressed in rags, picking up garbage and carrying it from one pile to another. 'Wait a minute,' stammered the woman to the Devil, 'I don't understand. Yesterday when I was here, there was a golf course and a country club and we ate lobster and drank champagne and we danced the night away, having a wonderful time. Now everyone's slaving away shovelling rubbish.' The Devil looked at her and smiled. 'Yesterday we were recruiting you. Today, you're staff!'

A woman died and found herself standing outside the Pearly Gates, being greeted by St Peter. She asked him, 'Oh, is this place what I really think it is? It's so beautiful. Did I really make it to Heaven?' To which St Peter replied, 'Yes, my dear, these are the Gates to Heaven. But you must do one more thing before you can enter.' The woman was very excited, and asked of St Peter what she must do to pass through the Gates. 'Spell a word,' St Peter replied. 'What word?' she asked. 'Any word,' answered St Peter. 'It's your choice.' The woman promptly replied, 'Then the word I will spell is love. L-o-v-e.' St Peter congratulated her on her good fortune to have made it to Heaven, and asked her if she would mind taking his place at the gates for a few minutes while he went to the bathroom. 'I'd be honoured,' she said, 'but what should I do if someone comes while you are gone?' St Peter instructed the woman simply to have any newcomers to the Pearly Gates to spell a word as she had done. So the woman is left sitting in St Peter's chair and watching the beautiful angels soaring around her, when lo and behold, a man approaches the gates, and she realises it's her husband. 'What happened?' she cried, 'Why are you here?' Her husband stared at her for a moment, then said, 'I was so upset when I left your funeral, I was in an accident. And now I am here? Did I really make it to Heaven?' To which the woman replied, 'Not yet. You must spell a word first.' 'What word?' he asked. The woman responded, 'Czechoslovakia.'

On their way to a Justice of the Peace to get married, a couple had a fatal car accident. They found themselves sitting outside the Pearly Gates waiting on St Peter to do an intake. While waiting, they wondered if they could possibly get married in Heaven. St Peter finally showed up and they asked him. St Peter said, 'I don't know, this is the first time anyone has asked. Let me go find out,' he said, and left. The couple sat and waited for an answer - for a couple of months - and they began to wonder if they really should get married in Heaven, what with the eternal aspect of it all. 'What if it doesn't work out?' they wondered. 'Are we stuck together forever?' St Peter returned after yet another month, looking somewhat bedraggled. 'Yes,' he informed the couple, 'you can get married in Heaven.' 'Great,' said the couple, 'but what if things don't work out? Could we also get a divorce in Heaven?' St Peter, red-faced, slammed his clipboard onto the ground. 'What's wrong?' asked the frightened couple. 'COME ON!' St Peter shouted. 'It took me three months to find a priest up here! Do you have any idea how long it will take me to find a lawyer?'

Clinton died and went to Heaven - or to be more accurate - approached the Pearly Gates. After knocking at the gates, St Peter appeared. 'Who goes there?' enquired St Peter. 'It's me, Bill Clinton.' 'And what do you want?' asked St Peter. 'Let me in!' replied Clinton. 'Soooo,' pondered St Peter, 'what bad things did you do on Earth?' Clinton thought for a bit and answered, 'Well, I smoked marijuana, but you shouldn't hold that against me because I didn't inhale. I guess I had extra-marital sex, but you shouldn't hold that against me because I didn't really have 'sexual relations'. And I lied, but I didn't commit perjury.' After several moments of deliberation St Peter replied, 'Okay, here's the deal. We'll send you someplace where it is very hot, but we won't call it 'Hell'. You'll be there for an indefinite period of time, but we won't call it 'eternity'. And don't 'abandon all hope' upon entering, just don't hold your breath waiting for it to freeze over.'

Hillary Clinton had an accident and an early demise. Arriving at the Pearly Gates, she stomped up to the head of the line at St Peter's desk. St Peter politely informed her that down on Earth she may have had privileges, but up here she would have to wait her turn in line.

A lawyer died and arrived at the Pearly Gates. To his dismay, there were thousands of people ahead of him in line to see St Peter. To his surprise, St Peter left his desk at the gate and came down the long line to where the lawyer was, and greeted him warmly. Then St Peter and one of his assistants took the lawyer by the hands and guided him up to the front of the line, and into a comfortable chair by his desk. The lawyer said, 'I don't mind all this attention, but what makes me so special?' St Peter replied, 'Well, I've added up all the hours for which you billed your clients, and by my calculation you must be about 193 years old!'

While waiting, she noticed one wall covered with hundreds of thousands of clocks and she noticed that occasionally one would jump ahead by 15 minutes. She asked the person sitting next to her what this was all about. 'Well, as I understand it, each of these clocks represents some man down on Earth. Each time he commits adultery, his time is advanced by 15 minutes.' 'Can you tell me which is my husband's clock?' Hillary asked St Peter. 'Oh, yes,' St Peter replied. 'God has it in his office. He uses it as a fan.'

A man arrives at the Pearly Gates. St Peter asks, 'Religion?' The man says, 'Methodist.' St Peter looks down his list and says, 'Go to Room 24, but be very quiet as you pass Room 8.' Another man arrives at the gates of Heaven. 'Religion?' 'Baptist.' 'Go to Room 18, but be very quiet as you pass Room 8.' A third man arrives at the gates. 'Religion?' 'Jewish.' 'Go to Room 11, but be very quiet as you pass Room 8.' The man says, 'I can understand there being different rooms for different religions, but why must I be quiet when I pass Room 8?' St Peter tells him, 'Well, the Jehovah's Witnesses are in Room 8, and they think they're the only ones here.'

Mother Teresa died and went to Heaven. God greeted her at the Pearly Gates. 'Are you hungry, Mother Teresa?' says God. 'I could eat,' Mother Teresa replies. So God opens a can of tuna and reaches for a chunk of rye bread and they share it. While eating this humble meal, Mother Teresa looks down into Hell and sees the inhabitants devouring huge steaks, lobsters, pheasants, pastries and wines. Curious, but deeply trusting, she remains quiet. The next day, God again invites her to join Him for a meal. Again, it is tuna and rye bread. Once again, Mother Teresa can see the denizens of Hell enjoying caviar, champagne, lamb, truffles and chocolates. Still she says nothing. The following day, mealtime arrives and another can of tuna is opened. She can't contain herself any longer. Meekly, she says, 'God, I am grateful to be in Heaven with You as a reward for the pious, obedient life I led. But here in Heaven all I get to eat is tuna and a piece of rye bread, and in the other place they eat like emperors and kings! I just don't understand.' God sighs. 'Let's be honest,' He says. 'For just two people, does it pay to cook?'

A man dies and is sent to Hell. Satan meets him and shows him the doors to three rooms and says he must choose one of the rooms to spend eternity in. So Satan opens the first door. In the room there are people standing in cow manure up to their necks. The guy says 'No, please show me the next room.' Satan shows him the next room and this has people with cow manure up to their noses. And so he says no again. Finally, Satan shows him the third and final room. This time there are people in there with cow manure up to their knees, drinking cups of tea and eating cakes. So the guy says, 'I'll choose this room.' Satan says okay. The guy is standing in there eating his cake and drinking his tea thinking, 'Well, it could be worse,' when the door opens. Satan pops his head around and says, 'Okay, tea break is over. Back on your heads!'

Satan greets Bill Gates: 'Welcome, Mr Gates, we've been waiting for you. This will be your home for all eternity. You've been selfish, greedy and a big liar all your life. Now, since you've got me in a good mood, I'll be generous and give you a choice of three places in which you'll be locked up forever.' Satan takes Bill to a huge lake of fire in which millions of poor souls are tormented and tortured. He then takes him to a massive colosseum where thousands of people are chased about and devoured by starving lions. Finally, he takes Bill to a tiny room in which there is a bottle of the finest wine sitting on a table. To Bill's delight, he sees a PC in the corner. Without hesitation, Bill says, 'I'll take this option.' 'Fine,' says Satan, allowing Bill to enter the room and locking the door after him. As he turns around, he bumps into Lucifer. 'That was Bill Gates!' cries Lucifer. 'Why did you give him the best place of all?' 'That's what everyone thinks,' snickers Satan. 'But the bottle has a hole in it.' 'What about the PC?'

'It's got Windows 95!' laughs Satan. 'And it's missing three keys.' 'Which three?' 'Control, Alt and Delete.'

Three men died in a car accident and met Jesus himself at the Pearly Gates. The Lord spoke unto them saying, 'I will ask you each a simple question. If you tell the truth I will allow you into Heaven, but if you lie - Hell is waiting for you.' To the first man the Lord asked, 'How many times did you cheat on your wife?' The first man replied, 'Lord, I was a good husband. I never cheated on my wife.' The Lord replied, 'Very good! Not only will I allow you in, but for being faithful to your wife I will give you a huge mansion and a limo for your transportation.' To the second man the Lord asked, 'How many times did you cheat on your wife?' The second man replied, 'Lord, I cheated on my wife twice.' The Lord replied, 'I will allow you to come in, but for your unfaithfulness, you will get a four-bedroom house and a BMW.' To the third man the Lord asked, 'So, how many times did you cheat on your wife?' The third man replied, 'Lord, I cheated on my wife about eight times.' The Lord replied, 'I will allow you to come in, but for your unfaithfulness, you will get a one-room apartment and a Yugo for your transportation.' A couple of hours later the second and third men saw the first man crying his eyes out. 'Why are you crying?' the two men asked. 'You got the mansion and limo!' The first man replied, 'I'm crying because I saw my wife a little while ago, and she was riding a skateboard!'

Three men die in a car accident on Christmas Eve. They all find themselves at the Pearly Gates waiting to enter Heaven. On entering they must present something relating or associated with Christmas. The first man searches his pocket and finds some mistletoe, so he is allowed in. The second man presents a cracker, so he is also allowed in. The third man pulls out a pair of stockings. Confused at this last gesture, St Peter asks, 'How do these represent Christmas?' 'They're Carol's.'

A woman knocked on the Pearly Gates. Her face was scarred and old. She trembled and she shook with fear. 'What have you done to gain admission here?' St Peter asked. 'I've been a loyal AOL user, Sir, for many, many years.' The Pearly Gate swung open wide. St Peter rung the bell. 'Come in and choose your harp,' he said. 'You've had your share of Hell.'

Two priests die at the same time and meet St Peter at the Pearly Gates. St Peter says, 'I'd like to get you guys in now but our computers are down. You'll have to go back to Earth for about a week, but you can't go back as humans. What'll it be?' The first priest says, 'I've always wanted to be an eagle, soaring above the Rocky Mountains.' 'So be it,' says St Peter, and off flies the first priest. The second priest mulls this over for a moment and asks, 'Will you be keeping track of us, St Peter?' 'No, I told you, the computer is down. There's no way we can keep track of what you are doing. This week's a freebie.' 'In that case,' says the second priest, 'I've always wanted to be a stud.' 'So be it,' says St Peter, and the second priest disappears. A week goes by, the computer is fixed and the Lord tells St Peter to recall the two priests. 'Will you have trouble locating them?' He asks. 'The first one should be easy,' says St Peter. 'He's somewhere over the Rocky Mountains, flying with the eagles. But the second one could prove to be more difficult.' 'Why?' asks the Lord. 'Because he's on a snow tyre somewhere in Alaska.'

Three nuns died and went up to Heaven, but before they were allowed to enter, St Peter told them they each had to answer a question. St Peter turned to the first nun and said, 'What were the names of the two people in the Garden of Eden?' 'Adam and Eve,' replied the first nun. At that, the lights which surrounded the Pearly Gates began to flash. 'You may enter,' said St Peter. Then he addressed the second nun. 'What did Adam eat from the forbidden tree?' 'An apple,' replied the second nun. At that, the lights which surrounded the Pearly Gates flashed and the second nun was permitted to enter. Finally St Peter

One day, a teacher, a refuse collector and a lawyer wound up together at the Pearly Gates. St Peter informed them that in order to get into Heaven, they would each have to answer one question. St Peter addressed the teacher and asked, 'What was the name of the ship that crashed into an iceberg? They just made a movie about it.' The teacher answered quickly, 'That would be the Titanic.' St Peter let him through the gate. St Peter turned to the refuse collector and asked, 'How many people died on the ship?' Fortunately for him, the refuse collector had just seen the movie and answered, 'About 1,500.' 'That's right! You may enter.' St Peter then turned to the lawyer. 'Name them.'

turned to the third nun. 'What was the first thing that Eve said to Adam?' The third nun looked puzzled. 'Gosh, that's a hard one.' And the lights around the Pearly Gates flashed.

At the Pearly Gates, St Peter greeted a minister and a congressman and gave them their room assignments. 'Vicar, here are the keys to one of our nicest efficiency units. And for you, Mr Congressman, the keys to our finest penthouse suite.' 'This is unfair!' cried the minister. 'Listen,' St Peter said. 'Ministers are a dime a dozen up here, but this is the first congressman we've ever seen.'

One day at the entrance to Heaven, a New York street gang walked up to the Pearly Gates. This being a first, St Peter ran to God and said, 'God, there are some evil, thieving New Yorkers at the Pearly Gates. What do I do?' God replied, 'Just do what you normally do with that type. Redirect them down to Hell.' St Peter went back to carry out the order and all of a sudden he comes running back yelling, 'God, God, they're gone, they're gone!' 'Who, the New Yorkers?' 'No, the Pearly Gates!'

A rich man is near death. He is very grieved because he has worked hard for his money and he wants to be able to take it with him to Heaven. So he begins to pray that he might be able to take some of his wealth with him. An angel hears his plea and appears to him. 'Sorry, but you can't take your wealth with you.' The man implores the angel to speak to God to see if He might bend the rules. The man continues to pray that his wealth could follow him. The angel reappears and informs the man that God has decided to allow him to take one suitcase with him. Overjoyed, the man gathers his largest suitcase and fills it with pure gold bars and places it beside his bed. Soon afterwards the man dies and shows up at the Gates of Heaven to greet St Peter. St Peter, seeing the suitcase, says, 'Hold on, you can't bring that in here!' But the man explains to St Peter that he has permission and asks him to verify his story with the Lord. Sure enough, St Peter checks and comes back saying, 'You're right. You are allowed one carry-on bag, but I'm supposed to check its contents before letting it through.' St Peter opens the suitcase to inspect the worldly items that the man found too precious to leave behind and exclaims, 'You brought pavement?'

Quick Quips 7

To me, funerals are like bad movies. They last too long, they're overacted, and the ending is predictable.
George Burns

I don't believe in an afterlife, although I am bringing a change of underwear.
Woody Allen

For three days after death, hair and fingernails continue to grow but phone calls taper off. ***Johnny Carson***

It's not that I'm afraid to die, I just don't want to be there when it happens. ***Woody Allen***

Eternity is a terrible thought. I mean, when's it going to end? ***Tom Stoppard***

I don't believe people die. They just go uptown. To Bloomingdales. They just take longer to get back.
Andy Warhol

It's funny how most people love the dead. Once you're dead, you're made for life.
Jimi Hendrix

They say such nice things about people at their funerals that it makes me sad that I'm going to miss mine by just a few days. ***Garrison Keillor***

You can spend your whole life trying to be popular but, at the end of the day, the size of the crowd at your funeral will be largely dictated by the weather. ***Frank Skinner***

Those who welcome death have only tried it from the ears up. ***Wilson Mizner***

Die, my dear doctor, that's the last thing I shall do! ***Lord Palmerston, on his deathbed***

My grandmother was a very tough woman. She buried three husbands. Two of them were just napping. ***Rita Rudner***

You give the people what they want, they'll turn out. ***A rival producer, observing the crowd at Louis B Mayer's funeral***

A friend of mine willed her body to science, but science is contesting the will. ***Joey Adams***

I know a guy who saved all his life to buy a cemetery plot. Then he took a cruise and was lost at sea. ***Norm Crosby***

'Here lies the body of Harry Hershfield. If not, notify Ginsberg and Co, undertakers, at once.' ***Harry Hershfield's suggestion for his own epitaph***

My Uncle Pat, he reads the obituaries in the paper every morning. And he can't understand how people always die in alphabetical order. ***Hal Roach***

The reports of my death are greatly exaggerated. ***Mark Twain***

If Shaw and Einstein couldn't beat death, what chance have I got? Practically none. ***Mel Brooks***

At my age I do what Mark Twain did. I get my daily paper, look at the obituaries page and if I'm not there I carry on as usual. ***Patrick Moore***

To lose one parent may be regarded as a misfortune; to lose both looks like carelessness. ***Oscar Wilde***

I don't want to achieve immortality through my work, I want to achieve it through not dying. ***Woody Allen***

I was with this girl the other night and from the way she was responding to my skilful caresses, you would have sworn that she was conscious from the top of her head to the tag on her toes. ***Emo Philips***

Death is not the end. There remains the litigation over the estate. ***Ambrose Bierce***

Everybody wants to go to Heaven, but nobody wants to die. ***Joe Louis***

When you've told someone that you've left them a legacy the only decent thing to do is to die at once. ***Samuel Butler***

Death is one of the few things that can be done as easily lying down. The difference between sex and death is that with death you can do it alone and no one is going to make fun of you. ***Woody Allen***

All our knowledge merely helps us to die a more painful death than animals that know nothing. ***Maurice Maeterlinck***

Dying is a very dull, dreary affair. And my advice to you is to have nothing whatever to do with it. ***W. Somerset Maugham***

I am ready to meet my Maker. Whether my Maker is prepared for the great ordeal of meeting me is another matter. ***Winston Churchill***

A single death is a tragedy, a million deaths is a statistic. ***Joseph Stalin***

Death does not concern us, because as long as we exist, death is not here. And when it does come, we no longer exist. ***Epicurus***

Everything is drive-through. In California, they even have a burial service called Jump-In-The-Box. ***Wil Shriner***

The fear of death is the most unjustified of all fears, for there's no risk of accident for someone who's dead. ***Albert Einstein***

I wouldn't mind dying – it's the business of having to stay dead that scares the shit out of me. ***R Geis***

It's impossible to experience one's death objectively and still carry a tune. ***Woody Allen***

For if he like a madman lived, at least he like a wise one died. ***Cervantes***

Eternal nothingness is fine if you happen to be dressed for it. ***Woody Allen***

Am I lightheaded because I'm not dead or because I'm still alive? ***Heidi Sandige***

After I'm dead I'd rather have people ask why I have no monument than why I have one.
Cato the Elder, 234-149 BC

religion

Have Faith

The plane had hit a patch of turbulence and the passengers were holding on tight as it rocked and reeled through the night. A little old lady turned to the minister who was sitting behind her and said, 'You're a man of God. Can't you do something about this?' And he replied, 'Sorry, I can't. I'm in sales, not management.'

Another 300 vicars were sacked last week, making a total of 2,000 holy unemployed.

An elderly couple, a middle-aged couple and a young newlywed couple were talking to the pastor about joining the Baptist church. The pastor says, 'Well, we have special requirements for new parishioners. You must abstain from sex for two weeks.' The couples agree and return to the pastor two weeks later. The pastor says to the elderly couple, 'Were you able to abstain from sex for two weeks?' The old man replies, 'Certainly, Pastor.' 'Congratulations! Welcome to the church!' The pastor then turns to the middle-aged couple. 'Were you able to abstain from sex for two weeks?' The man replies, 'I can't pretend it was easy, but yes, we managed it.' 'Congratulations! Welcome to the church!' 'So how about you?' says the pastor, turning to the newlyweds. 'I'm afraid we failed,' says the young man. 'What happened?' says the pastor. 'Well, my wife was reaching for a light bulb on the top shelf and she dropped it. And when she bent over to pick it up, I just couldn't help myself and we had sex right there where the bulb fell.' And the pastor says, 'Well, I'm sorry, but I'm afraid you're just not welcome in the Baptist church anymore.' 'That's okay,' says the young man, 'we're not welcome at Tesco's anymore either.'

Father O' Malley: When are you going to give up and treat yourself to a taste of pork?
Rabbi Weinstein: On your wedding day!

We've got the most incredibly inspiring preacher. After every sermon, the congregation give him a kneeling ovation!

I go to the bingo organised by my local church. The priest calls out the numbers in Latin so the atheists can't win.

The minister is driving home after a long day and is stopped by a traffic policeman for speeding. The policeman, smelling alcohol on the minister's breath and seeing an empty wine bottle on the passenger seat, says, 'Sir, have you been drinking?' And the minister says, 'Yes officer, but only water.' And the cop says, 'So why do I smell wine?' The minister picks up the bottle, looks at it and says, 'Good Heavens, he's done it again!'

This guy went to confession. I went with him, we were kids. And he confessed that he had had sex with a girl in his parish. The priest asked, 'Was it Mary Agnardi?' He said no. 'Was it Felice Endrini?' asked the priest. He said no. 'Was it Elise Guini?' He said no. The priest said, 'You're going to do 50 Hail Marys and give me half your allowance on the plate for the next three weeks.' My friend came out of the confessional and I asked, 'How'd you do?' He said, 'Not too bad, and I got three good leads!' ***Buddy Hackett***

Our church welcomes all denominations – fives, tens, twenties...

There was a very strict order of monks who lived by a rule that permitted speaking only once on one day a year, one monk per year. When the day came around, the monk whose turn it was stood up and said, 'I don't like the mash potatoes here, they're too lumpy.' And he sat down. A year later, another monk stood up and said, 'I rather like the mashed potatoes here, they're very tasty.' Another year went by and it was a third monk's turn. He stood up and said, 'I'm leaving the monastery. I can't stand this constant bickering.'

She's so religious she wears stained-glass spectacles.

Adam and Eve had an ideal marriage. He didn't have to hear about all the men she could have married, and she didn't have to hear about the way his mother cooked.

What did Buddha say to the hot dog vendor? Make me one with everything.

First priest: Hello, I'm sure we've met before. I'm Brother Michael.
Second priest: I don't remember the name but the faith is familiar.

So, after Adam was created, there he was in the Garden of Eden. Of course it wasn't good for him to be all by himself, so the Lord came down to visit. 'Adam,' He said, 'I have a plan to make you much, much happier. I'm going to give you a companion, a helpmate for you – someone who will fulfil your every need and desire. Someone who will be faithful, loving and obedient. Someone who will make you feel wonderful every day of your life.' Adam was stunned. 'That sounds incredible!' 'Well, it is,' replied the Lord. 'But it doesn't come for free. In fact, this is someone so special that it's going to cost you an arm and a leg.' 'That's a pretty high price to pay,' said Adam. 'What can I get for a rib?'

Why do Baptists object to fornication? They're afraid it might lead to dancing.

A Christian man is a man who feels repentance on Sunday for what he did on Saturday and is going to do again on Monday. ***Anon***

A priest asks a nun if he can walk her back to the convent. She says, 'Just this once.' Upon arriving, he asks if he can kiss her. She replies, 'Well, all right, as long as you don't get into the habit.'

First rabbi: We've got to do something. Many of the young people in our synagogue are converting to the Quaker faith.
Second rabbi: I've noticed that too. In fact, some of my best Jews are Friends!

I'm just a poor preacher. I know, I've heard your sermons.

A minister sold a mule to a priest and told him that the animal was trained to obey two commands: 'Praise the Lord' to go and 'Amen' to stop. The priest climbed on board the mule, said 'Praise the Lord' and the mule set off. The mule began to go faster and faster and the priest began to get worried. He wanted the animal to stop but couldn't remember the key word. He kept saying 'Whoa' but it had no effect. Finally he remembered and said, 'Amen'. The mule stopped immediately. The priest looked down and saw the mule had come to a halt right on the edge of a huge cliff with a 500-foot drop. Wiping his brow in relief, the priest sighed, 'Praise the Lord.'

I've joined a new church. It's very liberal. They've whittled it down to five commandments and five suggestions.

Religion is man's search for reassurance that he won't be dead when he will be. ***Anon***

The wife of the churchwarden was taking her seat in the front row of the pews when she tripped and rolled over, revealing her underwear to the congregation. Seeing her predicament, the priest stood in front of her and said, 'If any man should look at this poor, unfortunate woman, may the Lord strike him blind!' And a man in the third row turned to his friend and said, 'I think I'll risk one eye.'

I don't go to church much any more. I'm a Seventh Day Absentist.

If you want to see a man at his worst, see what he does to his fellow man in the name of God. ***Anon***

The Mother Superior was discussing the rising crime rate with one of her nuns. 'Sister,' she said, 'what would you do if you were walking along the street at night and were accosted by a man?' 'I would lift my habit,' replied the nun. The Mother Superior was shocked to hear this. 'Then what would you do?' 'I would tell him to drop his pants.' The Mother Superior was even more shocked. 'And then what would you do?' 'I would run off, because I could run faster with my habit up than he could with his pants down!'

Did you hear the one about the man who opened a dry-cleaning business next door to a convent? He knocked on the door and asked the Mother Superior if she had any dirty habits.

Three men of God were asked the same question: 'When does life begin?' The Catholic priest answered, 'At the moment of conception.' The Anglican vicar replied, 'When the child is born.' And the rabbi said, 'When the children are married and the mortgage has been paid off.'

And we are told in the Scriptures that at the beginning of time the Lord said, 'Let there be light.' But I've checked with a number of eminent Biblical scholars and they say the Lord's complete statement was as follows: 'Let there be light. Well, maybe not all day.'
Steve Allen

What do you get when you cross a Jehovah's Witness with an atheist? Someone who knocks on your door for no apparent reason.

Three nuns are walking down the street, when a man jumps out and flashes them. The first nun has a stroke, the second nun has a stroke, the third one doesn't touch him.

Paddy O'Casey was on his death bed when his wife Colleen tiptoed into the bedroom and asked if he had any last requests. 'Actually, my dear, there is one thing I really would like before I go off to that great shamrock patch in the sky,' Paddy whispered. 'A piece of that wonderful chocolate cake of yours.' 'Oh, but you can't have that,' his wife exclaimed. 'I'm saving it for the wake.'

A wife insisted that her husband accompany her to church every Sunday. But for him it was an ordeal and he always had difficulty staying awake. She was aware of this and so one week she took along a hat pin with which to poke him every time he fell asleep. Five minutes into the service, just as the husband was dozing off, the preacher asked, 'Who created the Universe?' The wife poked her husband with the hat pin and he yelled loudly, 'My God!' A few minutes later, the husband's eyes were shutting again just as the preacher asked the flock, 'And who died on the cross for you?' The wife gave a sharp poke with the hat pin and the husband shouted, 'Jesus Christ!' Shortly afterwards, the husband was asleep once more. The wife poked him with the hat pin just as the preacher asked, 'And what did Eve say to Adam the second time she was pregnant?' The husband woke with a start, jumped to his feet and yelled, 'By God, if you poke me with that thing one more time, I'm going to break it off!'

One Sunday morning a priest announced to his congregation, 'I have here in my hands three sermons – a £500 sermon that lasts five minutes, a £200 sermon that lasts 15 minutes and a £10 sermon that lasts a full hour. Now we'll take the collection and see which one I'll deliver...'

A rabbi and a priest were seated together on a plane. After a while, they started talking and the priest said, 'Rabbi, I hope you don't mind my asking, but I'm curious. Have you ever eaten pork?' 'Actually, yes, once I got drunk and temptation overcame me. I had a ham sandwich and, I hate to admit it, I enjoyed it,' replied the rabbi. 'Now let me ask you, have you ever been with a woman?' 'Well,' responded the priest, 'I once got drunk and went to a whorehouse and purchased the services of a prostitute. I, too, quite enjoyed the experience.' 'It's a lot better than a ham sandwich, isn't it?'

What is the biggest problem for an atheist? No one to talk to during orgasm.

A man entered a Trappist monastery and was told that once every five years he would be allowed to utter two words. After the first five years, he was approached by the monsignor and asked what he wished to say. The monk said simply, 'Bed hard.' The monsignor promised to look into the problem. Five years later, the monk was brought before the monsignor again. This time he said, 'Food cold.' The monsignor said that he would look into the matter. Another five years later and the monk told the monsignor, 'I quit.' The monsignor said, 'I'm hardly surprised you're quitting. All you have done over the past 15 years is complain!'

When I was a kid my mother switched religions from Catholic to Episcopalian. Which is what, Catholic Lite? One-third less guilt than regular religion! You could eat meat on Friday, but not a really good cut. ***Rick Corso***

God was talking to one of his angels. He said, 'I've just created a 24-hour period of alternating light and darkness on Earth.' The angel said, 'What are you going to do now?' And God replied, 'I think I'll call it a day.'

How do you make holy water?
Boil the hell out of it.

On the sixth day, God turned to the angel Gabriel and announced, 'Today I shall create a land called Canada. It will be a land of outstanding natural beauty, with snow-capped mountains, shimmering blue lakes, forests of elk and moose and rivers of salmon. And the air will be clean and pure. I shall make the land rich in oil so that the inhabitants shall prosper. I shall call these inhabitants Canadians and they shall be known as the friendliest people on Earth.' 'Don't you think you're being rather too generous to these Canadians?' asked Gabriel. 'Wait,' said God. 'You haven't seen the neighbours I'm going to give them!'

Jesus was really tired after the resurrection. So when he came to an inn, he put three nails on the counter and said to the innkeeper, 'Can you put me up for the night?'

The atheist was walking through the woods admiring the beauty of spontaneous life. He was looking at the trees, the beauty of the birds, the beautiful flowers, feeling the fresh wind in his face. While walking, he noticed a bear following him. He sped up his pace, looked over his shoulder and saw the bear was getting close. Starting to run, he looked over his shoulder again and saw the bear was closer even still. Now on a dead run he tripped and fell. The bear was on top of him getting ready to rip him to shreds when the atheist screamed out, 'Oh my God, no, no!' The wind stopped, the bear stopped, the clouds stopped and a bright light shown down from Heaven. 'I am God,' the voice proclaimed, 'Are you ready to believe in me for the rest of your days on this Earth?' The atheist said, 'Yes I am, but I also want the bear to do so.' 'Granted,' said the voice. The trees started to move, the wind started blowing and the clouds began to move again. The bear sat up, put his paws together and said, 'God, thank you for this meal for which I am about to receive.'

A priest and a rabbi went to a prize fight at Madison Square Garden. One of the fighters crossed himself before the opening gong sounded. 'What does that mean?' asked the rabbi. 'Not a damn thing if he can't fight,' answered the priest. ***Belle Barth***

Three pastors were discussing the problems they had been experiencing with bats in their church lofts. The first said, 'I introduced half a dozen cats, but nothing seems to work. The bats are still there.' The second said, 'I had the place fumigated, but even that didn't work. It's still infested with bats.' The third said, 'I baptised all mine and made them members of the church. I haven't seen one of them back since!'

A Sunday school teacher asked her young class, 'Why is it necessary to be quiet in church?' One boy answered, 'Because people are sleeping.'

What do priests and Christmas trees have in common? The balls are just for decoration.

A young boy and his grandmother were walking along the sea shore when a huge wave appeared out of nowhere, sweeping the child out to sea. The horrified woman fell to her knees, raised her eyes to the Heavens and begged the Lord to return her beloved grandson. Lo, another wave reared up and deposited the stunned child on the sand before her. The grandmother looked the boy over carefully. He was fine. But still she stared up angrily toward the Heavens. 'When we came,' she snapped indignantly, 'he had a hat!'

One day, God and Adam were walking in the Garden of Eden. God told Adam that it was time to populate the Earth. 'Adam,' he said, 'you can start by kissing Eve.' 'What's a kiss?' asked Adam. God explained, and then Adam took Eve behind a bush and kissed her. Adam returned with a big smile and said, 'That was great. What's next?' 'Now you must caress Eve,' said God. 'What's a caress?' asked Adam. God explained, and then Adam took Eve behind a bush and lovingly caressed her. Adam returned with a big smile and said, 'That was even better than a kiss. What's next?' 'I want you to make love to Eve,' said God. 'What is make love?' asked Adam. God explained, and then Adam took Eve behind the bush. A few seconds later, Adam returned and asked God, 'What is a headache?'

So far today, God, I've done alright. I haven't gossiped, I haven't lost my temper, haven't been greedy, grumpy, nasty, selfish or indulgent. I'm very thankful for that. But in a few minutes God, I'm going to get out of this bed, and from then on I'm probably going to need a lot more help. Amen

An atheist was fishing in Scotland one day when his boat was suddenly attacked by the Loch Ness Monster. The boat capsized and the man was tossed skywards. As he flew through the air towards the monster's open mouth, he screamed, 'Oh God, help me!' Immediately everything was frozen in place. The ferocious attack stopped and the atheist was left suspended in mid-air. A booming voice came down from the clouds, 'I thought you didn't believe in Me!' 'Come on God, give me a break,' said the man. 'Two minutes ago I didn't believe in the Loch Ness Monster either!'

What do you call a sleepwalking nun? A roamin' Catholic.

A married man went to confession and told the priest, 'Father, I had an affair with a woman - well, almost.' 'What do you mean, almost?' said the priest. 'Well, we got undressed and rubbed together, but then I stopped.' 'Rubbing together is the same as putting it in,' said the priest. 'Five Hail Marys and put £50 in the poor box on your way out.' The man came out and stood by the poor box for a few seconds, but didn't reach for his wallet. Instead he headed for the church door. The priest saw this and shouted, 'You didn't put any money in!' The man replied, 'But I rubbed against it and you said that's the same as putting it in!'

One Sunday afternoon, the vicar's wife dropped into an armchair saying, 'Boy! Am I tired!' Her husband looked over at her and said, 'I had to conduct two special services last night, three today and give a total of five sermons. Why are you so tired?' 'Dearest,' she replied, 'I had to listen to all of them!'

The meek will inherit the earth – as long as nobody minds.

Recently, at a theological meeting in Rome, scholars had a heated debate. One by one, they offered their evidence:

JESUS WAS MEXICAN
His first name was Jesus.
He was bilingual.
He was always being harassed by the authorities.

But then there were equally good other arguments:

JESUS WAS BLACK
He called everybody 'brother'.
He liked Gospel.
He couldn't get a fair trial.

JESUS WAS JEWISH
He went into His Father's business.
He lived at home until he was 33.
He was sure his Mother was a virgin, and his Mother was sure he was God.

JESUS WAS ITALIAN
He talked with his hands.
He had wine with every meal.
He used olive oil.

JESUS WAS A CALIFORNIAN
He never cut his hair.
He walked around barefoot.
He started a new religion.

JESUS WAS IRISH
He never got married.
He was always telling stories.
He loved green pastures.

JESUS WAS A WOMAN
She had to feed a crowd at a moment's notice when there was no food.
She kept trying to get the message across to a bunch of men who just didn't get it!
Even when She was dead, She had to get up because there was more work for her to do.

A new pastor visited a children's Sunday school. After standing quietly at the back for a few minutes, he asked the youngsters, 'Who tore down the walls of Jericho?' 'It wasn't me,' shouted young Tommy. The pastor was unfazed and repeated, 'Come on now, who tore down the walls of Jericho?' The teacher took the pastor to one side. 'Look, Pastor, Tommy's a good boy. If he says he didn't do it, I believe him.' The pastor couldn't comprehend what he was hearing and later that day he related the story to the director of the Sunday school. The director frowned. 'I know we've had problems with Tommy in the past. I'll have a word with him.' By now totally baffled, the pastor left and approached the deacon. Once again, he told him the whole story, including the response of the teacher and the director. The deacon listened patiently and smiled, 'Yes, Pastor, I can see your problem. But I suggest we take the money from the general fund to pay for the walls and leave it at that.'

Want a taste of religion? Bite a minister.

I am one of those cliff-hanging Catholics. I don't believe in God, but I do believe that Mary was his mother. ***Martin Sheen***

A cat died and went to Heaven. God said, 'You've been a good cat all your life. Is there anything you desire?' The cat replied, 'I lived on a farm and always had to sleep on a hard floor, so a soft pillow would be great. Then I could sleep peacefully in Heaven.' God provided a soft pillow for the cat. The following day, six mice died and went to Heaven. God told them, 'You have been good mice all your lives. Is there anything you desire?' 'Yes,' they said. 'We've always had to run everywhere, being chased by cats or people. We'd love a pair of roller skates each so that we can get around Heaven without having to use our little legs so much.' And God provided each mouse with a pair of roller skates. A week or so later, God thought he'd check up on the cat, who was fast asleep on his new pillow. 'Is everything okay?' asked God. The cat stretched out. 'I've never been happier,' he said. 'The pillow is so comfortable and those meals on wheels you've been sending over are simply the best!'

He charged nothing for his preaching, and it was worth it. ***Mark Twain***

Okay, so God made Heaven and Earth. But what has he done recently? [Bumper sticker]

'Sister Ann, aren't you putting on a little weight?' enquired Father Dan during his visit to the convent, suspiciously eyeing her bulging stomach. Why no, Father,' answered the nun demurely, 'it's just a little gas.' A few months later Father Dan put the same question to the nun, noticing her habit barely fit across her belly. 'Oh, it's just a bit of gas,' said Sister Ann, blushing a bit. On his next visit Father Dan was walking down the corridor when he passed Sister Ann wheeling a baby carriage. Looking in, he observed, 'Cute little fart!'

A church is a place where gentlemen who have never been to Heaven brag about it to persons who will never get there. ***H L Mencken***

One Sunday morning, the vicar noticed little Alex was staring up at the large plaque that hung in the foyer of the church. The plaque was covered with names, and small flags were mounted on either side of it. The seven-year old had been staring at the plaque for some time, so the vicar walked up, stood beside the boy and said quietly, 'Good morning, Alex.' 'Good morning, vicar,' replied the young man, still focused on the plaque. 'Reverend Smith, what is this?' Alex asked. 'Well, son, it's a memorial to all the young men and women who died in the service.' Soberly, they stood together, staring at the large plaque. 'Which service, the 9 o'clock or the 11 o'clock?'

Q: **WHY DIDN'T NOAH GO FISHING?**
A: **HE ONLY HAD TWO WORMS.**

I'm a Catholic and I can't commit suicide, but I plan to drink myself to death.
Jack Kerouac

Two little boys are looking for a way to cool off on a hot summer day. Dad won't let them play in the sprinkler because he's mowing the lawn, so the boys set out to find a way to get wet and cool without getting into trouble. They sit on the curb brainstorming when suddenly one of them jumps up and says, 'I know, let's go get baptised!' Both boys have seen enough to know that you can get wet at a baptism, so they trot down to the church on the corner and tell the priest they want to get baptised. The irritated priest finally relents after about ten minutes of begging. He drags the boys to the men's room and dunks them both head first into the toilet, then sends them on their way. The boys sit on the curb, slightly disappointed with the whole adventure, when one of them asks the other, 'What religion are we now?' 'I don't know,' replies the other. 'If we were Baptists, he would have filled up the big tub and dunked our whole body like he did for uncle Jim; and if we were Catholic, he would have poured it on our heads from a pitcher.' They sit and think about it for a while longer until the first one says, 'Since he stuck our head in the toilet, I think that it means we're 'piss-ca-pa-lians'!'

Q: **WHY DID MOSES WANDER IN THE DESERT FOR 40 YEARS?**
A: **EVEN THEN MEN WOULDN'T ASK FOR DIRECTIONS.**

Why is it when we talk to God we're said to be praying, but when God talks to us, we're schizophrenic? ***Lily Tomlin***

On the very first day, God created the cow. He said to the cow, 'Today I have created you! As a cow, you must go to the field with the farmer all day long. You will work all day under the sun! I will give you a life span of 50 years.' The cow objected, 'What? This kind of a tough life you want me to live for 50 years? Let me have 20 years, and the 30 years I'll give back to you.' So God agreed. On the second day, God created the dog. God said to the dog, 'What you are supposed to do is sit all day by the door of your house. Any people that come in, your job will be to bark at them! I'll give you a life span of 20 years.' The dog objected, 'What? All day sitting by the door? No way! I'll give you back my other ten years of life!' So God agreed. On the third day, God created the monkey. He said to the monkey, 'Monkeys have to entertain people. You've got to make them laugh and do monkey tricks. I'll give you a 20-year life span.' The monkey objected. 'What? Make them laugh? Do monkey faces and tricks? Ten years will do, and the other ten years I'll give you back.' So God agreed. On the fourth day, God created man and said to him, 'Your job is to sleep, eat and play. You will enjoy very much in your life. All you need to do is to enjoy and do nothing. This kind of life, I'll give you a 20-year life span.' The man objected. 'What? Such a good life! Eat, play, sleep, do nothing? Enjoy the best and you expect me to live only for 20 years? No way, man! Why don't we make a deal? Since the cow gave you back 30 years, and the dog gave you back ten years and the monkey gave you back ten years, I will take them from you. That makes my life span 70 years, right?' So God agreed. And that is why in our first 20 years, we eat, sleep, play, enjoy the best and do nothing much. For the next 30 years, we work all day long, suffer and get to support the family. For the next ten years, we entertain our grandchildren by making monkey faces and monkey tricks. And for the last ten years, we stay at home, sit by the front door and bark at people.

The priest was preparing a man for his long day's journey into night. Whispering firmly, the priest said, 'Renounce the Devil! Let him know how little you think of his evil!' The dying man said nothing so the priest repeated his order. Still the dying man said nothing. The priest asked, 'Why do you refuse to renounce the Devil and his evil?' The dying man said, 'Until I know where I'm heading, I don't think I ought to aggravate anybody.'

If God's got anything better than sex to offer, he's certainly keeping it to himself. ***Sting***

Discovering too late that a watermelon spiked with vodka had accidentally been served to a luncheon meeting of local ministers, the restaurant's owner waited nervously for the reaction. 'Quick, man,' he whispered to the waiter, 'what did they say?' 'Nothing,' replied the waiter. 'They were all too busy slipping the seeds into their pockets.'

I was recently born again. I must admit it's a glorious and wonderful experience. I can't say my mother enjoyed it a whole lot. ***John Wing***

A minister told his congregation, 'Next week I plan to preach about the sin of lying. To help you understand my sermon, I want you all to read Mark 17.' The following Sunday, as he prepared to deliver his sermon, the minister asked for a show of hands. He wanted to know how many had read Mark 17. Every hand went up. The minister smiled and said, 'Mark has only 16 chapters. I will now proceed with my sermon on the sin of lying.'

When I was growing up my mother wanted me to be a priest, but I think it's a tough occupation. Can you imagine giving up your sex life and then once a week people come in and tell you all the highlights of theirs?

Tom Dreesen

A young boy had just got his driving licence. He asked his father, who was a vicar, if they could discuss his use of the car. His father said to him, 'I'll make a deal with you. You bring your grades up, study the Bible a little and get your hair cut, then we'll talk about it.' A month later, the boy came back and again asked his father if he could use the car. His father said, 'Son, I'm really proud of you. You brought your grades up, studied the

Bible well, but you didn't get your hair cut!' The young man waited a moment and then replied, 'You know dad, I've been thinking about that. Samson had long hair, Moses had long hair, Noah had long hair and even Jesus had long hair.' His father replied, 'Yes son, and they walked everywhere they went.'

Two church members were going door to door, and knocked on the door of a woman who was not happy to see them. She told them in no uncertain terms that she did not want to hear their message and slammed the door in their faces. To her surprise, however, the door did not close and, in fact, bounced back open. She tried again, really put her back into it, and slammed the door again with the same result. The door bounced back open. Convinced these rude young people were sticking their foot in the door, she reared back to give it a slam that would teach them a lesson, when one of them said: 'Ma'am, before you do that again you need to move your cat.'

Q: **WHY DID GOD CREATE MAN BEFORE WOMAN?**
A: **HE DIDN'T WANT ANY ADVICE.**

The Sunday before Christmas, a priest told his congregation that the church needed some extra money. He asked the people to consider donating a little more than usual into the offering plate. He said that whoever gave the most would be able to pick out three hymns. After the offering plates were passed, the priest glanced down and noticed that someone had placed a £1,000 note in offering. He was so excited that he immediately shared his joy with his congregation and said he'd like to personally thank the person who placed the money in the plate. A very quiet, elderly, saintly looking lady all the way at the back shyly raised her hand. The priest asked her to come to the front. Slowly she made her way to the priest. He told her how wonderful it was that she had given so much and in thanks asked her to pick out three hymns. Her eyes brightened as she looked over the congregation, pointed to the three most handsome men in the building and said, 'I'll take him and him and him.'

Q: **WHEN WAS THE LONGEST DAY IN THE BIBLE?**
A: **THE DAY ADAM WAS CREATED BECAUSE THERE WAS NO EVE.**

One day a middle-aged Jewish man named Leo hears from his son attending university. 'I've decided to become a Christian, Dad.' Leo panics. 'What do I do?' he asks himself. The only thing he can think to do is call his rabbi. 'Funny you should come to me with this problem, Leo,' says the rabbi. 'Not two years ago my son comes to me with the same speech. I had no idea what to do. I panicked, and the only thing I could think to do was go to God.' 'What message do you think you got from God?' asks Leo. The rabbi laughed. 'God said to me, "Funny you should come to me with this problem..."'

Mahatma Gandhi walked barefoot everywhere, to the point that his feet became quite thick and hard. He also was a spiritual person. Even when he was not on hunger strike, he ate very little and became frail. Furthermore, due to his diet, he wound up with very bad breath. Therefore, he came to be known as a 'super calloused fragile mystic plagued with halitosis'.

A very religious man lived right next door to an atheist. While the religious one prayed day in day out, and was constantly on his knees in communion with his Lord, the atheist never even looked twice at a church. However, the atheist's life was good, he had a well-paying job and a beautiful wife, and his children were healthy and good-natured, whereas the pious man's job was strenuous and his wages were low, his wife was getting fatter every day and his kids wouldn't give him the time of the day. So one day, deep in prayer as usual, he raised his eyes towards Heaven and asked, 'Oh God, I honour you every day, I ask your advice for every problem and confess to you my every sin. Yet my neighbour, who doesn't even believe in you and certainly never prays, seems blessed with every happiness, while I go poor and suffer many an indignity. Why is this?' And a great voice was heard from above 'BECAUSE HE DOESN'T BOTHER ME ALL THE TIME!'

Muldoon, the farmer, lived alone in the countryside with his pet dog of many years. Eventually, his dog died of old age. Muldoon went to the parish priest. 'Father, my dear old dog is dead. Could you be saying a mass for the poor creature?' Father Patrick replied, 'Muldoon, I'm sorry to hear of your dog's death, but we can't be holding services for an animal in the church. However, there's a new denomination down the road, and maybe they would do something for the animal.' Muldoon said, 'Thank you, Father. Do you think £500 is enough to donate for the service?' The Father quickly responded, 'Son! Why didn't you tell me the dog was Catholic?'

A vicar passed a group of teenage boys sitting on the church lawn. 'Evening, boys. What are you doing?' Nothing much, vicar,' replied one lad. 'We're just seeing who can tell the biggest lie about his sex life.' 'Boys, boys, boys!' intoned the vicar. 'I'm shocked. When I was your age, I never thought about sex at all.' The boys looked at each other and then said in unison, 'You win, Vicar!'

There were two Roman Catholic boys, Timothy Murphy and Antonio Secola, whose lives paralleled each other in amazing ways. In the same year Timothy was born in Ireland, Antonio was born in Italy. Faithfully they attended parochial school from nursery school through to their final year at senior school. They took their vows to enter the priesthood early in college and upon graduation became priests. Their careers had amazed Catholics, but it was generally acknowledged that Antonio was just a cut above Timothy in all respects. Their rise through the ranks of Bishop, Archbishop and finally Cardinal was meteoric to say the least, and the Roman Catholic world knew that when the present Pope died, it would be either Timothy or Antonio who would become the next Pope. In time the Pope did die and the College of Cardinals went to work. In less time than anyone had expected, smoke rose from the chimney and the world waited to see who they had chosen. They had chosen Timothy. Antonio was beyond surprise; he was devastated because even with all Timothy's gifts, Antonio knew that he was the better qualified. With gall that shocked the Cardinals, Antonio asked for a private session with them in which he candidly asked, 'Why Timothy?' After a long silence an old Cardinal took pity on the bewildered Antonio and rose to reply, 'We knew you were the better of the two, but we just couldn't bear the thought of the leader of the Roman Catholic Church being called Pope Secola.'

IN HEAVEN

The cooks are French,
The policemen are English,
The mechanics are German,
The lovers are Italian,
The bankers are Swiss.

IN HELL

The cooks are English,
The policemen are German,
The mechanics are French,
The lovers are Swiss,
The bankers are Italian.

IN COMPUTER HEAVEN

The management is from Intel,
The design and construction is done by Apple,
The marketing is done by Microsoft,
IBM provides the support,
Gateway determines the pricing.

IN COMPUTER HELL

The management is from Apple,
Microsoft does design and construction,
IBM handles the marketing,
The support is from Gateway,
Intel sets the price.

An old priest got sick of everyone in his parish confessing to adultery. During one Sunday's sermon he told them, 'If one more person confesses to adultery, I'll quit!' Since everyone liked him, they decided to use a code word: 'fallen'. From then on, anyone who had committed adultery said they had 'fallen'. This satisfied the old priest and the parishioners, and everything was fine for years, until finally the old priest passed away at the ripe old age of 93. Shortly after the new young priest settled in, he paid a visit to the mayor. The priest was quite concerned: 'You have to do something about the pavements in this town, Mayor. You can't believe how many people come into the confessional talking about having fallen!' The mayor started to laugh, realising that no one had explained their code word to the new priest. But before the mayor could explain, the priest shook his finger at the mayor and said, 'I don't know why you're laughing, your wife fell three times last week!'

Upon entering the confessional, a young woman spilled the beans, admitting, 'Last night my boyfriend made mad passionate love to me – seven times.' The priest thought long and hard, then said, 'Take seven lemons and squeeze them into a glass, then drink it.' The young woman asked, 'Will this cleanse me of my sins?' The priest said, 'No, but it will wipe the smile off your face.'

One afternoon a little boy was playing outdoors. He used his mother's broom as a horse and had a wonderful time until it was getting dark. He left the broom on the back porch. His mother was cleaning up the kitchen when she realised that her broom was missing. She asked the little boy about the broom and he told her where it was. She then asked him to please go get it. The little boy informed his mum that he was afraid of the dark and didn't want to go out to get the broom. His mother smiled and said, 'The Lord is out there too, don't be afraid.' The little boy opened the back door a little and said, 'Lord, if you're out there, hand me the broom.'

Grant me the serenity to accept the things I cannot change, the courage to change the things I cannot accept, and the wisdom to hide the bodies of those people I had to kill today because they pissed me off. Also, help me to be careful of the toes I step on today, as they may be connected to the ass that I may have to kiss tomorrow. Amen.